OFF THE GRID FOR LOVE

RENA KOONTZ

Published in the United States of America by

Rena Koontz

2200 Kings Highway 3L

Suite 66

Port Charlotte, FL. 33980

ISBN: 979-8-9859109-4-0

Human Authored™, Reg #: 9389892, https://authorsguild.org/human

renakoontz.com

✸ Formatted with Vellum

For my husband, Jed, who dreams my dream with me,
And the friends and family who support me.
You know who you are and how much I appreciate you.

1

The mouth of the gray metal gun, aimed right at her midsection, looked as round and as wide as a beer can. Everything else blurred in Mackenna's vision.

Snippets of last week's FBI training session flashed through her mind and the agent's words replayed in her brain. He'd called it "situational awareness."

"Stay alert," he'd lectured, *"and take note of everything around you. Be aware of what's happening."*

At this moment, staring at the handgun, Mackenna McElroy became aware of several things. She was scared speechless. She'd tried to respond to the gunman but merely croaked.

All noise around her morphed into a monotonous drone, like a swarm of descending locusts. Her underarms were sticky with perspiration. She smelled her own sweat. The strawberry yogurt she ate for breakfast threatened to resurface, right on the neatly printed envelope that demanded she empty her cash drawer and not make a scene. Her heart thrummed in her ears. She barely heard the robber's words.

"Do it!"

His command was a sandpaper whisper. No, more like a snake's menacing hiss. Cold green eyes stared at her from beneath the rounded bill of the blue ball cap tugged so low on his forehead, it covered his eyebrows. An unfamiliar insignia decorated the front. Those eyes still hadn't blinked. Was he a robot?

A slow inhale filled her lungs with tepid air. She swallowed the boulder clogging her throat. The FBI agent had instructed them to stay calm if ever they were face-to-face with a bank robber and surrender the money. She eyed the weapon peeking out from the envelope bearing her instructions. The thief's hand lay beneath it. Was his finger poised on the trigger ready to shoot her?

"Don't risk your life," the agent had cautioned.

Mackenna stepped back on her right foot and opened the cash drawer, sweeping her hand across the counter surface, effectively whisking her pen to the floor. To her right, her co-worker Sandy remained oblivious to her plight, chatting happily with an elderly woman about winter finally ending. On her left, Matt studied a printout of his customer's checking account.

"No dye packs. Please hurry up."

A courteous bank robber. She'd have to remember that. Lifting the spring-loaded bill clips one at a time, Mackenna emptied the cash slots. Remarkably calm hands eased the collection of singles, fives, tens and twenties into an ordinary-looking bubble mailer. It distorted the flat envelope into a bulky lump. The room spun like a carousel, yet her hands remained steady. Every person in the bank faded into the background and time stopped. There was only the gun pointed at her chest and those ice-green eyes.

She allowed the cash drawer to hang open, hoping Sandy would notice the violation of bank procedure and realize what was happening.

"Close your drawer, please."

Wow. This bank robber was polite *and* smart. She shut the drawer and regarded her assailant.

"Thank you, miss. I hope I didn't scare you."

He pivoted, a soldier executing an about-face, and then released an ear-piercing scream like a wild animal before pointing the gun at the ceiling and firing a shot. The room erupted in screams. Bodies dropped to the floor. Hunched over like a running back carrying the ball, he bolted for the door. Mackenna pressed the alarm button at the edge of her station and sank to the floor into welcomed darkness.

VOICES BUZZED. Her nose burned from an ammonia whiff that clogged her throat and stung her eyes. She flailed her arms in the air and struggled to sit up. The sharp odor choked her.

"Give her some air."

"Back up."

"Are the paramedics on the way?"

Gagging and coughing, she swiped her nose with the back of her hand and raised watery eyes to her co-workers. The room still spun like a merry-go-round with their faces parading by. Her boss. Matt. Sandy. Strangers. Gawkers.

Sirens blared in the distance. She gasped for air and motioned for everyone to move back. "I-I'm all right. Pl-please. I'm fi-fine."

The bank manager's arm snaked around her waist. "Let me help you up, Kenna. Are you hurt?"

Never had he called her by her nickname, always maintaining a boss-employee relationship and addressing her as Miss McElroy. She'd always regarded Mr. Gleaner as somewhat feminine, but he lifted her off the carpet as easily as he might retrieve her pen, which remained stranded on the floor near

Sandy's station. Gently, he settled her into someone's roller chair and tucked her hair behind her left ear. Those errant strands always loosened from the ponytail she wore for work every day. Blue eyes leveled on her.

"Kenna? Speak to me. Are you hurt? What's my name?"

He grinned when she whispered, "Mr. Gleaner." Her throat felt raw, and her pulse raced. The veins in her neck hammered a bass beat to some unheard rap song.

"The paramedics are here, sir."

"Bring them back. Kenna? Would you like some water?"

She nodded and a plastic bottle of natural spring water materialized in front of her. Mr. Gleaner unscrewed the cap. "Just a sip, okay? The paramedics are here. I want them to check you out."

"I'm fi-fine, sir. I just fainted."

"Humor me." He rose to his full six-foot height and ordered Sandy and another woman to assist her into his private office, directing the paramedics to follow. The women each gripped an arm and helped her stand on wobbly legs. That's when she saw the sea of blue swarming the bank. Uniformed police were everywhere.

Bank protocol dictated that the doors be locked immediately after a robbery. She spotted the elderly woman who'd been talking with Sandy leaning against the counter fanning herself. Maybe the paramedics should check on her too. An officer interviewed Matt's customer. Several other customers were speaking with police and men in tailored suits. One by one, they'd shake the officer's hand and exit a door unlocked by a patrolman. How soon would they want to question her?

Once her blood pressure dropped to a more normal reading and the effects of the smelling salts wore off, the paramedics pronounced her healthy. Standing just beyond Mr. Gleaner's glass office door, Sandy wrung her hands and shook her head in response to a policeman's questions. Mr. Gleaner hovered, casting anxious glances toward her. He rushed in when the paramedics opened the door and said he could enter.

"Are you sure you're all right?" When she nodded, he stepped behind her and placed both hands on her shoulders. "Are you up to telling us what happened? The police are here and the FBI." He squeezed her shoulders lightly. "I can give you some more time if you think you need it."

She'd never thought of him as anything except a strict bank manager, a stickler for the rules and a son-of-a-gun when someone's cash drawer didn't balance. Now, he seemed tender. Did she bang her head when she fell? Concussions could cause delusions.

"I'm fine, sir. It's okay. I'll talk to them. I'd like to get this over with."

He stepped to her side. "I'll stay here with you. If you need to rest, just let me know."

The FBI agent's questions seemed endless. Even though she recalled the awareness training as the robbery happened, she'd noticed so little. Except for the blue ball cap, the robber might as well have stood at her window naked. She couldn't describe the clothes he wore.

She didn't think he had facial hair. Was she certain? No.

Height? Tall. Towering in the frame of the teller's window. But he'd been smart enough to double over and dart out the front door, rendering the measuring tape at the bank's entrance useless.

He definitely held the gun in his right hand, but she hadn't actually seen his hands once she stared down the cavernous gun barrel. The few words he muttered hadn't revealed an accent. All she recalled were the electric green eyes and the gray steel he slid beneath the mailing envelope.

Yes, she'd glimpsed the gun. No, she had no idea what kind it was. She didn't know anything about guns.

No, she didn't know him. Didn't recognize him. Pretty sure

she'd never seen him in the bank before. Couldn't tell them anything more.

It felt like she hadn't disclosed any useful information at all. But the FBI agents and the police seemed satisfied with her responses, despite urging her to contact them if she remembered additional details. Mr. Gleaner glided his hand across her shoulders and bent so that his face was next to hers.

"The bank will be closed for the rest of the day. Why don't you leave early and go home? I have to stay, otherwise I'd drive you."

Mackenna narrowed her eyes. Who was this man? "Thanks, but I have my car."

It had taken a gun pointed at her for Mr. Gleaner to treat her like a human, instead of a math android. Or, she really had suffered a concussion and hallucinated.

He continued to speak. "And take the day off tomorrow." His hand squeezed her shoulder, and she cringed. "I'll call and check that you're all right." His breath smelled like stale coffee.

She nodded. She wasn't in a rush to step into her cubicle again, that was for sure. Police still peppered the floor, both in the public area and around her teller station. Only a handful of customers remained. Her brain felt fogged, worse than any head cold she'd ever had. But her gait steadied once she gathered her purse and sweater and walked toward the entrance.

A young man stood behind her and they waited for the police officer to unlock the front door. The man stepped beside her and swung the glass door open. "Allow me."

"Thank you."

He strode to a copper-colored motorcycle parked in the front row of the bank lot and worked to loosen the strap on the helmet dangling from the seat. Apparently, he was in a hurry to drive home, unlike Mackenna. She couldn't go home, at least not yet.

Today was supposed to be a ten-hour shift at the bank,

scheduled from nine to seven and coordinated with a community event. Probably why the robber chose today to hit the bank. People were everywhere downtown.

The extra-long day at work allowed Arthur plenty of time to move out. It had been a long time coming and her ultimatum that brought them to this point. In her head, she knew it was the right decision and she was ready to let go. Her heart weighed heavier. She didn't want to witness his final moments in the apartment she'd considered "their" home."

The roar of the Harley jolted her from her reverie. She watched the helmeted young man walk his bike backward, rev the throttle one more time, lift both feet, and smoothly ride past her. He waved and she automatically nodded.

With no real destination in mind, she exited the parking lot out the same driveway as the motorcycle and drove to the mall. At least it would be easy to kill a couple hours there, although she wasn't in the mood to shop. How pathetic that she had nowhere else to go and no one to call. She'd devoted a full year to Arthur, at the expense of the few friendships she'd had. He hadn't liked her friends and, after a while, they grew tired of her excuses not to meet up. They stopped calling.

Did they sense that Arthur wasn't what he portrayed himself to be? Did they know he was a cheater? She'd known long before she actually acknowledged it. There were signs. The nights he rolled in at three a.m. The phone calls he left the room to answer. He hadn't touched her in months. Her heart eroded slowly, darkening a little more each day. She knew it. She just didn't admit it. Admitting it meant doing something about it. Knowing and acting are two entirely different challenges.

Thinking that a caffeine fix might settle her nerves, Mackenna walked to the coffee shop, barely noticing the window displays she passed. Usually she'd linger, admire, maybe even wander inside to try on a pair of shoes or feel the fabric of a pretty dress. But today was hardly usual.

An extra-large mocha coffee should help. The china cup rattled in its saucer as she carried the drink to the far corner of the deserted coffee shop and took a seat. The lunch crowd was at their desks by now. Thank goodness. She preferred solitude. Mackenna planted both elbows on the table and dropped her head into her hands. Her fingers trembled against her forehead and tears filled her eyes, surprising her. She wasn't one to cry, but this might have some therapeutic benefit.

"Hey, Kenna. You okay?"

Her head jerked up and she focused her blurred eyes on Motorcycle Man. He balanced his helmet on the back of the chair opposite her and leaned on it. "Sorry, didn't mean to scare you. Guess you've had enough of that for one day, huh?"

Mackenna wiped the tears from her right cheek with the back of her hand, then swiped at the left side of her face with her fingers. He'd startled her and left her wordless.

Motorcycle Man used his free hand to point to his chest. "I was in the bank this morning? We walked out together? I drove by you on the motorcycle?" His voice inflected with each statement, turning them into questions. "Remember?"

She gulped. "I-I'm sorry. Yes, I remember. I, you ... I apologize. This whole day has me rattled."

A smile, slow and easy, creased his face. "Don't apologize, ma'am. You have every right to cry after what you've been through." He waited, expecting a response.

Her mind registered his words as if it operated in first gear. He'd called her by name, yet he was a stranger. She didn't like the chills that crawled along her spine. "How do you know my name?"

His eyebrows shot up and lowered in one quick movement. He slanted his head slightly and dropped his gaze to her left breast.

She followed his eye movement and discovered she still wore her bank identification tag, displaying her name in bold black print. Normally, she clocked out and stuck the magnetized nameplate to the board in the employee lounge. But there was nothing normal about today. In her rush to leave the building, she'd forgotten to punch her timecard. Her cheeks grew warm. She lowered her gaze to her hands nested in her lap.

"Are you waiting for someone?"

Motorcycle Man asked too many questions for her comfort.

"Yes," she lied.

He slid the chair out from under the table. "Me too. How about if I wait with you?"

Yes, she was shaken, and her personal and professional worlds were falling apart in tandem. But that didn't render her stupid. If he was hitting on her, she wasn't interested and if he was a serial killer, the can of pepper spray in her purse would be a rude surprise.

"If you don't mind, no, I'd rather you not wait with me. Thanks, but I prefer to be alone."

He'd already dropped into the chair and plopped the helmet on the seat to his right. He folded his hands and set his elbows on the tabletop. "Really? Because it sure looks to me like you could use a friend."

Tears filled her eyes once more. Now, she had to contend with a stalker.

"You're not a friend. I don't even know your name. Please leave me alone or I'll call security."

His right hand shot toward her. "Jake's the name. Meeting you is my pleasure."

Mackenna's hands remained fisted together in her lap. She eyed his big, calloused paw, and mentally awarded him grooming points for his clean, neatly trimmed fingernails.

Finally, it registered that she didn't intend to shake his hand. He withdrew the bear claw and winked. "No harm. What do you say I simply sit here with you until my friend arrives? We don't even have to talk. But you've had a traumatic experience, the full impact of which probably hasn't hit you yet. You're not going to like being alone when it does. Sometimes it's just good to have another human being close by. I'm a body on the other side of the table and so," he shrugged, "you're not alone."

He swiveled in his seat, rested his left arm on the back of the chair, casually propped his right ankle on his left knee and centered his attention on three customers waiting for their orders. Faded blue jeans topped brown leather boots polished to a high sheen.

With both hands wrapped around her mug seeking the familiarity of the hot cup, Mackenna sipped her chocolate coffee. Its warmth caressed her throat. The sweet taste soothed her nerves. She studied her unwanted tablemate. Nicely shaped sideburns stopped just at the top of his earlobe and contrasted with his dark hair, which spilled haphazardly over his ear and lapped his collar in disarray. A little too long for her tastes but, on him, it worked. Just the shadow of a beard. In profile, long, dark eyelashes curled upward. Why did men always inherit the lush eyelash gene?

Today was a warm, spring day yet he wore a heavy black leather jacket. It looked worn enough to be comfortable. Tight thigh muscles stretched the denim on the leg he'd casually crossed. As more customers filed through the front door, Mackenna hated to admit it but, she was glad she didn't occupy the table alone. At least no one else would bother her. But why had he?

"Are you really waiting for a friend?"

"Yes, ma'am. She's habitually late, but I'm used to it."

"Isn't she going to wonder why you're sitting with another woman?"

"No, ma'am. She's not the jealous type."

Royal blue eyes gleamed at her. Dark hair and blue eyes were a rare combination. Which parent had he inherited them from?

"You don't have to call me ma'am. It makes me feel old."

That smile reappeared and the heaviness across her shoulders lightened. Under other circumstances, this guy might be charming if he wasn't so pushy.

"Yes, ma'am. It's how I was raised."

"Texas?"

"Damn. I tried hard to hide the accent. Alabama."

"You shouldn't. It's appealing. Women like a Southern gentleman."

He threw his head back and laughed hard enough to shake the table. "I've never been called that. But thanks."

His laughter shot a small thrill into her stomach. She ignored the sensation and averted her eyes to her cup.

"Are you feeling a little better?" His words were soft, like warm honey.

"Yes, thank you."

"I can give you a ride home if you like. Or follow you to make sure you get there safely."

Alarm bells sounded in her head. She lifted her purse from the floor and rested it in her lap. This didn't feel right.

"I think you should leave me alone. Now."

"Ah, we're back to that, are we?" He winked again and returned his focus to the front of the coffee shop. His chin tilted upward when a tall blonde approached. Jake rose and lightly grasped her elbow.

"This is my friend, Vicky. Vick, this is Kenna. Someone robbed the Good Neighbor Bank on Mound Avenue this afternoon. She was the teller at the other end of the robber's gun."

Vicky's mouth formed an oval. She reached out and placed her hand on Mackenna's shoulder, clasping it lightly. "Oh, my gosh, I'm so sorry. Are you all right? Is there anything we can do to help?"

Her skin was smooth and her eyes, several shades lighter than her boyfriend's, shined with concern. Mackenna liked her immediately. She loosened the grip on her purse.

"No, thank you."

She used a hitchhiker's thumb to point to Motorcycle Man. "Is he making you feel better or worse?"

A nervous laugh escaped Mackenna. "I'm not sure yet."

Jake canted his head and grinned, keeping his lips tight and denying her another bright flash of white teeth.

"I feel like that every day." Vicky laughed when Jake aimed a contrived glare her way and frowned. "He's harmless, I assure you. But seriously, you've probably had a hell of a day. You should go home and relax. Do you need a ride?"

"No, I have my car. And thanks. But for reasons I'd rather not go into, I can't go home yet. I'm going to sit here and finish my coffee and maybe do a little shopping. I'll be fine."

Vicky offered a warm smile. "Want me to ditch him and hang with you? Girl time is always a good thing."

For the first time that day, Mackenna laughed. She didn't know either one of these people, yet they seemed inclined to comfort her. It unnerved her, but was oddly reassuring.

"I appreciate it, but I'd rather be alone."

"Okay. We get it."

Vicky and Jake wished her well and strolled away, hand in hand. She got her wish. She was alone. And lonely.

J ake walked Vicky to her car and opened the driver's door.

"What was that all about?" she asked.

He shrugged. "She was pretty shaken at the bank. I followed her out and then spotted her sitting alone in there. I figured it couldn't hurt to talk to her a little more. But she's genuinely upset so I don't think she was in on it."

"Does she know you're a fed?"

"No. She likely thinks I'm just a pain in the ass."

Vicky laughed. "Beautiful and smart. I knew I liked her."

Jake tugged on the helmet chin strap. "You ready to do this? Remember, act pissed at me so they won't be suspicious when we break up."

"You piss me off on a regular basis. Give me something more challenging, please."

"Funny. Follow me to the public garage across from the Laundromat and I'll jump in the car."

This undercover assignment in Brighton City was the best gig he'd ever had. It had been sheer luck that he'd infiltrated the outer layer of the Cabacolli family, the city's biggest organized crime element and major drug-trafficking operation. Who knew that his instinct to rush toward the car that veered off the road in front of him, crashed through the guardrail and plummeted down the hillside toward the river would open the Cabacolli's front door. He'd yanked the unconscious driver out of the front seat of the BMW seconds before the engine caught fire, and dragged the guy to safety, spraining his ankle in the process.

Since he'd never been to Pennsylvania before and was miles from Brighton City, the local cops didn't know him. Consequently, he didn't identify himself as an FBI agent. Same with the paramedics who loaded him and the driver into the ambulance and hauled them to the hospital.

Not identifying himself as a federal officer wasn't unusual. He rarely revealed what he did for a living, even when he wasn't working undercover. People acted differently in the presence of Special Agent Jake Manettia. He didn't know why. Hell, he put his pants on one leg at a time just like every other jemoke. Women especially went all gaga once they learned he carried a badge and a gun and were much more willing to spend the night with him. In the early days, he'd taken all he could get, but that superficial attraction had grown old.

He was nothing special, just a boy from 'Bama temporarily assigned to a northern city and still trying to get acclimated to the cold and snow that accumulated in inches instead of a light fairy dusting that decorated the familiar horizons at home. Thank goodness it was spring now.

Jake didn't know it at the time of the accident, but the driver he rescued turned out to be Old Man Cabacolli's son.

Jake had limped by Vinny Cabacolli's room before leaving the hospital just to check on him, declined his offer to have a driver take him home, saying his girlfriend waited outside, and agreed to meet for a beer once Cabacolli was discharged as his way to say thanks. Even though he jotted his undercover cell phone number in the margin of the hospital dinner menu, Jake assumed he'd never hear from the dude again.

But Vinny made good on his promise, and a week later Jake found himself throwing darts, shooting pool and drinking beer with the sore but healing son of a major crime syndicate boss. Vinny Cabacolli had taken a shine to him and from there it progressed to a double date with the girls. He'd enlisted his partner's help, although working undercover was always better as a solo performance. Their planned breakup should ensure she'd only have to play the role this one time.

This was Vicky's first undercover challenge, but she knew the drill. Never let your guard down and never disclose the truth. She'd picked up on the ruse with the bank teller right away and played along. He felt confident she had his back, a given with partners.

LUNCH WENT WELL. Vicky played the role of a bitchy girlfriend perfectly. He was ready to send her packing and they weren't even an honest couple. She'd been that good. The flying eyebrows and quizzical looks told him Cabacolli noticed. When they said their goodbyes and hugged, Vinny whispered that they'd meet up real soon. Without the hoochies.

Jake nodded, but inwardly cringed at the disrespect. Women were creatures to be revered. His mama had burned that into his brain, as had his three sisters. He adored women. They were his equal for sure and, in his case, often his better. He loved a strong woman, but that didn't mean she didn't want pampered and comforted once in a while. And loved.

During lunch his mind had wandered to the bank teller and his desire to comfort her, a complete stranger. She'd smiled bravely, but her cow-brown eyes betrayed her. Such sad eyes. They reflected more than a bad morning staring down the nose of a gun. Prim and proper in a business suit with her hair tied back—did she transform into an exotic lover once the chestnut brown hair fell loose around her shoulders? When his jeans tightened in the crotch, he reined in his thoughts. Undercover meant total attention to the task and the subject. Diversions could be deadly.

The bank teller reappeared in his thoughts while he drove home. Kenna was an unusual name. It had to be short for something more formal. If his day cooperated, he'd wander into the bank tomorrow to make sure she was all right. He'd ask about her real name then. Right now, he needed sleep. Working his primary assignment by day—Vicky's corruption case—and hanging out with Vinny at night was taking its toll.

3

Mackenna would think twice the next time anyone suggested they spend a day at the mall. She visited every store, used every restroom, and watched two movies at the mall cinema. Her eyes burned, her head pounded, and her feet ached. Surely Arthur was moved out by now. It was after seven.

She drove past the visitor's parking spot assigned to her unit where Arthur always parked. When she saw the space was empty, her shoulders relaxed. The load of the day's events sounded in her heavy footsteps as she climbed the stairs to her floor. Evicting Arthur should free her. But Motorcycle Man was right. Tonight, it would've been nice to come home to somebody.

She didn't reach for the light switch until she entered the kitchen, kicked off her shoes, and deposited her purse on the counter. She flicked the switch twice, yet the room remained dark. No matter. The apartment had been home for three years now. She knew the layout like she knew her birth date. She strode to the adjoining dining room. Odd. The chandelier didn't switch on either. A power outage? She took a few backward steps toward the kitchen and checked the microwave clock, which shined like a star through the darkness. Her stomach knotted.

She strolled into the TV area and squinted, allowing her eyes to adjust to the dim light spilling in from the balcony door. No bulky shadows filled the room. She couldn't discern the outline of the loveseat, didn't see the shape of the lampshade on the magazine table between the two overstuffed chairs, nor any reflection on the flat screen. *Oh my God, he didn't.*

Suddenly, the home she knew so well became foreign. She stretched her arms in front of her and felt the air while she maneuvered tentative steps back to the kitchen table. The flashlight on her phone confirmed her worst fear. The rooms were empty. Arthur hadn't merely moved out with his belongings, he'd taken everything. She executed a slow three-hundred-and-sixty degree turn in the living room twice, as if seeing the empty space the first time wasn't enough.

A sob caught in her throat when she entered the bedroom. Her lingerie, casual tops, and dressier T-shirts that she folded neatly and stacked in the bureau drawers lay piled in heaps along the back wall. He'd dumped her lotions and perfumes into the clear plastic waste basket from the bathroom and balanced it on top of the mountain of clothes. They hadn't shared a bathroom because Arthur complained she was too messy. Nevertheless, the lights didn't work here either.

The linen closet was empty except for a box of tampons and a four-pack of toilet paper. How generous of him. At least her makeup, bath products, and grooming accessories were still there. Of course, what need would he have of mousse and a blow dryer? He shaved his head.

The sinking feeling she'd had at the bank staring at the gun barrel returned. Suddenly, the room was incredibly hot. Her throat dry. Her head pounding.

She rushed to the spare bedroom. Empty, except for the gray linen futon that converted to a sleeper. They'd only hosted overnight guests twice. The thing was practically new, albeit not the best substitute for an actual bed. Both times the visitors were Arthur's friends too drunk to drive who needed a place to sleep it off. Neither had complained about comfort.

She waved the flashlight beam around the room and spotted a sheet of printer paper sitting on top of the cushion. He'd left a note. *Have a nice life, bitch.*

Mackenna spun around in disbelief. The bastard had taken everything, including the light bulbs. She sank to the floor, dropped her head in her hands, and wept.

~

MACKENNA'S PHONE rang beside her ear, jolting her awake. In the daylight, the townhouse was bright and as empty as could be. She'd cried herself to sleep on the floor, curled in a ball, exhausted from the previous day's events. Her neck ached. Her tongue moved inside a mouth as gritty as sand. She walked into the spacious living area and peered into the kitchen. No coffeemaker in its usual place on the counter. She'd kill for a cup of coffee right now. Finally, she answered the ringing phone.

"Kenna? It's Ted."

"Who?"

The voice on the other end chuckled. "Your boss? Ted Gleaner? Remember me?"

She shook her head to clear her brain and stared at her watch. Almost nine-thirty. "Yes, sir. I'm sorry. You said I could take the day off."

He laughed again, but it sounded forced. Had he expected her to report to work? "I'm not calling because you're not here at work, I'm calling to check on you. Are you all right? Do you need anything?"

How about a house filled with furniture? Her stomach growled. Had Arthur cleaned out the pantry too? The fridge?

"No, sir. Thank you, I'm fine." She was getting good at lying. First to Motorcycle Man and now her boss.

"I'd like to see for myself. May I take you to lunch today?"

She was so stunned, she took a step backward. "Sir?" Not another man hitting on her. Right now, she wasn't too fond of the species.

"Lunch. You know, two people sit down at the table and share a light meal. Like soup and sandwich or a chef's salad. I know you eat lunch because I've seen you doing it in the breakroom."

"Are you asking me out, sir?" Wasn't that an HR violation?

He paused. "Well, I guess I could tell the higher ups that I'm ensuring the welfare of my employee but that doesn't sound too appealing, does it? So yes, I'm asking you out. To lunch, not a lifetime commitment."

How was she going to get out of this? "Isn't there a policy against employees dating, not to mention a supervisor and an underling?"

"Is that a no?"

Was it? "Would you mind holding for a minute, sir?"

Without waiting for an answer, she laid her phone on the floor and walked to the kitchen. Even before she opened the refrigerator, she knew it was empty. Just like the pantry, except for a bag of condiment packets they'd collected from various take-out meals. No coffee. No food.

"Mr. Gleaner? Lunch sounds like a good idea. Where shall I meet you and what time?"

"You don't have to meet me, hon, I can pick you up at your place."

Hon? That set off warning sensors in her head. And god no,

he couldn't come here. "Thank you, sir, but I have some errands to run. I prefer we meet at a restaurant."

"Ted."

"Sir?"

"Not sir. And not Mr. Gleaner. My name is Ted."

"Yes, sir, er, Ted. What time for lunch?"

4

For at least the tenth time today, Mackenna released a chest-heaving sigh. She'd started the morning sipping water from the kitchen faucet. An oversized sleep shirt substituted for a bath towel after she showered without a washcloth or her mesh body scrubber. She'd applied her makeup standing in front of the balcony door. Without the glamour bulbs above the vanity, the windowless bathroom was too dark.

The clothes she chose, a pair of peanut-colored slacks and a tan and peach top, were wrinkled. Arthur had taken the iron, which surprised her. She doubted he knew how to use it.

Now, the gas pump rejected her card. The clerk insisted the pump operated just fine and the problem was on Mackenna's end. There wasn't time to debate the point so she handed the woman a twenty-dollar bill and hoped that would at least move the gas gauge needle beyond half.

She had no appetite as she parked in front of the restaurant where Mr. Gleaner stood like a sentry at the door, waiting for her. But she hadn't eaten since yesterday when she picked at a side salad in the food court at the mall. And his lunch invitation was a kind, somewhat human gesture. Even Sandy said so when she called to check on Mackenna and see how Arthur's exit had gone. Mackenna's answer was vague. "He took some furniture he shouldn't have. I'll explain later." She avoided going into detail by saying she had to dress for her lunch meeting.

That's what this felt like, a meeting. Definitely not a social occasion. She was certain Mr. Gleaner merely wanted to reassure her that the robbery was a one-in-a-million occurrence. That probably wasn't the correct statistic, but they didn't happen that often. And the chances of it ever happening to her again were likely infinitesimal. No doubt this lunch was bank protocol.

He greeted her with a wide smile, reaching to grasp her elbow as he opened the door for her. "You look like you barely slept. I hope you didn't have nightmares about what happened yesterday." He signaled the hostess. "Two, please."

Guess the undereye concealer hadn't worked. "I did have a bad night, yes."

"I'm so sorry. Do you live alone? I don't think I've ever asked."

He'd never asked her anything personal beyond "how are you?" and that inquiry always followed "good morning," and seemed automatic. Had he asked her last week, the answer would be quite different.

"Yes, I do. I had a roommate who recently moved out so, right now, yes, I'm alone." Those last two words killed her, but Mr. Gleaner didn't notice.

"Had I known, I might have suggested one of the other women stay with you, or you stay with them. Or I might have volunteered myself."

Her stomach lurched. Would his wife have been okay with that? The look on his face was dead serious, his eyes riveted on her, watching for a reaction. What the heck?

"I'm fine, sir. I actually preferred being alone." She

squirmed beneath his scrutiny. Fortunately, the waitress arrived to end that line of conversation, but Mackenna wasn't interested in food. She ordered a bowl of soup, hoping it might ward off the internal chill causing her heart to stall. All she wanted was to get the hell out of here.

Mr. Gleaner had other ideas. "I thought we could discuss your future at the bank."

"My future?"

"Why, yes. You don't want to be a teller forever, do you? I see you as a candidate to advance within the system. This isn't common knowledge yet, but the position of assistant bank manager will be opening soon. I can help you into that vacancy."

From teller to assistant bank manager without any intermediary advancement? She doubted it. "How so?"

He smiled. "We can talk about it."

That was a borderline creepy answer and suddenly, she wanted this lunch to be over. Now.

"It sounds interesting, but my immediate concern is returning to work tomorrow and not reliving the whole bank robber ordeal. I don't want to fear every customer who walks up to my window."

"I want that too." He tapped his knuckles twice on the table. "If you're uncomfortable at your station, I can arrange for you to work at another branch for a few weeks, perhaps one closer to your home. New surroundings and fresh faces might help. And then you won't be concerned about our seeing each other."

"Sir?"

His smile patronized her. "Ted."

"Mr. Gleaner, I appreciate—"

"As I said, we can discuss all of this later." He checked his watch. "Right now, I better get back. Take your time finishing, I've got the check. Enjoy the remainder of your day and I'll see you tomorrow. Try to get some sleep." He stood, dropped a ten dollar bill on the table for the tip, and sauntered toward the cash register.

HER SOUP BOWL WAS EMPTY, not because she was hungry, but it had given her something to focus on other than her boss leering at her from across the table. Despite the clean bowl and empty iced tea glass, she waited twenty minutes after his car exited the parking lot before she departed. If this lunch was meant to console her, it backfired. Maybe she read too much into his words, but it didn't feel like that. No, he was coming on to her and dangling her job at the bank as bait. Or was she overreacting? Over the last twenty-four hours, her emotions had been stripped raw. Maybe Sandy was available to meet after work. They could hash it out together. Plus, she'd be able to fill her in on Arthur's departure.

For now, she needed some basic household goods. A coffee pot and coffee first and foremost, light bulbs and towels, a pillow and maybe a throw. The floor was chilly this morning. She headed to the discount store.

5

The depth of her humiliation couldn't be verbalized. With five impatient customers lined up behind her, Mackenna argued with the store clerk about the available balance in her checking account. Then she challenged the computer system after it rejected two different credit cards.

Finally, she stepped to the side and checked the amount of cash in her wallet. Fifty-two dollars and some change. If she paid cash for all the items in the shopping cart, she'd have about twelve dollars left. Whatever caused the bank snafu could take longer than twenty-four hours to resolve.

She prioritized her needs and bought only the coffee maker, on sale for fifteen dollars, a pack of filters, an eleven-ounce can of coffee that wouldn't last long, and a handful of pre-packaged foods, all on sale for two dollars each.

Once inside her car, she dialed Sandy's desk phone.

"Hey, girlfriend, how was lunch with the boss man?"

"A little weird. Wait 'til I tell you. But right now, I have a problem. Do you have time to check my account balance? My debit card wouldn't work." She repeated the account number and listened to Sandy's manicured fingernails tap the keyboard.

"Wow, Kenna, did you make a mistake? Your balance shows seventy-three cents and a pending ten-dollar service fee for sinking below the daily minimum."

How could that be? "What about my savings account?"

Several more key tabs. "It's telling me the balance is zero and the account was closed, let's see, yesterday. What's going on?"

Mackenna's stomach clutched. "Can you check the credit card linked to that account?" She recited the security information to allow Sandy access.

"It shows a reported stolen card. All activity is suspended. You didn't tell me your card was stolen."

"It wasn't. Nevertheless, I think that's true. I'll call you back."

Using the search engine on her cell phone, she called up her other charge card to discover the same notation. She tried to sign in to her cell phone bill, but the screen rejected her attempts. Same with the light company, the gas company, and the city utilities. Then she tried her personal email. All of her logins and passwords were rejected. Arthur.

He knew where she kept a written log of every password and user ID for her electronic transactions. She had no reason to hide that binder. After all, she'd trusted Arthur. He'd wiped out all her money and sabotaged her credit accounts.

The rent would fall due in three days and was set up as an automatic withdrawal from her checking account, as was every other bill she paid. The bastard had left her high and dry.

She drove to the Mound Avenue branch, clutching the steering wheel with a white-knuckle grip. Sandy might be able to help with a loan, but it would be a temporary fix. Mackenna had no idea what to do.

Only two customers stood at the teller counter when Mackenna entered, her fingers crossed that Mr. Gleaner wasn't on the floor. Sandy's smile froze when she saw her.

"You look like hell. Did you forget makeup today?"

Mackenna grasped the edge of the counter to steady her trembling hands and support her shaking legs. "I'm in trouble. Can you loan me some money? Arthur wiped me out. He cleaned out the apartment and emptied the bank accounts. I have no money. I have nothing."

Sandy gasped.

"I can't get into any of my accounts. He-changed my logins and passwords. I don't have anyone to turn to. Can you help me?"

"Of course," Sandy said, her eyes still wide. "Did you call the police?"

Mackenna shook her head. "I don't know how I would prove it was him."

"Who else would steal all your furniture? You should call them so there is an official report on file. Could be one of your neighbors saw him moving out and can substantiate the report."

Mackenna squeezed her temples with her forefingers. Sandy was right, but she doubted it would do any good. "Okay, I'll call as soon as I leave here. In the meantime, can you lend me a little money? I don't have a morsel of food."

Sandy's caught her breath. "You mean he took everything?"

"Everything, including the light bulbs. He was kind enough to leave one pack of toilet paper and my tampons. Can you hurry? I don't want to see Mr. Gleaner."

"Mr. Gleaner has been locked in the conference room with three corporate execs since he returned from lunch. He was whistling when he came in. I want to hear everything about your meeting. I'm on break in five minutes. I'll make a withdrawal and meet you at the picnic pavilion outside."

Mackenna breathed a sigh of relief and stepped away from the window. At least this was a small step out of this mess.

"By the way, some guy was just in here asking about you?"

Her heart jumped. "Who?"

"He said to tell you Jake on the motorcycle stopped in to check on you. I thought he was kind of good-looking in a scruffy sort of way. Who is he?"

"A creepy stalker who was in the bank yesterday when we were robbed. I ran into him at the mall. He must think we shared a life experience together or something. He tried to take me home."

Sandy's eyebrows arched to her hairline. "He seemed nice."

"I bet they said that about Charles Manson too. I'll meet you outside."

The fresh spring air smelled sweet, and Mackenna smiled for the second time since her life had been threatened. Spring was such a happy time of year when everything bloomed again and the world burst into color. She loved it. Her joy proved short-lived.

She rounded the corner of the bank en route to the picnic pavilion in the side yard and encountered Motorcycle Man perched on his bike, his legs stretched long, his arm resting on his helmet and a phone to his ear. Her step faltered. She considered turning around, but she wasn't quick enough. He saw her and smiled as she walked by, searching for anything to study but him.

Not wanting to turn her back on him for fear he'd surprise her, she stepped onto the bench seat and perched on the table. It didn't work. Less than a minute elapsed when Motorcycle Man swung his long, blue jeaned leg over his bike and started in her direction.

Her hand shot out traffic cop style. "Just stop. Don't bother me. I've had it with you and everyone else." The strain of the last two days overcame her, and her voice cracked.

Through tear-filled eyes, she stared at him. "Just leave me alone."

He stopped dead in his tracks the minute she extended her unsteady hand. He tilted his head, a habit she already recognized, and spread his arms wide, palms to the sky.

"Take it easy. I'm not moving another step."

Her wobbly hand remained in the air. "Please leave me alone."

Motorcycle Man shrugged. "Sure. I'm just concerned about you. What you went through is traumatic and, from the looks of things, you aren't handling it too well. You might want to talk to someone."

"I have plenty of people to talk to, I don't need you."

That slow, deliberate smile creased his face. "I meant a professional."

"I'd be fine if everyone would stop telling me I look like hell and leave me be."

Sandy came around the corner, glanced at Motorcycle Man, and continued toward the table. "That's the guy who was asking about you." Behind her, he still smiled. She pushed a white envelope into Mackenna's hand.

"This is the best I can do. It's not quite five hundred. Why don't you stay with me tonight? Dave won't mind."

Motorcycle Man hadn't moved. Dammit, she didn't like him knowing her business. "I asked you to leave."

"Yes, ma'am." He returned to his bike, strapped on his helmet, revved the engine more than she thought necessary, and sped away.

Sandy marked his exit with a soft whistle. "I wouldn't mind riding him, ahem, with him on his motorcycle, I mean."

Mackenna's head jerked toward her friend. "Sandy, you're married."

"Well, yeah, but just because I said 'I do' didn't render me blind. He's kind of hot."

"He's annoying. Listen, I'll pay you back when I'm solvent again. With interest, I promise."

Sandy waved off her words. "I meant it when I said you should stay with us. That man is right, you have been through a lot. And he doesn't know the half of it. And who knows if Arthur is done screwing with you."

"I don't want to impose. It's bad enough I have to borrow money from you. I'm not going to infringe on your personal time. You and Dave are still newlyweds. I'm fine. I'm going to pick up a few groceries, go home, and regroup. Tomorrow I'll be good as new."

"Well, please call me tonight so we can talk. And call the police about Arthur taking all your things. That's so low, I can't even fathom it. I've got to get back inside. I'll see you tomorrow."

The money would help, but it wouldn't pay for her rent or her utilities or make her car payment. Come the first of the month, she'd have major money problems.

At least she could buy a few staples for the pantry. In college, she'd lived on instant noodles, macaroni and cheese, a loaf of bread and a jar of peanut butter. That menu gagged her now. After batteries of tests and trials, doctors determined she had a mild case of wheat intolerance that could escalate at any time. Since she adjusted her diet, she felt immensely better. She jumped off the picnic table, dusted off the seat of her pants, and headed for the grocery store.

Instead of the boxed dinners, she now preferred salads and fresh vegetables, which would be cheaper in the long run. The vegetable bins always had older produce on sale and a poor man's salad wouldn't be so bad. That's what she called a bowl of lettuce with only oil and vinegar. No cheese, tomatoes, or other extras. Solely lettuce was healthier anyway, wasn't it? She eyed the variety of produce while she waited for the vegetable sprayers to stop, oblivious to the people around her.

"No fair, sugar. I was here first."

She jumped when his deep voice sounded beside her. Motorcycle Man. Her anger flared. "What are you doing here? Are you following me?"

A red plastic shopping basket swung from his arm already loaded with milk, cheese, and mouthwatering ripe, red tomatoes still on the vine. Motorcycle Man shook his head.

"No, ma'am. I'm trying to decide if I want the organic lettuce or the store brand. For some reason, their prices are the same."

Before she could speak, a man's voice from behind interrupted them.

"Jake? I thought that was you. Pretty far from home, aren't you?" The man assessed Mackenna as if she were a side of beef, rolling his eyes down her body and back up, pausing at her waist, her breasts, and then her face. "You didn't waste any time, my man. This one's much softer looking. Introduce me."

Motorcycle Man appeared speechless. At the man's first words, he'd spun around and taken one step in front of her, protectively, as if shielding her from the guy's scrutiny. "Vinny, what are you doing here? Slumming? You're far from home as well."

The man grinned. "I don't often get down this way, but I wanted to visit a cousin at St. Mary's. Is this the new love of your life?"

Jake cast a quick glance over his shoulder and shook his head. "No, not at all. I don't know this woman. I'm here by myself picking up some grub."

"Truly? It looked like you too were talking." He flashed a blindingly white smile at Mackenna. "Allow me to introduce myself. Vincent Cabacolli. This is my friend, Jake Manfred. And you are...?"

Motorcycle Man spun around, leveled a stern gaze at her and whispered, "Leave. Now."

"C'mon, Jake, share the wealth. Sweetheart? I didn't catch your name."

Vincent was the same height as Motorcycle Man. She guessed a little over six feet. But he was fairer, blond, more weathered, and even from a distance the odor of cigarette smoke clung to him. He dripped in jewelry. His blue shirt was unbuttoned from the neck one button too low. Cabacolli was a name associated with the underworld, wasn't it?

Whatever was going on, Motorcycle Man didn't like it. Her heart rate spiked a beat or two sensing that, while the two of them appeared friendly, she didn't think they were friends. It was payback time. Motorcycle Man had been a thorn in her side for the last two days. She tilted her chin upward and smiled.

"My friends call me Kenna. Nice to meet you, Vincent." She extended her hand, and he clung to it like a life preserver, forcing her to take a step forward, drawing her out from Motor-cycle Man's body shield. Vincent tugged on her arm until her hand was at his mouth. He gallantly kissed the top of it. Beside her, Motorcycle Man stiffened.

"Jake, if you claim not to know this woman then I shall happily forge a friendship with her, or"—he paused and leered —"whatever else I can accomplish. Please tell me, dear Kenna, that you don't currently have a man in your life."

He hadn't released her hand and now she resisted his grasp, suddenly not as comfortable with her payback plan. Motor-cycle Man wrapped his arm around her waist possessively. "Give a man a chance, jerkoff." He leaned to whisper in her ear. "Now isn't the time to fuck me over. Trust me on this. Walk away."

Maybe it was the way he squeezed her waist or the urgency in his words. His royal blue eyes darkened to purple and drilled into hers. She freed her hand from Vincent's grip and placed it against Motorcycle Man's chest to push out of his grip. Beneath her fingertips, his heart raced. She nudged Motorcycle Man backward, forcing him to drop his hand from her waist, and smiled at Vincent.

"Actually, this man is correct. We don't know each other. And as charming as both of you seem, I'm in a relationship. But it was nice to meet you both." Jake's rigid posture relaxed.

"Have a good day, gentlemen." She didn't look back as she drove her cart to the juice aisle.

6

———

Jake was never so happy to watch a woman walk away from him. Still, he pretended to be disturbed.

"Thanks for nothing, man," he said. "What the hell are you doing here anyway?"

Vinny chuckled. "I already told you, I visited a friend in the hospital. And I wanted to grab a cold six-pack for the ride home." He tilted his head to see around Jake in the direction Kenna had gone. "She's cute. A little curvier than your last one but I like it. Too bad she said she's involved with someone." He spread his arms out. "Look at it this way, I saved you the pain of being shot down." He laughed at his own joke. "What are you doing so far out of your neighborhood, bud?"

Jake's undercover assignment had all the safety measures in place to prevent discovery. A different state, lodging under his assumed name, and a safe distance from the fraud and public corruption case he worked with Vicky. He'd been riding his motorcycle, exploring on his bike the day Vinny drove off the road in front of him. Jake had logged more than one-hundred miles and was two-plus hours away from his apartment.

Running into Vinny here, in the nearest grocery store to the undercover apartment was highly improbable. None of the Cabacolli clan had ever been observed by other agents in this neck of the woods. The Bureau's Special Agent in Charge had deemed it safe for Jake to pursue the friendship with Vinny. Apparently, it wasn't far enough.

The FBI knew the comings and goings of every member of the Cabacolli family and never once in the two years they'd tailed him had Vinny grocery shopped. What the hell was he doing here? And the bigger question—was *his* cover blown?

Nothing to do but play it out. "Well, there's a lesson for you, Vinny, never travel far from home without adequate refreshments in your car. I'm surprised you didn't send your driver in for the beer."

Vinny shrugged. "The parking lot was so crowded it would have taken longer to find a spot than for me to jump out of the car while he circled around. But you're right. Supermarkets aren't really my thing." His eyes dropped to the basket dangling from Jake's arm. "What about you?"

Jake mimicked Vinny's shrug. "Unlike you, I don't have someone to do my shopping. I rode my buddy up this way to pick up a car he bought. I'm not even sure where we are but like you, a cold beer sounds good." He nodded to his basket. "I figured I could grab a few groceries while I'm here. I'm on the bike, though, so I'm limited to one bag."

Vinny nodded. "Let's hang this weekend. You free?"

If he was suspicious, Jake couldn't tell. "I think so. I'll give you a call." He didn't wait for Vinny to ask more questions and instead set off for the beer aisle. He wanted to find Kenna and make sure she didn't leave the store until Vinny was gone. Ensuring that Vinny didn't see the car she drove or spy her license plate would ease his mind.

Fortunately, Vinny introduced him using his undercover

name. That was another safety precaution. An undercover identity always included the agent's actual first name, so there'd be no missteps if someone hollered from across the room, but a different last name.

Had he introduced himself to Kenna yesterday using his full name? He couldn't remember.

Jake grabbed a six-pack and walked toward the front of the store. Reading the informational signs hanging over each aisle, he glanced down the rows in search of her. Vinny moved through the express checkout as Kenna emerged from the far aisle. Jake rushed to block her cart, and she rolled her eyes.

He placed both hands on the front of the shopping cart. "Look, I know I'm a pain in the ass. I promise to leave you alone. Just do me this one favor and don't check out yet. Wait before you leave the store."

Her head shook slowly in disbelief. "Why, pray tell?"

"Because I'll go away and leave you alone if you do."

The corners of her mouth tipped up. "For that, I'd do just about anything. How long do I have to wait?"

He raised his forefinger to signal one minute and sauntered to the front window. No sign of Vinny's new black BMW. Maybe Jake was paranoid, and it had all been just a coincidence. But he didn't believe that. Walking back toward Kenna, he noted she didn't have many groceries in her cart beyond juice, lettuce, oil, and vinegar. She must not cook meals for that boyfriend of hers.

"I can't go into detail but, believe me, you don't want to socialize with Vinny. He's not a good person."

She arched one perfect eyebrow. "Oh, and you are?"

He had to hand it to her, she made him smile. The feeling pleased him. "Yes, ma'am, I am. I promised to leave you alone and I will but please take this." He removed a pen and pocket-sized notebook from inside his leather jacket. After jotting down his first name and undercover cell number, he tore the sheet from the spiral binding. "Don't throw this away. Just tuck it in your purse and if you ever see Vinny again, let me know. I swear, it's important."

Kenna eyed the paper for so long, he didn't think she would accept it. Finally, she reached for it. "I'll be happy to never see either of you again."

That hurt. But he promised to leave her alone, so he muttered his thanks and walked away. He fiddled long enough at his bike to see Kenna carry one plastic grocery bag to her car and drive away. He scanned the parking lot for five more minutes, long enough to reassure him that no one followed her.

JAKE IMMEDIATELY CALLED VICKY, knowing this encounter with Vinny had to be documented and dissected. Vicky was his lifeline to the administration, his contact agent, since an undercover agent never went into the office. Her phone number was blocked so if any unsavory characters stole Jake's cell phone, there would be no connection to the FBI. The coincidental runin with Vinny didn't sit well with Vicky either. They agreed on a neutral meeting spot where Jake's supervisor could hear the details first-hand.

At the restaurant, Vicky planted a friendly peck on Jake's cheek in case they were being watched. But Jake assured her he hadn't been followed. He'd driven miles out of his way before heading to the restaurant. The milk and cheese might be a casualty of the trip, but he was okay with that.

"Do you want out?" his supervisor asked after Jake recounted Vinny's appearance.

"No, not yet. Let's run this a tad further. He wants to meet this weekend. I'll gauge his attitude toward me and then we'll decide. I might simply be overreacting."

"What the hell was he doing so far from his home base?" the boss asked, knowing there would be no answer. "You watch your back, Manettia. This feels bad."

"Yes, sir. Don't worry. It's probably just a fluke."

At least he hoped so. For his sake as well as Kenna's.

7

The main room of this bank branch was housed in a tighter area, but it had more customers than the one he last robbed. It was his second cruise through the parking lot, and the majority of the spaces were filled again. One empty spot in the last row caught his eye and he backed into it. He'd checked it yesterday morning and on two other afternoons at different times. If he couldn't find a window when the bank was mostly empty, he'd select a safer target.

This was his habit, making sure he knew every inch of the building inside and out, staking it out long enough to recognize the tellers and sometimes, the regular customers. His planning was precise. Same as his precautions. Despite the assurances of his partner, it was his neck on the line if something went wrong.

Last week's hit had gone so well, he'd been tempted to call the bank and thank them. This must be how a drug addict feels. He couldn't wait for his second high. But he still had a lot of homework to do.

He cinched his tie tighter, slipped into his suit jacket, and sauntered toward the building. Behind his sunglasses, his eyes skimmed the rooftop and entrance for surveillance equipment. A blinking red light no bigger than a pencil eraser confirmed his suspicions. Once inside, he strolled to one of the two customer service desks, picked up a white deposit slip, and reached for the pen chained to the desk. Removing his glasses, he casually surveyed the room.

Three teller windows, in addition to the drive-thru window, all located left of the front door. About a dozen desks on the right side of the room. Close. Too close. Anyone sitting at one of those desks could easily view customers at the counter in these confined quarters. That was less than ideal. Too easy to see suspicious activity and call for help. This particular bank branch was too small, too risky. He'd have to regroup and find another mark.

He retrieved his cell phone from his breast pocket, stared at it for thirty-seconds, and then shook his head slowly. He balled up the deposit slip and dropped it in his coat pocket. Affecting a frown, he continued to shake his head and nudged his sunglasses onto his face. An unarmed security guard stood near the entrance with his hands folded in front of him. They made eye contact, and he nodded.

"I'll have to come back. It's an emergency."

If the guard watched him walk to his car, he didn't know. It would be a mistake to turn around and look. He was simply a man interrupted by a text message. Nothing suspicious about that.

A financial competitor stood on the opposite corner, but it was a Good Neighbor branch, the same outfit he robbed last week. Hitting the same bank in back-to-back gigs was dicey. Still, he was here in the parking lot. It couldn't hurt to wander in and get a feel for the place. Reaching into his back seat, he unzipped a duffel bag and searched for a pair of dark-rimmed fake eyeglasses. In another life, he might have been the nerdy accountant he'd gone to school to become.

But he preferred investing his own money instead of managing someone else's.

He smoothed his suit coat and straightened his tie. No harm in looking.

AFTER FIVE MORE DAYS OF research, his plan for this heist was faultless. He'd driven the distance between this Good Neighbor branch and the police department and calculated the cops' arrival once an alarm sounded. Even though this was the same bank as his last hit, it was perfect. Big enough to approach the teller without arousing suspicion and easy exit out one of two driveways. Ideally, the light would be green at the main exit, and he could drive straight through and zoom to the interstate. If it was red, he'd turn right and head toward the highway.

Upon leaving the bank, if that exit didn't feel right, he'd speed to the back of the building and get lost in the neighborhood streets. He'd already plotted and timed all the routes.

It surprised him that his partner was on board with this. He'd expected objections to robbing the Good Neighbor Bank twice in a row. But the first gig only netted a couple thousand dollars, which they'd split. Chump change compared to the potential in those drawers. His share was gone, which was why he wanted to roll again. Plus, he champed at the bit to make another hit, like a junkie waiting for his next fix. This was the ultimate high.

The self-tanning lotion he'd applied to his face over the last few days darkened his skin to a yellow-tan tint. He tugged the black curly wig over his shaved head and pushed the fake eyeglasses up his nose with his forefinger. He'd wait to wedge the black licorice between his front teeth, giving him the appearance of a gap. The candy lodged there annoyed him. He didn't want to insert it until necessary.

As he entered the bank he smiled, feeling as calm and serene as if he walked into church. Only one teller wasn't busy, so he sauntered up to her window and slid the mailing envelope in front of her. He'd learned the bigger bills were kept in a lower, second drawer. The instructions read: 'Put all the money from both your drawers in this bag. I have a gun.'

Holy shit. She was the same teller from the first Good Neighbor Bank. He'd been to this bank seven times and she'd never been behind the windows. What the hell was she doing here?

Her eyes widened, and he suppressed the urge to react. He recognized her. But did she realize it was him? Her eyes filled with tears and her hands trembled when she stepped back and opened the cash drawer. The gun remained in his jacket pocket. He felt sorry for her. The color drained from her face. Slow tears rolled down her cheeks. But she followed his instructions exactly. In seconds, the bulky mailer was in his left hand. His right hand eased the gun from his side. "Sorry, miss."

The room exploded with the sound of the gunshot, and he ran to the door amid the chaos. Once inside his car he sped to the traffic light, which conveniently shined green, and breezed through the intersection. In less than thirty seconds, he was on the interstate, yanking off the wig and the glasses. Oh, man, he had a hard-on. Easy peasy, lemon squeezy.

8

Mr. Gleaner insisted that morning that she clerk at a different branch today. When she arrived at her regular station at Mound Avenue and opened her window, the robbery replayed in her mind as it had every day. Her hands shook while she cashed a check for her first customer.

Mr. Gleaner hovered and watched. His proximity didn't help matters. Her nervousness caused her to miscount the first time, and she double-counted the amount out loud the second time.

Running his hands up her arms from her elbows to her shoulders, Mr. Gleaner leaned close and whispered, "Step into my office so we can talk."

Dutifully, she'd propped the closed sign in her window and followed him into the glass-enclosed office, grateful for the interruption. Mr. Gleaner furrowed his brow. "Have you been sleeping, sweetie? You look..." He probably couldn't think of a word horrid enough to describe her appearance.

She shook her head. "Not so much, no."

Folding his hands in front of him, he nodded in sympathy. "I know it's hard to get back up on the horse."

The metaphor confused her, but she knew what he meant. From now on, when she stepped into her station, a spot that was once as comfortable as a second home, she'd recall the gun barrel aimed at her stomach and the icy look in the robber's eyes. Her hands trembled with each new customer.

"I think a location change will be best for you, right now. I'm assigning you to the East Seventh Street branch for the next two weeks. They are short-handed with vacation requests. Head over there now. I'll pop over this afternoon toward the end of the day. We'll go to dinner. How does that sound?"

"Yes, sir." This felt like punishment, but she hadn't done anything wrong.

Sandy looked skeptical, but remained silent while Mackenna signed off the computer and shut down her workstation.

Because each branch was a mirror of the next, Mackenna walked into the East Seventh Street Bank completely familiar with procedures. Mr. Gleaner was right. The new surroundings boosted her confidence and after the second customer, she was as comfortable as if she'd always worked there. The other tellers welcomed her and, since communication between banks occurred regularly, Mackenna was happy to connect faces to familiar names.

The morning breezed by without incident until he walked in.

The different environment lightened her mood. She smiled when she raised her eyes to the new customer and repeated by rote, "Hi, I'm your good neighbor. How can I help you today?"

And then the envelope slid into her line of sight. This time she looked up at her robber, determined to notice every detail about him. Tan. Glasses. Thick curly hair. The top of his head about five inches higher than the edge of the glass partition.

She didn't see a gun, but his note stated he had one. She assumed it was true.

He smiled. An obvious gap in his teeth. Surely that would be a detail police would welcome.

Once again, the FBI agent's training instructions echoed in her head. *"Stay calm and give the robber the money."*

She carefully emptied the upper and lower drawers, mentally calculating how much she removed. He'd escape with thousands of dollars this time. So much, she could barely stuff it all into the mailer. Unlike the first robbery, she looked up as she nudged the envelope toward him.

"Sorry, miss," he whispered. It sounded like an apology. And then he raised his gun and fired a deafening shot. He was out the door before her finger released the panic button.

At least she didn't faint this time. Instead, she grabbed her pen and retrieved a BRSD form from the lowest drawer. The East Seventh Street branch was newer than Mound Avenue and more progressive. Tellers had Bank Robbery Suspect Description forms designed to aid in identifying an assailant. The blanks were intended to help jog the employee's memory.

She quickly filled in the blanks. Height. Build. Eye color. Complexion. Teeth. Tattoos. Whether a note was used and the wording. Method of escape, and description of vehicle. All the questions the police had verbally asked at the Mound Avenue office. She wrote furiously, filling in as many blocks as she could. All hell would break loose when the police swarmed the place. She didn't want to forget a single detail. His manicured fingernails. The tooth gap. A young, white man with a bad tan.

The teller beside her screamed when the gun fired. Remarkably, Mackenna remained calm. As if her life wasn't pathetic enough, now even gunshots didn't upset her.

Just like before, the bank went into lockdown, and police in uniforms and FBI agents in three-piece suits crowded into the building. She recognized two of the agents who also investigated the first robbery. One of them, a bear of a man, straightened his tie as he approached her.

He extended his hand to display his credentials and identified himself, apparently not making the connection. "Hello. I'm Special Agent Demond Crews. And you are?"

The minute she said her name, he remembered. She could tell by the quick jerk of his eyebrows. She offered him a confident smile. "I think you'll be happier with my observations this time, Agent Crews."

9

J ake spread his notes across the kitchen table and grimaced when he burned his tongue on the fresh coffee. Once his paperwork was caught up, he'd meet Vicky in a public place and hand off the information. Although the FBI office was off-limits, the paperwork remained a requirement, so his reports found their way to the boss via his handler.

Today, Jake arranged the meet at the mall coffee shop where he'd seen Kenna, even though it was unlikely she'd show up there again in the middle of the day. But the locations for these meetings changed regularly, so no one would be the wiser. And who knows? He might get lucky.

Just as he opened his laptop, Vicky rang his cell phone. "Did you hear the news?"

"What news?"

"The Good Neighbor Bank was robbed again. Different branch but same teller. Your little friend might not be so innocent after all."

"What?"

"Yep. Sorry to burst your bubble, partner. Two branches in a little over two weeks with the same teller at both windows. What does that tell you?"

"You mean Kenna? Why was she at a different branch?"

Vicky chuckled. "Exactly. That's the seven-thousand- dollar question because that's about what the guy's take was today. Seven thousand and some change. Smart enough to know about the bottom drawer. Or did your friend clue him into that? It's a nice haul for about five minutes of work. And a handsome hourly rate if you ask me. I'm definitely in the wrong profession."

On the surface, the same teller in two robberies was highly suspicious. He couldn't imagine that Kenna was a co-conspir- ator with a criminal. On the contrary, the word victim popped into his mind when he thought about her. Which he'd been doing a lot lately.

"Did the bank robbery squad interview her? What was their take on the hit?"

"I don't know any more than what I just told you. Demond called in from the scene looking for the boss and I picked up the phone. I think they're still there. I take it from the sound of your voice, you're surprised."

That was an understatement. "And you seem amused."

"Well, I do find humor in this. Once again, your track record with women exceeds all expectations. She's a criminal, and you have the hots for her. Gotta run. See you at the meet."

Vicky disconnected the call before he could challenge her claim. He stared at the blank phone screen while a gazillion questions launched in his head. Why was Kenna at a different branch on the exact day it was robbed? What were the odds that the robber targeted her again? Didn't he worry that she would recognize him? Or was she part of the scheme? Was it the same robber today as last week?

With any luck, the bank surveillance photos would be clear and give them a good facial shot, which they'd compare to the surveillance tape from the first robbery. They'd also study Kenna's mannerisms during both robberies. And run a background check on her now. Why her twice in a row?

He wanted answers but he couldn't call Kenna, primarily because he didn't have her phone number. But also, he couldn't blow his cover, and how else would he know she'd again been the targeted teller for a robber? He'd been in the bank the first time as a legitimate customer and hadn't participated in any of the official police interviews to maintain his cover. Instead, he stood on the sidelines, an extra pair of eyes observing the aftermath for his fellow agents. Kenna couldn't be involved. Her eyes were sad, not sinister. He'd have to talk to Demond.

THE MOUND of paperwork in front of him wasn't shrinking, despite the two solid hours and his full attention devoted to it. He'd relocated temporarily to Brighton City after being assigned to Vicky's fraud and public corruption case, which was ongoing. It had allowed him to work closely with Vicky, and they'd even shared a few happy-hour beverages together. She was a good agent with a dry sense of humor. He liked her. More importantly, they trusted each other.

Yanking Vinny out of his wrecked car and gaining access to the Cabacolli family had been a bonus. But that assignment was still in its infancy. Although Vinny befriended him, Jake hadn't been privy to the Cabacolli inner sanctum yet. His primary assignment remained the public corruption scam, which required detailed documentation of his activities for the case to hold up in court. This was the part of the job he hated most.

Jake welcomed the interruption when his cell phone rang, even though the display revealed an unfamiliar number. At this point, even a telemarketer would be eagerly received. "Yeah?"

The woman's voice on the other end sounded tentative. "Hello? Um, is this Jake?"

"Who's this?"

The caller exhaled into the phone. "My name is Mackenna McElroy. I'm the bank teller at Good Neighbor Bank who you kept bothering. I was going to throw this piece of paper away, but I didn't. Hello? Are you there?"

He bolted upright. His colleagues likely were looking into her background at this exact minute, searching for a connection between the two bank robberies. So far, she was it. They'd be dumping her phone records too, and see this call.

"Sure, Kenna, I know who you are. I'm surprised you kept the number." Why was she calling him? Did she know he was a federal agent?

"Me, too. I almost didn't. Listen, I've had a hell of a day so please don't turn into the jerk I think you are. Actually, the last few weeks have sucked." Her voice caught in her throat as if she suppressed a sob. "Remember that guy in the grocery store? The one you told me to let you know if I ever saw again."

Holy hell.

"I think he's following me. No, I'm certain he is."

His pulse skipped. "Why do you say that?"

"Well, unless it's a coincidence that he has business at the discount store, and that he needed something from the drugstore and now, he wants to pick something up at the mall, he's following me. I've been to all those places and so has he."

Why the hell was Vinny following her? "Are you sure it's him? Vinny?"

"Yes. I saw him sitting in the back seat of a black car with tinted windows. The window was down while he spoke to another man and then that man came into the discount store. The behemoth didn't buy anything, just searched the aisles until he spotted me, then he walked back to the car. I didn't think anything of it until I saw the car in the drugstore lot, parked far down at the end. And now, it's outside the mall entrance, waiting three lanes over from my car."

She'd described Vinny's car and bodyguard. The man resembled an Army tank on steroids. Vinny never went anywhere without him. He detected an edge in Kenna's voice, like she was ready to lose it.

"I don't know who he is but, I gotta tell you, I don't need any more stalkers. If he's your friend, I wish you would tell him to back off. I think I'm in trouble with the FBI, and I don't need more complications in my life."

She couldn't see him, but he raised his hand in the air anyway. "Hold on a minute. Where are you? Tell me and then promise you won't move until I get there."

"You're kidding, right?"

He'd grabbed his keys and rushed out of his apartment toward the elevator. "No, ma'am. I'm dead serious. Where are you?"

"The last thing I need today is you giving me grief. I've had a terrible day. I was robbed again. All I want to do is go home and, I don't know, throw myself out the window." Her voice trembled. Was she afraid of being caught or upset about the situation she was caught in?

"Don't drive home. Not if he's following you." Vinny probably already knew where she lived if he'd seen her car. He would have noted her license number. The administration suspected Old Man Cabacolli had someone within the local or state police departments on his payroll. Maybe even more than one cop. The Cabacolli family had come out clean on too many attempts to take them down not to have a mole on the inside.

Crap. Jake didn't even know where Kenna lived but he'd bet his last dollar Vinny already did.

"Please tell me where you are."

Another loud exhale, as if the day exasperated her. "In the department store."

"Where in the department store?"

"Women's purses."

"Please stay there. Don't leave. Promise me. I can be there in fifteen minutes. I'm getting in the elevator now, so I'm going to lose this call. But I'm on my way. Just stay there. Please."

The call dropped.

Once inside his car, he called Vicky. "I'm heading to the mall. We've got trouble. Mackenna McElroy just called me. Vinny is following her."

"Vinny is tailing your bank robbing babe? Do you think there is a connection?"

"I don't think she's a bank robber or that Vinny is in any way related to the robberies. Vinny is dicking with me because he thinks I like her. That's the real question. What game is he playing with me and why? Tell the boss what's going on."

"What exactly is going on?"

"I'll call you as soon as I know."

RELIEF WASHED over him when he spotted Kenna standing at a handbag clearance table, so much so that he rushed to her, grasped her face with both hands and kissed her. Her eyes widened and she planted both hands on his chest and shoved him backward.

"What the hell do you think you're doing?"

Well, the kiss surprised him too. "Sorry, sorry. I'm just glad to see you. Are you all right?"

She wrapped her arms around herself and took one step away from him. "Look, I don't like you. I don't like anything about you. I'm also not fond of being manhandled by strangers and followed around. So go tell you buddy to leave me alone and you do the same, okay?"

Dark circles ringed her eyes, either from lack of sleep or

mascara smeared by tears. Growing up with three high-mainte-
nance sisters had taught him more about women's grooming
than he cared to admit. But the shadows under Kenna's eyes
were difficult to identify. She looked haggard.

"Will you let me buy you one of those chocolate coffees you
like first? You look beat up. You said you were robbed again?
Man, that's rough."

Her chin quivered and she caught her breath.

His most charming smile might win her over. His face
slowly creased in half. "I'm not that bad, honest. Let me buy
you a coffee. Have you had lunch? I'll even throw in a sandwich. Maybe by then, Vinny will have given up."

He doubted it. More likely he'd send his henchman in to
locate Kenna, and he'd wait her out. But why?

AT THE MENTION OF LUNCH, Mackenna's stomach growled. And
her mocha coffees were an addiction. A simple reference to one
kicked her taste buds into salivate mode. But she wasn't up to
dealing with Jake the Jerk today. He misinterpreted her hesitation,
stepped forward, and gently placed his hand on her arm, rotating
her toward the department store exit. The mocha triumphed.

"I promise I'll be on my best behavior." With his hand
placed on the small of her back, he nudged her toward the food
court. "You said on the phone that your name is Mackenna.
That's unusual. I've never heard it before, but I like it. I
wondered if Kenna was short for something. Which do you
prefer?"

They walked side by side toward the coffee shop. She was
keenly aware of his hand riding her waistline. Arthur rarely
touched her when they were out. He shunned public displays
of affection.

"Most of my friends call me Kenna."

He winked at her. "What am I allowed to call you?"

Okay, he could be charming when he wanted to be. A light laugh escaped her. "You've been calling me Kenna, why change now?"

He guided her to an empty, round table-for-two in the corner and slid back a chair. "Thank you, ma'am. What may I get you besides a coffee?"

Her appetite disappeared the day of the first robbery.

"Nothing, thanks."

He texted while he stood in line. This would be the perfect opportunity to stand and walk out of the coffee shop. Just go straight to her car and drive home. Except, there was nothing for her at home, not even furniture. At least here, surrounded by people, she didn't feel like such a loser.

Jake returned with two coffees and a supersized chocolate chip muffin. "I know you said nothing, but I skipped breakfast and lunch."

He settled across from her, and split the muffin in half with a plastic knife. Placing a napkin in front of him, he relocated his half to it and eased the paper plate toward her. "Help yourself, please."

She broke off a tiny bite, conceded she was hungry, and it was truly fresh and tasty, and reached for one more bite. It wasn't a portion big enough to make her sick, and what did it matter anyway? The way things were going, maybe she should try to overdose on the stuff.

She moved her muffin half to the side and sipped her coffee, peering at Jake over the rim of her cup. He appeared engrossed in his treat.

"Why is your friend following me?"

Jake's royal blue eyes locked onto hers. "I plan to ask him about that. He's not my friend, more like a business acquaintance. In my opinion, he's not a good guy. I wish he wasn't tailing you."

"What does he do?"

"He's what you might call a shady businessman."

"And what are you?"

He blinked twice and swallowed. "I'm in security."

"Like a guard some place?"

"Yeah, something like that. Must be why I'm a little overprotective. Tell me about getting robbed again. It might help if you talk about it. What are the odds that the same bank gets robbed twice in what, two weeks? Why do you think you're in trouble with the FBI?"

Her stomach dropped at the recollection. "My boss moved me to a different branch. He thought I might feel more comfortable there. And I did at first. And then, it was like a bad dream that I already had. I looked up and there he was. He had a note—"

"The same guy?"

"No, it wasn't the same man. This one had a gap in his teeth." She touched her own front teeth to show where. "And he wore glasses. He had a bad tan, close to looking jaundiced. But he did the same thing. Slid a note under the glass written on an envelope in the same neat printing. Just like the first time. I was stunned."

The details flooded to the front of her mind like a deadly tsunami wave. She straightened in her chair, bracing for impact. "It felt like I was in a trance, having an out-of-body experience. I watched myself emptying my cash drawers and sliding the money into the envelope, just like the first time. He smiled at me, but I didn't smile back. And then, like the robber at the Mound Avenue branch when you were there, he aimed at the ceiling and fired his gun. The explosion scared the hell out of everyone in the bank, but I didn't even flinch. Like I viewed a familiar movie and expected it. And then it all hit the fan."

All the air left her lungs and her shoulders sagged. Her confession was over, but her hands still trembled when she again raised her cup to her lips. Jake's expression remained blank. "Did you tell the police all that?"

She nodded. "I paid better attention this time and I thought they'd be glad that I remembered so many details. But the way they grilled me, their skeptical looks, I think they think I'm in on it." Saying it out loud made it real. Unchecked tears began a slow stream down her cheeks. What did it matter if she cried in front of this man? She was losing everything.

"I could tell by the questions they asked this time. They don't believe me. I think I'm in trouble."

Jake stared at her for at least thirty seconds before asking, "Are you in on it?"

The question didn't even surprise her. She only felt numb. "No, god no. I swear to you I'm not." And then she cradled her head in her arms on the table and wept. The crying jag was overdue and the culmination of splitting up with Arthur, coming home to find every possession she owned stolen, looking down the barrel of a gun, and being followed by a man she didn't know but sensed she should fear. She'd no idea how long it lasted, but it was cleansing. When she raised her head, Jake wore a sad smile and extended a handful of napkins.

"I'm sorry," she said. "How embarrassing for you. You must think I'm one wacked-out woman."

He shrugged. "I'm not the least bit embarrassed. I have three sisters and one of them was always crying about something. Do you feel better?"

"A little."

"What about you? Sisters? Brothers? Parents who can help?"

She missed her mother more than she could express. "My brother is in the service, overseas. I don't hear from him much. One sister, but we're estranged. She's on the other side of the country. My dad is in an assisted-living facility. He's been ill for years." She was revealing too much personal information to this man. It told him she was vulnerable. "I should go home."

Jake reached across the table and gently grabbed her forearm. "Listen, sugar, why don't I give you a ride home. That way Vinny won't follow you. I'll get a buddy, and we'll come back for your car. I'll feel much better if you let me do that."

Hell's fire, she couldn't let him do that. What if he wanted to walk her to her apartment door? He'd see she had no furniture, nothing.

"But then you'd know where I live. Sorry, but I don't know you, and I'm not comfortable doing that."

He grinned and wagged a finger at her. "That's good, ma'am. You can never be too careful. How about this plan, then? I'll take you to my place and call Vicky. You remember her, don't you? She'll meet me back here, drive your car back, and then you can head home."

It was likely she was in shock from the day's events because his so-called plan made her laugh outright. "That's the worst pick-up line I've ever heard. Come back to my place and wait for my girlfriend. Sheesh, I thought I was pathetic, but you might have me beat."

His eyebrows shot up in surprise, then his face relaxed into a laugh. "It didn't come out the way I meant it to sound."

"I just want to go home. Thanks for the coffee and for listening to my tale of woe. If your friend is out there, I'll tell him to leave me alone or I'll call the police. Unless he points a gun at me too, I'm not afraid of him." She stood and retrieved her purse from the floor.

Jake rose as well. "At least let me walk you to your car. A Southern boy always does that." He didn't wait for her to agree and, instead, lightly held her elbow as they wove through the department store aisles and out the North Entrance.

"Where'd you park?"

"Aisle Seventeen, under the light fixture. I always park in that area and use this door to go in and out of the mall. Otherwise, I'm afraid I'd forget where I left my car."

They reached her driver's door. Jake squeezed her elbow before she reached for the door handle. "My number is in your phone now, since you dialed me. Will you add it to your contacts, just in case Vinny turns up again? I'd like to know if he does."

The black car approaching behind them caught her attention. "I don't think you'll have to wait long."

It cruised up behind her thirteen-year-old Ford Taurus and the rear window eased down.

"Well, what a coincidence. Jake, I thought you didn't know this young lady and yet, I find you two together again."

Jake's arm wrapped around her waist. His hand splayed across her hip, causing her to gasp. He drew her close to his side. "I'm trying to rectify that, asshole. What the fuck are you doing here?"

The question surprised both of them, judging by the way Vinny's mouth dropped open. They couldn't be friendly business associates if Jake spoke to him like that. He didn't give Vinny a chance to reply. "She's off-limits. Or don't you abide by the Bro Code. You don't hit on a friend's girl. We are friends, right? So back the fuck off and quit following her. Do I make myself clear?"

Vinny's brows furrowed. "Take it easy, pal. I just happened to be in the neighborhood, and I spotted the two of you leaving the mall. No harm meant. In fact, let me help you with your love life. Be my guest for dinner tomorrow night at my restaurant. My treat. I'll reserve the best table. Say, seven o'clock? If you want to impress a lady, Cabacolli's Casaria is the place to take her."

The conversation confused Mackenna. Was Vinny a restaurant owner? Jake described him as a shady businessman.

Would she have to eat dinner with Jake? She hardly knew him, despite the sense of security she felt with his arm around her. And the tingling from his long fingers that rested on the top of her butt cheek. Her body and her heart were starved for attention. But Jake wasn't the solution.

Jake apparently had the same thoughts. "No, thanks. We have other plans."

Vinny shook his head. "Aw, c'mon. I've been telling my pop about you. He'll be there. I'm sure he'd enjoy meeting both of you."

Her shoulders tensed when Vinny's eyes roamed over her body, as if he pictured her standing there naked. Jake must have picked up on it as well because he inched her behind him. "Some other time."

"Talk it over with your girlfriend. The food is excellent, and reservations are hard to come by. I'll look for you at seven tomorrow night." The rear window rose slowly, like a stage curtain lifting for the first act. But it signaled the end of Vinny's performance. "A coat is required and most of the clientele wear ties so dress appropriately." He disappeared behind the tinted window. The car eased away.

Jake whirled and smacked the roof of her car with his open palm. "Son of a bitch."

She waited for an explanation. The color of his eyes deepened to that eggplant purple she'd seen in the grocery store. Already she was becoming familiar with this man, the impish way he canted his head, the feel of his hands on her, and those eyes that darkened when he sensed trouble. Before either of them spoke, her cell phone rang. She fished it from the bottom of her purse and frowned. Mr. Gleaner.

"Hello?"

"Hello, sweetie. I'm calling to check on you. How are you feeling?"

"I'm fine, Mr. Gleaner." She eyed Jake, and he backed up

several steps to allow her some privacy. Not far enough away, though, that he couldn't hear her side of the conversation.

"I told you to call me Ted. Listen, I'm sorry about what happened today. I make an administrative decision and send you to another branch so you'll be more comfortable, and you are victimized again. And I wasn't there to comfort you. I want to make sure you're all right. I'd like to see you tonight. How about dinner?"

Maybe she really would go home and throw herself out the window. All these strange men favoring her with their unwanted attentions suffocated her. Killing herself had to be less painful.

"I can't tonight, Mr., er, Ted." She stared at Jake as she spoke. "My friend is already with me and we're making plans for tonight."

"That's good. I don't want you to be alone. What about tomorrow night?"

"Um, we already have dinner plans. She's planning to stay with me for a couple of days, so you don't have to worry."

Jake's head tilted to one side.

"I'm at the mall, sir. Truly, I'm fine. And I'll be at the East Seventh Street branch first thing in the morning. I don't need the day off. It's better if I keep busy. Listen, I have to go. Thanks for calling." She disconnected before he could say any more.

Jake closed the distance between them and touched her elbow. "What was that about?"

She shrugged. "I guess we're both lying to our business acquaintances."

He grinned and wrapped his hand around hers, easing the phone from her fingers. "May I see this for a minute?" After punching a few keys, he returned it. "I'm saved in your contacts."

"Thank you. Now, may I go home, please?" She pressed her key fob, and her door unlocked.

Jake reached to open it. "Yes, ma'am. I'd still like to follow you, though, just to make sure Vinny doesn't. My bike is around the other side of the mall, but you could drive me to it."

"I'd prefer you didn't."

"Don't think your boyfriend would understand a motorcycle escort?"

"My who?"

"Your boyfriend. In the supermarket, you said you were in a relationship. Where I come from, that means you have a boyfriend. No ring, so it's not a husband."

The emptiness of her life resurrected in her heart, which lay heavy in her chest. She locked her lips between her teeth to control their quivering. She'd already had an emotional breakdown in front of this man so there was no need for pretense. "I threw him out. I'm done with men. So, I'd rather you not follow me. Thanks for the coffee."

She turned the key in the ignition and drove away.

10

He stacked and re-stacked the piles of money, each the same height according to denomination and an inch apart from the next, all neatly displayed like stepping stones along the baseboard of his bedroom. These were his friends. George Washington faced to the left on all the one-dollar bills heaped in three six-inch-high piles at the farthest end. Abraham Lincoln stared at George from the fives in an even stack. Old Abe required more real estate. Five mounds of fives. He liked it.

He nodded respectfully to Alexander Hamilton and Andrew Jackson, the two in a neck-and-neck race at the moment for their space along the wall and beating Abe by two piles, both approaching the eight-inch mark. The stacks were banded in bundles, easy to tally. But he had no need to count his friends. He knew their exact number.

He snapped his heels together and saluted Ulysses S. Grant. "Don't worry, you'll grow," he whispered to two three-inch stacks of fifties.

Last, but perhaps his most cherished friend, Benjamin Franklin, kept a watchful eye on his comrades, like a doting father. Ben eyed him from atop a short stack of one-hundred-dollar bills, only three inches high. Ben and he were buds. Both geniuses in their own right. Both men of vision with goals and the commitment to achieve those goals. He winked at Ben. "I'm graduating to the vault. You'll be the tallest soon."

He caressed the hundreds, so clean and crisp it aroused him. Ordinary people didn't regularly carry bigger denominations, so they weren't handled as often as the others.

They even smelled different.

Stepping back to admire the exhibit, he smiled, carefully nudging one stack a centimeter to the left. People said he suffered from an obsessive-compulsive disorder, but they were wrong. His IQ had tested near genius. That was why he'd outsmarted the FBI so far. He had a brilliant mind. Just like Ben Franklin.

And now, a new opportunity loomed. He wasn't out of money and normally, this would be the time to lay low. Every news cycle featured a story about the rash of bank robberies carried out by unknown persons. They broadcasted blurred pictures from bank surveillance tapes that might as well have been pencil drawings scrawled by a toddler. That's how useless they were.

He loved hearing himself described in the plural. Persons. No one knew one smart dude was getting the best of the state and local police, and, as a bonus, the FBI. Well, that fact registered more like a boner. And better still. No one knew it was him.

Ordinarily, he'd just enjoy the ride. But next week, opportunity would knock. He'd have the advantage of driving a different vehicle for a full week. Not that anyone had picked up on the car he drove, at least not according to the news reports. In fact, the reporters said no one had noticed a getaway vehicle. He'd counted on people inside the bank being too scared to look at him once he fired his gun at the ceiling. As for the general public, well, they were too busy with their own lives to pay attention to him. God bless cell phones and texting.

All the police could view was film from both bank's surveillance cameras, one that showed him hunched over and running out the door, and one that depicted a nerdy-looking man who kept his face down at the teller window.

With little fact to report, the media speculated about the robbers, whether the incidents were connected, if someone had a vendetta against the Good Neighbor Bank, or if each hold-up was a random act of violence. They were clueless.

And now, another chance.

His friend owned and drove a two-seater pickup, but was part of a carpool with his workmates. So, one week a month, they swapped vehicles. Next week, he'd be driving around town in his friend's green pickup, instead of his own beat-up Chevy.

The prospect of another job and escape in a different vehicle appealed to him. Usually, he smeared his rear license plate with mud to partially cover the digits and letters, making them difficult to identify. Not so dirty that a cop would pull him over. But he had an ingenious idea to disguise his friend's license. The inspiration came to him as he watched late-night TV and a commercial for women to temporarily conceal their gray hair by spraying an aerosol product on it. The darker color lasted until the woman washed her hair.

Knowing that his friend's license plate included the numbers five, nine, and zero, he planned to use the color spray to change the five to a six, the nine to an eight and the zero to an eight. Even if someone noted the plate as he drove away, the number would be bogus.

Starting research on his newest target titillated him, like the promise of sex at the end of a dinner date. The objective definitely could not be a Good Neighbor branch this time. That would tempt fate. As always, he'd be methodical. By the time he strolled in the building ready to make his demand, he'd know everything about the branch, including the number of tellers and guards, the distance to and from the police station, all highway accesses, peak hours, and more. And if he didn't complete the spreadsheet he carefully filled out for each job, he could afford to wait until next month. He definitely liked the idea of driving another vehicle.

A new disguise was necessary as well. This time, it just might be a woman behind the wheel of that pickup. A donation center in the next town would have everything he'd need. A dress, wig, pocketbook, shoulder shawl, even plus-size bras that he could stuff. He'd look for women's shoes as well, something orthopedic.

Switching on the bathroom lights he studied his face in the mirror. His skin was smooth, his features sharp. He'd add a swipe of lipstick and red color on his cheeks. And false eyelashes to wear behind a new pair of pink glasses. Laughing, he strolled to his desk to get started. This was going to be fun.

11

J ake's boss slammed his hand to the table. "I don't like it. That's twice now that Cabacolli shows up eighty miles away from his home base and just happens to run into you. Something's fishy."

"I'm not sure it's me, boss, I think it's the girl. It seems like he's tailing her."

"Well, who the hell is she to you? A nobody bank teller, right? You have no interest in her so just let her be. If she gets involved with Cabacolli, that's her business."

No way could Jake let that happen, for a whole host of reasons. "It's not that simple. If I hadn't been talking to her in the produce aisle, Vinny would never have introduced himself to her."

"You don't know that as a fact. He's a mongrel where women are concerned. I tell you, this whole thing stinks."

Jake raised his hands to calm his boss. "Don't yank the plug yet, sir. I already called Vinny and told him I wouldn't be at his Casaria tomorrow night. Although it's too bad because from all the intel we have, the restaurant is the front for their dirty businesses, the drugs, prostitution, black market goods. This would be an opportunity to meet his father and move me one step closer to infiltrating the family. With the girl in the picture, though, it's too risky. But if he invited me once, he'll invite me again. For whatever reason, Vinny likes me. He probably doesn't have many friends."

His boss's shoulders slumped. "I'm not sure I agree, but you're the one in the trenches with Cabacolli so I'm not going to pull rank on you yet. But this is the last coincidental meeting, do you understand? You've accomplished in a few weeks what we've tried to do for two years, place someone next to that family. But it doesn't feel right to me. Be sure to stay alert and question anything that, well, you know the drill."

"Yes, sir. Thank you, boss."

He poked his finger at Jake. "And don't chase that skirt. You and your new best friend don't need to be fighting over that."

Was that a direct order?

"Remember, if Cabacolli just happens to show up on your doorstep again, it's over. Case closed. Is that clear?" He made air quotation marks around the words 'just happens' to emphasize that he didn't believe in coincidence. Jake wouldn't argue. Several missing persons cases were directly connected to the Cabacolli family, but how and when they disappeared were mysteries. He didn't plan on becoming one more.

Their lunch meeting at a neighborhood Mexican restaurant ended once his boss was appeased. Jake waited at the table for another fifteen minutes after the boss left, which allowed him time to call Demond, who headed up the bank robbery squad. The African American agent was a human oxymoron. Muscular to the point of being bulky. Fierce looking with his shining bald head and gruff mannerisms. And as gentle as a teddy bear.

Often, when an agent transfers to a new field office on a

temporary assignment, the regulars don't take much notice. Not Demond. He'd welcomed Jake on his first day, practically crushing his hand when he shook it, and bought him dinner that night, where he recommended restaurants and dry cleaners, shared driving shortcuts, and filled him in on office politics. Every bureau had them.

Jake imagined his giant face splitting into a wide grin when he answered Jake's phone call. "I was wondering when I'd hear from you. How's it going, my friend?"

"Why were you wondering that? Do you miss my Southern charm?"

Demond's rich laugh rolled through the phone. "Sure I do. And those pretty blue eyes that Vicky tells me you have focused on my victim bank teller. She's not bad looking. Not my taste, but that's okay."

Jake laughed. One amorous hug from Demond could crush a woman's ribs. "And how do your tastes run, may I ask?"

He released another laugh that sounded as if it formed in the bottom of his belly and rumbled up through his massive chest. "Me? I like my women like I like my coffee. Sweet and black." Jake couldn't resist laughing when Demond roared.

"Tell me about the bank teller, Demond. Do you like her for the robberies?"

The levity in his voice disappeared. His tone deepened into all business. "Hard to tell. Ask me after the first time I interviewed her, and I'd say no. She was an emotional wreck. I wasn't certain she'd get her own name right. But this time, there was something different about her. As if she remembered too many details. She said that, after the first robbery, she resolved to be more aware. But who anticipates being robbed again? And her body language contradicted her words. Her chin quivered, she flipped her pen in her fingers, fiddled with the strap on her purse, she was as nervous as a nun in a sperm bank."

Jake exhaled. "Maybe she was just that. Nervous."

"Maybe," Demond conceded. "I'm putting together a dossier on her for a more in-depth look. She's a puzzle, that one."

"How so?"

"Barely a dollar in her bank account yet all her bills are paid, and she has good credit. I've seen people who live paycheck to paycheck but she's penny to penny. She could have a sugar daddy, but she doesn't seem the mistress type." His chair squealed under his weight as he leaned back. "What is she to you, exactly?"

Jake frowned. "Don't believe Vicky, I hardly know the woman. I told you I chatted her up at the coffee shop after the Mound Avenue incident, but didn't get anything to help your case. Vicky exaggerated that chance meeting into a rendezvous and has been needling me ever since.

"But our paths crossed again today. Kenna called me so my number will show up on the log when you dump her phone. That's a whole other story. I had the chance to talk to her some more, though, and she told me about the second robbery. She claims she made a concerted effort to pay attention to the robber this time. She also senses that the police don't believe her."

"Do you?"

"I can't say for sure. There's definitely something going on with her. Whether or not it's connected to the bank robberies, I don't know."

Demond breathed heavily into the phone. "Are you opposed to getting closer to her, feeling her out a little more?" He laughed. "Not feel her out in the physical sense but if that happens, you don't have to share the details."

"What do you mean?"

"I'm bringing her in here tomorrow along with some other tellers from both branches. I want them to look at our photo files. Maybe someone will look familiar. I could ask a couple customers in as well, which would drop you into the mix. Give you a chance to talk to her again, maybe get a little friendlier. Might be too risky, though, since you've got Vicky's case going. This building is off-limits to you."

Off limits was an understatement. But if Vinny was suspicious and spying on him, Jake had a legitimate reason for being at the FBI office, since he'd been a real customer that day. And if Vinny asked, Jake could play up the angle that he balked at going there but didn't know how to decline the FBI's invite.

The idea of seeing Kenna again appealed to him, but deceiving her to gain intelligence didn't. He had no other reason to contact her, particularly since she flat-out asked him to leave her alone. Meeting her at the FBI's request wouldn't arouse suspicion and Demond was right, it would give him one more opportunity to talk to her. The unanswered question was how close did he want to get? The boss's words echoed in his head. Had he issued a directive?

Jake hadn't been able to stop thinking about that impromptu smooch and her surprised response. Albeit briefly, she'd returned the kiss. Or had he simply imagined that because the idea enticed him? He'd resisted cuddling her and cooing words of reassurance when she broke down and cried at the coffee shop. But he sure wanted to take her in his arms at that moment.

Demond misunderstood the silence when Jake didn't immediately answer. "Forget it. It was a bad idea. Too risky for you and you already have a full plate. Don't worry about it."

Jake wasn't going to close the door on this opportunity. "No, no, this could work. Let's just keep it between me and you if it gets personal with Kenna, okay? Make sure the boss knows I'm coming in with the customers because you think I can work the suspect teller. He'll balk, but if Cabacolli has eyes on me, this might flush them out. What time is everyone coming in? I'll be there."

What could it hurt? Kenna likely didn't know anything anyway.

MACKENNA ADMONISHED herself for picking at and chewing the cuticle on her right thumb to the point where it started to bleed. Just a droplet at first, and then a growing bright red bubble. She took great care with her appearance, which included her hands and nails, especially since she presented that part of herself daily to each customer. But she was nervous as hell walking into the federal building. The very structure was intimidating, with its guarded entrance and metal detectors, darkened window panels, and the FBI insignia as big as a VW bug inlaid in the tile at the entrance. She pressed a tissue to her thumb.

Even though Sandy, Matt, and several of the other tellers were also summoned to this photo line-up, she feared the agents would pay particular attention to her. After all, she was the true eyewitness. The others had merely been bystanders. Mr. Gleaner explained this morning that the agents scheduled the photo array after bank hours, even though there were no suspects. One today and one tomorrow, to accommodate everyone's schedule. But they had specifically requested that Mackenna attend today's session. Mr. Gleaner told her in private that he tried to delay her appearance so he could accompany her tomorrow but the case agent, Demond Crews, insisted she attend this particular session.

In one sense, she was grateful for the command performance today when Mr. Gleaner was unavailable. He'd stepped up his efforts to see her outside the office and, in fact, was adamant that she meet him tonight after he finished his dinner meeting and her appointment with the FBI concluded. Sandy advised her to simply decline, but the vibes Mackenna sensed were that Mr. Gleaner wouldn't accept that. As if she didn't have enough to worry about.

She blotted her bleeding thumb while everyone sat in silence in the conference room, reminding her of a wake. That's what it felt like. And she was the deceased. Whenever the door opened, each person looked up and nodded at a fellow teller or the handful of recognizable customers who apparently had also been contacted. Mackenna nodded to the elderly lady who'd been at Sandy's window during the first robbery, and smiled at a few regulars from her home branch. Her stomach grabbed when Jake the Jerk walked in.

Same tight blue jeans, brown boots, and black leather jacket. He carried his helmet and ran his hand through his long hair, which fell back into place in an orderly unmanaged style, as if it were cut to do that. Inwardly, she smiled at her new designation for him. He'd transcended from the anonymous Motorcycle Man to the more personal Jake the Jerk.

He spoke briefly to the agent signing everyone in, surveyed the room, and nodded when his gaze fell on her. Instead of taking the empty seat to Mackenna's left, or any of the other available chairs, he chose to stand in the corner, his feet spread for balance and his hands crossed in front of him, the helmet dangling from its strap. The stance resembled a soldier standing guard. He must have a military background, despite his rebel appearance.

Agent Crews introduced himself to the room and explained the purpose of the meeting. "I'm going to break you up into groups of fours and show you some photos of known felons. I ask that you don't exchange impressions so as not to influence the person next to you. Take your time to ensure that everyone has a chance to view each photo before moving on."

He checked his clipboard, pointed at people in no particular

order, and relocated them. If there was a method to his selection process, Mackenna couldn't detect it. The next thing she
knew, she sat at a round table with a rotund man and an older
woman, both unfamiliar to her, and Jake the Jerk. Wordlessly,
he nodded to her a second time and perched at her elbow.

The agent placed a tablet-sized computer screen in the
middle of the group. "The screen is pre-set to show one digital
picture at a time. Raise your hand if you have any questions."

Jake nudged the screen toward her. "You had the best view.
You might as well do the honors."

With an unsteady hand, Mackenna tapped the screen. She
held her breath until the first face appeared. The two strangers
on her right moved in closer for a better view as did Jake, who
casually placed his arm on the back of her chair. He leaned so
close, his cologne teased her nose. It was the faintest scent of
cedarwood, transporting her outdoors and into the woods.

"C'mon, lady, I ain't got all day. Can't you move those
pictures a little faster?" Beneath the table the man she didn't
recognize bounced his right leg vigorously, causing the table to
vibrate. Beside her, Jake tensed.

"I want to be sure I don't miss him, sir. I plan to take my
time. Perhaps you should ask to move to another section if you
are in that great a hurry."

He expelled a heavy breath, leaving little doubt he ate a
hoagie with onions for lunch, but he didn't comment further. In
her ear, Jake whispered, "Atta girl." His words warmed her.

She could pick out distinctive features from the various
pictures—a square chin, eyebrows trimmed as if they'd been
tweezed, a tan complexion—but none of the pictures combined
to portray the faces of either bank robber. Around her some of
the tables emptied, but she took the time to study each photo,
sometimes closing her eyes to bring the real robbers' faces
clearer to the forefront of her mind.

When all the images started to blur, she sat back and rubbed her temples.

"It isn't any of these," she said to the table. "Neither one of the men are in this array."

The big man shoved his chair back. "Well then, that's it. I'm out of here." He saluted his tablemates and strolled to the agent running the meeting. After signing something, he left.

Beside her, the woman gathered her purse and sweater. She touched Mackenna's arm. "Don't worry dear, they'll catch him. I watch a lot of police shows. The FBI always gets their man." She teetered off toward the door.

Mackenna smiled at the woman's attempt to reassure her. Once again, she'd been unable to contribute to the investigation. She looked up when Agent Crews approached the table.

"No luck?"

"No, sir. I'm sorry."

When he focused on Jake, he shook his head. "Nothing. Sorry."

The agent faced her again. "What bank branch will you be working at tomorrow, Miss McElroy?" He closed the tablet and slid it off the table. His hands were huge.

She caught her breath. Why did he ask that?

"I'm assigned to the East Seventh Street branch for two weeks, agent. I'm filling in for someone on vacation. Why do you ask?"

He smiled, or smirked, she wasn't certain. "We want to keep an eye on you, that's all. Thank you for coming in. We'll be in touch." As he moved away from them, she felt her shoulders sag with the weight of his words. Her intuition had been correct. They suspected her.

Jake cleared his throat. "They do that kind of thing to intimidate you. Don't let him scare you."

She leveled watery eyes on his. "But I am scared. My whole

life is going to hell right now. And they think I know more than I'm saying. But I swear to you, I don't."

His arm moved from the back of her chair to squeeze her shoulder. "If you told the truth, you have nothing to worry about. C'mon, I'll walk you out." He stood and waited for her as the last table of four also rose.

Having him hold her elbow once they signed out and moved down the hall comforted her somehow. They rode the elevator in silence to the first floor. He resumed his grasp out the front door and to the parking lot where, once again, life dropped her to the mat. Her left rear tire had gone flat. Was it possible to sink any lower? She had no money for car repairs.

"Are you kidding me? Am I cursed, or what?" It didn't help but she kicked the traitorous tire.

Jake knelt for a closer look at the flat. "Looks like you're waiting on the auto club to fix this. Unless you let me rescue you. I'll call my buddy who runs a towing service. He'll pick up the car, fix the tire and haul it to your place no charge. He owes me a couple of favors."

"You don't need to do that."

He scanned the visitors' parking lot. Only three cars remained. "Well, I can't very well leave you standing alone in this empty parking lot. My mama would skin me alive if she found out. I'll be happy to give you a ride. It's after six and will be dark soon. The rest of your co-workers are already gone, so your options are limited. I haven't eaten all day, and I'm famished. We can grab a fast bite on the way home."

"Look, Jake, I appreciate that you're trying to be friendly and twice now, you've kind of rescued me. But I don't know you and I don't want to be your friend. I'll handle this. I—"

~

WHEN MACKENNA VIEWED her ringing cell phone screen, she cursed. "Damn it."

Jake inspected the tire more closely while she spoke, pretending not to listen. No obvious reason for it to be flat unless one of the agents inside made sure the air escaped. Leave it to Demond to go the extra mile.

"Hi, Mr., er, Ted. Listen, I can't meet you tonight. I just left the FBI office and I have a flat tire." Ted was the same name she identified as the caller in the mall parking lot, the one she avoided seeing by fabricating a lie. Whoever the caller was, he was persistent. Competition? He'd back off if she was interested in another man. Begrudgingly, but he'd do it.

Only from the sounds of this conversation, Mr. Right wasn't on the other end of the line.

Kenna spoke again. "That won't be necessary, sir. Oh, you're right, Ted. My friend is already here with me and he's going to make sure I get home and that my car gets towed. No, he's already called someone and I, um, yes, I think the truck is coming now. I better hang up. I'll see you at work tomorrow."

She ended the call and looked at him like a six-year-old caught telling a whopper of a fib. But those eyes of hers looked more than guilty. She looked defeated.

"Someone you work with?"

"My boss. He's pressuring me to see him, and I don't know what to do."

A quick shot of anger surged through him. Had he seen her boss at the bank? He hated men who preyed on vulnerable women. "That's called harassment. You don't have to put up with that."

Her gaze dropped to her feet. "Yeah, well, that's easy for you to say. He can make my job miserable if he wants, even fire me. And believe me, I can't afford that."

Barely a buck in the bank, Demond had said. She was well dressed, educated, and she held her head high with an air of sophistication. Why was she broke? Gambling? Drugs? Booze? She didn't fit any of the profiles.

"That's exactly why it's illegal. He can't force you to see him. I have—"

She raised her hand and her voice at the same time. "Please don't. I can't handle a lecture about sexual harassment tonight. I can't handle much more of anything. I swear I'm on the verge of a breakdown. If one more thing goes wrong in my life, it will be my undoing. So please, leave me alone so I can think this through and figure out what I'm going to do about my car."

She didn't need to be left alone, she needed help. He recognized borderline despair when he saw it.

"Are you an auto club member?"

"No." Her response resembled a croak, as if she choked back tears.

He reached into his jacket pocket and retrieved his phone. As he dialed, he gifted her with his most charming smile, hoping to reassure her. "Well, now I know what to buy you for Christmas." Her jaw dropped as he spoke into the phone and recited the make, model, and license number of her Taurus, offered up the location, and requested it be towed as soon as possible.

"What's your address, Kenna?"

She stammered and shook her head no.

Damn, she was so secretive. Maybe she *was* a freakin' criminal. "Tow it to the Good Neighbor bank on East Seventh Street. She'll be working there tomorrow. Put the keys in an envelope and toss them in the bank's night deposit box. Thanks."

He tucked the phone back into his pocket. "Yes, I'm butting into your business. I'm being as pushy as your boss. Except my intentions are honorable.

"You, on the other hand, are being stubborn and bull-headed because right now, you need help." He spread his arms wide. "It's a no-strings-attached offer. I'll give you a lift wherever you want to go. I'd like to stop and get something to eat, but if you're not comfortable doing that, then fine. My stomach can growl all the way to our destination."

At least that made her smile.

"You don't like me, I get that. I'm a stranger. But if you called a ride right now, you'd be accepting a ride from a stranger so what's the difference? Leave your keys under the floor mat. There's a security guard at the end of this parking lot. Your car won't disappear. We'll tell him about the tow truck on the way out."

She hesitated.

He stretched his hand toward her. "C'mon, let's get out of here."

She eyed it warily before slipping her hand into his, sending a surge of heat up his arm. Her cold hand trembled when he wrapped his fingers around it and tugged lightly. "I'm parked over here."

Her first steps were tentative before she fell in beside him as she eyed the shining copper bike.

"Well one thing went right today. I'm glad I wore a pantsuit. I've never ridden a motorcycle before."

"No? I think you'll love it. It's a sense of release, like a rush of freedom."

"What if I'm afraid?"

His head jerked involuntarily. "You don't have to be afraid of anything with me, sugar." Their eyes locked.

"Let me adjust this helmet so it fits you better."

He handed her the spare helmet and, once on her head, he adjusted the angle and tugged at the chin strap, keenly aware of the smoothness of her cheek against his knuckles. "I can tuck your purse into this saddlebag if you like, or you can hold on to it." Wordlessly she handed him her bag, and he stowed it. Then he slipped out of his leather jacket and held it open expectantly.

"Just in case we wipe out, this will protect you."

Her eyebrows hiked. "Are we going to wipe out?"

"No, ma'am. But my mama taught me to take care of precious cargo. And you fit the bill perfectly." She slipped into his jacket and drew it close, causing him to smile. Too bad it wasn't his arms wrapping her in warmth.

He dropped the passenger foot pegs and instructed her to keep her legs away from the exhaust pipe.

"I'll board and then you climb on behind me. Just extend your right leg over the seat and slide gently up onto it. Drop your feet on the foot pegs and keep them there. Don't put them down when we stop. Do you think you can throw your leg over the seat with those heels on?"

Sexy, tan stilettos peeked out from the hem of cream pants with thin, coffee-colored stripes. The pattern of her jacket was the opposite, threads of white on brown. Conservative yet hot. Did she know how provocative she could be?

Mackenna scrunched up her face. "The heels aren't a problem."

"Okay. Once we're moving, you'll be able to talk to me through the microphone in the helmet. But tell me your address now so I can plug it into the navigation system."

Her eyes widened. She sure as hell didn't want him to know where she lived, although he remembered her address from the dossier Demond emailed him. An apartment building in a nicer part of town. Maybe she did have a man in her life. But then, why hadn't she called him for a ride?

"I don't want to go home. Is the offer for something to eat still on the table?"

Finally. His face split into a wide grin. "You bet it is."

After strapping on his own helmet, he threw his right leg over the bike and settled into the seat. She used his shoulder for balance and eased into place behind him. He instructed her to lean with the bike as they turned a corner, even though she might feel like she was falling off. He assured her she wouldn't.

"Don't take this the wrong way but you should wrap your arms around my waist and hold tight until you feel comfortable."

All he heard was her breath in his earpiece. And then her arms went around his middle and her thighs encompassed his butt and hips in a nest of warmth. It was a sample of heaven. Would she notice if they rode like that for the next two days?

Or forever?

12

He knew just the spot. A bar he'd discovered that wasn't too rowdy and catered to the more genteel rider, like himself, rather than the Hell's Angels type. Although some of the friends he'd made there might certainly be members of that group. He never asked.

Plus, the food was good, dancers were encouraged to strut their stuff, and a live band played every night after nine. He might not be able to keep Mackenna there that long, but he'd give it a shot. A night of dancing and laughing might do her good. And he wanted as much time with her as he could steal.

She tensed when he made a left turn out of the parking lot, squeezing her arms tight to his side and pressing against his back, and a second time when he went right at the intersection. But in no time at all, she relaxed behind him, even though she kept a tight grasp around his waist.

"What do you think?" His words startled her, and her breasts poked into his shoulder blades, prompting him to smile.

"You were right. This is exhilarating."

"Maybe we can take a long ride in the country some time.

It's much better to smell fresh grass than exhaust fumes." When she remained silent, he added, "No strings attached."

That made her chuckle. "Maybe."

He eased the Harley into a parking spot at the end of the crowded lot. After shutting down the engine, he waited for her to slide off before he dropped the kickstand. She shook out her shoulder-length brown hair and straightened her clothes. "I feel windblown."

"You look beautiful."

"How can you tell? It's dark."

He laughed. She seemed more comfortable with him now. He gently placed his hand on her waist as they walked through the parking lot. "I'm pretty sure the ladies' room has hair products and stuff that you can use to smooth everything back into place."

This time, she laughed. "How would you know what's in the ladies' room? No, wait, I already suspect you're a rogue so don't tell me anything that will confirm it."

A couple strolled out the door as he attempted to look shocked. He held it for Mackenna to enter. She took three steps inside and stopped, glancing around the bar. Country music blared from speakers in all four corners and everywhere, groups and couples talked and laughed. Jake grabbed her hand.

"C'mon. It's slightly quieter on the patio. You don't mind sitting outside, do you?" He didn't wait for an answer and instead, forged a path through the crowd toward the back of the room with her in tow. The waitress recognized him and motioned toward an empty table just outside the door.

He slid a chair out for Mackenna as the waitress wiped the surface clean and handed them each a menu. "The usual, Jake honey?"

"Sure, Evey. Give my friend a minute to decide, okay?"

"Be right back."

Mackenna eyed him. "What's the usual, Jake honey?" Her

voice had a teasing lilt in it. He liked how it made him feel. Giddy. "Let me guess. A cold beer in a frosted mug."

Jake settled into the chair to her right, his back to the building. "That sounds delicious, but I never drink when I'm on the bike. Feel free to order one though, if you like."

SHE SHOOK HER HEAD. "I'm not a very good drinker. I think I'm missing the alcohol tolerance gene. I get drunk too easily and do really stupid things."

He suppressed a grin. "What's your cut-off limit?"

"Why?"

In his mind it was an innocent question, but she was suspicious of everything. He inhaled deeply and shook his head slowly. "I think you're missing the trust gene, too, sugar. I only asked so I know when to cut you off. Do I bring out the worst in you or are you this guarded with everyone?"

Her mouth dropped into a tiny circle. His eyes were drawn to her lips. The memory of the department store kiss whet his appetite for more.

"I'm sorry. It's just," she shrugged, "I don't know. I'm in a bad emotional spot right now and I have a low opinion of all men. My limit is two drinks. After that, I'm toast."

The waitress returned and set a tall, ice-filled glass in front of him. She cracked her gum and asked, "What's for you, honey?"

Mackenna studied Jake's glass. "What are you drinking?"

"I'm a 'Bama boy. It's sweet tea."

"I'll have the same, please." The waitress winked and walked away. Mackenna studied the menu. "What's good here?"

Me, honey. Can't you see that?

He recommended his favorite black-and-bleu burger with seasoned fries. While she reviewed the menu he checked out the crowd, nodding at a few familiar faces and taking note of the people standing around the bar and clustered near the door.

"Are you looking for someone in particular?"

He hadn't realized Mackenna studied him. "No, not at all. Just looking around."

"Hoping you don't run into your girlfriend when you're with another woman?" Her voice teased him, but the look on her face was serious.

"No, ma'am, that's not a concern at all. It's always good to familiarize yourself with the surroundings. You know, where the exits are, what parts of the room might be more crowded, stuff like that. In case there's an emergency and you have to get out quick."

"Aren't you already familiar with this place? I thought you were a regular here."

He nodded. "It's a habit I have. So, tell me, how'd you like your first motorcycle ride?"

A smile brightened her face, and she conceded she'd enjoyed it. As they made small talk about different topics, her shoulders dropped. She sat back in the chair and stopped folding and refolding her napkin, all positive body language indicators that she was beginning to feel more at ease with him. Until her phone rang and she spied the identification of the caller. Immediately, her torso locked up tighter than her bank vault.

"Would you like me to step away?"

She grabbed his forearm. "No. Please stay."

It was the boss again. Jake couldn't hear what he said, but he didn't allow Kenna much time to answer. She stuttered a few no's and yeses and with each one, the hold on his arm tightened. Finally, Jake couldn't keep quiet.

He waved his hand in front of her face and whispered, "What's he want?"

"Hang on a minute, Ted, the waitress is asking me a question." She covered the phone with her hand and moved it beneath the table. Her teeth clattered like a set of castanets. "He wants to know what time I'll be home. He wants to meet me there."

The bastard. "Tell him you're spending the night with a friend."

Tears rimmed her eyes. "But I have nowhere to go. And he's going to ask. He'll check, I know he will."

That didn't jive. What about her friend from the bank, the one who handed her money the day after the first robbery? Why couldn't she go there?

"What about staying with a girlfriend?"

Water welled in her eyes. "I can't. To be honest, I haven't been a very good friend to most of my friends. It's a long story."

Warning bells sounded in his head as words passed through his lips that surprised even him. "You can spend the night on my sofa. It's quite comfortable. I fall asleep on it most every night."

She caught her breath. "I can't spend the night with you, I don't even know you. I'm not sleeping with you."

He canted his head. "I didn't invite you into my bed, sugar. If you prefer, I'll take you to a motel."

"I can't afford a motel."

"Well, from where I sit, you can't afford to go home either unless you want to screw your boss because we both know that's what he's after." He slid his hand under the table into her lap and pried the phone from her grasp.

"Hey, Ted, is it? Jake Manettia here. Kenna's staying with me tonight. I'll see that she's at work on time tomorrow morning. Thanks for checking on her, man, but I got this." He ended the call and returned the phone to her. "Problem solved."

Her jaw sagged and her hand flew to her mouth. "Are you crazy? What'd he say?"

"I didn't give him a chance to say anything. If he gives you a hard time tomorrow, please call me. I'll come to the bank and have a talk with him."

"You're going to get me fired, and then I'll truly be screwed."

The waitress arrived and when Kenna ordered her burger without a bun and substituted the fries for coleslaw, he made a mental note. His younger sister suffered from Celiac's disease, a gluten intolerance, so he was quite familiar with the diet. Kenna must also be sensitive. Good to know the next time he took her out. Because he definitely wanted a next time.

13

"How long have you worked at the bank?" Jake waited to ask until the waitress left. "Don't you have seniority or protection from being arbitrarily dismissed?"

"Theoretically, yes. But don't forget I'm a bank teller who has been held up twice and who the FBI is suspicious of. I doubt seniority would factor into something like that. But even without that, it'd be so easy to fabricate a case against me. Mr. Gleaner could fudge my end-of-the-day numbers and make it look like my drawer was short. Or he could say he received complaints about my demeanor or my attitude. If he wanted, he could fire me within a week."

"Is he the reason you detest the entire male population?"

She laughed. "One of them. But..." She cast her gaze away from his inquiring eyes, found nothing else to focus on, and raised her chin as she looked straight at him again. "You might as well know the whole sad saga that has become my life. I told you the other day that I threw my boyfriend out. Arthur and I lived together for a year. I thought he was my king." She regarded Jake with a half-smile. "That's a reference to Camelot. You probably don't know that."

A challenge. He loved it. "Knights of the Round Table. King Arthur. A Broadway play and a movie starring Richard Harris, I believe. Also used to refer to the presidency of the late John F. Kennedy. I'm pretty sure it only rains in Camelot after sundown."

A smile exploded across her face and the light in her eyes ignited a spark in his heart. Suddenly the stress of the past days evaporated. He saw more teeth in that grin than he'd seen since he met her.

She bowed her head in tribute. "You surprise me, sir."

Wouldn't be the only time, he hoped. He returned her grin.

"Well, my King Arthur turned out to be king creep. A liar and a cheat. It took me a while to admit it because, well, quite frankly I let my pride dictate my life. That was a mistake I'll never make again."

Jake studied her as she spoke, still assessing her body language. Her control remained steadfast. "I'm sorry."

A deep breath as she resigned herself to the facts. "Don't be. Any feelings I had for him, or thought I had, are long gone. Mentally and emotionally I'm fine, even happy to be out of that relationship. I was totally prepared to move on.

"What I wasn't prepared for was Arthur's parting stab in the back. It was my apartment to begin with, so I ordered him to move out. The day that I was robbed the first time was the day he was supposed to remove all of his belongings. I was scheduled for a longer day because the bank was participating in the town's community celebration and staying open until seven. I figured that allowed him plenty of time to get in and get out without my seeing him. That's why I was hanging around the mall instead of going home after the bank closed. I was giving him time to take everything out.

"Only the joke was on me because that's exactly what he did. He took everything from my apartment, right down to the light bulbs. He left me a lumpy futon and a nasty note. He also wiped out my bank accounts, closed my credit cards, and changed the logins and passwords on everything. Utilities, phone, you name it. I figure I have about sixty days to recoup before I'm evicted and once this month's bills aren't paid, my credit will start to tank. I'm one of those people who lives beyond their means. It was easy to do with his paycheck supplementing my whims."

She spread her hands to indicate their dinner plates. "The list of creditors will be long so I'm afraid you'll have to wait in line for repayment of this meal and my car repairs."

"Jesus, Kenna, did you call the police? Do you know where he went? That's theft. He committed a crime."

"Yep, that's my luck. Robbed twice in one day. I didn't call the police because I don't know where he went. And I can't prove anything. My bank account was emptied from my computer using my identity. It looks like I did it."

"You should still get a report on file. You know his contact information."

She shook her head. "I tried calling him, but the cell phone number is no longer in service. He must've changed it."

He nodded. Victims usually possessed more personal knowledge about someone than they realized. "You know more than you think, honey. I assume you know his birth date, maybe even his Social Security number. You know the type of car he drives, possibly the license number. You know where he works, where he takes his dry cleaning, where he likes to shop, what organizations he belongs to, who his insurance carrier is. All that is valuable information the police could use to locate him."

Her eyes narrowed, her fork dangling in the air. "You're some kind of cop, right?"

"Who? Me?"

"Yeah, that's what you said in the coffee shop when I asked what you did. You said security. What exactly do you do because you sure seem to sit on the right side of the law."

Tread carefully, Manettia. "Maybe it's just that I know right from wrong. And what Arthur did is wrong, not to mention illegal."

She tilted her head, closed one eye halfway, and studied him. "Come to think of it, you told Mr. Gleaner on the phone that your name is Jake Manettia. But when we were in the grocery store, that's not the name your friend Vincent used. He called you something different, didn't he?"

Dammit. Ted's attempted manipulation of Kenna had him so worked up, he'd identified himself on the phone using his real name, instead of his undercover name. He should have heeded his boss's advice and stayed away from her.

"Vinny never gets his facts straight. I don't recall what name he used. And you're trying to change the subject. You should call the police and file a report. And while you're being assertive, you should let Old Boss Man Ted know you aren't going to stand for his harassment."

She propped her elbow on the table and dropped her chin into her hand. "Tell the police and tell Mr. Gleaner. And what should I tell you, Mr. Mystery Man?"

MACKENNA FELT A SURGE OF SATISFACTION. The question had surprised Jake. He dropped back into his chair. Good. Jake the Jerk was a little too confident for his own good. Although after having her arms around him on the motorcycle and now sharing dinner, he was hardly a jerk. Rather attractive and she liked his wit. Lots of muscles were concealed beneath his clothes.

She'd felt them while pressed against him on the bike. A flat, firm stomach and taut back muscles that flexed with his movements. The proximity of their bodies coupled with the vibration from the motorcycle ride had been rather stimulating. After he suggested it, she'd imagined them taking that ride in the country on a sunny afternoon, stopping for a picnic lunch in a grassy pasture, and tasting each other on the blanket for dessert. It'd been too long since she'd been loved, truly adored. Arthur had been disappointing in the affection arena and rather bland between the sheets, like she was fragile glass that he feared would break. And so, he hardly touched her. And if she were honest with herself, he'd only used her, never really loved her.

Contact with Jake had been minimal, yet she'd welcomed his hold on her elbow and his hand riding her hip, easily gliding her through the mall. Being physically near him was pleasant. Jake, in his black leather with thighs strong enough to balance a Harley and a rider, might be a bad boy but he sparked a fire in her belly. She'd always been a good girl. Maybe it was time to cross over to naughty. She smiled at her thoughts while his royal blue eyes studied her.

"You haven't answered my question, sir."

He wiped his mouth with his napkin. "Yes, ma'am. I'm afraid if I answer you honestly, you'll be offended. I'm enjoying this meal with you, and I don't want to make you mad again."

She felt empowered. "You told me earlier at the FBI office that as long as I tell the truth, I have nothing to worry about. You must believe honesty is a good policy. I encourage you to be honest."

He mirrored her posture, propping his elbow on the table and settling his chin in his hand. They were face to face and her eyes dropped to his mouth when he spoke.

"What should you tell me? You should say 'Jake, I like you and I'd like to spend more time with you.' And you should say

'Jake, later when you ask if you can kiss me, I'm going to say yes.' Then you should add, 'I want to make love with you some-day, Jake, because I know you're a good man and that's what I need.'"

She jerked back as if the heat of his words scorched her face. He sat back as well. "You requested honesty, sugar."

Her heart fluttered. "Well, you didn't have to be quite so honest. I'm not interested in another relationship. I told you, I'm off men. And I barely know you."

He pushed his chair back. "Let's head home and I'll tell you all about my Southern mama and three sisters while I'm making up the sofa."

She remained seated and stared up at him. "Can I change my mind? It's nothing against you, I'm just not comfortable going home with you. I'm certain your girlfriend wouldn't appreciate it either. I'd like to go back to my place. I don't think Mr. Gleaner will bother me tonight. He thinks I won't be there."

She wasn't confident of that fact but sleeping in the same building let alone the same apartment as Jake seemed dangerous and, as tempting as it sounded, she wasn't quite ready to cross over to naughty. At least she assumed he lived in an apartment. She knew practically nothing about this man who still held out his hand, waiting for her to stand. She didn't trust her desire to learn more about him.

"It's fine if you'd rather go home. I'll camp out at your place then, just in case. I'm on my best behavior, so you don't have to worry."

Her hand slid tentatively into his and she rose. "No furni-ture, remember? The only option would be to sleep on the floor. I doubt that would be very comfortable."

"I've slept in foxholes, sugar. A carpeted floor will be heaven. And once we get there, we'll call Vicky so she can assure you she's just my friend."

Mackenna remained still. His hand clung to hers, but she

hadn't moved with him when he took his first step. He paused, silently questioning her hesitation.

"One more thing."

He waited.

"No kiss."

"No, ma'am. Not until you're ready."

14

On the ride home Mackenna convinced herself there was no need for Jake to sleep on her floor. She persuaded him to leave with the promise he'd be the first phone call she made, even before the police, if she sensed trouble. Although the events of the last few days had dulled her senses to the point where she might not recognize trouble when it presented itself. If an asteroid crashed through her sliding glass door right now, she'd probably reach for the vacuum and clean up the mess with the thought that she somehow deserved the intrusion. Except she no longer owned a vacuum cleaner.

She didn't own anything anymore, not even her identity. That was the real reason she couldn't let Jake get a glimpse into her sorry life. No one should see how low she'd sunk.

She didn't fear Mr. Gleaner knocking on her door as much as she dreaded the embarrassment of Jake seeing the conditions she lived in. He *was* a nice guy. Under other circumstances, she'd be thrilled by his interest. He escorted her to her apartment door, but she'd insisted he begin his walk back toward the elevators before she slipped inside. Her stomach

fluttered when he winked, reminded her "no kiss," and sauntered away.

She'd immediately recalled the kiss in the department store
when he seemed so happy to see her and regretted establishing
that boundary. His lips had been firm and his kiss possessive.
Despite her shock at his actions, a tingle of excitement coursed
through her that day. A sweet kiss before stepping into the
darkened abyss that now was her home might have eased the
pain.

But she'd drawn the line, and Jake made no attempt to cross
it. *Dumb move, McElroy.*

The night passed without incident. She barely slept. The
futon was not made for an adult to spend the night comfortably
with a cheap pillow and small throw blanket. She slept in her
clothes, her cell phone clutched in her hand.

This morning, she operated on automatic pilot, rising,
showering, and making her way to the East Seventh Street
branch. Her sense of relief that Mr. Gleaner would be at the
Mound Avenue branch was short-lived. He strolled into the
East Seventh Street building shortly after nine. Her morning
coffee turned to acid in her stomach. Ten minutes after his
arrival, he stood behind her waiting for her to complete a
customer's transaction. His mere presence turned her fingers
into thumbs as she clumsily concluded the withdrawal.

"After this customer, close your window and step into the
manager's office please, Miss McElroy."

He shut the door behind her and lowered the privacy
shades on the glass panels that fronted the office and allowed
the manager full view of the tellers and customers when it was
raised.

Two chairs for visitors were positioned in front of the desk.
He didn't indicate she should occupy one, so she stood tall in
between them braced for a speech. On what, she'd no idea. The

room fell silent while he remained behind her. Finally, she twisted her head to see him over her shoulder.

"Face forward, please."

She refocused on his empty leather chair, half expecting to be paddled like a mischievous child called to the principal's office. But schools didn't do that anymore. When Mr. Gleaner finally spoke, she jumped.

"It's my understanding that you recently parted ways with your live-in boyfriend, is that correct?"

Damn, Sandy. She was a good friend, but she thrived on gossip.

"Yes, sir."

"Who is the man on the motorcycle? A new beau already?"

He knew about Jake? How? Her eyebrows knitted at the antiquated reference to a boyfriend.

"No, sir. He's only an acquaintance I recently made."

"Yet, you allow him to take you home?"

Had Mr. Gleaner been there? Spying on her? She twisted her head, and he snapped at her to face his empty chair. What the hell?

"I needed a ride, sir."

"I offered to come and pick you up."

"Yes, sir, but Jake was already there. The FBI summoned him along with some other customers. When we left—"

He cut off her words. "Never mind about him."

More silence, punctuated by her boss's heavy breathing. Her pulse increased to the same tempo, and a foreboding prickled her arms with goose bumps.

Mr. Gleaner cleared his throat. "I see that you are in dire financial straits, is that correct?"

It shouldn't surprise her that he knew about her zero bank account balance. He had full access to all the bank transactions and accounts and, probably some automated delinquent notice had been generated when the bills set for payment directly from her checking account bounced for lack of sufficient funds. Her email inbox likely was full of payment notices and reminders. Without a computer, she hadn't checked. Ignorance was bliss.

"Yes, sir."

Mr. Gleaner stepped behind her. He laid his hands on her shoulders. "Let me help you out." Puffs of air hit the back of her neck when he spoke. Her spine stiffened. He was that close.

"When you walk out of this office, I'll deposit five hundred dollars into your account. And tonight, after I leave your apartment, I'll deposit another nine hundred, which will cover your rent payment for this month. It was due five days ago, I believe."

Her heart exploded in her chest. A wave of nausea overcame her.

"I-I don't understand, sir."

His grip on her shoulders slid south, across her chest. He cupped her breasts and drew her backward into an embrace. Automatically, she raised her hands to release his hold, but he held her tight.

"I can make it better or you can make it worse."

Tears welled in her eyes. "Sir?"

His hands squeezed her breasts, dropped to her waist and settled on her hips. "I think you understand perfectly. You like men, that's obvious. You'll learn to like me. And your financial future will be guaranteed." His fingers moved slowly, in a walking motion, coaxing the jersey material of her dress upward. "You won't have to worry about money. Your career here at the bank can soar. It's your choice, Miss McElroy."

She began to hyperventilate. And perspire. He'd hiked her dress up to her hips and leaned against her, pressing his erection into her backside.

"You can't afford to lose your job, can you?"

The arms she planted on the desk to steady her wobbled. "No, sir."

"Let me make it better for you. Bend over."

She held her back stiff. "Please, Ted. Don't do this. I don't want you to touch me. Please. Don't."

"You have two choices, Miss McElroy. Bend over or pack your shit and get out."

MACKENNA RUSHED TO THE LADIES' room and vomited. Kneeling on the tile floor, she sobbed against the side of the cool, porcelain commode. This was no way to live, and she had nothing to live for. Mr. Gleaner would have raped her right there at the desk if the intercom hadn't buzzed and interrupted him. He'd cursed, said to expect him tonight, and zipped his pants. She'd used the distraction to bolt from the office. But that was simply a temporary escape. Mr. Gleaner expected to have sex with her tonight and who knew how many nights after that. She couldn't do that. She wouldn't.

Another teller entered.

Mackenna tried but couldn't contain her sobs.

"Are you okay?" the woman asked.

"I-I'm fine. I just keep reliving the robberies and it's upsetting. No need to call anyone."

She wiped her face with a wet towel and returned to her station. She could file an HR complaint, but what good would that do? His word against hers. And it could cost her job. Once her landlord evicted her, she'd end up one of those dirty, homeless women begging for money and doing who knew what to get it. But wasn't that what Mr. Gleaner wanted her to do? Give him sex in return for financial gain. No way.

Mr. Gleaner whistled through the rest of the day, smiling at customers and employees alike. The other tellers noticed and twittered about his good mood. Two of the younger women mooned over him, expressing their desires to spend one-on-

one time with him. She'd gladly surrender her place in his demented mind.

Toward the end of the day, he approached and touched her elbow, standing close enough that his crotch rubbed her bottom. "Before we go to your place tonight, let's have dinner. I know an Italian restaurant with a fantastic wine list. I'll ask you to stay late and we won't leave until everyone else is gone. That way we won't arouse suspicion." He hadn't waited for her to accept the offer.

Even Arthur's meager attempts at civility were posed as a question when he'd ask, "Do you wanna cook or go out tonight?"

She wouldn't have believed she could find someone lower than Arthur.

Riding in the passenger seat of Mr. Gleaner's Cadillac felt like methodical torture. He made small talk, as if he hadn't nearly raped her hours earlier and didn't plan to soon. Chitchatting about bank operations, profit margins, and her potential for promotion within the company. As what, his personal whore? She responded with obligatory grunts in the appropriate places, her mind frantic with what was to come and how she could avert it.

One idea continually resurfaced. Jake. If she could call Jake, he might be able to help. Even rescue her. Again. Sheesh, she was becoming so dependent on him, calling him when someone followed her at the mall, letting him fix her car, and now, on the verge of rape, needing a knight to save her.

As soon as they arrived at the restaurant, she asked about the ladies' room. Mr. Gleaner scowled but said he'd wait for her before taking a table. Her fingers trembled while she searched for Jake's name in her contact list. Her heart sank when the call went to voicemail. Other women had come into the bathroom, so she quickly spoke into the phone. "Please call me. It's important. This is Mackenna."

Mr. Gleaner looked at his watch when he saw her come out. "Are you all right? You were in there a long time."

She nodded. "There's always a line in the ladies' room." Her stomach soured as she followed the waitress to a candlelit table for two in the corner. Mr. Gleaner made a show of ordering wine, sniffing the cork, and swirling a taste in his mouth before nodding his approval. Mackenna simply wanted to throw back a couple glasses, get smashed, and make it through the remaining hours of this agonizing interlude.

He insisted on ordering for her. A cream-heavy pasta dish with fresh Italian bread. Fried cheese sticks as an appetizer. Maybe she could eat her way to death.

Her phone rang by the time their entrée arrived and she was on glass number three. Or four? Who was counting?

"'Lo?"

"Kenna? Is that you?"

She giggled. "Un-huh."

"Kenna? Are you okay?"

"Hey, Jake, ole buddy. How's it hangin'?"

"What's the matter with you? Where are you?"

"Nothin's matter, JakeyBoy. I'm enjoying a wonerfull pasta dinner with my boss. At a restaurant."

His voice grew louder. "Are you crazy? Pasta will make you sick. What the hell are you doing with him? Are you drinking? Where are you?"

She giggled and burped. "Oh, 'scuse me. It's a fine wine. Tastes like grape juice. I like it. Oops, I gotta go. Mr. Gleaner isn't happy that I'm talkin' to ya. Bysey-bye." She held her glass out for a refill.

≈

JAKE STARED AT HIS PHONE. Dammit. He was still an hour outside of town. How the hell was he going to find her? What time did they arrive at the restaurant. How long until that bastard hauled her drunken ass home and took advantage of her? He'd kill the fucker.

He dialed Demond. "Any chance you're keeping an unofficial eye on Mackenna McElroy?"

"I thought that's what you were doing."

"Yeah, well, I also have to placate Vinny Cabacolli and keep tabs on my day job. Never mind, I'll find her."

Damn Vinny. He'd taken Jake on his collection runs tonight, confirming the FBI's intel that businesses paid the Cabacolli family for protection. Jake hadn't actually witnessed any payoffs because Vinny wouldn't dirty his hands with a shakedown. They remained in the back seat of Vinny's BMW while one of his goons entered the establishments. There'd been one casualty. A store owner who didn't have the full amount. Jake held his breath when Vinny's enforcer removed a tire iron from the trunk and disappeared inside the building. Fearing the worst, he reasoned with Vinny.

"If you kill him, doesn't that shortchange you in the future?"

"They won't kill him, just inflict pain. From now on, he'll fear me. Trust me, fear is a weakness. When I learn a man's weakness, I win."

Jake fought to keep his dinner down.

Vinny's invitation to tag along moved Jake one-step closer to the Cabacolli inner circle, despite his disgust over the evening's activities. The bosses would be happy.

He only wished Vinny hadn't chosen tonight to open that door. His thoughts were consumed by Mackenna. He'd wondered how her boss had reacted today to Jake's dismissal of his phone call last night. He'd worried that she'd pay the price for the rebuff.

His day hadn't allowed him time to go to the bank to see her. He'd dialed her cell phone twice; fully aware she wouldn't answer. Bank tellers stowed their cell phones when working the windows. He'd hoped she might call him over her lunch hour, but she hadn't returned either call as he'd requested. When she did finally call, he wasn't in a position to answer.

He cursed again. Half of the restaurants within a fifty-mile radius of her apartment were unfamiliar to him. That was if her boss decided to feed her somewhere close. Hell, they could be anywhere. Better to camp out at her apartment and wait. Assuming he arrived there in time.

Last night when he drove her home he frowned when he noticed her apartment building didn't have a security system for the front door. Now, he was grateful. He took the stairs two at a time to the fourth floor and banged on Mackenna's apartment door. No response. The chances were fifty-fifty that her boss would bring her back here to seduce her, in which case Jake was in luck. If the joker coaxed her to a motel or his place, wherever that was, all Jake would be able to do was clean up the mess. Because sure as hell, Kenna was caught in one hell of a predicament.

Leaning against the wall he braced his shoulders and slid to the floor, stretching out his legs. Nothing to do but wait.

About an hour passed, his anger escalating with each minute, before the elevator bell pinged down the hall. The door opened and a man stepped out, his arm wrapped around Kenna, supporting her. It had to be her boss, Ted. They made a loud and raucous entrance into the hallway. Jake jumped to his feet, his fists clenched. Mackenna and her boss laughed and wobbled toward the wall. "Whoa, whoa, whoa, sweetie. What's your apartment number again?"

Kenna laughed and pointed with a limp wrist. "There. Right there. Where the man is standin'."

Ted halted their progress. The pair stood together, swaying. The boss blinked several times. Kenna's head bobbed while she appeared to focus on the figure approaching them. Jake advanced slowly. The urge to punch the man into oblivion was surpassed by his concern for Kenna. Her eyes were bloodshot. Her makeup smeared. More strands of hair escaped the elastic ponytail band than stayed captured. A red blotch stained her shirt. She flashed him a ridiculous grin and kept her arm in the air as if to welcome him.

"Lookie! It's Jakey. Wha a nice sapprise."

Jake grabbed her arm and tugged her toward him. "I've got her now, Ted. You can leave." Kenna fell into his arms and slumped toward the floor.

"Who the fuck are you?"

Jake understood each word, spoken clearly and distinctly. Ted wasn't one bit drunk.

Jake hoisted Kenna into an upright position and hugged her to his chest. "I'm the guy who just ruined your seduction plan. She is hardly in a condition to consent so, I'd say I did you a favor. I saved your ass from rape charges."

Mackenna's head snapped up. "I canna afford to lose my job. He-he already tried. I..." a loud belch blasted stale breath in his face, "...I puked after." Her eyes closed and her head rolled back onto his shoulder. "I don feel so goot."

Ted's eyes widened. He shook his head to deny her words. Heat rocketed through Jake's entire body. "What did she just say?"

Kenna's boss waved his hand in the air. "She's drunk. She doesn't know what she's saying. I don't appreciate you being here, buddy. Mackenna and I are dating. We both had too much to drink." He spread his arms wide. "I'm merely making sure she gets home safe. Who did you say you were?"

Jake's chest heaved. Standing toe-to-toe with the prick, he had about three inches on the guy. Even with Mackenna sagging in his arms, he could lay a mighty hurt on the piece of shit. "I know who you are and you're not dating. And believe me, *buddy*, you don't want to know who I am, not really. Stay away from her or you'll find out."

He tucked his hand beneath Mackenna's knees and lifted her into his arms. As he approached her apartment door, he yelled over his shoulder, "You better be gone when I turn around. And if you ever touch her again, I swear I'll kill you."

He pivoted at Mackenna's apartment door and viewed an empty hallway. Old Ted must have taken the steps because the elevator hadn't pinged. After feeling inside the entire contents of Mackenna's purse, which she clung to with one hand, he located her keys and opened the door.

She'd said Arthur took everything but Jesus, this was like walking into a cave. No wonder she hadn't wanted him to enter last night. How was she living like this for even one day?

They stumbled through the main room, and he spied the kitchen to the right and a coffeemaker. "How about some coffee, sugar?"

"I jus wanna sleep."

"I know, but let's pour a little caffeine in you first. You're going to be sick soon. We might as well get it over with." Ordinarily, he'd settle her on the sofa or in an easy chair but that wasn't an option. He leaned her gently against the wall and held her shoulders. "Let's ease down to the floor, okay? C'mon."

Gravity took over the minute her knees unlocked, pulling her downward. She landed on her backside with a thud. The wall supported her head, and she stretched out her legs.

"Stay here. I'll brew the coffee."

"I don feel so goo, Jakey."

Despite the pathetic look on her face, he grinned. No one had called him Jakey since the third grade.

Mackenna's eyes closed. She might have already drifted off but at least she was upright. He started the coffee and wandered around the rest of the apartment. One futon in a bedroom and her clothes neatly folded and stacked in another bedroom. No surprise there. She was careful about her personal appearance. It made sense her home would be neat as a pin. Although, there wasn't much to keep clean in this vacuum.

The bathroom looked the most normal with cosmetics, toiletries, and accessories arranged in an orderly line against the back of the sink. Curious, he opened the linen closet and found three bath towels bearing the discount store's label. This was no way to live especially for a woman like Kenna.

The coffee sputtered and spouted its final brewing stages. Strolling toward the kitchen, he eyed Mackenna's designer purse, still dangling from her arm. The polite thing to do would be to remove it and deposit it on the kitchen counter. But a good investigator never passed up the chance to scrutinize… what? What did he suspect the contents of her purse might reveal? Something to implicate her in the robberies? Or proof of her innocence? Which did he want to find?

Gently, he eased the purse off her wrist and peeked inside. A clutch wallet and her cell phone mixed with a tissue pack, cosmetics, hand cream, a comb, three pens, eye drops, and a few cash register receipts. She'd had to buy the linens he saw and the coffee pot at the discount store just weeks earlier. She wasn't kidding when she said her ex had taken everything. What would make a man do that?

Her cell phone asked for a code to unlock the screen. He clicked it off and dropped it back inside. A couple charge cards and her driver's license filled her wallet. The compartment for bills held three dollars. His stomach sank. Demond said her bank account bordered on empty. Was that all the money she had?

He snapped the wallet closed and set the purse on the counter. Time to pump some coffee into her. He'd done his share of worshipping the porcelain throne after a night of over indulgence. As ugly as it could be, she'd feel better once she got that over with. After that, he wasn't sure what to do.

15

Midnight blackness suffocated her. Mackenna hyperventilated and sprang up into a sitting position. Two green dots flashed in the distance and to her left, the orange glow of a digital clock illuminated the time. Seventeen minutes after three.

"Relax, Kenna. You're okay." A man's deep voice sliced the darkness. Dear God, was it Gleaner? Where was she? Her throat clogged with fear. She skittered backward until the wall halted her escape.

She blinked once, twice. Too dark to see.

Someone moved beside her. "Take it easy, sugar. I'll turn on the light."

The luminosity blinded her. She squinted and tugged on a sheet? A blanket? Some type of cloth protection that she plastered to her heaving chest. Jake cocked his head.

"Easy, honey. You look like a frightened puppy. I won't hurt you."

Mackenna blinked again. She gulped. Her mouth was as dry as dirt. She laid her palm against her throbbing forehead. Jake was next to her in bed, naked from the waist up. He boosted himself into a sitting position on arms that bulged with muscles, then arranged the pillows and relaxed into them. Immediately she recalled the muscular system poster displayed in her doctor's office, the one that defines every muscle in the human body. Had he been the model for that placard?

A thin layer of tan skin barely covered every ripple and swell in his chest, which was topped with a smattering of dark hair. Some sort of tribal tattoo decorated the left side. She may have a hangover and be disoriented about her whereabouts, but she certainly was able to appreciate the fine specimen sharing a bed with her. Her pounding heart switched gears from fear to outright attraction. Holy cow. He was hot!

So was she when all of a sudden, the room became uncomfortably warm. Or was that her reaction to Jake, whom she might now mentally refer to as Juicy Jake. Her mouth watered for him, eliminating the dryness.

Mackenna drew the sheet closer to her chin and tucked her hair behind her ears. What happened to her ponytail? "Where are we?"

Jake folded his hands in his lap. When he spoke, his words were soft. "We're at my place. I wasn't about to leave you alone in that hole, and the idea of sleeping on your apartment floor didn't appeal to me."

"How'd I get here?"

He filled his chest, drawing her eyes to his chiseled pecs. "It was a little bit of a chore, believe me."

She squeezed her eyes shut. No recollection of the past... How many hours? She glanced at the clock again. No idea. What was the last thing she remembered? Certainly not crawling into bed with Jake. A body like his would be impossible to forget no matter how drunk she'd been.

She eyed his chest and taut stomach. "Are you naked?"

The corners of his mouth edged upward. "Normally I would be but, out of deference to you, I kept my skivvies on."

She glanced down at the white cotton T-shirt she wore, aware that she was braless and wore only panties. "You took my clothes off?"

Jake flat out grinned. "No, ma'am. You did that all by yourself. You were quite entertaining, too. If you lose your bank job, I'm certain you have a future at a strip club."

She gasped. Her cheeks burned.

"I'd like a replay of that performance someday when you're sober. I must say, you tempted every bit of my manly restraint. You are quite the vixen."

Her hand flew to her mouth in horror. "Oh my God. What did I do?"

"Now I see why you say you can't drink. A lesser man would have succumbed to your attempts at seduction." He raised one hand, stacking his thumb and forefinger a half-inch apart. "I came this close to saying yes."

"Some Southern gentleman you are. Didn't you try to stop me?"

She could swear his eyes beamed. "Sugar, if I hadn't stopped you, you'd be naked right now and we'd know each other a lot more intimately than we do."

She dropped her head into her hands. "Dear Lord. I want to die."

His voice deepened and assumed a serious tone. "That's the other reason I wasn't about to leave you alone. Look at me, please." She raised water-rimmed eyes to him.

"You kept saying you wanted to die. Throw yourself off the balcony or run into the middle of the highway. You scared me.

"Thoughts like that are unacceptable. You think you're unlovable, that men only want you for sex and not to see the real you. Sugar, you've no idea how alluring you are. I'd like the chance to show you how a real man treats a woman. When you're ready, that is. If you're interested."

Her head dropped against the headboard. A tear escaped

the corner of her eye. "I've never been so humiliated." She pressed the heel of her hand to her forehead.

"No need, honey. We've all hit low points in our life. But that's over for you now. I'll find some aspirin for that headache." He threw the sheet off his legs and stood, bringing to life the bottom portion of the medical muscle illustration. Sinewy thighs and a tight butt tucked into blue boxer briefs strolled from the bed into the adjoining bathroom. Had she been standing, her knees would have weakened.

She crawled to the edge of the bed and stood as Jake returned with a glass of water and two colored caplets in his palm. Her eyes feasted on his torso. The man was ripped. She swallowed the pills with a sip of water, unsure how they'd sit on her stomach, and then excused herself to use the restroom. Jake had placed a cellophane-wrapped toothbrush and tooth-paste on the sink. He certainly wasn't like any man she'd ever known.

One look at her pale complexion and raccoon eyes and she groaned. She brushed her teeth, pressed cool water to her face with her palms and scrubbed her teeth a second time. When she returned to the bedroom, Jake perched on the edge of the bed waiting.

Her gaze dropped to her feet. "Thanks for the toothbrush. My mouth feels disgusting."

A deep, sexy chuckle escaped him. "Your mouth is beauti-ful. I hope I get to kiss it some more."

She coaxed her hair behind her right ear. "You kissed me?"

Now a richer laugh that could heat a cold cup of coffee.

"You started it. But I confess I happily obliged."

This was beyond humiliation. Could she will her heart to cease beating and drop dead right this second?

Jake grinned and waved his hand to the side, indicating she should return to bed. "You first, ma'am."

Mackenna tugged at the hem of his T-shirt, cognizant that

with the light behind her, it likely was transparent. "Maybe one of us should sleep on the couch."

"Not necessary. I'm not the rapist, remember? We still have that to discuss, by the way."

Her stomach pitched. Bits and pieces of the night replayed in her mind in foggy snippets. But the events of the prior day remained clear.

Wordlessly she crawled across the queen-sized bed and backed up against the wall again, drawing the sheet to her chest. "Wh-what do you mean?"

Jake resumed his place, plumped the pillows, and leaned back, covering himself to the waist. "I believe your boss forced you to have some type of sex, I'm just not sure when. I hoped I could prevent it. That's why I waited for you at your apartment. But I think I was too late. For that, honey, I'm truly sorry."

Mackenna swallowed the lump in her throat. "I don't know what you're talking about."

His head bobbed slowly. "And now I know two absolutes about you. You're a poor drinker and a terrible liar."

She raised both hands to her head and twisted her hair into a ponytail, only she had nothing to secure it with. A few more twists and she draped it over her shoulder.

"Please, Jake. It's not what you think. I can't afford to lose my job. You saw my apartment. I have no money, nothing. If I don't play along with Mr. Gleaner, I'll be out on the street."

"That's a load of crap. The man used his authority to rape you."

"He didn't. He would have but the intercom buzzed and interrupted him, and I ran from his office. But he told me last night that since I agreed to go to dinner with him and whatever else, I could never accuse him of sexual assault because I'd be a willing participant." The aspirins sat like a rock in her stomach. She squeezed her mid-riff to ease the ache.

"That's a lie. There's a difference between a choice you

make and an ultimatum he gives you. Do you want to sleep with him?"

She gasped. "No. God no. He makes my skin crawl when he touches me."

"Is your job on the line?"

This was too degrading. She dropped her head into her hands, wishing it would all go away. But Jake didn't let it go. His voice was slow and silky. "Answer me, honey. Did he imply that you'd lose your job if you didn't consent to his advances?"

Her palms muffled her response. "Yes."

Jake took a deep breath and lightly caressed her arm. "Tell me what happened."

"I don't want to. I'm ashamed."

"You have nothing to be ashamed of unless you let him get away with hurting you again. Did you tell him no?"

She hung her head. "I never used that word. No."

"What did you say?"

"I think I said I didn't want him to touch me. Something like 'please don't.' That's not the same thing. He explained it to me at dinner."

"Dammit, it *is* the same thing. Tell me what happened."

Tears rolled down her cheeks, unchecked by her trembling hands. "Please, don't make me tell you. It's too awful. He'll fire me, I know he will."

Time stopped while he filled his lungs with an audible breath and exhaled slowly. Then he tugged on her wrists to draw her hands away from her face. He lifted her chin with his forefinger. Those blue eyes of his had deepened to purple and she saw into them, into a man with a kind, gentle soul. A man who for some reason seemed determined to protect her and was apparently destined to play a role in her life whether she wanted it or not.

Jake extended his open hand toward hers. "Give me your hand, honey. Please trust me."

She wanted to cry herself to death. Sob until her lungs exploded or simply evaporate into nothingness because at this precise moment, that's what she was. Nothing. Jake whispered her name.

Slowly, she slipped her trembling hand into his and immediately, his fingers wrapped around it, strong, warm, and comforting. "You're not in this alone. I'm here," he whispered. "Tell me when it happened."

Her fingers closed around his. She clung to them, praying for courage.

"Yest-yesterday afternoon."

"Where?"

"At the bank."

"Where specifically?"

"The manager's office."

"Did he force you to have oral sex with him?"

He held tight when she tried to draw her hand back. She barely shook her head. This was mortifying. She shook her head.

"Did he penetrate you?"

"No."

"Please tell me the specifics. It's important."

"He-he stood behind me and pressed himself against me. He was aroused and he-he rubbed himself against me. He—" A sob escaped her, and Jake tightened his grip.

"He told me I had two choices, either let him...you know... or pack my things and get out. He-he ordered me to bend over his desk, and he raised my dress. He shoved my panties down. I heard his zipper go down. I felt his.... Then the intercom buzzed. He swore, smacked my ass and moved to the front of his desk. He couldn't reach the phone from where we stood. I ran out of his office."

Despair took over and she wept, shaking her head in denial. Jake released her hand and edged toward her. He positioned himself beside her, his back against the wall just like she sat, and gently wrapped his arm around her shoulder. As if his muscles were magnets, she felt the tightness in her body release and she leaned into him. As her tension eased, her emotions overflowed. She hung her head and cried harder.

Jake cooed to her like she was an injured toddler, raising her hand to his lips to kiss it, and then drawing her closer. She wanted to crawl under his skin and stay tucked away from bank robbers and sexual predators and the FBI. How long they stayed in that position, she didn't know. Long enough for her to cry her heart out. At some point, he eased her head to a pillow across his thighs. His thumb drifted along her arm in a slow rhythm and every so often, he raised her fingers to his lips and lightly kissed them.

When Mackenna awakened, her head rested in Jake's lap. Behind her, soft snores. She lifted herself up an inch at a time so as not to disturb him. He'd propped the other pillows beneath his arm and laid his head on them. The forty-five-degree angle couldn't be comfortable. His neck would be stiff when he woke.

Exhaustion enveloped her. But the breakdown and extra sleep cleared her head. She studied the man who, even in sleep, clung to her hand. Those long eyelashes and the unkempt hair that now fell over his face. Why couldn't a man like him desire her instead of that monster of a boss?

Glancing around the bedroom, she frowned. On top of the bureau Jake had deposited his watch and wallet. Aside from that, the space was empty. The blinking green lights belonged to a router, which sat next to a laptop on a kid–sized desk. No drawers, no piles of paper on top.

Mackenna surveyed the rest of the room. It was so impersonal. One abstract painting of a wildlife scene hung behind the bed. It would have been centered except Jake had the bed shoved against the wall. No family pictures, mementos, or other clues about the man she was in bed with. Even the nightstand held only a digital clock, a pen and pad, and his cell phone. Had he not been truthful? Were they in a motel instead of his apartment?

The minute she attempted to ease her hand from his he awakened and sat up straight.

"I'm sorry. I tried not to disturb you," she whispered.

Jake blinked as if he was surprised to find her beside him, smiled and glanced at the clock. It was minutes before seven.

"Good morning, sugar. I hope you feel better. I turn into a human once I drink my coffee."

He edged toward the side of the bed and rose, retrieving his phone from the nightstand. "I'll start the pot."

He was unaffected by his state of undress, so she feasted her eyes on him as he walked toward the door in his underwear. Her head was clearer now, her eyes focused and her first impression the same as last night's. Wow!

Mackenna tucked her hair behind her ears. "I have to go home, shower and change. I can't be late for work."

He stopped in the doorway and regarded her through half-closed eyes. "You're not going to work this morning. You're going to the police station."

16

J ake dialed Vicky while he walked to the kitchen. Having Kenna here was a major violation of undercover conduct, one that would surely result in a written repri- mand, probable internal inquiry, and possible termina- tion if he were found out. He'd weighed all those consequences last night with Mackenna in his arms in that empty hole she called home. She'd been too distraught to leave there.

So that made bringing her here to his undercover apart- ment the only option. And risking everything. The decision wasn't as hard as he thought it should be. This woman who'd declared more than once that she didn't like him had inno- cently seeped into his pores and penetrated his soul. He couldn't leave her alone in that empty apartment last night because he couldn't leave her. He'd meant what he told her last night, that he'd babysit her every minute of the day if he had to.

A wry smile crossed his face while he waited for Vicky to pick up. Maybe they'd both end up homeless.

The bureau kept a tight leash on its undercover agents, always needing to know where they were and what they were doing. The monitoring was necessary in the event a case went bad, and the agent required backup. Tight supervision was reassurance for an agent under cover, but it also limited one's privacy. Jake couldn't simply go off the grid for a few hours without raising suspicion.

Vicky sounded cheerful when she answered his call. "What's up, partner?"

"Vick, I've got some personal things to take care of this morning. I'll be here at the apartment most of the morning, but off the clock."

Behind him, Mackenna snapped, "How dare you?" Loud enough for Vicky to hear.

"You entertaining?"

He couldn't admit that a possible suspect in two bank robbery cases had shared his bed the night before. "Just cover for me, will ya? Personal business this morning if anyone asks."

On the phone, Vicky remained silent while Mackenna huffed behind him. All the experience he had with three emotional sisters should have better prepared him to handle women. It hadn't.

Vicky broke the silence. "I hope you're not thinking with your dick, pal. Meet me at two o'clock at the usual place. Make sure you show up or I'll log it." She hung up before he could respond. Another female furious with him.

He plastered a smile on his face and pivoted to face Mackenna's wrath.

"You can't tell me what to do." Her hangover must have subsided because the level of her voice was two decibels below a shout. "I'm done with men who try to run my life. I want to go home. Now! If you won't take me, I'll call a ride."

Well, he liked the sound of that. At least she was back in fighting mode and not whining about a miserable existence and ending her life. He counted the scoops of coffee into the filter and pressed the brew button.

"Did you hear me, Jake?"

Wiping up the counter where water dripped, he nodded. "Yes, ma'am, I surely did. I'll be happy to take you home. And then I'll drive to the police station, and I'll file the report."

Her mouth dropped into a cute oval. Memories of her kisses from the night before flooded his brain and aroused his manhood. She'd begged him to make love to her, make her feel like a woman again. Damn, he'd wanted to. Real bad. He stepped closer to the sink, hiding the bulge in his underwear. He should've slipped on his jeans before leaving the bedroom.

"What do you mean?"

He shrugged. "I can file an attempted rape report based on information received. Whether it's because of you or me, police will question that bastard this afternoon."

"You wouldn't. I'll lose my job."

"How long do you think you're going to keep that job, anyway? You were babbling in the hallway last night about how you puked after he touched you. He knows that I know."

She stared at him, speechless, her hair disheveled and her makeup smeared from not scrubbing her face last night before falling asleep. Mackenna remained motionless, looking sexy as hell in his T-shirt.

Her eyes narrowed. He imagined her brain working. She stepped closer to the granite counter that separated the kitchen from the TV area. "Are you an attorney?"

He jerked his head slightly backward, surprised by the question. "No, ma'am."

"Then you're a cop."

He froze, striving for a blank facial expression. "You're changing the subject, sugar."

Her eyes flashed. "No, this is the subject at the moment. You." Her index finger pointed at him. "And exactly who you are. Earlier you asked if I was penetrated. Now you use words like information received? Who talks like that if not a lawyer or a cop?

"You've said before that as long as someone tells the truth, they have nothing to worry about. That's what you advised me to do and, much to my chagrin, I've been completely honest with you about a slew of things that are none of your business. I can blame some of that on the wine, I think. But I'm sober now."

The forefinger dropped to the countertop and tapped. "I'd like to know who you really are, Jake Manfred or Manettia or whatever your last name is today. Let's start with that."

His eyebrows betrayed him and shot upward. She recalled his alias and his real name? Fuck.

Kenna was on her toes this morning. She caught the eye movement. "That's right. I remember both names. I'm not stupid, all actions of the past weeks to the contrary. Who are you? What do you do for a living? And why are you so interested in me?"

Her cheeks flushed with anger. Standing there barely dressed she drummed her finger impatiently, her other hand perched on her hip. Under different circumstances, he'd scoop her up and make love to her into the middle of tomorrow, she was so damn attractive like that. And his desire raged. *Get your head in the game, Manettia. This is a major fucking problem standing in front of you.*

The number one rule of undercover work is never, ever, disclose your true identity, under any circumstance. Even in the face of death or, in this case, an intense attraction to a woman. Well, there it was. An admission in his head that his heart figured out days ago and his body agreed with one hundred percent. For whatever reason, this woman mesmerized him. If she shared even the slightest bit of affection with him, he'd be under her spell. Maybe he was already.

He wanted to know her so much more personally, physically as well as in every other way. What was her favorite color?

Her family background? Her dreams for a future? For a husband?

Certainly not a man who lied to her. He knew her well enough already to know that. She'd already said Arthur cheated and lied. Last night she'd rambled on and on about that loser and about her boss, whom Jake wanted one-on-one time with in a dark alley. She'd been an open book, candidly answering any question he asked, including his curiosity about both bank robberies. She wasn't involved in either of the hold-ups, he was certain. But she was caught in a lair of life's complications. And then, she'd turned the tables and sweetly asked, "That's my wretched life in a nutshell, Jakey. Now tell me who you are."

"Someone you can trust," he'd said. Because she could. But that opened the door to her attempted seduction, complete with the striptease, her straddling his lap and kissing the hell out of him. She was the most sensuous woman he'd ever had in his arms, even under the influence. He'd wanted to say yes to her requests to love her. But that'd make him no better than her boss, who'd taken advantage of her vulnerability and planned to exploit it. The man expected to have sex with her last night. Kenna fretted that Jake's interference angered him, which she thought would result in consequences for her. A police report wasn't going to make matters any worse than they already were.

Through tears last night, Mackenna was completely truthful about her life, even though she didn't recall telling him most of it. And now she expected the truth from him.

But he couldn't reciprocate, not without risking his career and possibly his life. He was glad Kenna's self-pity from last night had disappeared. But now, her chocolate- brown eyes bore a hole through him.

"Answer my questions, you son of a bitch. Who are you really?"

Both palms flattened onto the counter in an attempt to

steady his hands. He didn't want to lose her. But truth was not an option.

"My name is Jake. I—"

"Jake what? What's your last name?"

Why was the kitchen so damn warm? He wore only underwear and yet, perspiration soaked his back.

He filled his lungs with air and exhaled slowly, trying to calm his raging thoughts. "Will you listen to me for a minute without interrupting, please?"

A stall, but she bought it. Her hand cut the air between them. "The floor is all yours, sir."

"I'm someone you can trust, but I can't answer your questions. I can't tell you why and I know that's a conundrum." She opened her mouth to speak. He raised his hand in a halting motion.

"No interruptions, you agreed."

Mackenna clamped her jaw shut.

"My name is really Jake. I'm from a small town in Alabama where my mother still lives. She would love you. I have three sisters who drive me crazy, but I can't wait for you to meet them. Those are all truths."

He stopped talking, hoping that might end the conversation and knowing it wouldn't.

"What's your mother's last name?"

God, she was smart. He broke out into a wide grin.

"If she remarried, it would be different than mine."

"Has she?"

"No. She said there would never be another man like my daddy. He passed three years ago."

Her finger resumed beating on the counter. "Sorry. So. It's Jake...what?"

"Look, sugar, my last name doesn't matter. You ask valid questions that I'm not prepared to answer. I can't explain why. All I can do is ask you to trust me because you already know you can. And I beg you not to shut me out of your life because I know I want you in mine. It's a hell of a predicament we're both in. I'm asking for blind faith but in time, I'll be able to answer your questions. And you'll understand, I promise."

Mackenna's eyes widened and her face flushed. "Why in the hell would I trust you? After all I've been through, you stand here and ask me to have blind trust in someone I barely know but whom I already suspect is deceitful. I've had enough lies and betrayal. I'm done being used."

"Yes, ma'am, I agree with everything you say." He raised one finger. "I'd like to clarify one thing. I haven't lied to you. I haven't answered your questions, but that's not the same as not being truthful."

Her eyes narrowed as if honing her thoughts and giving weight to his argument. He took advantage of the moment.

"I'll tell you why you should give me the chance I'm asking for." Jesus, his heart raced like an express train. "You're standing in my apartment, in my T-shirt, and you spent the night in my bed. I could've taken advantage of you last night as many times as I wanted and honey, I sure wanted to. But I didn't because I want more than a hot night of sex with you."

He laid a hand on his chest, his heart muscle exploding beneath it. Did she see it? "Believe me, it's a shock to me too. As for trusting a total stranger, I don't care how drunk you were last night, you knew instinctively you could trust me. You know it now, standing here arguing with me. That's all I'm asking, to please trust me and give me a bit of time."

She arched one eyebrow. "Are you married?"

"No. That's the truth."

She studied him, perhaps considering his words, so he drove home his position.

"I understand you've been used and abused by men recently. I'm not one of them and even falling down drunk you knew that last night. You reached for me to get away from Ted.

For crissake, we're standing here in our underwear. You're not afraid of me, not one bit.

"Have one iota of faith in me, sugar. Please. And give me time. I promise, it will make sense."

Her chest heaved, and her lips formed a thin line while she studied him. Time stopped for him. His heart raced. Was she debating a future with him?

"I'd like to go home now."

His emotions tanked. Despair seeped into his bones, and he nodded slowly. He hadn't convinced her of anything. He'd take her home and lose her. "I need ten minutes to shower and dress, unless you want to shower first. You're welcome to."

She shook her head. "I just want to go home."

17

S tanding in her empty kitchen cradling a cup of coffee, Mackenna assessed her situation, disgusted by what her mind's eye viewed. Over the last six months, she'd let Arthur wreck her self-esteem, destroy her confidence, and rob her of her independence. She'd been so desperate to hold on to him, she'd let an overheard remark made by a jealous co-worker cloud her perspective about their relationship.

Mackenna turned thirty next year and her co-worker implied Arthur was Mackenna's last chance to snag a man. Ironic since the woman struggled with her own unhappy marriage. Yet, the comment powerfully affected Mackenna and although she'd enjoyed her single life, she'd been determined to make it work with Arthur. For their first three months, he'd been a dream companion. Everything changed once he moved in. The secretive texts. His unexplained lateness more evenings than she cared to number.

Finally, after searching his pockets while he showered, she'd discovered a motel receipt. That tiny slip of paper carried a wallop of a message. Sharing a bed with someone isn't the same as sleeping with someone who loves you. That was when she decided Arthur had to go.

And no, dammit, Arthur wasn't her last resort for happiness. No man was. Let the gossips have a field day. Throwing him out was the right thing to do. Sure, it'd be great to spend her golden years with someone special but if that didn't happen, she'd rescue a dog.

Begrudgingly, she admitted that Jake was right about Ted Gleaner. She couldn't let him sexually exploit her. She wouldn't. Yes, she was in a hell of a financial mess, but she'd work it out somehow. Even if it meant flipping burgers or working a night shift in a gas mart.

The ride home from Jake's apartment to hers had been silent. She'd been surprised when they exited the elevator to the underground garage of his apartment building, and he guided her toward a Jeep. Jake attempted conversation, saying that he'd driven the Jeep last night otherwise it would have been difficult to balance her on the back of his motorcycle for the drive to his place. She refrained from commenting, in part because she had no recollection of the trip. And this morning, it hadn't occurred to her to wonder how he'd gotten her there.

She remembered stumbling off the elevator with Mr. Gleaner and spotting Jake in front of her door. And feeling relief that he was there, waiting for her. Jake was spot on about one thing, she trusted him.

It was a hard lesson, but she learned definitively that alcohol was not her friend. She vowed to abstain completely in the future. But she hadn't consumed all that wine only to get drunk. She'd tried to block out Mr. Gleaner, fearing his plans.

Jake also was right that he could've taken advantage of her in her drunken state. But he hadn't. Instead, he'd realized she was drinking when he called her, suspected the worst, and rushed to her rescue. Maybe he actually was a knight in shining armor, worthy of a seat at the round table. After all, the knights in King Arthur's court lived by a code of chivalry. So did Jake, apparently. Was that another lesson to learn?

After she deflected his attempt at conversation en route to her apartment he remained silent until the Jeep stopped in front of her building. "Call me, please. Don't shut me down."

Those eyes of his had deepened to eggplant purple and misted. The look on his face mimicked a young boy who'd lost his best friend. She didn't know what to think or how to interpret her conflicted feelings. All she did was whisper, "Thanks for bringing me home," before exiting the passenger seat without looking back.

In retrospect, she had a hell of a lot more to thank him for. The heaviness in her heart included confusion about Jake. She didn't know a thing about him yet, he certainly was a good man. She knew it intuitively. He was right about that, too. She enjoyed being with him, manifested goosebumps recalling their closeness in his bed and conceded the mystery surrounding him both infuriated and infatuated her. Maybe she'd call him later.

But this morning, Jake wasn't a priority. After toweling herself dry she called the East Seventh Street Bank to say she had an appointment at the police station, and she'd be late. The clerk who answered the call assumed the meeting pertained to the bank robbery and Mackenna didn't correct her.

She applied her makeup carefully, concealing the dark circles beneath her eyes, dressed in a navy blue flowered sheath dress and stepped into red stilettos. One glance around her empty apartment, a fortifying deep breath and she lifted her chin a notch. Mackenna McElroy was done being used.

FILING two police reports took longer than she expected and involved dealing with two different police officers. The female officer who assisted her with the sexual assault report was full of compassion, even as she explained that without physical evidence, the charge against Ted Gleaner was weak. The officer recorded Mackenna's preliminary statement before asking questions designed to provide more details. When she asked if Mr. Gleaner had penetrated her, Mackenna snapped her face up from the paperwork.

"I'm sorry, Miss McElroy, but the more specific you can be, the stronger my report will be."

Mackenna shook her head. "Yes, I understand that it's just, a friend of mine asked me the same question, using the same words."

The policewoman smiled. "Is he a cop?"

"I think so." He had to be. But why wouldn't Jake simply admit that?

Essentially, the attempted assault accusation would boil down to Mackenna's word against her boss's. The officer advised her to also file a complaint with the bank's human resources department as a way to protect her job. She conceded that Mackenna's standing might be tenuous. Mackenna planned to report Mr. Gleaner's conduct to HR, but she suspected it would be futile. He'd been with the bank ten years. She was certain he'd wheedle his way out of the allegation.

She doubted she was the first woman he sexually intimidated but, again, she had no proof. It wasn't exactly something the ladies discussed on their breaks. Unemployment could be in her future but if it meant an end to his demands, it was worth it.

The theft report proved more difficult. While she could provide details about who, when and how Arthur had robbed her, the question about what was taken overwhelmed her. "Everything. He took everything," she explained to the detective.

"I need a complete list," he said, sliding a pen and yellow legal pad across the table.

Her shoulders sagged. "Furniture, dishes, electronics." She spread her hands wide. "He stole it all. And he hacked into my bank accounts and stripped me of my personal identity."

"I'll need as complete a list as you can compile, Miss McElroy. If you need time to write it, that's fine. It might be easier if you went home and looked around, room by room, and noted everything you remember. You can return the pages tomorrow. In the meantime, I can start a general search for Arthur, since you have no idea where he might be. Maybe we'll get lucky."

Her spirits had been high when she drove to the police station, bolstered by her decision to take action and stand up for herself. She left the building deflated. But the definition of a fighter is someone who doesn't surrender. She didn't plan to.

It was one o'clock when she arrived at the East Seventh Street Bank branch. Thankfully, Mr. Gleaner wasn't at this branch today. When the manager asked about her meeting with the police, she said she needed to give them additional information. It wasn't exactly a lie, although he assumed the information pertained to the bank robberies. While her failure to clarify that impression was deceitful, she reasoned that she misled him for good reasons.

Did that explain Jake's conduct? Did he firmly believe his reasons for deceiving her were solid? Was that different from a lie? Neither one of them revealed the truth about certain events. Why was it okay for her but wrong for Jake to take that posture?

The dilemma played in her mind through most of the day. Until about an hour before closing when the employees started buzzing. Two police officers had escorted Ted Gleaner out of the Mound Avenue branch. No one knew why but the murmurs said he didn't look happy.

18

J ake tucked his cell phone into his jacket pocket when Demond approached. Five phone calls to Kenna since he'd dropped her off two days ago and still no response. Nothing. Stone-cold silence. Each call bounced right to voicemail. He didn't bother leaving a message this time. Maybe if he waited another day, gave her more time. Or maybe he should take the hint.

He focused on his colleague, who'd called earlier with a request to meet somewhere since Jake in his undercover capacity couldn't go to the FBI building. Given that he had laundry to do anyway, Demond agreed to meet Jake at the Laundromat.

The neon green plastic chair next to Jake's groaned when Demond stuffed himself into it. "You don't look too happy, friend. Trouble in paradise?"

Jake shrugged. "I've been trying to call Mackenna but she's not answering. I assume you're logging her calls by now, so you'll see those. If you can keep them off the boss's radar, I'd appreciate it. They're strictly personal."

Demond raised his eyebrows but didn't commit to the deception.

Jake's stomach twisted. "What's up?"

Demond's massive chest expanded to twice its size after he took a deep breath. "Got some bad news for you. Your bank-teller girlfriend has moved to the top of our suspect list." He slid a printout from his coat pocket and handed it to Jake.

"A couple days ago, she barely had enough to keep a bank account open. Now, some interesting deposits have appeared. Here's five hundred bucks and another nine-hundred deposited in a two-day period." His round finger moved down two lines.

"This one appeared this morning. Maybe it's a coincidence that it's fifty-two dollars less than the amount taken from her cash drawer in the first robbery. I doubt it, but I like to keep an open mind." His finger redirected Jake's attention. "And this one? This deposit equals the take from a bank robbery seven weeks ago clear on the other side of town. We didn't think they were connected but now, we're re-examining it. She's flush again."

Jake was dumbfounded. "There has to be another explanation. I'd bet my career that she isn't involved."

"I think that's exactly what you're doing, my friend. You should step back from this." Demond studied a woman standing at a folding table across the floor, robotically stacking children's clothes. "I admit I'd be surprised but then, it wouldn't be the first time a beautiful woman fooled me. We talked about you getting closer to her but now, that isn't advisable. I wanted you to hear from me that we're looking at your bank teller harder now. I plan to bring her in for more intensive question-ing. This time I'm taking off the gloves."

He shrugged and hoisted himself out of the seat using the chair arms. "Get out of this while you can, Jake. And watch your back. She could be the next Bonnie Parker or worse," he said, referencing half of the infamous bank-robbing duo, Bonnie and Clyde.

Demond ambled away, and Jake reached for his cell phone. He was in too deep to get out. Should he leave Kenna a message saying it was important that he speak with her? For what purpose? He certainly couldn't tell her the FBI monitored her financial activity, not only because it would blow his cover, it would also be against the principles he'd sworn to uphold when he took his oath as a new agent. His allegiance was to the Bureau and the Constitution of the United States.

The wiser move would be to leave her alone.

Vicky's public corruption case that originally brought him to Brighton City was in a position to finalize. The prosecutor's office expected to have the arrest warrants ready next week, launching a major sweep of the key players. The police would arrest Jake too, in order to maintain his cover. He'd been dropped into the case as the money man who served as the liaison between city officials and the shady contractors. It afforded him a bird's eye view of a dozen corrupt politicians, two secretaries who would be caught in the sweep and the night watchman, who willingly admitted Jake after hours with his payoff pouches. Under ordinary circumstances, that would end his temporary assignment in Brighton City, and he'd head back to his home office.

It would be months until he appeared in court in a suit and tie to testify. Prosecutors would do their best to protect his identity until then. He'd be listed only as a confidential informant in any paperwork requested by defense attorneys. As far as Vinny Cabacolli was concerned, Jake was simply a Good Samaritan who'd become his friend. His credibility as a man on the wrong side of the law could be enhanced if after the sweep and his arrest, he called Vinny to bail him out. That was a risk Jake would have to convince his boss to take. Doing that would extend his assignment in Brighton City, immerse him deeper into the Cabacolli case, and keep him close to Kenna. That's what he really wanted, more time with her.

Of course, he could opt out of the Cabacolli case and head back home. Then he could tell Mackenna the truth about his job. But that would leave him in Alabama and she'd be here, too many miles away to build a relationship. He'd tried long-distance love. It didn't work.

Jake wrestled with his options while he finished his laundry, mentally rehearsing the pros and cons he'd present to the boss. He was making good headway on the Cabacolli case, meeting Vinny tonight, in fact, just to hang out. Better progress with Vinny than Mackenna.

Demond's revelation puzzled him. Even if Kenna were part of the bank robberies, she wouldn't be stupid enough to deposit the money in her personal account. Would she? If she did take Jake's call, he didn't know how he'd approach the subject anyway. He'd have no way of knowing about her bank balance.

The quandary occupied his thoughts most of the day while he caught up on paperwork, and on the ride to the sports bar where Vinny would be camped out watching the different sports contests he made book on. That had been somewhat of a surprise to the administration. Vinny ran his own small-scale sports betting operation, separate from the family businesses. Jake wondered if Old Man Cabacolli even knew about it.

Jake spotted Vinny's black BMW parked in a prime spot as he drove into the lot in his Jeep. He expected it to be a late night, and he hadn't wanted to ride the motorcycle, knowing Vinny enjoyed beer by the pitcher. He chose a parking space at the far end of the parking area, wondering if subconsciously it was an effort to distance himself from Vinny.

Entering the bar, Jake found exactly what he expected. Vinny sitting like a king in one of the overstuffed chairs grouped in twos and threes, all facing a bank of screens. Two of his lackeys milled around ready to fulfill his every command, like dogs waiting for crumbs. The regular bimbos flitted about as well, smiling and jiggling their parts as he approached. Busting this arrogant thug would be an extreme pleasure.

Vinny jumped up when he saw Jake, embraced him and signaled the waitress. Jake sighed and ramped up his enthusiasm. It was going to be a long night.

Hours later, Jake swallowed the remnants of his beer, passed a handful of darts to Vinny, and offered to buy another round for them both. His cell phone rang as he headed to the bar. He squeezed it when he read the caller ID. Mackenna. Close to midnight. Was something wrong?

It wasn't hard for him to sound upbeat about her phone call. His heart actually fluttered.

"Hey, sugar, I've been calling you."

"I know. I had some things to sort out before I returned your messages. Is it too late for me to call? Are you busy?"

"Ah, kind of. I'm working tonight."

She paused. "Oh, I'm sorry. I didn't realize you work a night shift. I shouldn't have bothered you. Should I call back tomorrow?"

"No, no, don't hang up. Is everything all right?"

"Yes, I guess. I need a friend to help me with something. I thought you could do it."

"I'm your man." *I wish.* "Is it something we can do tomorrow? I can change my schedule and help you with whatever it is any time that you need."

Geez, Manettia, could you sound more eager? If you were a puppy, your tail would be wagging and you'd be humping her leg. Come to think of it, you are a dog where Kenna is concerned.

"Won't you have to work tomorrow night too?"

"My schedule is flexible. Tell me what time and where."

"Can you meet me at my apartment after I get off work, around five?"

"You bet, honey. See you tomorrow." He disconnected, not

wanting to give her time to change her mind and hoping she hadn't identified the background noise as a bar. A grand slam on one of the broadcasts had generated a roar of applause.

He hadn't asked what she needed help with. It didn't matter. Just the fact that she'd called him and wanted to see him again was enough.

Vinny noticed his improved mood when Jake returned with fresh beers. Jake threw three darts and hit the bull's eye twice, landing the third arrow in the triple ring, effectively leaving Vinny in his dust.

She needed a friend, she'd said. He could be that and more if she let him.

19

Arriving thirty-five minutes early to meet Kenna wasn't a sign that he was eager, more like he was punctual. And the long-stem white rose he purchased? Well, that was a symbol of a new start, which is what he wanted. With her. He looked up when the exit door at the end of the hallway opened and she stepped out of the stairwell. She appeared thinner and her clothes hung slightly loose. Her eyes widened, as if finding him there surprised her.

He summoned up his sweetest smile. Not too difficult, considering his heart detonated at the sight of her and his desire jumped to full attention. Man, he had it bad.

"You look surprised to see me. You asked me to meet you here, remember?"

At least she kept advancing toward him. She offered a tentative smile.

"I didn't expect you to be waiting for me. I thought I'd have time to change clothes." Her eyes dropped to the rose, and he held it out for her.

"I can wait out here if you like." Why, he didn't know.

They'd already paraded around in front of each other in their underwear.

"What's this for?"

"I wanted to make you smile." Her eyes lit up. She rewarded him with a wide grin. Visible tension released from her shoulders as she relaxed them and reached for the flower.

"Thank you. That's a sweet thing to do. I don't think I have a vase for it, though."

He extracted the half-empty bottle of water from his jacket pocket and held it out. "It's not fancy but it will work."

Mackenna unlocked the door, stepped inside, and waved him in. She placed her purse on the kitchen counter on top of a yellow legal pad then stepped out of her heels and put the rose to her nose. Still smiling, she reached for the bottle, uncapped it, and plopped the rose inside.

"It's lovely. Thank you. Give me a minute to change and I'll explain what you can help me with."

Jake tucked his hands in his pockets and leaned against the counter, since there was no place to sit. "Take your time."

When she returned, he felt faint. She'd slipped into a tight pair of faded blue jeans and a pale blue V-neck T-shirt. Just the slightest bit of cleavage tempted him. Her hair hung around her shoulders, freed from the workday ponytail, and she was barefoot. Her polished red toes titillated him. She had no idea how hot she was.

"You look great. I thought I liked the business woman but the after-work-casual Kenna could drive a man insane." He folded his hands in front of his crotch to conceal just how crazy.

"Thank you." Her breasts rose when she took a deep breath. So did the heat in the room. "I went to the police station." Her smile was tentative, her eyes seeking validation.

A grin broke out across his face. "Atta girl. I'm proud of you. I would have gone with you if you'd asked, but I'm pleased that you went. How'd it go?"

"The police woman asked me about penetration, just like you did." She leveled a steady gaze at him now. His internal alarm sounded. *Careful, Manettia.*

"I smiled when she said that and when she asked why, I told her that my friend used the same words. Then she asked if my friend was a cop."

Until now, he'd never known what a pregnant pause meant. Electricity charged the space between them. His hard-on disappeared, replaced by a thudding heart. Where was she going with this?

"And?" His question hung in the air between them.

"I answered yes, I think he is." She reached into the refrigerator for a bottle of water, uncapped it and drank. Somehow, an invisible windstorm had blown every grain of sand from the Sahara Desert into his mouth. She extended the bottle to him, and he gratefully accepted it.

"Say something, Jake."

Another swallow, his eyes never leaving hers. "You're a smart woman, Kenna. Think it through."

"It's all I've thought about. If you aren't a cop, you're into something illegal, like a drug dealer." She left the statement hanging in the air, just as he'd done.

It was brilliant. If he denied dealing drugs, it confirmed her suspicions. She had him cornered. Checkmate. "Can you respond to me, please?"

"No, ma'am, I can't."

"You have to say something. Either that or get out."

He hated ultimatums. Usually, he chose the 'or' option simply because he detested being forced into anything. But this time, door number two meant walking out on Mackenna.

And that was unacceptable.

"Don't shut me out of your life, sugar."

She sighed, shaking her head slowly. "What do you want from me?"

He locked on to her dark-brown eyes, widely innocent and questioning. His heart pounded. This was a make-or-break moment. He chose his words carefully, holding her gaze as he softly repeated her question.

"What do I want from you? I want to be inside you. Not just between your legs as your lover. In your heart and in your head. I want to be the voice in your ear and the taste in your mouth. The last face you see before you close your eyes at night and the first thought on your mind in the morning."

She stared at him wide-eyed. "You say that and yet you can't tell me the truth."

"Stating it like that implies that I lied to you, honey, and I never have."

"That's just semantics. You know what I mean."

"It's where we find ourselves at the moment." Five seconds of silence. Ten seconds. A stand-off.

Mackenna's shoulders sagged. "I'm on a precipice here. My whole world is upended. I'm about to fall off the edge and out of nowhere you appear to save me. But I don't know anything about you. I don't know where or how you fit into my life, and you won't talk to me. Why can't you be honest?"

He stepped toward her, his pulse racing. Slowly, he lifted his hands to her arms and eased her into his embrace. "I won't let you fall."

Her hands settled on his waist. He kissed the top of her head, inhaling the coconut scent from her shampoo.

"I promise, sugar, I won't hurt you and I won't let you get hurt."

She leaned into him, her body conforming to his, her arms wrapping around him. They fit together so perfectly. Didn't that count for something?

"Just trust me a little longer. Don't ask me questions I can't answer right now."

With her face against his shoulder, she mumbled, "Are you sure you're not hiding a wife somewhere?"

"That answer is the same honest answer. No, I'm not married." He hugged her tighter. "But I'm not free anymore. I'm a puppet and you could control all the strings if you allow me the chance to win your heart and be a part of your life."

"What about Vicky?"

"I swear to you Vicky is a good friend. She always has my back. That's the truth."

She raised her face to his. His heart splintered at the tears that edged her eyes. "Will you please answer just one question?"

Could he? Did he dare? Silently, his whole life teetering on that precipice she feared, he waited.

Her voice cracked. "Are you a bad guy?"

The breath he held released slowly. So many ways to interpret that question. But the answer remained the same for all of them. He lowered his mouth to hers as he spoke.

"No, ma'am. I'm one of the good guys."

His lips touched hers and he detected the slightest tremor. Soft and full. Different from the kisses she'd delivered in her drunken performance, when she'd pressed her lips to his mouth, forceful and demanding. Now, she hesitated. He thirsted for this mouth, for every inch of this woman. And so, he drank.

He raised his hands to her face and kissed her harder, his tongue touching her lips until she willingly opened her mouth, and he plunged into paradise. The kiss was like fourth of July fireworks. Her hands clung to his biceps while he devoured her mouth, interchanging short, playful pecks with lustful, long dips into heaven. Somehow, Mackenna McElroy crawled through the portal that was his mouth and saturated his whole body, taking sweet possession of his heart and soul. Her kisses not only gave him life, they sucked it right out of him.

Her body tensed when he leaned against her, essentially pinning her to the counter. Immediately, he released her face and drew back.

"I didn't mean to press you. I'm sorry if I scared you. I would never force you to have sex with me." His arms glided down hers and he took both her hands in his and squeezed.

Desire raged through him, making him grin like a teenager about to get laid for the first time. "I can't pretend I don't want to make love to you, but I'm not pushing. I'll wait until you're ready. Just don't add me to the men-you-hate list."

She swallowed and cast her eyes downward. "Jake, I..."

"Relax, sugar. No strings, remember?" He stepped backward in a gesture meant to give her space, even though he desperately wanted strings with this woman. He wanted to tie himself to her in every way possible. The room remained charged with the electricity between them. He took another step back.

"You said you needed my help with something. Was that a ruse to lure me here or do you need a good ole boy for a chore?"

Mackenna's eyes sparkled. "Some of your sayings make me laugh. Yes, you can help me. I filed two police reports yesterday. One against Ted Gleaner and one against Arthur. The officer asked for a detailed list of everything missing. I tried to tell him my entire apartment and my identity are all gone, but he couldn't comprehend that. He said he needs specifics. I thought we could go from room to room, and I could recite everything I had in each room and you could record it. Plus, you can help me remember things I don't list."

He shrugged, confused. "I've never been in your apartment before Arthur cleaned you out. How can I help you with that?"

Mackenna presented her back to him as she searched her purse. "Well, the truth is I don't think you're a security guard. You're some kind of lawman. You can use your cop brain to help me think it through." She swung around, grinning, with a pen and the legal pad in her hand. "Ready?"

20

As they moved through each room, Mackenna's spirits dragged like a boat anchor caught in sludge. It was one thing to stand in an empty kitchen and see nothing. But to close her eyes and describe the décor, down to the cutest knickknack, or to open each cupboard and recall the bowls, dishes, pots, and pans that once cluttered the bare shelves, redefined the word 'everything' into an itemized list of losts.

Sentimental objects, like her mother's crystal stemware, and cherished gadgets like the mini-chopper she used daily and the singing bottle opener that never failed to make her giggle were all gone.

By the time she and Jake walked into the bedroom, the task overwhelmed her. She suppressed a sob when she eyed the neatly piled stacks of clothes against the wall, which once filled her dresser drawers.

Sensing her despair, Jake moved behind her and squeezed her shoulders. "Do you want to take a break?"

He was a stranger and yet so in tune with her emotions, an up to her down, the smile for her frown. Like salt and pepper.

Or peanut butter and jelly. One didn't work as well without the other.

Well, considering they'd shared a bed in their underwear, the word stranger didn't truly apply either. She knew so little about him and still, his hands on her shoulders and his breath in her ear comforted her. She leaned back, inviting him to wrap his arms around her and he did. He excited her, with his face next to hers and their cheeks touching. She clung to his muscular forearms.

"Somehow writing everything down makes it so much more invasive. The bastard stripped me of it all."

Jake tightened his hold. "It's just stuff, sugar. I know it was important to you, and it will be costly to replace all of it. But he didn't strip *you* of anything. You're an incredibly strong, intelligent woman. He didn't touch that. You're beautiful, warm, loving, and sexy as hell. None of that's gone."

Once again, he knew exactly what to say to lift her up. She shivered at his nearness, and a nervous laugh escaped her. "You're only saying that because you want in my pants." She eased her head to one side, presenting her neck to him and when he kissed it, tingles of desire shimmied into her chest.

With his lips on her skin, he murmured, "Well, I can't deny that. But you're all that and more. That's the truth."

She tilted her head up and he stopped immediately. There was no doubt about his respect for her. She stepped out of his embrace. "Sorry, I'm not ready to take that step. Too much has happened."

"No worries."

She spun around to face him. "I'm not talking about sex. Hell, I'm ready to jump into bed with you right now. Fortunately, there's no bed in this room. I meant I'm not ready for a new relationship. I'm quite comfortable in your arms and, yes, I have to admit for all the mystery surrounding you, I trust you. But I think I should spend some time alone, for myself. When you and I," she paused, "if you and I go down that road together I want to be the woman I used to be, confident, independent and yes, desirable. I need to reinvent myself. I—"

He lifted his hands, fingers spread wide and interrupted her. "I understand and it's not a big deal. Don't think for one minute you're not desirable. But I want us to be friends first. Would I like more? Yes. Anything beyond friendship will be a bonus, like extra innings. Do you like baseball?" He had such a quirky way about him, it made her laugh.

"Yes, I like most sports."

"Good. Someday we'll go to a game together. How about we finish this missing-items list and go out for dinner? My treat. We can discuss our favorite teams and even place a friendly wager." He moved his head from side to side. "This place isn't healthy for you. I have an idea I'd like to run by you. But standing in this empty apartment is not the proper setting to present it."

She nodded. The rooms were becoming hateful. In less than an hour, the inventory was complete. Locking the door behind her, she conceded it was a relief to be out of there. Once outside, they discovered a light rain falling. Jake frowned.

"I'm on the bike and I only have rain gear for me. Would you mind if we took your car?"

She handed him her keys and led the way to the tenant's parking lot adjacent to the building.

Jake opened the passenger door for her and then squeezed into the driver's seat, releasing a breath once the seat rolled back and the steering wheel no longer compressed his diaphragm. She giggled at the sight. His long legs stretched to the pedals. She recalled those muscles flexing when he rose from his bed wearing only boxer briefs. Her thighs tightened together while she snapped her seatbelt closed. No denying a physical attraction to the man.

"Why is it I feel so comfortable with you, and I hardly know you?" She hadn't meant to verbalize her thoughts. Still, Jake grinned like a Lottery winner and winked at her.

"Kismet?"

When she laughed, he beamed.

"You have a great laugh. It's like fine bourbon. It warms me from top to toe and makes me want another taste. Do you have any place special you like to eat?"

Her stomach somersaulted. "Not really. Arthur favored a Mexican restaurant around the corner that I hated. The glasses always looked dirty, and the food gave me heartburn. We went there regularly, though, I think because the waitresses all wore low-cut, off-the-shoulder tops and I'm certain enormous breasts are a pre-requisite for working there."

Jake smiled at her description. "If you don't mind my asking, how come you stayed with a loser like Arthur for as long as you did?"

She shrugged. "I believe in loyalty, I guess."

Thirty minutes later, Jake steered the car into a crowded parking lot. "How about here? I know for a fact the glasses and silverware are clean. They also have a good selection of gluten-free dishes."

She caught her breath. "I don't remember telling you I'm gluten sensitive."

He shut off the ignition and grinned. "You didn't, honey. I figured it out."

Before he stepped out of the car, she grabbed his forearm, one eyebrow arched. "You mean like a cop trained in investigative techniques might figure it out?"

The grin faltered but only for a second. "Nah, more like a man with a younger sister who has Celiac's." He winked again and butterflies invaded her stomach. "Nice try, though."

Once they were seated and ordered, she leaned back in her chair. The restaurant was new to her, and not that far from her apartment. Why had she and Arthur never tried it? Jake made her laugh when he used his napkin to wipe her silverware and held their water glasses up to the light for inspection.

"I think you're making fun of me."

The corners of his eyes crinkled when he smiled. "No, ma'am. Just trying to please you."

It'd been so long since someone ranked her interests first, she didn't know what to say. Her cheeks heated at the attention. She searched for a change of topic.

"How was your day?" Maybe his answer would provide a clue about what he did.

The question didn't appear to faze him. "Today was a paperwork day. Not my favorite thing to do. How about you?"

"It was okay. Everyone is still buzzing about the police escorting Mr. Gleaner out of the building. Nothing more has surfaced about that. I filed a report with HR, but that feels like it backfired."

"Why's that?"

"HR said they would launch an investigation and in the meantime, I'm being transferred to another bank branch. This one is out of Mr. Gleaner's supervision so he can't show up there. But it means a longer drive for me to a part of town I'm unfamiliar with and a different clientele. So, it feels like I'm the one being reprimanded."

Jake shook his head. "That doesn't sound fair. But at least it keeps you out of his clutches. If you need a driver, I'd be happy to ride you to and from work, kind of like your personal bodyguard." He flashed a quick smile and a jolt of current shot through her.

"I can't ask you to do that. You work nights and come home to sleep. I'm at the bank before the doors open."

He shrugged. "I told you my hours are flexible. If you want my escort, I'll make it work."

That made no sense. A job was a job. Its hours were stipulated. But she was too tired mentally to dissect it further.

"Thanks for the offer but it's not necessary. I'm working on finding that independent woman again, remember? You mentioned an idea you wanted to run by me. What's that about?"

Jake nodded and sat up straighter, as if he were about to negotiate a business deal. "I don't think you should stay in that apartment any longer. It's full of negative energy and I hate to think of you spending long, lonely hours there without so much as a TV to watch or a sofa to sit on while you read a book. I can't imagine how you do it."

Her stomach clenched. What did he propose? She halted his words with a raised hand. "Hold up a minute. I admit I'm starting to like you, but if you're about to suggest I move in with you, please don't. You always say no strings attached and I'd like to hold you to that."

He responded fast enough to startle her. "Jesus, I think you're the one who is the cop. You're suspicious of anything I say, as if I have an ulterior motive for everything. Your King Arthur screwed with your head, and it makes me feel like I'm banging mine against a brick wall."

His words rushed out angrily and she jerked back. And then he smiled, and the color of his eyes darkened. "I'm glad to hear you're starting to like me, though. And for the record, my intentions are honorably dishonorable."

He was contagious, like being in the company of a laughing baby that brings joy. An automatic smile creased her face and lightheartedness surged through her. Being with Jake was fun.

"It's only a smidge of a like so don't push it." Now, his grin matched hers but guilt over her reaction surfaced. "I apologize for jumping to conclusions. I will try in the future not to compare you to the rest of the despicable male species. Finish what you were saying."

His smile disappeared. "And I didn't mean to snap at you." He leaned back and shrugged. "My proposition could be misconstrued as moving in with me. At least I hope your boss will see it that way. There are several furnished apartments currently vacant in my building, some of them owned by businessmen who sublet on a monthly basis at a lower rent rate rather than let the units sit empty. I think it would be a good idea for you to move into one of them. You'd at least have furniture to sit on, actual dishes to eat off, and a decent bed to sleep in."

He spread his hands out, palms up. "And if I'm being truthful, the idea of you living closer to me is damn appealing. So," he raised and lowered his eyebrows in Groucho Marx fashion, "I might have ulterior motives."

Again, she laughed. He wasn't like any man she knew, secretive and yet so open. His concern felt genuine. She'd sensed that the first day he spoke to her in the coffee shop. Unfortunately, he didn't grasp the depth of her financial plight.

"I'm not opposed to the idea of leaving that empty apartment, but I can't afford to move. I have no money for a deposit or even for one month's rent. I've been eating corn chips for lunch from the vending machine at work and refilling my bottles from the water cooler. I'm afraid the machine will take my last dollar tomorrow. I already owe Sandy money. She loaned me some that day you saw me under the gazebo. You buying me this meal is a real treat, one I can't return. I can offer to cook you dinner. I'm a good cook. But you'd have to buy the groceries. I'm the closest thing to destitute you'll ever meet."

JAKE STUDIED her as she spoke, analyzing her body language, assessing her facial expressions for signs of deception, employing his FBI training as if she were a suspect. Not a hint of fraud. Full eye contact, steady hands, and honest, if not sad, facial expressions. Demond had shown him the printout of her bank account. The balance exceeded two thousand dollars. Snack foods from a vending machine? Why?

Either she staged one hell of a con or...or what? How did that thought finish?

"I don't want to pry but you do receive a paycheck, don't you?"

She didn't flinch. "Yes, I'm paid every other week. An automatic deposit goes into my account. All of my bills are set up as electronic deductions. But I told you, my salary doesn't cover my monthly expenses. I kept a reserve in my account to supplement the shortage. In about two years, I would have been out of debt completely and capable of saving extra money. But Arthur wiped out my reserve. I'm quite sure all my bills are bouncing to high heaven."

"Have you contacted your creditors and explained the situation? Did you check your account?"

"Without a computer, I've no way of checking. Arthur changed all my user names and passwords so I can't access any of the accounts. I'm afraid to check the status of my bank account when I'm at work because once I sign into it, I have to acknowledge that I'm aware of the negative balance and the overdue payments. It's bank policy to maintain good credit and keep all debt financially current.

"Once I look in there, it's ammunition that can be used against me."

Stunned, Jake said, "You mean you don't know if you have money in your account or not?"

"Sandy checked my balance for me the day after Arthur moved out. It was less than ten dollars then so I'm certain it's in the red now."

Was it possible that the bank robber deposited funds for her without her knowing? Maybe their agreement was no communication between them so he wouldn't know that

Mackenna was unaware the money was there. But that assumed she was a part of the robbery schemes.

Admittedly, he wasn't a financial wizard but what Mackenna described didn't add up. And it was the opposite of what Demond reported. Apparently, Kenna didn't know she was flush. Either that or she was a damn good actor.

All the more reason to keep her under surveillance. When he first entertained the idea of having her live in his building, it was predominantly to save his ass. Getting involved with Mackenna was against Bureau regulations while he worked an undercover assignment. Having her in his apartment—worse, in his bed—was grounds for dismissal. But he couldn't walk away from her. He didn't plan to.

Convincing her to move into his building would allay any suspicion that he was seeing her if agents saw her coming and going. Sure, the Bureau kept a close eye on its undercover agents, sometimes without them knowing about it. But once inside, they wouldn't know if she was in her apartment or his.

Thus far, only Demond knew that Jake planned to pay closer attention to Mackenna than was necessary. That was between them, and he trusted the man. Vicky sensed his attraction, but he could easily deflect that. All he had to do was talk about the bimbos who threw themselves at him and Vinny. He could relate their offers for anything he wanted and some things he'd never thought of without elaboration. After all, a Southern gentleman never besmirched a lady's reputation.

But first, he must convince Mackenna to relocate. Their food arrived while she explained her financial predicament and she used that to end the discussion.

"Are you amenable to the idea of sub-letting if something can be worked out?"

"Yes. You're right about staying at my place. It's horrible. But I don't see how I can get out of it."

"Will you let me pay the security deposit for you?" He

ignored her head snapping up so fast, it must've hurt. "Only as a loan, no strings attached. Just until you get a couple of paychecks under your belt. I'll insist that you pay me back."

One of his sisters would be good for the loan. They'd be ecstatic to hear it was to help his girlfriend.

"Thank you, but I can't ask you to do that. Besides, money that goes into my account now will automatically pay my delinquent bills, including the rent for my apartment. There won't be leftover money for additional rent on another place to live."

The urge to grab her by the shoulders and shake her threatened to surface. She wasn't in arrears on any of her accounts. Why the hell didn't she know that? Or did she and she was simply playing him for a fool?

"At least give me the chance to talk to one unit owner in particular and see what he says." She nodded, her mouth too full to speak. "And, if you'd like, I'll sleep on the sofa tonight and you can have the bed. I'd feel better knowing you're not in The Hole alone for the whole weekend. Your building doesn't have a secure front entrance. Your boss could knock on your door and you'd be helpless."

Her fork stopped in mid-air. Apparently, she hadn't considered that.

"Wouldn't that be a mistake on his part? If I went to the police once, he must know I'd do it again."

"That presumes he's thinking rationally. If he isn't, the consequences won't matter once he beats the hell out of you. Or worse. You shouldn't be there alone. If not my sofa, how about staying with your friend, Sandy? Or someone else? I could call Vicky." *Christ, Manettia, what are you thinking?*

She seemed to have lost her appetite. "I don't even know Vicky. I won't impose on anyone. Sandy might be a witness for the robbery case. The police cautioned me not to compromise her. I think that's the word they used."

He started to nod but caught himself. No need to give her more hints about the true Jake Manettia.

"Probably good advice. So, temporary quarters at my place it is. Let's swing back to your digs and you can pick up some clothes and essentials. You can stay the weekend. I have to work tomorrow and might have to log a couple hours on Sunday, so I won't be underfoot. And by then, we could have a unit for you to stay in. If not, I have a spare key."

Never mind that he'd likely be arrested within the week and she could have his place to herself.

21

Mackenna waged a half-hearted argument against staying at Jake's apartment, in part because she couldn't bear the thought of a full weekend in The Hole, as Jake kept referring to the place. She now thought of it that way. It no longer felt like home.

And he was right. What would she do all day Saturday after she finished her laundry? Spend another marathon day walking the mall? She couldn't afford to buy anything. And the idea of sitting cross-legged on the living room floor reading by the balcony door for eight or twelve hours didn't appeal to her either. And what if Mr. Gleaner did knock on her door? She hadn't considered that he might contact her outside of work. That possibility frightened her.

Begrudgingly, she conceded to Jake's way of thinking. It didn't make sense to stay at her place when another option was available. Sadly, his apartment was her *only* option.

What was it her grandmother used to say? Turn lemons into lemonade? Maybe it wouldn't be so bad spending the weekend with him. He said he had to work and wouldn't be around much. Besides, he was starting to grow on her. He made her laugh.

Wherever his hands touched, her skin heated. And the way he looked into her eyes excited her. His gaze was packed with expectation. He aroused her sexually, unlike Arthur who nursed a low libido. That'd been another disappointment in that arrangement. She no longer thought of her time with Arthur as a relationship.

Jake, on the other hand, was the long-haired bad boy type, clad in leather and straddling a motorcycle. The image screamed sex. Damn appealing. She wouldn't mind if he strutted around in his boxers again.

She gathered her cosmetics and essentials and packed them into a duffel bag Jake had in the motorcycle's saddlebags. "I'll follow you, okay? That way I'll have a car and be mobile if necessary."

Why she phrased it like that, she didn't know. She had nowhere to go, and she'd become miserly about saving gas. As she followed his motorcycle, the decision to accept Jake's offer felt right. Something about Jake implied safety and comfort.

"Make yourself at home, sugar." He motioned for her to enter and carried the duffel to the bedroom. She stopped in the middle of the living area and waited, unsure what to do. Jake returned with a sheet and pillow, tossed both on the sofa, and shrugged.

"The sheets on the bed have only been slept on once. I'm afraid I only have two sets but if you'd prefer these, we can swap them out." He nodded to the set he'd plopped on the couch.

She shook her head. "It's fine."

"I'm going to have a beer. Can I get you something? Afraid all I have is water, sweet tea, and a couple sports drinks."

He handed her a bottle of cold water and dropped onto the couch. Reaching for the remote he popped the top on his beer and focused on the TV when he spoke.

"You can stand in the middle of the room if you like but I

think you'll be more comfortable if you sit and relax. I won't bite. You already know that. And it's not as if you haven't been here before."

She clasped and unclasped her hands in front of her. "This is different."

"How so?"

"This feels more, um, intimate."

Jake's grin split his face in half. "Or it's simply two friends hanging out together. Take a deep breath, let it out, and get comfortable. You said you like sports. How about hockey? I hate the captain on this team."

She perched on the edge of the oversized chair positioned to the right of the sofa and surveyed the room. Friends, he said, yet she knew so little about him and his home provided no further insight.

"How long have you lived here."

"About six months." He concentrated on the hockey game.

"Your apartment doesn't look lived in. It's, um, rather impersonal."

Jake nodded, his concentration still on the screen and the action on the ice. "It needs a woman's touch."

"For all the talking you do about your mother, I'm surprised there isn't one photo or ten of her."

Well, that grabbed his attention. His head jerked up and he studied her. Did the comment surprise him?

"Most of my stuff is in storage. I'm not certain I'm going to stay here."

Confused by her immediate reaction, she clenched her teeth to keep her jaw from dropping. "Do you mean stay in this apartment or remain in Brighton City?" Where she lived was what she wanted to add. Why did it matter if he lived here or somewhere else? She barely knew the man.

He chuckled and allowed the corners of his mouth to tilt

upward into an easy grin. "Would it upset you if I moved away, sugar? The look on your face says it might."

Flustered, she dropped her gaze and inspected her cuticles. "It just surprised me, that's all. You can do what you want."

Except for some reason, the notion of Jake leaving the city bothered her.

An hour later, she contemplated those feelings as she stared at his bedroom ceiling in the dark. The pillows held his scent and the room, albeit impersonal, felt like him. How was she supposed to sleep with him all around her and the niggling fear that he might no longer be there?

Yet sleep she did and more soundly than she could remember. Jake was gone when she awoke. She didn't hear him leave, but his toothbrush and a travel-size toothpaste tube lay on the sink in the spare bathroom. A note beside the coffee pot informed her he went for a run. It wasn't quite seven-thirty. What time had he left?

And how long would he be gone? Long enough for her to nose through his personal belongings and learn more about him? He was her host and her protector. Was that fair? She recalled a poet who wrote "The rules of fair play do not apply in love and war." She cupped both hands around her coffee mug. Which applied to Jake? Battle? Or something more personal?

A key in the door ended all thoughts of snooping. Winded, Jake strolled in, his white T-shirt plastered to his upper body, outlining every muscle and bulge in his arms and chest. Strands of hair curled at the ends with droplets of sweat clinging to them. She leaned with her back against the counter, and his face exploded into a wide grin when he saw her. She wore an oversized sleep shirt. His eyes cruised down her body to her bare feet and back up.

Jake retrieved a water bottle from the fridge and winked as he opened it. "You're beautiful in the morning."

She watched as if hypnotized when he lifted the bottle to his lips, his head back, eyes closed, gulping the refreshing liquid, his Adam's apple rolling slowly, the slightest overflow of water streaming from his mouth, down his chin, navigating his jawbone to ease down his neck and settle at the base of his throat. An urge to step forward and lick the spot dry overcame her. She clutched the edge of the counter, digging her fingernails into the underside of the granite.

His chest rose and fell in slow breaths as he drained the bottle. A drop of moisture dotted his lips when he lowered the plastic container. Mackenna licked her own dry mouth. Heat emanated from his body and engulfed her. She gripped the cup tighter and swallowed hard.

"Good morning." Was the octave of her voice higher than usual? "I didn't hear you leave."

Wordlessly, Jake nodded and reached into the refrigerator. "I'm glad. You needed a good night's sleep." He handed her a pound of bacon and pointed at her knees.

"There's a pan right behind your legs. You start the bacon, and I'll jump in the shower. Then I'll whip up some breakfast. It's the only meal I'm good at." He walked away as he spoke, reaching behind his shoulders with both hands to grab his shirt and yank it over his head. Back muscles as thick as electric cords competed for her attention with bulging triceps and deltoids. Involuntarily, Mackenna made the sign of the cross. The guy was a living miracle of muscle.

She pivoted, her eyes never leaving his body, to follow his progress toward the bedroom. Jake stopped when he saw the look on her face. Her eyes dropped to his bare chest, still glistening with sweat. Good Lord.

"Are you all right?"

A knot in her throat the size of her fist kept her from speaking.

Jake offered an impish smile. "You want to shower with me? You could soap my back."

She did. Lord help her, she wanted to lay her hands all over the man. "Sorry, I, ah, you, um, sorry. I didn't mean to stare."

Now, his right eyebrow rose with his question. "So, that's a 'no' to the shower invitation?"

Heat crept up her cheeks. But two could play this game. "Maybe next time."

Jake's eyes rounded and he laughed, pointing at her as he disappeared into the bedroom. "I'm gonna hold you to that promise."

She wanted him to do just that.

22

J ake contemplated his teeth in the Jeep's rearview mirror, all of them exposed by the grin that wouldn't disappear. What a great morning! He and Mackenna cooked breakfast together, sat in the kitchen chatting while they ate, and teamed up to rinse and load the dishwasher as if it was a routine they performed daily. Damn, it felt right. A schoolkid with a crush on the girl who sits in front of him couldn't feel giddier.

Although laundry was on her agenda Mackenna said she had no real plans for the day. He encouraged her to relax and make herself at home. He had a meeting with Vicky to turn over his most recent reports. Of course, he wasn't that specific with Mackenna. She believed he had to meet a friend and hadn't asked for details.

Jake suggested they go together to the management office and inquire about available apartments upon his return. Then he took it a step further, offering to take her to dinner before he went to work tonight. Given a choice, he'd much rather spend time with Kenna than hook up with Vinny. But he feared Vinny

would become suspicious if Jake cancelled their planned atten-
dance at a bachelor party for one of Vinny's boys. Tonight was
an opportunity to meet some of Vinny's so-called associates,
moving Jake one step closer inside the Cabacolli circle.

But that meant it'd be a late night. Mackenna would be
asleep when he returned, if indeed the festivities didn't turn
into an all-nighter. So, the dinner date was important. Well, he
hadn't exactly used the word "date" when he suggested they get
something to eat. Come to think of it, the whole scenario he
suggested was veiled in half-truths. It was a hell of a way to
build a relationship.

Still, she seemed agreeable to it all and, as if it was the most
natural of actions, he kissed her goodbye before he left. She'd
been smiling as he closed the door behind him. He grinned like
a buffoon.

Unbeknownst to Mackenna, Jake had already contacted the
owner of a corner apartment with an extraordinary view two
floors above his. He'd laid down one month's rent as a security
deposit, with the understanding that Mackenna not be privy to
that information. Instead, the office manager agreed to tell
Mackenna that, since Jake knew the owner, he would accept
Jake's reference and guarantee for the condition of the premises
and waive the required deposit. As for the rent, Mackenna
would be charged half the asking price. Jake planned to pay the
other half.

He imagined his mama tsk-tsking and waving a cautionary
finger at him. Mama liked to quote her favorite poets to her
children. Her voice echoed in his head: "Oh, what a tangled
web we weave, when first we practice to deceive, child." And
Mama didn't know the half of it.

Still, he could justify the deceit. He continued to work his
undercover job—two of them, technically—and still protected
Mackenna. Jake countered Mama's nagging voice with his own

quote, although he didn't know from whom: "The end justifies the means."

The meeting with Vicky went well. He finally confessed about his interaction with Mackenna, stopping short of the whole truth. Vicky lectured him again about the risks of compromising his identity, reminded him it was unwise to have women at his apartment, no matter how drunk they were, and seemed satisfied with his assurance that it was a one-time thing. Yet another layer of deception to his pyramid of lies. The rest of the meeting was all business. There was no indication the Bureau suspected he harbored their number one Good Neighbor suspect. And Jake couldn't wait to get back to her.

MACKENNA NAPPED on a lounge chair on his balcony when Jake returned home, a popular gossip magazine opened across her stomach. Seeing her wrapped in his Mobile BayBears baseball sweatshirt made him grin. She'd covered her legs with the afghan from the couch to ward off the crisp spring air. The gentlest of nudges scared her, causing her to cry out and swat the air, wild-eyed and frantic before focusing on him.

"I'm sorry, sugar, I tried to make enough noise to wake you, but you were out."

An easy smile spread across her face. "I feel so comfortable here, so relaxed. I realized I haven't truly enjoyed time alone for a long time." She yanked the front of his sweatshirt away from her chest. "I may have overstepped my bounds as a guest, though. I wanted to sit outside and enjoy this sunshine, but I didn't pack anything warm enough. I'm afraid I invaded your privacy and rummaged through your drawers until I found this. What are the Mobile BayBears?"

"Not a what. They used to be a minor league baseball team

back home in Mobile. Now, they're based in Madison, about four hours away, and called the Rocket City Trash Pandas. They're the farm team for the Los Angeles Angels. Harder for me to catch the games when I'm home but my buddy plays for them. He's a natural ballplayer. I expect to hear any day that he's moved up to the majors. I'll take you to a game some time."

Mackenna's face immediately brightened, turning on a light in his heart. "In Alabama?"

"Hell ya, honey. Mama will love you even more if you root for the local boys. Let's get going. We have an appointment with the management company. I called them on the way home."

Mackenna loved the available apartment. His heart tugged watching her balance on the sofa as if she'd damage it, caressing the coverlet on the king-size bed, and breaking into a toothy grin opening the kitchen cabinets to find dishes, glasses, and tableware. When she pulled the cords of the blinds to the outdoor balcony she gasped, then threw open the sliding doors and stepped out with her arms wide and her face lifted to the sky, as if she could hug the world. She spun around to look at him, her face beaming.

"Jake, I can't possibly stay here. This is much nicer than where I live now. Even the furniture is an upgrade for me. It must be terribly expensive."

The building manager stepped up beside Jake and cleared his throat. "It's a seasonal rate right now, Miss McElroy, and that has been reduced further since Jake here is a friend of the owner. Based on Jake's assurances, you won't be responsible for a security deposit. The owner doesn't plan to start charging you rent until the first of next month."

Jake relaxed his shoulders. The manager played his part perfectly.

Mackenna's eyebrows knitted. "Are you certain?"

The manager cleared his throat again and extended a set of keys toward her. "Absolutely. You can assume occupancy right away if you like. We'll just need a few forms signed back at the office."

Mackenna nodded. "If you don't mind, I'll look around a minute more. Jake and I will be right down."

When they were alone, she propped her hands on her hips. "How big a role are you playing in this, my friend?"

His stomach jumped. He'd achieved friend status. "All I did was make a phone call."

"I don't believe you. Does your buddy know I'm in dire financial straits right now and not only might I be unable to pay the rent, I could be arrested by the FBI?"

She didn't let him respond and advanced toward him. "I've never heard of an owner allowing a stranger to live rent-free." Now she stood toe-to-toe with him. "This has you written all over it. My knight." Her arms snaked around his neck. She drew him toward her. "I will pay you back every penny, I promise. Right now, I'm not going to look a gift horse in the mouth. Instead, I'd like to kiss that mouth."

He wouldn't have argued even if there was time. But there wasn't. Before he knew it, his arms wrapped around Kenna, his opened hands splayed across her back and pressed her closer. The sweetest lips God ever created settled on his own. Soft, lush, and giving. General Robert E. Lee couldn't have surrendered more completely. He was all hers.

Mackenna withdrew the slightest bit and spoke against his mouth. "Thank you. I'm not sure why you walked into my life when you did or what I did to deserve you. But I'm glad you're here. Thank you."

He didn't want the embrace to end. He could stand there for eternity kissing her, holding her, needing her as much as he wanted her. And that was a hell of a lot judging by his body's reaction. More than just a physical erection, his emotions soared, taking with it his stomach, his heart, and his head.

Decency forced him to step back and ease Mackenna out of his arms.

"We better get those papers signed before I carry you into that bedroom and make love to you until we both pass out from exhaustion."

She didn't flinch at the suggestion, perhaps because she knew he'd never force her. Or maybe she was warming to the idea of being in his arms.

In the elevator, he reached for her hand. "I have time before I go out tonight. Would you like to move your clothes over here? With two vehicles it should only take one trip. We can grab something to eat on the way back."

"Won't that make you late? What time do you have to be at work?"

"I'll have time."

~

IT ALL SEEMED to be working out so effortlessly, which should have been Mackenna's clue not to relax. Nothing ever was easy for her.

With Jake's help, she loaded the trunk and back seat with her clothes and toiletries. Thirty-nine shoeboxes stacked up neatly in the backseat of Jake's Jeep. She was beginning to believe he really did have sisters. He didn't blink an eye at the number of shoes or all of the cosmetic bottles, jars, and tubes.

Spending time with him felt so natural, reminiscent of the easy camaraderie she shared with her brother. Except the feelings blossoming for Jake were hardly sisterly. On the contrary, seeing him bend over in skin tight jeans, his butt and thighs stretching the denim like plastic wrap across a salad bowl stimulated her desire for a man again. The urges were more than sexual. She craved his touch and his taste. His laughter and his attention. He felt like a new adventure.

When they stopped at a deli known for its soups, salads, and wraps she teased him about his menu selection. A lesser man would be uncomfortable with such a light meal, she suggested, laughing. Jake simply shrugged and smiled. "That should tell you something about me. I'm in touch with my yin and yang."

He punctuated his words with a wink, and she'd giggled like a teenager. It told her he was pretty self-assured. Playfully, she picked chips off his plate. Arthur forbade her from eating from his plate or even sampling from his fork, saying it was unsanitary. As a test, she spooned up her black bean soup and stretched it toward Jake, inviting him to taste. He smiled, accepted the offered spoon, and said it was good but his Mama made better. Someday she'd taste it, he promised. It was starting to feel like she wanted that.

Her heart was lighter than it had been in months. That was when the ax fell. Jake checked a text message and said the manager wanted them to stop at the office when they returned. They'd waved to him on their way out of the building.

The tenant living above Mackenna's temporary apartment had fallen asleep in the bathtub with the faucets open. Water overflowed through the floor and ceiling and her new temporary bathroom flooded.

"We have repairmen on staff for this building, but I'm afraid you won't be able to stay there tonight. Fans are running, but it will take a couple of hours to dry out everything. They can replace the drywall tomorrow and that's the soonest I can let you in, although we'll paint the following day so if you think the fumes will bother you, you might want to delay your move." Her shoulders slumped.

Jake's arm slid around her waist, and he squeezed her side gently. "It won't hurt you to camp out at my place one more night. I'm ready to head to work. I'll be back late. You'll have the apartment to yourself. I'll be quiet as a mouse when I come in and I'll sleep on the sofa. It's not a big deal."

So here she sat, her legs tucked under her on Jake's couch searching the TV channel guide for something to entertain her. But her mind relived the events of the day and questions swirled through her brain. Jake hadn't been in a hurry to leave. It was after seven when he casually kissed her goodbye and said he'd see her in the morning.

Mentally she calculated an eight-hour shift and tried to match it to a law enforcement profession. Eight at night to four in the morning? A security guard might work those hours at a warehouse or some type of overnight operation. But where was his uniform? In a locker at work? That was feasible. But if that was the case, why did he leave wearing dress pants and a dress shirt with his sports jacket hooked on his finger over his shoulder? Did his company require employees to dress to report to work? Did they also require he smelled as good as he did?

A pang of guilt pierced her thoughts. She'd done more than search for a sweatshirt earlier today. She poked around in his drawers, studied the contents of his closet, and deliberately moved the mouse to awaken his computer. The screen asked for a password. She didn't dare attempt to figure one out. Jake remained a mystery. Nothing in his home revealed anything more about him than she already knew, which was minimal at best.

That compounded her confusion about the man. She wanted more.

HIS WORDS WERE SOFT, whispered. "Hey, sugar. Wake up, honey." That's what they were in her sleep-addled brain, sweet as honey. She inhaled a slow, calming breath. Jake was so sweet. "Kenna. Wake up."

Consciousness rolled over her in slow waves. She opened her eyes and blinked at the light from the television. Jake bent and nudged her shoulder. "Wake up, sugar. What are you doing sleeping here? You're supposed to be in the bed." Slow awareness of her surroundings surfaced, the afghan sliding from her legs to the floor when she sat up on the couch and offered Jake a lazy smile.

"What time is it?"

Jake bent to retrieve the blanket and folded it as he answered. "Not quite four in the morning. C'mon, let's get you in bed."

She slipped her hand in his proffered one and stood, her nose crinkling at his odor. "You reek of cigarette smoke."

Jake led her toward the bedroom. "I know. It's one of the hazards of the job. I usually have to scrub down before I turn in. I'll be quick." He stopped at the side of the bed, and she closed the distance between them, grimacing again.

"You also smell like cheap perfume. I thought you were working tonight?" Ouch. That sounded like something a jealous girlfriend might say.

"Also one of the perils of the job. Sometimes I want to rub mentholated cream underneath my nostrils, you know, like the detectives do in the movies when they find a decomposing body. But I'd look kind of funny with shiny blotches on my upper lip." He drew back the covers. "In you go."

Dutifully, she perched on the edge of the bed then slipped her feet beneath the covers and drew them to her stomach as she curled onto her side. Jake bent, lifted his right pants leg, and unsnapped a strap around his ankle. Without glancing at her, he tucked a gun in the top nightstand drawer and eased it closed. Then he gifted her with a charming smile and a wink.

"Don't fret about that. Sometimes, the job is unsavory." She'd never been around guns and having one so close made her nervous. Was he qualified to own one?

"What is your job again?"

Jake switched off the light on the nightstand as if he hadn't heard her question. "I'll jump in the shower and then hit the sofa. See you in the morning."

He disappeared into the bathroom, closing the door behind him. She stared at the drawer, halting her hand in mid-air. There was no need to yank it open and verify what she'd just seen. Did a warehouse security guard need to wear a concealed gun? It didn't make sense.

The hot water faucet squealed, indicating he turned it on, and her thoughts took a different path. She pictured him shedding his clothes and stepping naked into the downpour. Immediately, her pulse quickened. Maybe all the mystery surrounding Jake was part of her attraction to him. She barely knew anything about him, yet here she was in his bed. Again. Less than six feet away from her, with a simple sliding door separating them, he stood naked, water cascading down his perfectly sculpted body. Would he balk if she stepped into the shower with him? After all, he'd invited her to do just that. And the more time she spent with Jake, the more tempting the thought. Another squeal from the faucet and the water ceased. Too late.

Mackenna switched on the light, propped herself against the wall, and positioned the blanket across her lap. She didn't want to sleep alone. Not tonight. Not after what had happened. Before opening the bathroom door, Jake switched off the light, expecting the bedroom to be dark. His eyebrows arched when he saw her sitting up, waiting. He stopped in the doorway, a bath towel draped around his waist.

"That doesn't look like a comfortable sleeping position."

She had nothing to lose if he rejected her offer.

"It's late and we're both tired. You'll sleep better here in bed rather than on the couch. We're both adults, I think we can share this bed without issue. We've done it before."

He extended both hands to the top of the doorway and caught his fingers on the woodwork, causing the towel to dip dangerously low around his abdomen. Tendons and muscles stretched tight. Sweet Jesus.

"Is this some kind of test, sugar?"

Her head jerked higher at his comment. "Not at all. I'm not sure why you'd ask that. I simply think we'll both sleep better in a bed. I don't mean to offend you. I don't feel right displacing you like this."

He stood silently, a lone muscle in his jaw twitching, and studied her. What was he thinking? She held her breath, deciding against pleading her case further. Her chin inched up and she waited.

Finally, he ran his hands through his damp hair and shrugged. "You're right, I'm bushed. I'll turn out the kitchen light."

Her heart raced waiting for him to return. When he entered the room, he stopped in front of his bureau and opened the top drawer. The towel dropped to the floor, and she glimpsed his bare butt before he stepped into a pair of wine-colored boxer briefs. His cheeks were smooth and round, just as she'd imagined. He folded the towel and disappeared into the bathroom. And then he stood beside the bed.

Wordlessly, she sunk below the covers and waited. Jake switched off the lamp and eased in beside her, stretching out on his back and drawing the blanket to his chest. They lay there in silence, listening to each other breathe, until his words cut the darkness.

"Did something happen tonight that you want to tell me about?"

How could he possibly know? No man had ever been so in harmony with her. The phone call frightened her so badly, she'd called Sandy for reassurance.

She spoke to the ceiling. "He called tonight."

Jake's head turned on his pillow. "Who?"

"Mr. Gleaner."

"What'd he say?"

"I-I don't know. I didn't answer."

"Did he leave a message?"

"No."

"You did good not answering."

He should know the whole story since he was being sucked slowly into her quicksand of troubles. "I called Sandy right away and talked to her for an hour. Seeing his name on my phone frightened me."

"Why didn't you call me?"

She'd thought about it. Debated the consequences of calling him at work, wherever work was. She turned her head toward him. "I wanted to. But I don't know where you work or what you do, not really. Hell, I hardly know you. I wasn't sure I could interrupt you or if you can take calls."

In the dim light, Jake's white teeth flashed. "You can call me anytime, sugar. Did you tell Sandy where you're staying?"

"No. I figure the less she knows, the safer she is. I just needed to talk to someone about...everything."

Now, Jake rolled on his side and propped his head on his hand. "What's everything? Do you mean about your boss harassing you or the robberies or both?"

The darkness provided a sense of security, as if secrets exchanged between them would never see the light of day. Talking to him like this was safe.

"Not so much about the robberies because, as I said, the police advised me not to compromise her. I told her about Mr. Gleaner, about what happened in his office and about him getting me drunk. She was stunned. He presents such a respectable persona at work, quite detached from his employees. Some of us questioned whether he had feelings because he's always so aloof.

"And we discussed Arthur and how he screwed me. Sandy never liked him, but she tried to console me anyway."

In the shadows, he stared at her. "Did you talk about me?"

"A little. I told her you saved me when Mr. Gleaner got me drunk and took me home. That you were waiting. I said I thought you were stalking me, but I was happy that you were. And that I wasn't afraid of you."

"What did Sandy say to that?"

"She asked why but I couldn't explain it. How can I explain that you keep coming to my rescue when I don't understand myself? She doesn't know much about you beyond the day you showed up at the bank asking about me. She thought you were cute. What do you think she'd say if she knew I was in your apartment, in your bed? She'd be dumbfounded.

"I tried to sound like it was just a lucky coincidence. When she asked where I was, I said my neighbor's. I was just so scared when I saw Mr. Gleaner's name. I think if I'd been at The Hole I would've thrown my phone against the wall and run. Just run away from everything. That's the real reason I wanted to talk to Sandy. I needed to hash out my feelings."

Another silent pause before Jake asked softly, "What are your feelings?"

The question caused her to laugh. "You name it, I'm good with it. Scared. What if the FBI doesn't believe me? Betrayed. By Arthur and Mr. Gleaner, both people I thought I knew and could trust. Angry. At them for what they did to me and myself for being so vulnerable. Worried to death about my finances. I've worked so hard to keep good credit. How am I going to bounce back from this?"

Mount St. Helens couldn't spew its lava faster than her fears tumbled from her lips. "Lost. I have nowhere to go. I'm ready to fight for myself, but I'm confused by all of it. Why me, I want to ask? Safe is another word that comes to mind. When I'm with you, I feel safe. And excited. When I'm with you, I'm also afraid.

And that adds to the confusion and thoughts of running away from it all."

She took a deep breath. "Shall I continue?"

"Jesus, that's a hell of a lot of stuff bouncing around in your brain. You'll never get to sleep with all that going on. We should talk about all this. Maybe I can help you work through some of it. But not tonight, it's late. And as you said, we're both tired. You'll think more clearly in daylight." He shifted toward her and edged his hand beneath her shoulder blades. "Come here."

She scooched nearer to him, readjusted the oversized sleep shirt she wore, and stretched out along his right side. He was boiling hot, like a furnace. Jake rested his hand on her hip and placed a gentle kiss on the top of her head.

"I like that you feel safe with me because you are. I'm not sure why you're afraid of me. I'd never hurt you. But that douche bag you lived with probably told you the same so I can understand your doubt. Maybe it's not me who scares you, maybe it's you. Could be you see what's happening between us and that scares the hell out of you. It frightens me too, but I think together, we can figure it out."

She caressed his stomach, causing him to inhale sharply, and eased her hand to the waistband of his underwear. "Jake?"

This time he planted a gentle kiss on her forehead. "Not tonight, honey. It'd be for the wrong reasons. Sex is a great escape from just about anything that's ugly. But I want better than that for us. You're not looking for me tonight. You had a scare and you're looking for someplace to hide. I don't want you because you're running from someone else. I want you because you're running to me."

He dropped another kiss on her forehead. "Like you said, I'm tired. Go to sleep. We'll talk tomorrow."

∿

Forty-five seconds later, Jake's chest rose and fell rhythmically. His breathing slowed to a constant pattern. Mackenna settled in closer, stretched one bare leg across his thighs and relaxed her head on his shoulder. He was right about one thing, she was hiding this weekend. She could hide in this make-believe world for one more day before she returned to work and the reality of her life. But she still had tomorrow with Jake and whatever that might bring.

23

M ackenna stirred, waking Jake. She cuddled behind him in a spoon position, generating an immediate hard-on. Her face nuzzled between his shoulder blades. One arm lay across his hip, her fingers dangling in his crotch. He couldn't take much more of her being so close without making love to her. And that would be the mother of all mistakes.

Who was Jake Manettia? A decorated Marine who wanted nothing more than to serve the Bureau as he'd served his country, and to make his mama proud. Yet here he was in bed in his undercover apartment with a prime robbery suspect, which was against every regulation on the books. And his body worked to betray him. Every one of his cells screamed in heat for Kenna.

She thought she was confused by the situation she found herself in, but she didn't know the whole truth. She was sleeping with the FBI, the very agency she feared most. What would she do when she found out he was an agent? And if he faced arresting her, this woman who trusted him with her life, could he? Would he?

He shifted his weight to lie on his back and her eyes opened. Drawing her into his arms, he whispered. "Go back to sleep. It's still early."

A soft murmur floated up from her face, nestled in the side of his neck, after she repositioned herself and stretched her leg across his groin. Her hips gyrated. "Mmmm, is that for me?"

His erection stood tall. Thank God the room was dark, preventing her from seeing his flaming cheeks. His voice croaked. "Yes, ma'am. I'll behave, though. Don't worry."

Somehow Mackenna's sweet voice turned sultry when she rose up on one elbow, then rolled on top of him. "What if I don't want you to behave?"

He didn't dare breathe. This had to be an incredible dream and if he exhaled or uttered one word, he'd wake up and be majorly disappointed. "Sugar, you don't know what you're doing to me. I'm only a man and we're all weak creatures."

Mackenna caressed his cheek. "I can feel exactly what I'm doing to you. Last night you said I was running away from something and last night in the dark, you were right. But it's dawn now and my eyes are wide open. I know what I want. Give me a minute to pee and brush my teeth," she whispered. "Keep a good thought."

She slipped out of his side of the bed and floated to the bathroom while his brain turned to mush. This had to be what an LSD trip was like. He'd never done drugs, but this hallucination was mind numbing. What'd she say? Did she mean what he thought she meant?

Maybe his mind didn't comprehend her words, but his body sure did. He retained one lucid thought. *Stop this now, before it gets out of hand. You've already committed innumerable errors. Don't cross this line.*

Jake threw the covers off and planted his feet on the floor. He stood beside the bed when the door slid open and she glided toward him. He lifted his hands to stop her. "We should talk about this. Give me a minute."

With the door closed, he splashed cold water on his face and brushed his teeth. He regarded the bulge in his underwear. The delay had no effect on his desire. The only way to stop this was to tell her the truth, confess who he was and explain why he'd deceived her. But that would be a violation of Bureau policy, equally as flagrant as the sins he'd already committed and the one she tempted him with now. Which misstep was the right one? Or the wrong one?

No, he couldn't let it go that far. He'd stop this now.

He slid open the door and spied Mackenna on her side facing him, wearing only white lace panties. The argument he'd planned to make evaporated. She reached her hand toward him and against his will, his feet walked him to the bed. "Sugar, this is a bad idea. There's too much you don't know."

She coaxed him onto the bed beside her and pressed her fingers to his lips, suppressing his words. "Shhh, don't say anything. Don't ruin the mood by being logical or rational or protective. We both want each other. That's all I need to know right now. I haven't felt like this for a long time. Let's just get lost in the moment." She kissed him tentatively. Sweet and minty.

He moved her hair behind her ears. "Jesus, yes, I want you. But I've never been a one-and-run kinda guy, especially with a woman like you. We do this and it changes everything between us. I'm not sure you'll like that."

She smiled and rolled on top of him. "I'm a grown woman. I can be intimate with a man without expecting a marriage proposal. Without expecting anything, for that matter. If we never have sex again, that will be fine. But right now, this is right for us. Don't worry about tomorrow or even later today. Let's just be together. I want you for all the right reasons. Now."

This was crazy. He was an undercover agent on special

assignment and about to violate every conduct code established by the Bureau. Mackenna shouldn't even be in his apartment, let alone in his bed. And no way in hell should he get involved with her on any level.

Too late for that. He already was involved. On all levels. The only thing he could do was pray that he didn't get caught.

Straddling his hips, she sat up, allowing him full view of her creamy, round breasts. His arms involuntarily settled on her waist. His heart thudded. First his feet and now his hands operated of their own volition. He was a mere puppet in her presence, and she jiggled the strings. Jesus, he was as nervous as a virgin.

Beautifully shaped breasts topped by perky nipples beckoned. His fingers eased up her ribs and cupped them. To his delight, he discovered skin as soft as a Georgia peach. He smiled.

Mackenna dropped her hands on either side of his head and fell forward, her hair enclosing him in a brown cloak of coconut scent. His palms slid to her round bottom and her breasts dangled in front of his face. He placed a light kiss on each nipple and then stared into her eyes, dark with desire.

"I want you," she whispered. There was no going back now. Slowly, she lowered her face to his, her mouth inching closer and closer. And then, nirvana. Minty kisses so sweet they could compete with his Mama's tea and skin as soft as a puppy's ear. His hands skimmed upward to press her to his chest. He welcomed her mouth eagerly, his tongue doing a slow dance of desire with hers. Her hips rocked on top of his in concert with their kisses and a moan, barely audible, escaped him.

"You're the sexiest woman I've ever held in my arms. You're driving me crazy."

She giggled and murmured against his mouth, "Good. My plan is working."

She drew back a few inches, balancing herself on her forearms. "I'm not running away. More like I'm finally running to. You. No strings attached."

His hands skated along her velvety skin to caress her breasts some more. She purred as his thumbs teased her nipples into peaks that tempted his taste buds. "Come here, sugar."

It was difficult to decide which he enjoyed more, kissing her soft mouth or bathing her lovely breasts with his tongue. He alternated between the two, forging a path with his lips and tongue along the side of her neck, nuzzling the hollow of her throat and nibbling her ear lobes. Based on her moans and the heightened movements of her hips on his erection, she enjoyed it all.

She delivered three quick pecks to his mouth and sat upright. "Can we shed the clothing?" Without waiting for an answer, she sat back on her haunches and tugged at his elastic waistband. He lifted his hips to assist in the removal of his underwear. No hiding his desire now.

His fingers moved to the lacy edge of her panties. She rose up on her knees, sliding out one leg and then the other. She settled back down on his thighs and admired him.

A wide smile creased her face before she placed a gentle kiss on the head of his penis. "Hi, handsome." Then she crawled up his body, her eyes hazy with longing, straddled him and reached down to grasp him.

"Mackenna, wait." He grabbed her arms in a weak attempt to move her backward. "I don't have protection here. We can't do this."

When her hand closed around him, he groaned. She had total control over him and could negate the need for a condom with only a few quick hand strokes.

"It's okay, I'm on birth control. Even if I wasn't, this is a safe time of the month in my cycle."

Panic replaced every lustful thought that clouded his brain.

From the time a boy first hears about sex, he learns never to take a chance on the rhythm method of birth control and never to trust a woman who says it's a "safe time." His hand shot down between his legs and closed around hers.

"Wait one minute. Let's not be too hasty."

Her eyes rounded and she stared at him for several seconds before she laughed, dropped closer and placed a tender kiss on his mouth. Then she sat back on his thighs. "This is rich. Suddenly the tables are turned, and you don't like it, do you?"

"Huh?"

"Not long ago you stood in your kitchen and begged me to trust you, asked me for blind faith and yet right this second, you can't give me the same. I tell you I'm on birth control, but you aren't certain you believe me." Her hand tightened around him. His breath snagged.

"I saw the panic in your eyes when I said the time of the month is safe. You aren't so sure you trust me, are you?" Her lips landed on his, this kiss more demanding. Then she drew back, leaving only inches between their faces.

"What's it going to be, *sugar*? I want to make love with you right now and it's quite obvious you like the idea." She squeezed his penis again. Hot desire electrified him. "Trust me? Believe me? Or stop me?"

Their kisses had left her lips exotically swollen, her beautiful breasts brushed his chest, and her fingers enclosed his pulsing erection. There was no need to contemplate his decision.

Smiling, he released her hand to caress her bottom. "Take me to heaven, sugar."

She hesitated but a second before rising up on her knees and lowering herself onto him. Her desire equaled his and he slid into paradise, warm, wet, and pulsating. She set the pace of their coupling, slow at first, the two of them learning about each other together.

With her on top of him, she controlled the action. Within minutes it felt as if she followed a set pattern of movements rather than indulged in the delight of intimacy. In a sitting position, she caressed his chest and rode him, all the while rolling her head from side to side and keeping her eyes closed. Her gyrations increased in intensity as did her breathing until he witnessed a one-woman show imitate sexual ecstasy.

While he enjoyed the sensations and their nakedness, it dawned on him that Mackenna didn't know the first thing about making love.

She dropped her head to his chest and kissed his breastbone, her breathing ragged. "I wondered what it would be like to be with you. It was all that I imagined."

He was grateful she didn't see his face. If it reflected the amusement he felt, she'd be disappointed. Her performance had been admirable, but not genuine. He doubted she'd been satisfied.

With a firm hold on her Jake rolled over, eliciting a dainty yip when Mackenna suddenly found herself on her back and beneath him. He balanced on one arm and studied her face. With his free hand, his forefinger outlined her eyebrow, her cheekbone and finally her mouth. When she smiled at him, he whispered words he hoped wouldn't hurt her feelings.

"Is that what you're used to, honey?"

Her eyebrows knitted.

"Is that what pleased Arthur, you riding him until he was satisfied, which I'm guessing was a matter of minutes, and you never getting anything out of it?"

She swallowed hard. "I-I don't understand. Didn't I please you?"

He lowered his mouth and kissed her gently, before murmuring against her lips. "It's not about pleasing me. It's about our shared pleasure." Another slow, deliberate kiss. Her breath caught.

"I'm pleased just being here with you, skin on skin, kissing you and touching you." His hand glided down her side to her hip. "You're as soft as cotton. And as beautiful as the white sandy beaches back home. They're breathtaking."

He kissed her again, settling his hand between her legs, hoping to communicate with his actions what words wouldn't. When he touched her, she gasped.

"Have you ever experienced an orgasm, Kenna?"

Her eyes widened. "What do you mean?"

That was his answer. Mackenna McElroy had never been truly worshipped, loved like a woman deserved to be loved, every inch of her flesh kissed and caressed until she screamed on the edge of fulfillment and shuddered once she reached it. Jake rolled over top of her, careful not to settle his full weight on her. He smiled, already anticipating the most exciting sexcapade he'd ever indulged in.

Mackenna stared at him wide-eyed. A smile crept across his face as he moved toward her head. "My turn, sugar," he whispered before placing his lips at her hairline, kissing each eyelid, her nose, and finally settling on her lips. She was so easy to kiss. She responded to his intensity, playful when he offered light pecks and passionate when he allowed his desire to dictate. He kissed her throat, the cleft between her breasts and then cherished each beautiful mound, growing harder when she moaned with pleasure.

He kissed his way to her belly button and down her left thigh to her knee. He sucked her toes and caressed her right leg with his tongue before licking a path to the center of her legs. Mackenna tensed and nudged his shoulder. "I'm not comfortable with that."

Undaunted, he refocused his attentions on her belly button and kissed his way back to her mouth, hovering over her so that their skin barely rubbed. Her breath came in quick spurts. Her eyes were half-closed. His hand found its way between her legs again and he teased her with his fingers. She was slick with desire. Her back arched each time he touched her core.

"What are you doing? This is...I've never...I'm losing control. This scares me."

He repositioned himself and rubbed her center with his erection. "Never be scared in my arms, my sweet. Just let yourself go."

MACKENNA'S EYES flew open when Jake plunged into her. Half in surprise at how much she wanted him and partly because she'd never experienced such intense physical reactions to a man's touch. He'd sucked her toes for Pete's sake. It had been the most erotic thing anyone had ever done to her. Slow and deliberate, he'd taken command of her body. The new sensations were equally frightening and electrifying.

Sex had never been a gratifying act for her. She'd enjoyed the handful of partners she'd had in the past, relished the intimacy of being naked together, or touching each other in private spots. But there had never been that moment when she lost her mind with lust and screamed for her partner, like she'd read about in various magazines and novels. The men had always achieved orgasm and complimented her ability to satisfy them afterward. But she'd never truly enjoyed the encounters. Instead, she learned to follow a pattern of key moves she knew worked.

Lying here with Jake became a completely new experience. Her body heat rose even as goose pimples peppered her arms. He elicited responses with the simple brush of his fingertips or feather breath blown on her skin. Instead of concentrating on her breasts and between her legs, Jake expertly explored her entire body, kissing the crooks of her arms and behind her knees, licking each finger and caressing her feet. And her toes. Wow, that had been a turn on.

When he finally entered her he paused, smiling, his mouth inches from her, his eyes hooded, then slowly pressed his weight into her. She gasped as the inner sensation to open up and draw him in further overtook her. She uttered his name and clung to his shoulders.

"Feel me inside you," he whispered between kisses.

She could feel nothing else.

"Give yourself to me, honey." There wasn't anything left to give. He had it all.

"Let it go, sugar." And then one slow gyration followed another as he probed deeper, capturing her innermost soul. Other men pounded and ground against her. Not Jake. His slow, calculated moves, each one deeper, harder, sent her soaring high into an unknown. She breathed faster. Her heart raced. Sweat formed on her back and behind her knees. And then she clawed at his back, raised her hips to meet his thrusts, tightened her legs around him and screamed. His name burst from her mouth as an explosion of spasms engulfed her, catapulting her into a world where nothing existed except him and her.

The room spun. Tears sprang to her eyes. She shuddered, clinging to him, her face buried in his neck where she felt his pulse beating wildly. He breathed as fiercely as she did. His back was a sheet of muscle dotted by sweat. Neither of them moved. She didn't dare let go. What if she never felt like this again? What if he was capable of taking her to these heights every time? Those were two equally intimidating thoughts.

Jake sighed and lifted his head from her neck. His mouth tilted upward in the tiniest of smiles before he gently kissed her. This man, whom she didn't know, hadn't liked, and thought she feared was a man she never wanted to leave. But she didn't dare tell him that. What could possibly attract him to her? A woman with nothing in the bank and the FBI nipping at her heels. Her chin quivered, and a look of concern crossed his face.

"Did I hurt you?"

She shook her head, barely able to find her voice. "That was scary, wherever it is that you took me. I've never had sex like that."

They were still connected and now, Jake eased out of her and fell to one side, drawing her into his embrace.

"That was more than just sex, sugar." He kissed her forehead. "We don't have to get up yet. Lie here with me a little longer." She no sooner stretched out beside him than his slow, rhythmic breathing cut the silence. He drifted off to sleep, a half-smile on his face.

She snuggled closer, more than content to wait for him to awaken. Maybe they could spend the day together, if he didn't have to work today. It was Sunday. Didn't he get a day off? Curiosity about his employment still nagged her but what did it matter? Whatever was between them wasn't anything that would last. After all, he'd already indicated he didn't plan to stay here, whether that meant this apartment or this city, she didn't know.

Her hand glided over his chest and washboard stomach. Even in sleep, his manhood was admirable. Kenna reached to tug the sheet over them, afraid that if she continued to stare at his nakedness, she'd want to make love to him again. Was that what he'd meant when he said their experience wasn't just sex? For the first time in her life, at the age of twenty-nine, she'd made love with a man.

24

J ake hadn't slept beyond nine o'clock since he was an unemployed teenager. His silenced phone showed one missed call and two texts from Vicky. He quickly typed "All good. Call soon."

Kenna snored softly on her side, turned away from him, presenting a lovely view of her backside. Slowly, he drew the sheet over her and slid out of bed. Now what?

Mere hours ago, he'd experienced lovemaking like never before with a woman he desperately wanted to spend the rest of his life with. And couldn't. At least not yet.

He wanted to talk to someone he could trust, someone who wouldn't judge and wouldn't tell him he'd just thrown away a career he'd worked damn hard to achieve. With brains as scrambled as breakfast eggs he dialed his friend, Adam Michaels. They'd met at a training seminar, both Southern boys with an immediate connection. Adam was from Oklahoma and worked for a state agency. He'd been in a similar predicament. While he worked an undercover assignment, he became enamored with the woman he eventually married.

Whether federal or state, undercover rules are the same.

Adam had been suspended three months without pay despite both he and Valerie risking their lives to apprehend a serial arsonist. Like Jake was doing now, Adam had harbored Valerie in his undercover suite when she'd needed protection. And he'd fallen in love with her. Same scenario for Jake.

"Boy, you're itchin' for a scratchin." Adam chuckled after listening to Jake's dilemma. "What's the evidence look like against her?"

Jake exhaled. "On the surface, it's damn incriminating. The same teller robbed twice, one of those incidents in another location. What are the odds? Money pouring into her bank account in amounts matching what was stolen. But the thing is, she's living like a pauper. She says her bills are bouncing and she's eating snacks from a vending machine for her meals. I swear, she doesn't know she's flush. Even if it's all an act, she doesn't know who I am. Why waste the energy on me? Save the performance for Demond."

"Do you believe her?"

He laid his hand over his heart, even though Adam couldn't see him. "In my heart, yes."

"It's gotta be more than a good roll in the hay, bud."

He exhaled again, but it didn't relieve the burden on his shoulders. "Last night was the first time I crossed that line. This isn't about sex.'

Adam cleared his throat. "What's it about?"

Jakes response was automatic, like breathing. "Love. I fell like a rock. Face first, full body, all in."

"Then there's your answer, my friend. The job is how we make a living. A woman to love is how we make a life. We risk everything for her. I did.

"I can't tell you what to do. I can tell you being on the beach is no fun. Your colleagues look at you differently. It takes time to live it down."

"On the beach" was the FBI's slang reference for a

suspended agent. It meant time off without pay and a permanent page in his personnel file. Jake didn't have near the years of experience that Adam had, nor the track record for solving major cases. No mitigating arguments to wage in his favor. Unlike Adam's bosses, who suspended rather than dismissed him, the FBI might simply terminate him. The question Jake faced was simple. Was Kenna worth it?

"Was it worth it, Adam?"

"Boy howdy, it was. Listen, call me when you need a loan." That was a polite way to say when he got suspended. In the past, when agents were suspended, coworkers pitched in to help with the missed paychecks. Jake was a transplant in this office. He doubted there'd be a collection for him.

"And if it really goes south," Adam continued, "call me. I might be able to get you on board here." Another polite way to imply he'd be fired.

After an hour talking with Adam, Jake wasn't any less certain about his course of action. He only knew one thing for sure, he couldn't let Kenna go. The men promised to visit soon with their respective ladies. If he found himself unemployed, Adam might be a lifeline. He and Valerie lived in Pittsburgh now. Would Kenna be willing to leave everything she knew and all her friends to follow him?

No sooner did he disconnect with Adam than Vinny called. Jake was glad he'd settled into the lounge chair out on the balcony for the phone calls so Kenna didn't overhear the conversations. Vinny wanted Jake to make another set of collection runs with him.

"You're like a good luck charm, man," Vinny coaxed when Jake didn't immediately commit to the evening. "Last time we only encountered that one problem and he made good the next day. Ever since you dragged me from the wreck, I've been sailing through life. It's because of you, I can feel it. You gotta come tonight."

He'd have the full day to spend with Kenna. Perhaps it was better if there wasn't another night together. Reluctantly, he agreed but insisted it'd be later than usual.

When she finally appeared, Mackenna had showered and made up her face. The sliding glass door slid to the side, and she stood in the opening, her hands locked in front of her.

"Hey, sugar. You look great. It's past breakfast time but I'm starved. Brunch? Or lunch? Your choice."

Mackenna cast her eyes downward and picked at her cuticle. "I think we should talk first. I feel like I owe you an apology but," she paused, reluctant to look at him, "what happened... well, you're right. Things are different now." She stood wringing her hands.

Jake's stomach dropped. "It must not be a change for the better. You can't even look at me."

Her head sprang up, and she focused on his face, causing him to immediately smile. "Much better, thank you. Listen, what happened, happened. It doesn't have to happen again if you don't want it to, but I sure hope it does. I don't want to mess this thing up between us, whatever it is. How about we enjoy being together and let nature take its course? I'm a no-strings guy, remember?"

The slightest smile lifted the corners of her mouth. "I told you I'm a big girl. Having sex with you is not what has me off balance. It's the way you made me feel. I totally lost myself in your arms. That's what scares me."

He rose and walked to her, taking her hands in his. "News flash. It scared me too. Kinda it hurts so good feeling." He lightly squeezed her hands. "Neither one of us is in a position to start a new relationship. Let's not fret about it, okay?" His head lowered and he kissed her gently, the taste of toothpaste still lingering on her tongue.

"I'm going to shower. And then I want to head to some all-you-can-eat diner. My stomach thinks my throat's been cut. We should be able to move you in upstairs today before I go to work."

Her eyes widened. "You have to work tonight?"

"Yeah. I hadn't planned on it, but something came up. See? There's nothing to worry about. Tonight, you'll be in your own bed and I'll be working so your virtue will be safe."

He brushed past her before she could agree.

HOURS LATER, Jake struggled to concentrate on Vinny's ramblings. Mainly because every time he thought about Mackenna, he got hard. She was so easy to be with. Maybe it was because he wasn't actually courting her, which allowed them to drop all pretense and simply relax in each other's company. But what passed between them in the wee hours of the morning brought them closer in little ways.

Mackenna easily slid her hand into his as they walked. When he leaned and brushed crumbs from her cheek, she didn't bristle. They tasted food off each other's plates and play-fully bumped shoulders when they shared corny jokes. He hadn't wanted the afternoon to end.

Together, they relocated her clothes and personal items to the apartment two floors above his. He hated leaving her standing in the new place, piles of clothes and shoeboxes precariously balancing on every piece of furniture. Not that he would've helped her unpack. He simply wanted to be with her.

It made the evening with Vinny and his bimbos more intol-erable than usual. Jake found himself snapping at the women to leave him alone. His short temper paid off when Vinny suggested he needed a good Italian meal to improve his mood. He invited him to the next Cabacolli family dinner. Vinny wanted Jake to meet his father.

Good news for his bosses. This was a giant leap for their

investigation. This was a case that could accelerate Jake's career. And all he could think about was rushing back to Kenna.

He ended the night early by Vinny's standards and unlocked his apartment door shortly before two in the morning. The place seemed emptier than usual without her. By now, Mackenna was sound asleep. Even as he dialed her cell phone the thought that he shouldn't be waking her crossed his mind. After all, she had to go to the bank in a couple of hours. And he? Well, he'd probably be headed to jail.

25

Pey McCann was at odds with his partner. The dude wanted another heist. Right away. Like yesterday.

And this time he wanted to choose the bank and had a specific teller in mind. What the hell. The idiot identified the same woman he'd already robbed twice. It was a crazy idea. Right now, he was sitting pretty. He couldn't ask for more perfect days. After the last heist, he'd returned the freshly washed pickup to his buddy and treated himself to a steak dinner, which included a hefty tip for the waitress. He could afford it. The last bank haul would keep both of them rolling in dough for months, even after the major deposit he made into his savings account. After all, a man had to ensure his future financial security.

Still, he was an odds man, and the odds were against another heist too soon. Seven bank robberies in three months without a hitch. No one hurt and no problems. And best of all, the cops had no idea who they were looking for. A kid? A woman? An executive? The briefcase, three-piece suit, and canted fedora had been inspired by a late-night gangster movie.

The Feds had turned to the news media with grainy photos and the offer of a reward for information. He laughed the night he listened to the newscaster ask the public, "Do you recognize this robber?" Laughed so hard, his pop bubbled up and out through his nose.

That would only help him. Every wacko who watched television would call the hotline, convinced they knew him. It was bound to cause confusion and send the cops chasing false leads.

He wanted to leave well enough alone. But his partner pushed for another hit. Pushed hard. Flat-out insisted and threatened to expose him if he didn't agree. The reality was he had more to lose than his partner. Hell, he wasn't positive he knew the man's name. But for sure his partner could identify him.

Would he turn him in if he didn't agree to rob another bank? Sure he'd collect the reward money, but he'd also be killing a good thing. Like cutting off the nose to spite the face. It would be a stupid decision to rat him out.

He eyed the stacks of money that lined the baseboard of his bedroom. Two walls now. One more hit and the procession would be halted by the legs from the bedroom bureau. That would balance the display, running it end to end from bureau leg to nightstand leg. A beginning and an end. Another haul would accomplish that. And then he could take a break. Maybe even disappear. He doubted his partner knew where he lived and he'd be unable to track him down. He could relocate and think about going out on his own. There wasn't much more inside information he needed about a bank. Especially since he'd learned his way into the vault. Man, that robbery had been a trip.

So, it was settled. One more job that he'd split fifty-fifty with his partner. That would complete his money train around the room, like a sign to take a new road. He'd leave town and fly solo after this. It'd be easy, especially since the Feds weren't on to him yet. And this was too much fun.

26

The phone startled Mackenna. She didn't immediately recognize her surroundings. Sweat broke out on the back of her neck when she panicked. The screen from the ringing phone cast the slightest beam of light through the darkness. She honed in on it. Her heartbeat switched from panic-mode to excitement. Jake.

"Hey, sugar. Did I wake you?"

"Yes, but that's okay. Is everything all right?"

The breath Jake released filled her ear. "Yeah, I, ah, I just thought I'd check on you. I shouldn't have called this late."

Mackenna sat up in the dark. "No, it's fine. I'm glad you called." Glad was an understatement. She'd crawled into this huge bed wishing he waited for her under the covers and now, hearing his voice, her thighs tingled. "How was work tonight?"

"Not the best night tonight. I couldn't keep my mind on what I was supposed to do. A certain homeless brunette kept creeping into my thoughts. You all settled in?"

She was grateful he couldn't see the grin that erupted on her face. He'd been thinking about her. As much as she'd been unable to think about anything else besides him? "Pretty much.

I still can't believe I'm staying in this apartment. It's like a palace. This king-sized bed is huge. I'm lost in it all by myself."

Did Jake just catch his breath? It sounded like it through the phone. Seconds of silence ticked off between them before he spoke, his voice a chord tighter. "Well, I'm only two floors away if you need anything."

Him. She needed him. Even if it was only for one more night. "Two floors. That's rather far away. What if the elevator doesn't come quick enough? And you get a cramp and can't climb the stairs?" Her hand throbbed a silent protest at her tight grip on the phone. She wasn't usually this coy. Why didn't she simply invite him up? That's what she wanted.

As always, Jake was on her wavelength, even via an electronic connection. His voice was low and suggestive when he asked, "You want some company in that big ole bed?"

She purred her answer. "Know anybody on their best behavior? No strings attached?"

Jake laughed. "Give me ten minutes to shower and I'll be up. Wait for my knock before you unlock the door and check the peep hole to make sure it's me, please." He disconnected the call, not giving her the chance to ask why.

An intercom system secured this building against unwanted visitors, and residents had individual ID numbers they punched into the keypad. She'd never considered that anyone other than people who lived here could gain entrance to the building. Would Mr. Gleaner know how to get in if he discovered where she was? Jake obviously considered it a possibility.

Mackenna suppressed a shiver and jumped out of bed, splashed water on her face and brushed her teeth. She tossed the oversized sleep shirt in the hamper and evaluated the contents of the underwear drawer. She couldn't answer the door in a bra and panties, and she didn't own any sexy lingerie. Arthur scoffed at such displays. Sexy wasn't the look she wanted anyway, was it? She didn't want Jake to think she was cheap. Or easy. Or too eager. But the mere thought of his hands on her titillated her.

Slamming the first drawer closed and searching the second, she scowled. The pair of pale-blue cotton boxer shorts and matching tank top were hardly suggestive. Arthur hated the pajama set, claiming it made her look like a young boy. He'd used the word ridiculous, which likely meant it was bland enough to wear in front of Jake. Let him decide how the next few hours would progress.

When she opened the door and stepped back to let him inside Jake's jaw dropped. His eyes raked over her before he stepped over the threshold, kicked the door closed and cupped her face, just as he'd done that day in the department store.

"Sweet Jesus, how am I supposed to be on good behavior when you open the door looking like this?" His mouth swooped down to capture hers in a kiss so hot with longing it could reshape steel. Never had anyone made her feel so desired.

His arms wrapped around her. She melted into his embrace, her body reacting to his touch and taste. The muscles in his back bulged when he tightened his hold. She ran her fingers through his hair, still damp from the shower, to press her mouth tighter to his. It would be better if she could crawl under his skin or have him slip beneath hers.

Like a sponge, she was ready to soak up and absorb all the sensual water he poured over her. She wanted to drown in this craving.

A pang of disappointment shot through her when Jake ended the kiss and drew back an inch from her mouth. "I'm sorry," he said, hoarsely, "you didn't invite me up to manhandle you."

He made to step backward out of her arms, but she clung to him. "Shut up, Jake."

∽

Was it possible to reach a higher level of satisfaction than their first encounter? Mackenna wouldn't have thought so but, dear Lord, Jake sent her on an outer space mission, soaring to heights she hadn't known she was capable of. His lovemaking was a combination of tough and tender.

Sometimes he barely touched her, and she begged for more. Other times the thinnest of threads couldn't weave itself between them when he pressed closer than she thought humanly possible. And still, she wanted him nearer.

When he finally brought her to orgasm, she screamed his name and burst into tears. Never had she surrendered to a man so completely and yet felt so empowered. Even then Jake cradled her, kissing her wet eyelashes and licking the tears from her cheeks, gently rocking them both. They drifted off to sleep like that.

She'd always hated Mondays but this morning she dressed for work with an eagerness to start the day. Mostly because she hoped Jake would be at the end of it.

Standing at the kitchen counter drinking a cup of coffee, she felt her cheeks grow warm and her thighs tighten when Jake strolled out of the bedroom shirtless and barefoot, wearing only blue jeans. She could get used to this picture. Wordlessly he took her face in his hands and softly kissed her. She was beginning to like that habit. It felt like he wanted to hold on to her.

"Good morning, sugar. I didn't hear you wake up."

"I tried to be quiet. You must be tired. You didn't get much sleep."

He hadn't moved away, and he delivered one more playful kiss to her mouth. "Sleep is the last thing I want to do in bed with you. How soon do you have to leave?"

She checked her watch while she poured him a cup of coffee. "About now. I'm not sure what traffic will be like. Remember, I'm heading across town to the Ninth Street branch today, out of Mr. Gleaner's clutches. That will be my new home for who knows how long. I don't want to be late on my first day."

Leaning against the opposite counter, Jake nodded. "Call me if you have any problems."

"What's your day going to be like? Do you have to work tonight? Will I see you?"

His expression turned serious. His lips locked. He set his cup down and stepped toward her, reaching for her shoulders. "Do me a favor, will you? Have faith in me. No matter what you read or what you hear. Believe in me, okay?"

She raised her hands to his biceps, loving the feel of his stone hard muscles beneath her fingertips. "I don't understand. What do you mean?"

He shrugged. "It's one more thing I can't explain. I'll get out of here now. Don't forget what I said. And you better get moving."

THE NINTH STREET bank felt different. She hadn't dealt with any of the employees in this branch. Each name was new. Every face regarded her suspiciously, like she was an interloper. Did they know why she'd been transferred here? Filing an HR complaint was supposed to be confidential but every company had its rumor mill. Was she today's grist?

At least the banking procedures were identical, and she was able to do her job efficiently. She headed to the lunchroom with her cell phone in hand, ready to call Jake and let him know her new assignment was going smoothly. Butterflies danced in her stomach in anticipation of hearing his voice.

But a breaking news report playing on the flat screen TV made that impossible. The minute she viewed the screen, the butterflies morphed into dive-bombing moths that soured her appetite and ruined her mood. A list of names crawled along the waistline of a news reporter speaking to the camera in front of the same FBI building she'd been summoned to for the photo identification session.

The morning's activities involved a series of major arrests in a scheme to steal millions of dollars from the city, the reporter informed her audience, and it promised to have a rippling effect through several government agencies on the local and state levels. The TV station replayed a film clip of the agents, bright yellow FBI letters emblazoned on the backs of their jackets, walking out of City Hall with more than a dozen executives in handcuffs.

And there he was. Jake. His chin lowered to his chest and his hair partially covering his face. But she'd already read his name in the news scrawl at the bottom of the screen. Jake Manfred. Wasn't it Manettia? He wore a blue shirt and tie over blue jeans. His hands were cuffed behind his back. She'd never seen Jake wear a tie.

Where was his security guard uniform? Why had agents arrested him? What was he doing at City Hall today when he worked nights? Who exactly was the man she was falling in love with?

THE TAKEDOWN by the FBI agents came off without a snag. But Jake wasn't one bit pleased about it.

First, some pissant in the corner immediately whipped out his cell phone to record the action and post it live to his social media account. That tipped off the news stations and reporters swarmed City Hall. Naively, he'd hoped the raid might go unnoticed until he was out of the building and in custody.

Secondly, out of deference to the deputy sheriffs permanently assigned to City Hall, the FBI informed them of the arrests minutes before they occurred. The deputies accompanied the agents to the various offices. Jake was supposed to mouth off to the agent who confronted him, thereby removing him separately and safely from the bigger mix. But the deputy sheriff didn't know that. When Jake insulted the agent and attempted to resist, the deputy punched him on the left side of his head. The kid was obviously on a power trip, puffing out his chest like a bull leaving the barn. The square gold ring the deputy wore inflicted a one-inch cut over Jake's eyebrow. No doubt his eye would be black and blue in hours. Blood that rolled into his eye stung.

It was all Jake could do not to fight back. He made a note of the deputy's name on the badge over his pocket though. He'd come back some other time and deal with the jackass.

Jake didn't have to fake embarrassment at being paraded out the front door like a criminal because he truly was humiliated. He belonged on the right side of the law, where Mackenna suggested he stood, and this experience affirmed it. At least she was at work today and wouldn't see any news broadcasts.

But thanks to his meddling, she now resided in an apartment with two perfectly good working televisions. She was bound to see the reports tonight. Dammit.

On the flip side, the coverage might reach Vinny's eyes and ears and add to Jake's credibility as a criminal. The FBI already had fabricated a criminal history for him prior to parachuting him into Vicky's public corruption case. That was standard operating procedure because the underworld always checked. When Vinny Cabacolli befriended Jake, there was no concern that his true identity would be uncovered, no matter how many contacts Old Man Cabacolli had on the inside.

In all, the first round of arrests netted about a dozen city employees and two elected officials. They sat in chairs lining the walls of a caged holding area in the bowels of the federal courthouse, most of them silent. Someone was in the men's room puking his guts out. Two women whimpered into balled tissues in their hands. No one spoke.

One by one, agents accompanied by public defenders escorted someone out of the room to what Jake knew were interview rooms. Each person would be questioned, arraigned before a federal judge, and allowed to make bond arrangements if the judge permitted it. Jake would be the last one released.

Vicky was among the agents at the courthouse guarding the prisoners. Jake made a show of yanking out of her grasp when she approached him and raised his face to assess the gash over his eye. "You okay?" Her question was gruff, but the concern in her eyes was genuine.

Despite a headache starting to take hold, he was fine. "Piss off," he spat. The slightest upturn to the corners of her mouth let him know she read him loud and clear. She crinkled her nose like a bunny before walking away.

He must have dozed off in the chair because the next thing he knew, hot stings cut through his dreams. His arms flung out like a wild man, and he jumped up. Vicky laughed and held up a cotton ball in one hand and bottle of alcohol in the other.

"Relax, partner. That blood is dried over your eye. It needs to be cleaned so I can see it better."

He gratefully accepted a cold bottle of water, only then realizing that his hands were no longer locked in handcuffs. The aroma of takeout wafted through the air. He followed his nose to a bag from his favorite burger joint. Vicky nodded.

"I figured you'd be hungry."

Reaching for the bag he asked for a status report. Everyone arrested today had been interviewed and arraigned and other than the two top dogs, had already posted bail. Per the plan, Jake was last. As a formality, he'd appear before the judge who'd been keyed into the specifics of this corruption sweep this morning and made aware of Jake's role. Once paperwork was in place establishing a bail amount, Jake would call Vinny.

It had been Jake's idea to reach out to Vinny once he was arrested and claim he didn't have money for bail. Afterall, Vinny owed him for saving his life. That ensured that the Cabacolli family knew Jake Manfred was dirty.

"Unless he's living in a vacuum, he's already seen the news reports," Vicky told him while he devoured the burger and onion rings. "It's the top story on every channel. You shouldn't have to explain anything." She held up a butterfly bandage. "I don't think you need this but let's apply it to that wound anyway. It will enhance your boyish looks."

He'd love a shower but that was out of the question. He couldn't be released from federal custody smelling fresh and clean. He also wished he could call Mackenna. Again, not possible. It was close to four o'clock. She'd be leaving the bank soon. Had she seen the news yet? What must she be thinking?

He didn't have a safe way to get a message to her, at least not until Vinny arranged for his release. And at that he wasn't comfortable talking to Mackenna in Vinny's presence. He had to let it go and hope for the best. Whatever that turned out to be.

Surrounded by agents and a recording device, Jake dialed Vinny from a courthouse desk phone, knowing Vinny wouldn't recognize the number.

"Yeah?"

"It's Jake. I need help."

"So I've heard. Stay put." To everyone's surprise, Vinny ended the call. No need for an explanation. Not even an inquiry into Jake's location. Was he blowing Jake off? Or was this confirmation that Cabacolli had a mole inside?

Less than a half-hour later, Vicky locked the handcuffs behind Jake's back and held his elbow as they took an elevator to the first floor. A tall blonde in a dress that cinched at the waist and hugged her curves offered him a practiced smile, dark red lips outlining whitened teeth.

"Mr. Manfred? I'm your lawyer. Please don't say anything." She scowled at Vicky.

"Get those off of him! Now! He's been released."

She didn't see Vicky give Jake's fingers a quick squeeze before unlocking the handcuffs. Jake extended his hand toward the attorney. She shook it with a firm grip. She reached for the briefcase positioned beside her four-inch heels and pivoted. "The car is waiting."

Jake followed his new lawyer like a child walking behind a parent, wanting to ask where they were going but too afraid of the reprimand the question might spawn. He wondered who this woman was and how legitimate her connection to the Cabacolli family was. She was stunning and way too classy for Vinny. The association had to be through the Old Man.

A driver held the rear door open. She slipped inside and slid across the seat. Jake stepped in and sat beside her.

The car eased away from the curb into traffic and she regarded him, nodding toward his eye. "Does that hurt?"

"Not anymore. They sprayed it with something so it's numb." He knew better than to ask their destination. The tiny tracking device in his watch would keep him on the FBI's radar. He leaned his head back on the headrest and closed his eyes. No turning back now.

27

T he old-lady wig and oversized glasses transformed his face into his grandmother's image, unrecognizable even to her, he'd bet. But he still didn't like it. He hadn't had time to case this bank and learn the layout. He didn't feel comfortable inside the building. And he especially didn't like robbing the same teller again. But his partner insisted. In fact, he demanded this hit.

He wasn't worried about this disguise. It was top notch. Ruby red lips and excessive cheek blush stared back at him from the mirror. His mother's mother resurrected. A baggy dress and stuffed bra completely disguised his male form. Thick support stockings and orthopedic shoes rounded out the masquerade. He'd be hard pressed to recognize himself. The teller wouldn't either.

But confronting the same woman three times in a row was too big a gamble. He felt bad for the poor girl, although the last time she'd handled herself admirably. But wasn't he tempting fate, looking her in the eye again and ordering her to empty her cash drawers? He'd protested, but to no avail.

His partner was the brains of the operation and had

assured him the woman would be so startled, she'd barely remember a detail. After all, what were the odds of the same bank teller being robbed three times in three different branches by three different people? In truth, it was a brilliant plan and would immediately shift suspicion to her. But even as he strolled into the bank and searched for her window, he didn't like it.

MACKENNA WAS DISTRACTED. During her lunch break, she watched and re-watched the newscasts, stunned in disbelief by what she saw. She'd wanted to call Jake, had her cell phone in her hand, but decided against it. She needed to distance herself from him. Obviously, he was a liar and a thief. No different than Arthur.

She'd halfheartedly resumed her post at the teller window and greeted her first customer. "Good afternoon. I'm your good neighbor. How can I help you today?"

Mackenna waited for the older woman with curly brash-blond hair and a glittery cord attached to her thick black eyeglasses to respond. The well-rehearsed smile froze on her face when the barrel of a gun edged over the counter. The old lady shoved printed instructions beneath the Plexiglas divider.

Instantly, her head throbbed as if her brain expanded in a skull too small. Her lungs locked. Her vision blurred when tears pooled in her eyes. A jumble of questions pummeled the front of her brain. Why her? Again. Why didn't the woman just shoot her and put Mackenna out of her misery? Would the old lady do it if she asked?

Jake had been arrested and taken to jail. She wouldn't be able to call him for help. No matter. He was no better than this thief sticking up the bank. There wasn't anybody she could call. And then back to the first painful thought. Dear God, why me?

~

AFTER GIVING a statement to a young FBI agent, Mackenna waited per his instructions in the manager's office. She rehashed the entire incident, searching her memory for anything more she could give them. The old lady had fired a bullet into the ceiling, just like the other robbers. Panic rolled through the bank. People screamed and dropped to the floor. The bank guard looked around startled. The old woman ran out the door barely noticed. She'd moved rather quickly for someone her age. Mackenna hadn't thought to mention that to the young agent.

Special Agent Demond Crews approached her with a stern look on his face. Gone was the amiable smile she'd seen at the photo array. He dispensed with the amenities, his credentials displayed in his left hand.

"Miss McElroy, do you remember me?"

How could she forget a man as massive as a volcano always looming on her horizon, intimidating, like Italy's Mount Vesuvius? She nodded.

"I'd like you to accompany me to the FBI office, ma'am. We'll leave now."

"Are you arresting me?" she managed to ask. Her throat had closed.

"I'd like you to come voluntarily, if you will, Miss McElroy."

"I can give you a description of the robber, Agent Crews."

But Crews wasn't interested in her observations. He'd merely repeated his request that she accompany him to his office.

That hadn't answered her question, but it also hadn't presented any other options. She nodded and allowed him to take her elbow as they walked out the front doors, the eyes of her co-workers riveted on her. Gossip traveled fast. By now, everyone in the building from the janitor to the manager knew she'd been a robber's target already. Did they suspect she was involved? Did Agent Crews?

She strived to hold her head high. Agent Crews clutched her elbow differently than when Jake took her arm. The agent's grasp was tighter. Meaner. Christ, she shouldn't be thinking about Jake at a time like this. She was being arrested. At least that's what it felt like. She should concentrate, convince this agent that she wasn't part of these robberies. How the hell could she do that? He looked like his mind was already made up. He didn't merely look at her, he glared.

Riding in the back seat of an unmarked car, her mind swirled. This was a living nightmare. What were the odds? Robbed three times. At three bank branches. By three different robbers. And she couldn't tell the FBI anything concrete. Except they'd all had a gun. And each one of them shot into the ceiling. That was something, wasn't it?

She leaned forward. "Agent? Sir? I've been thinking—"

The seatbelt anchored his massive form so tightly, Agent Crews was only able to rotate his head toward her. "Please don't say anything yet, Miss McElroy. It's for your own good."

She clamped her jaw shut. What was the line in all those old movies? Anything she said could be used against her. Holy crap.

No front door entrance this time. They drove to the back of the building to an underground garage. Once again, Agent Crews held tight to her arm when they entered the building. He flashed his badge at the security monitor and walked through the metal detector, setting off all sorts of alarms. The attendant punched several buttons, and the ear-piercing siren silenced.

The screener directed Mackenna to place her purse in a bin that slid through a scanner, just as if she were at the airport. The metal detector stayed silent when she stepped through. She breathed a sigh of relief. Nevertheless, a female attendant used a wand to inspect her body and then patted her down, an action that bordered on personal violation. The woman nodded to Agent Crews. He extended his hand, this time locking his fingers on her upper arm in a death grip.

They rode the elevator in silence and emerged on a floor sectioned off into cubicles. A din of voices, keyboard clicks and ringing phones permeated the room. Agent Crews guided her down a narrow path between the wall and the desks to a cheery conference room and directed her to sit to the right of the head position.

"Would you like some water?"

"Yes, please."

He leaned out the door and verbalized his request, then closed it and sat in the head seat. Her father always sat at the head of the table. It was a treasured family tradition. This wasn't one bit the same.

From his jacket pocket Agent Crews retrieved an oblong tape recorder no bigger than a pack of cigarettes. "Do you mind if I record our conversation?"

Did she have a choice? She shook her head.

One pudgy finger snapped a red button. Agent Crews directed his words toward the black square. He recited his name, the time, date, and place and said the session was a recorded interview with Mackenna McElroy. Then he aimed his words, cold and calculated, at her.

"This is just a formality, Miss McElroy, but you have the right to remain silent and refuse to answer questions. Anything you say may be used against you in a court of law. You have the right to consult an attorney..."

The rush of blood to her head drowned out the rest of his words. His lips moved, but nothing sounded in her ears. Her breathing spiked along with her body temperature. She immediately had the urge to use the restroom. She couldn't fathom what was happening in this oversized conference room that suddenly seemed no bigger than a linen closet.

Agent Crews stared at her like a robot, reciting his cautionary words by rote.

"Miss McElroy?"

She forced herself to hear him.

"Knowing and understanding your rights as I have explained them to you, are you willing to answer my questions without an attorney present?"

Equally as robotic, she nodded.

"I need you to speak your answer so it is recorded, please."

"Ye-yes. I'll answer your questions. I have nothing to hide."

He nodded and folded hands as big as baseballs with fingers that resembled Italian sausages in front of him.

"How you holding up, Miss McElroy?"

"I'm scared out of my wits. Call me Kenna, please."

The slightest hint of a smile touched his face. Maybe he was human after all.

"Why are you frightened, Miss McElroy?"

Her breath expelled in a huff and she spread her hands out. "Isn't it obvious? I'm being questioned by the FBI about three bank robberies that involve me. Who wouldn't be nervous?"

Agent Crews nodded. "So, you admit you are involved with the robberies?"

She bolted upright in her seat. "No. No, I don't admit that. That's not what I meant at all. You're twisting my words."

Her heart raced at record speed. Breathing any faster would surely implode her lungs. If she were a horse, she'd win the Kentucky Derby.

He shrugged. "What did you mean then?"

"I meant that I was the teller working the window in three bank robberies. The victim teller. The one the robbers pointed guns at. That's how I'm involved."

He nodded. "Fair enough. Let's talk about these robbers. Did you know them?"

She gasped. "Know them? No! I've never seen any of them

before. They pointed guns at me, for Christ's sake. I thought they were going to shoot me."

His mouth stretched into a straight line. "What made you think that?"

Fear gave way to anger. "Are you dense? The gun was pointed right at me each time. Why else would someone point a gun unless they were capable of using it? I know what you're searching for, Agent, but you're barking up the wrong tree. I had nothing to do with any of the robberies. I never saw any of those people before and I can't tell you any more than that."

"Oh, I think you can tell me a lot more, Miss McElroy." His words hung in the air, heavy like fog over a lake in mid-August. Mackenna clenched her teeth. He was goading her, trying to throw her off balance.

Jake's voice echoed in her ears from when they looked at the suspect photos. *"They do that kind of thing to intimidate you,"* he'd said. *"Don't let him scare you."*

Easier said than done. But she refused to respond to the agent's comment. When he continued to glare at her, she dropped her gaze to the table.

Needing a diversion, she reached for the water he'd placed in front of her and drank slowly, her mind recalling the erotic way Jake swilled his water after his morning run. *Where are you when I need you? Locked up in jail somewhere?*

The FBI arrested him too. Could she ask to see him? Maybe they could share a cell.

As if reading her thoughts, Agent Crews drew in a deep breath, his chest puffing up to the size of a hot air balloon.

"How's your love life, Miss McElroy?"

She caught her breath. "My what?"

"We've had you under surveillance. You're pretty chummy with a petty felon named Jake Manfred. Care to tell me about that?"

Her heart sank like a cement brick. They'd been monitoring

her. She was their suspect. Worse, his comment confirmed her fears about Jake. He was a criminal who'd lied to her. Instantly his kiss and murmured words, *"No, ma'am. I'm one of the good guys"* resurfaced in her brain. A fresh heartache took root and began to tunnel deep into her chest.

Agent Crews waited for an answer.

"No. I don't, Agent Crews. My personal life is none of your business."

Now the bastard smirked. "I beg to disagree with you. But we'll leave your boyfriend out of this for now. Let's talk about your present financial situation."

She felt her cheeks burn hot. This was intrusive. Offensive. Another form of rape. Was he fishing or did he know she was destitute?

"If you must know, I'm in dire financial straits at the moment. Is that why you think I'm involved with the hold- ups? I assure you, I'd never stoop so low as to rob a bank for my own personal gain. And certainly, I wouldn't agree to be a target for a robber holding a gun."

His hands spread wide. "You seem like a nice lady. I doubt you'd want to hurt any of your colleagues so that wouldn't be your plan. You'd be the pretend target."

Her jaw dropped open. "You really think I'm a part of this?" The thought stunned her. "My regard for the FBI's investigative skills just took a nosedive. I'm a victim here. Not a co-conspirator."

His face sobered. "How exactly do you define 'dire financial straits,' Miss McElroy?"

It humiliated her when she told Jake the whole ugly Arthur saga. Agent Crews was a complete outsider. But if he knew the details of her life the past few weeks, he might be more sympathetic to her plight. She inhaled a fortifying breath.

"I recently ended a relationship with a man I lived with. The day that I was robbed at the Mound Avenue bank was the day he moved out of my apartment. He took everything. Right down to the light bulbs. There's a police report on file if you don't believe me." Thank goodness Jake had persuaded her to file an official report against Arthur.

"He also emptied my bank accounts and hacked all of my creditors, changing the passwords so that I'm unable to pay them. I paid everything electronically and I'm behind on all my bills. I can authorize you to check my bank account if you'd like to verify that."

A deep belly laugh exploded in her face, lasting a full minute. Then Agent Crews grinned, shaking his head emphatically.

"I'll give you this, Miss McElroy, you're quite a storyteller."

She choked on her indignation. "It's not a story, you son of a bitch. It's the truth. I don't have a dime to my name."

Still chuckling, he reached for a manila folder and shuffled through several pages before extracting two that he slid across the tabletop toward her.

"Care to explain this?"

Mackenna studied the top page in disbelief. It was a screen-shot of her bank account. She recognized the first page bearing the bank logo in the upper left corner and the summary balances of her checking and savings accounts. The saving account showed a zero balance. The line for the checking account listed a balance of more than four thousand dollars.

Her hand shook when she lifted the second page for a closer look at the detailed line items of her checking account ledger. Her bills were paid. Deposits in various amounts were interspersed with the automatic payments. Five hundred dollars. Nine hundred. A deposit of thirty-four hundred dollars made last week. Her monthly paychecks didn't even total that.

"I-I can't. I'm sorry, I've no idea what this is. It must be some mistake. This can't be my account."

Agent Crews raised a skeptical eyebrow. "Isn't that your

Social Security number on the top line?" His fat finger tapped the spot.

"It-it is, yes, but there must be a clerical error or something."

"Where's the money coming from, Miss McElroy?"

She shook her head, speechless. Her world was coming to an end right here in this conference room. Agent Crews didn't believe a word she said. She struggled to find her voice. "I want a lawyer."

28

M ackenna's whispered words hung between them. Agent Crews stared at her before finally leaning forward. "My apologies. I didn't hear what you said."

She straightened her spine and repeated words she never thought she'd utter. "A lawyer. I'd like a lawyer present. You said it was my right."

Agent Crews tilted his head. "Only guilty people ask for their lawyers, Miss McElroy. Are you sure that's the position you want to take?"

How much did an attorney cost? Where would she find one? Would the lawyer believe her story? Mackenna wasn't sure she believed it. She studied the bank statement. How could this be? Where did the money come from? Five-hundred dollars. Nine hundred.

Suddenly, the afternoon Mr. Gleaner attempted to rape her leapt to life. Hadn't he said he'd deposit money into her account if she gave him what he wanted? What were the amounts he said he'd deposit? Nine hundred dollars to cover her rent payment. She remembered that clearly.

Mackenna raised her eyes to Agent Crews's unwavering stare. Could she tell him about Mr. Gleaner and her sexual harassment complaint against him? Was it possible to be even more humiliated?

"I might know the origin of some of these deposits, sir."

Agent Crews sat up straighter. "So, you're willing to discuss this without a lawyer present?"

Mackenna's eyes widened. "No. No, I think I should retain an attorney."

"Then this conversation is over. Have your attorney contact me. Soon. The sooner the better for your sake. And I caution you, Miss McElroy, don't make me come after you."

He flipped a business card toward her. "The next time we meet, I'll expect you to be more forthcoming. Or you can plan to spend the night in a federal holding cell."

She was unable to stop the tears that leaked from the corners of her eyes. Agent Crews rose and without looking at her said, "Stay here. I'll arrange to transport you back to your car at the bank."

The space closed in on her despite him leaving the door open. Every bone in her body turned to mush. She couldn't stand if her life depended on it. The agent had to help her out of the room.

The return ride in the backseat of an unmarked car was solemn, like a funeral procession. Her funeral. A sign announcing the bank was closed due to a robbery hung in the front door. All the lights were out inside. Hers was the sole car in the parking lot. The dinner hour was long past, but she felt no hunger pangs.

One foot in front of the other to reach it while the agent who chauffeured her watched. Unlock the door and slip into the driver's seat. Close the door and start the engine. She was numb, operating on autopilot. No appetite. No plan. No desire to live.

She drove to her temporary apartment, her eyes automatically finding Jake's balcony. Was he home? She'd want to talk to him before...before what? Her arrest?

The FBI had her under surveillance. She prayed it was while she lived at The Hole. Did they know she'd relocated to Jake's building? If they knew about Jake, maybe they'd seen them move her clothes inside. But that required waiting inside the underground garage that day, which was unlikely. She favored the odds that their information was limited to the knowledge that she dated Jake.

After parking in the tenant's underground parking lot, she walked outside to the front of the building and surveyed the area. The street was quiet. She didn't see any cars that resembled dark, unmarked cars like the FBI agents drove. Nothing appeared out of the ordinary. Maybe they were waiting for her to arrive at her old apartment. *Dear Lord, please let that be the case.* If the agents were at her old building, it bought her some time.

But if they knew she'd relocated, knew she was in this building now, would they know which apartment she was in? What if in the middle of the night they broke down the door and arrested her? She'd seen it happen on TV. The building manager was an amiable type and certainly someone who'd cooperate with a group of feds who flashed badges in his face. He'd spill his guts immediately.

No, she wasn't safe in the new place. But she should be safe at Jake's. She'd known that instinctively the first time she woke up there, nursing a hangover. Was he home? Was he in a similar situation, looking for a lawyer to save his ass? Maybe they could negotiate a two-for-one deal with someone.

She dialed Jake's cell. Her call went to voice mail. Instead of leaving a message, she hung up and rode the elevator to his floor. After knocking twice and calling to him, she accepted that he wasn't home. Certainly, he wouldn't mind if she hid out there. But that wasn't possible if she couldn't get in. Her thoughts returned to the manager who'd seemed friendly with Jake. Maybe he could be persuaded to give Mackenna access.

But time was of the essence. The management office closed at nine on weeknights. Fifteen minutes from now. Mackenna stood outside his office and counted to ten. Then she took two deep breaths in through the nose and out through the mouth, tilted her chin upward, and mustered a bright smile. The manager looked up from his desk when she entered.

"Hi, Miss McElroy. I was just locking up. How can I help you?"

Her phone buzzed, and she slid her hand into her pocket to silence it. She couldn't lose her nerve now.

"Have you heard the news about Jake?" He didn't appear the news channel type. Behind him, a black-and-white Andy Griffith rerun played on a thirteen-inch flat screen.

"No. What news?"

She shrugged as if it was no big deal. "He's in a bind. Says it's all a misunderstanding." Was it? She wanted to believe that with all her heart. What had he asked of her this morning? Have faith in me, he'd whispered. Did she dare? He'd believed in her when he barely knew her.

"He asked me to find him a fresh shirt and some important papers. Can you let me into his apartment to collect the items? I was at work all day and wasn't able to see him to take his key."

The manager hesitated. "Sorry, but that's not company policy."

She nodded. "Yeah, Jake told me. But listen, you can let me in and stay right there with me while I grab the things he needs. That way I'm not in the place alone and you can lock up behind me. That shouldn't violate the rules, should it? Jake needs several files he left on his desk to, um, clear up this mess."

The manager looked up at the wall clock. "I'm about ready to leave for the night."

Mackenna smiled and nodded her understanding. "It's extremely important that I find those files for him tonight. I'll be quick, I promise."

He mulled the idea for all of thirty seconds before rising and going to a cabinet comprised of three-inch-by-three-inch drawers. Her phone vibrated against her thigh while his finger coasted down the columns until he found Jake's apartment number and extracted a key. If she missed a call from Jake, she'd kick herself.

"Nah, I don't need to come with you. I know you and him are," he paused, blushed, and grinned, "well, he told me when he set up the rent payments that you were special to him. I know you're a lot more than casual friends. Based on the way he talked, I didn't understand why you didn't move in with him to begin with. But I guess appearances matter."

Mackenna stopped breathing for a second when he said Jake arranged to pay her rent. She knew it. There wasn't an apartment owner on earth who'd allow a squatter to stay scot-free. She tucked that bit of information in the back of her mind for now. She'd have it out with Jake later.

She was special to Jake? He'd told the manager that?

Her heart fluttered. She'd ask about that as well.

She shrugged. "Yeah, well, things aren't always what they seem."

He stretched his hand toward her. "Try to hurry, okay? I'll wait on you. I shouldn't leave until you return the key."

Mackenna reached for the shiny gold key. "Fifteen minutes tops including elevator time. I'll bring it right back. Thank you."

She closed her eyes and said a silent prayer of thanks as she rode the elevator back to Jake's floor. He'd shown her the spare key he stowed in the medicine cabinet in the guest bathroom.

She tucked it in her skirt pocket and remembered the missed call when her fingers touched her phone.

It hadn't been Jake calling. A voice message left by a personnel supervisor she didn't know replayed, terse and to the point. "Miss McElroy, we've been advised by the FBI that you are a person of interest in a series of robberies targeting Good Neighbor banks. You've been placed on unpaid administrative leave pending the outcome of their investigation. Your employee identification card has been voided until then and your Good Neighbor account frozen. If you have any questions, feel free to call me. Have a good day."

Have a good day? Was he kidding? She wanted to throw her phone against the wall. They must be desperate to distance themselves from her to call this late at night.

Unemployed. Homeless. And wanted by the FBI. Even her worst nightmare wasn't as frightening as her real life.

Eyes closed, she stood motionless. Breathe in. Breathe out. She couldn't afford to panic. No one could help her but herself. One final inhale and she strode to Jake's bedroom and opened his clothes closet. The aromatic scent that rushed out smothered her in Jake's essence, fortifying her. Soapy clean and woodsy. Even when he wasn't present, his strength prevailed. She closed her eyes to contain it in her lungs, immediately reliving their lovemaking last night. He'd asked her not to believe anything she read or learned today. Apparently, he'd known he'd be arrested. How had he known that?

Well, when you came right down to it, wasn't she in the same position? Wasn't it a matter of time before Agent Crews located her and arrested her? And she was innocent. She had to believe Jake was too.

Mackenna made a scene of rushing back to the business office to return the key and thanked the manager profusely for staying ten minutes beyond quitting time. He locked the office door and watched her walk to the elevator, so she tapped the button for her floor and waved to him as the double doors closed.

She walked down two flights to Jake's apartment. When had she become so cautious?

Nothing to do now but wait. For what, she wasn't certain. For Jake to come home? For Agent Crews to track her down? She drew the balcony drapes closed and snapped on the television, casting the apartment in black-and-white shadows like the TV show the manager viewed. The only other light she switched on was the guest bathroom, which didn't have a window and would cast no reflection beyond Jake's walls. It was enough to illuminate the rooms.

Jake's refrigerator contained a case of water, a six-pack of beer, two sports drinks, and two leftover food containers. How did the man live like this? She reached for a can of beer. It was the only way she'd turn off her brain and sleep tonight. Tomorrow, in the daylight, a clearer picture of what to do might materialize.

Her nose crinkled when she sipped the beer, but it was cold and vaguely reminded her of Jake's kisses. Absentmindedly she strolled to his bedroom and eyed the bed. A smile crept across her face remembering the way he'd made her scream in ecstasy.

Another gulp of brew and she stretched across the bed on her belly. *Oh Jake. What's going to happen to me? What should I do? Where are you when I need you? You've always been here for me.*

That was true, she realized, drinking again. She needed Motorcycle Man. Her own Jake the Jerk. He'd materialized on her darkest day and shined light into her life. A light she hadn't known was extinguished. And now, she lay in the dark, missing him, wanting him, feeling emotions she'd never known. For him. Was this what love felt like? Painful yet pleasing? Hot and cold. Exhilarating one minute, scary frightening the next?

Jake was in trouble too. Was he in a cold jail somewhere?

This wasn't the time to worry about herself. She must find a way to help Jake. She hadn't lied to Agent Crews and Jake had said that day in the FBI building that if she told the truth, she'd have nothing to worry about.

Tomorrow she'd put aside her personal concerns and try to locate Jake. He'd rescued her more than once. Time to return the favor.

The air conditioning clicked on. Mackenna took one last sip of beer before reaching for the bottom of the bedspread and drawing it up over her legs. She dragged the opposite top corner over her shoulders as her eyelids drooped. Tomorrow. She'd find Jake tomorrow and rescue him.

29

Vinny's penthouse apartment resembled a scene from a bad gangster movie, all chrome and leather. The lawyer dropped him off outside the high-rise in an upscale part of town and drove away after nodding to the doorman to admit Jake. They hadn't spoken beyond her inquiry about the cut on his eye. Before he exited the car, he asked, "What happens now with my arrest?"

She smiled that phony smile. "Don't worry about it." He shrugged, thanked her, and stepped onto the sidewalk.

Once inside the lobby, another uniformed bellman escorted him to the penthouse elevator, tapped the button for him, and waited until the elevator arrived, touching the brim of his cap when Jake entered.

When the doors opened, Vinny stood with his arms spread wide, a wineglass clutched in one hand.

"Jake. Mio fratello." He embraced him, patting him vigorously on the back. "It's good that you called me, brother. Come in, come in. How about some wine? Or do you prefer beer? A cold one sound good after the day you've had? What about food? I can have something sent up. How long were you locked up, man?"

Jake ran his hand through his hair. "Yeah, a beer sounds good. Thanks for bailing me out. I couldn't call anyone else."

Vinny waved it away as he walked to the stainless steel kitchen and retrieved a beer from the double-door refrigerator. "Don't mention it. Glad to help. It doesn't pay you back for saving my life but it's a step closer. You want to talk about it? The news wasn't clear about the case, and we couldn't find out much on our end. I figure the feds are keeping a tight lid on things. What was your involvement? You never said you worked at City Hall."

Vinny's comments surprised him. Jake hoped his internal reaction didn't register on his face. They weren't able to find out information? From whom, he wanted to ask. If nothing else, it confirmed that Cabacolli had inside contacts. But where?

"It's not a real job. I'm more or less a bagman, doing a guy a favor to work off some gambling debts. I didn't know anything about the payoffs. That's my luck. The wrong place at the wrong time."

Best if he changed the subject. "Thanks for sending the lawyer. Man, she was a hottie. Worth getting arrested just to meet her."

Vinny slurped his wine and bobbed his head. "Yeah. Pretty sure my old man is banging that, but I don't know. I'd sure like some of it."

Same old Vinny. Put the man in a penthouse with a state-of-the-art kitchen, high-end furnishings, and expensive artwork on the walls and he was still a low life.

Jake sipped his beer and nodded as if he agreed. "Thanks for bringing me here, man, but I gotta get home. How 'bout we hook up tomorrow?"

By now, Mackenna had seen the news. When she called,

he'd been unable to answer, and she hadn't left a message. Was that a good sign or a bad one? He wanted to hold her in his arms when he told her his version of today's events. It'd be the same story he just related to Vinny. Caught in the wrong place at the wrong time. She'd ask questions. She was too smart not to. He'd tell her anything to keep from losing her. Except the truth.

Vinny shook his head. "You should stay here for a couple hours. Let the dust settle. My people will make sure the feds aren't scoping out your place. That's how they operate, you know. Turn you loose, then sneak around spying. You're better off here, outta sight. There's a guest room you can use. And friends are coming over later. You remember, Misty, don't you? I invited her special. Sink between those thighs and you'll forget all about today."

Jake ran his hands across his face, frowning at the stubble. "Thanks but, after the day I've had I'm not sure I can get it up. I need a shower, and my head is splitting from a punch I took. Some overzealous deputy trying to prove his worth. I'd prefer to crash at home."

"Not until I get an all-clear from my men," Vinny said, reaching for his phone. "I'm ordering dinner. Clean up in the guest bathroom if you like. Everything's in there you should need. I'll try to rustle up a shirt that might fit you. Or just wait for the ladies to arrive. I'm sure Misty will be happy to wash your back for you."

Already making his way toward the guest room, Vinny's lecherous laugh smacked Jake in the back. Good thing Vinny couldn't see the disgusted look on his face.

Fuck. Reaching out to Vinny for bail might've been a mistake. The last thing Jake wanted was a goddamn pajama party with him and his cheap entertainment.

Standing in the hot shower, Jake debated calling Mackenna. He wanted to talk to her, but a phone call wouldn't work. This rationalization required face-to-face time so he could look into those beautiful brown eyes when he explained about his arrest. His FBI training kicked in while he scrutinized the bathroom, scanning all the corners, rummaging through the drawers, suspicious that Vinny would have a listening device planted somewhere. He couldn't take the chance.

Jake stepped into his jeans and yelled, "Enter" when Vinny knocked on the door. He held out a black undershirt, the type often referred to as a wife-beater shirt. Vinny's eyes widened when he saw Jake shirtless.

"Fuck. You don't look that built with your shirt on. I don't know if this will fit. It's the only thing I have without sleeves and your shoulders are twice the size of mine. I can send someone to your place for your own clothes if you want."

Vinny's goons nosing around his undercover apartment was the last thing Jake wanted. He shook his head. "Nah, this is fine." The soft cotton undershirt hugged his chest like a layer of skin. But he'd already gotten a whiff of the dress shirt he'd worn all day. It definitely couldn't stand another wearing.

Vinny canted his head. "You look like something off a magazine page, man. Misty's gonna love it. The girls are on their way with dinner."

"I'll be right out." Standing in front of the mirror, Jake laughed. What magazine? Guns and gangsters? Hang a few gold chains around his neck and dangle a cigarette from his mouth and he'd resemble the stereotypical mob guy. If she saw him right now his mama would have a fit of the vapors, a condition she always threatened but he'd never witnessed.

Misty couldn't keep her hands off him, but her attentions turned him off. She wasn't the woman he wanted falling all over him. At least the meal Vinny ordered from his family's restaurant was superb. Vinny reiterated his invitation to the upcoming family dinner and hinted that he might have a job for Jake since he was now gainfully unemployed. That was all good. But Jake was on edge. And wary of the whole buddy-buddy performance.

Half-heartedly, he placed a kiss on Misty's cheek. "Listen, honey, I've had a helluva day and my head is pounding. You and me will happen some other time, okay? But not tonight." He rose. "Vinny, I gotta crash for the night. Too much has happened today. I'm turning in."

Misty jumped to her feet. "I'll come with you, baby."

He shook his head, said "no thanks," and started toward the bedroom. But she followed him, closing the door and leaning against it with her hands behind her back.

"I can make you feel better if you give me the chance. You'll forget everything that happened today, I promise."

"Not tonight, okay?" He sat on the edge of the bed with his back toward her. God he wanted out of this place. The mattress sagged behind him when she crawled onto the bed and his back stiffened. She leaned in from behind and extended her arm in front of his face. A black lace bra dangled from her fingers. Her enhanced breasts pressed into his back like torpedoes. He immediately recalled the rush of excitement he'd felt with Mackenna behind him on the motorcycle. This was nothing like that.

Misty blew into his ear. "Mommy can make it all better," she cooed.

He rocketed up out of her reach and strode to the window, startled by the sudden realization that he was a one-woman man now who would opt for celibacy if he couldn't lie in Mackenna's arms. The depths of his feelings for her drowned him, at the same time bringing him a sense of peace. Finally, he'd found his soul mate.

But he couldn't let Misty, and by extension Vinny, know that. He turned to find her stretched out on the bed wearing only black lace panties. Her pose mimicked the way Mackenna had beckoned him that morning they first touched each other. Misty missed the boat when it came to arousing his desire.

He clenched his teeth and forced a smile. "I'll tell you what, sugar, give me about an hour to catch a power rack and I'll be all over you." She knitted her eyebrows.

"You know, a quick nap. Let me get some sleep, get rid of this headache, and I'll be all yours."

Misty patted the bed. "Sure, honey. Let's both take a nap. I have a unique way of waking up my men." Her tongue wiped her upper lip. His stomach turned.

"You can go out and watch TV or something. You don't have to stay with me."

She held out her hand, long shiny red talons summoning him. Not even close to Mackenna's invitation to join him on the bed. "I'll be right here beside you when you wake up."

Reluctantly he climbed onto the bed and stretched out on his back beside her.

"Don't you want to take off your clothes?"

He didn't. Not even his shoes. He wanted to escape this lair as fast as he could. Out of Misty's claws and away from Vinny's scrutiny.

Jake mumbled his response. "I'm too tired. Just let me rest." He closed his eyes and slowed his breathing, lying perfectly still so she'd think he was asleep. Endless minutes ticked by while she rolled her fingers along his arm and across his chest, blew warm breath on the back of his neck and ear and plastered her body against his side, stretching her leg over his groin and rubbing. It took every ounce of self-control not to move. Once Misty realized her attempts to interest him were futile, she dropped onto her back and hummed softly, eventually falling asleep. When she began to snore, Jake decided it was safe to move.

As gingerly as he could, he eased off the bed, grabbed his shirt and tie from the chair, and tiptoed to the door. No sounds came from beyond and after opening it ever so slowly, he slipped out of the bedroom. Raucous laughter and muffled moans emanated from Vinny's bedroom across the hall, causing Jake to smile. He doubted the elevator ding even disturbed them.

AFTER SNEAKING out of Vinny's apartment, the building doorman asked his destination. Jake nodded to the twenty-four-hour drugstore on the corner. "Condoms." He walked the block, sensing the doorman's eyes on him until he entered the store. He exited the building out an employee's entrance. Just to be safe, he strolled two more blocks before he called for a ride home.

Even though it was after midnight, he was determined to talk to Mackenna. He rode the elevator to her floor, grateful the business office was closed, and he didn't see any other tenants. But she didn't answer his knock. His phone call went straight to voice mail. Dammit. Where the hell was she?

Jake stopped dead the minute he entered his apartment. He hadn't left the television on yesterday morning. Or the light in the guest bathroom. Automatically, he reached for his ankle. But he'd left his gun home yesterday knowing the arrests would go down and not wanting his colleagues to confiscate it, which they'd be forced to do if anyone knew he carried.

Since he'd ended up back at Vinny's it had been advantageous not to have his weapon. He felt certain Vinny searched the guest room while he showered. Nothing to find but his dirty clothes. Jake carried his cell and wallet into the bathroom with him.

No, he walked out of his apartment yesterday unarmed.

And now he felt naked.

He slipped out of his shoes and socks. Bare feet could be a

viable weapon in a fight. After his eyes adjusted to the shadows, he crept down the hallway in a rehearsed step, rolling from heel to toe in a fluid movement while he scanned the rooms. Nothing seemed out of the ordinary. Arriving at the kitchen he eased an eight-inch chef's knife from its wooden block holder. He was much better with a gun, but he'd been trained to defend himself with and without various weapons. The knife was better than nothing.

Jake tapped the flashlight app on his phone to better search the rooms. The beam wasn't nearly as powerful as his bureau-issued tactical flashlight but again, better than none. He'd have about a five-second advantage if the light momentarily blinded his intruder. He could do a lot of damage in five seconds.

The guest bedroom and bathroom were vacant. No one under the bed or hiding behind the doors or furniture. He turned his attention to the master bedroom, his senses heightened by his diminished vision. He smelled beer. Soft, easy breathing reached his ears. Distributing his weight evenly so the floor didn't creak, he advanced a step and studied the mound on his bed. Now a waft of familiar perfume grabbed him. He saw the outline of one dainty hand hanging limp over the edge of the bed. The sight of Mackenna wrapped up like a burrito in his darkened bedroom instantly made him grin.

He clicked off the light beam and placed the knife on top of his bureau. Starting by her feet he crawled onto the bed, his hand running over her hip to her shoulder. She stirred and rolled toward him.

"Sugar, what are you doing here?" The emotions that surged through him choked his words. Elation that she was here. Grateful he'd have the chance to talk to her, to somehow explain about today. And desire so intense he forgot his pounding head and lack of sleep.

No, the only ache he felt right now was his need for her. To touch her and taste her and be inside her. To never let another day pass without her being a part of it. He wanted that more than anything. And then he acknowledged the pang of disappointment because he knew it would never be. Once she found out his true identity and learned that he'd weaved a web of mistruths about his life, she'd run for the highest hill. And the woman who completed him would be gone.

But he had her now, this minute. And if he had to, he could live on this memory for the rest of his solitary life.

Jake brushed the hair out of her eyes and whispered again. "Sweetheart, why are you here?"

Mackenna smiled and freed her arms from the blankets to cup his face like he always held hers. "I didn't want you to come home to nothing."

His heart exploded simultaneously with the smile on his face. Her fingertips touched the butterfly bandage over his eye, and she caught her breath. "You're hurt."

He turned his face to kiss the palm of her hand. "It's nothing." Then he dropped a light kiss on her mouth. "I always want to come home to you. I don't ever want to lose you."

She blinked the sleep from her eyes and rewarded him with a slight nod. Her thumb eased over his bottom lip while her eyes roamed his face. "Make love to me."

The hell of the day faded away and Jake kissed his way to heaven.

JAKE AWAKENED SLOWLY, feeling as if he'd had no sleep at all. His limbs were heavy. He wanted to reposition and go back to sleep, but Mackenna sprawled across him, her breasts pressed to his chest, one leg stretched between his. Their legs were entangled in the sheets. He closed his eyes reliving their lovemaking, marveling at the heights Kenna sent him. He'd methodically kissed every inch of her body and when she allowed him to bury his mouth between her legs, he discovered a new and exciting nirvana. Never had a woman so captivated him. If she wasn't in his life, he had no reason to exist.

She stirred and he stretched his hand over her hip to caress her velvety smooth bottom. Nothing to do about his erection right now. There wasn't time. If she didn't get moving, she'd be late for work.

Jake kissed the top of her head. "Sugar, wake up. You're going to be late."

She murmured a negative response.

"C'mon, honey, you have to go to work."

Her breasts pressed into his chest when she took a deep breath. Her eyes fluttered open. "I don't have to go to work today. I just want to hide here. In your arms."

He rolled his head sideways to see her face. "What do you mean you don't have to go to work today? Did something happen with your boss?"

She tried to nuzzle closer to him, but he nudged her back. "Mackenna, tell me what's going on. What happened yesterday?"

"Oh, all right." She jabbed him in the chest, sat up and moved her hair behind her ears. "You sure know how to ruin a nice moment." His eyes were drawn to her beautiful breasts. This was the first time she hadn't reached for a sheet or a shirt to cover up in front of him.

"I don't have to go to the bank today because yesterday I was suspended without pay."

He bolted up into a sitting position. "Why? Because you filed an HR complaint against Ted? They can't do that."

Mackenna's gaze dropped to her lap. "No, Mr. Gleaner has nothing to do with this. The Ninth Street Bank was robbed yesterday. I was the teller she robbed."

"Wha-at?" His question came out loud and long. And more reproachful than he intended.

She glared at him.

"What the hell did you just say?"

She drew the sheet over her breasts. "I'm saying I was robbed again yesterday. Thanks for the sympathy."

Sympathy, hell. She couldn't possibly be an innocent victim three times in a row. After one day of rookie training with the FBI he'd know better than to believe a story like hers. Sweet Jesus, he was in love with a con artist. A damn thief, no better than Vinny.

He all but yelled at her, "Tell me what the fuck happened? Tell me everything."

She straightened her back. "Don't swear at me. You're as bad as Agent Crews. How about a little support when I need it? Don't you think I'm traumatized having a gun poked in my face for a third time?"

She was right. He strived to regain control of his emotions. But Jesus, God, this was beyond bad.

"He held the gun in your face?"

Mackenna shrugged. "No, not exactly. But I saw it. And it was a she this time, an old woman."

"Tell me. Every detail. Don't leave out a single thing."

Her eyebrows knitted and she stared at him. "Who do you think you are? The FBI? That's all you're worried about is what happened? Not if I'm okay? If I was hurt? You only want the gory details? I think I've greatly misjudged you. I was a fool to think you cared about me."

Jake grabbed her arm when she moved to crawl out of bed. "I do care about you. More than I can express. But this is so goddamn serious. Did you give the FBI the whole story? Did you tell them the truth?"

She wrenched from his grasp and jumped out of bed, hiding her nakedness with the sheet. "How dare you ask that question? What do you think I told them? Lies? You're the one who lies.

"I was scared out of my mind. They took me down to their office and Agent Crews questioned me. I felt like a criminal. You should know that feeling. I saw you in handcuffs yesterday on TV."

He ran his hands through his hair. "I can explain that."

"Don't bother. Agent Crews didn't believe me and it's apparent by your reaction you don't believe me either. I made a mistake coming here expecting you to understand. I'm leaving."

She bent and began retrieving her clothes. Jake jumped out of bed and tried to take her in his arms. She shoved him away. "Don't touch me."

His arms shot up as if someone pointed a gun at him. "Okay, okay. Please, can we talk about this? I overreacted. I'm sorry."

With her clothes in a bunch, she raced to the bathroom. "I'm sorry too. I thought I was in ..." She burst into tears and disappeared behind the sliding door. He listened to her crying while she dressed. Her cheeks were dry when she emerged minutes later, her hair in disarray, her nose red and tiny droplets clinging to her eyelashes.

He reached for her, but she avoided his grasp. "Sugar, wait. Don't leave like this. Don't leave at all."

"Go to hell." She never looked back.

30

Blinded by her tears, Mackenna raced up the stairwell to her temporary apartment. How could she have been so stupid to believe in Jake? He was a rebound relationship, just as Arthur had been, and once again, she was the fool. The only difference was this time, her heart hurt. She thought Jake wasn't like other men, that he was a good guy and that he'd look out for her, believe her when the chips were down. But no. He thought she was guilty of collusion in a series of bank robberies. Seriously? Her? The mere idea was laughable. But she didn't feel like laughing now.

The satchels she transported her clothes in lay folded on a chair in the bedroom and she snatched the top one from the pile. Running into the bathroom, she swept the vanity with her arm, dumping everything into the bag, not caring if the bottles broke or the jars popped open.

A second bag caught the handful of lingerie she grabbed from the dresser drawer. She stuffed a fistful of T-shirts and shorts from the drawer below into the sack. It didn't matter if anything matched. She had to get out of here. Out of this building and away from Jake. Away from everything.

Sobbing, she scooped up her keys and hurried to the elevator. She'd held out a thin thread of hope that when she opened the apartment door, Jake would be standing there. But he wasn't. The bastard hadn't even chased after her.

So, there it was.

Jake the Jerk was indeed one. Well, he could kiss her ass. This whole town could. Her cousin in New York had been arrested some years back for shoplifting and minor drug possession and was anti-police. Surely, she would understand Mackenna's need to hide out with the law breathing down her back. And New York was a perfect city to disappear in. She might even change her name.

The tires on her car screeched when she tore out of the underground parking garage. Thankfully, Jake had filled the gas tank for her. Well, at least he was good for something. How far a full tank would take her she had no idea. No matter. Once she ran out of gas, she'd call her cousin for bus fare. That way the feds couldn't track her car if they were looking for her.

How long would it take them to discover she'd left town? That was a directive always issued on the TV cop shows. They told the criminals not to leave town. Well, Agent Crews hadn't said that to her, so she wasn't disobeying any FBI orders.

She drove blindly, knowing she had to reach the turnpike. New York was at least eight hours away if not longer. After she put some distance between herself and Jake, she'd plot a more definite route. She didn't want to run out of gas alongside the highway. Tears streamed down her face unchecked. *Damn you, Jake. I thought you were different. I thought you cared. I thought I loved you.*

Her cell phone played Jake's designated ring. She'd programmed the theme from the *Rocky* movie to play when he called thinking he was her champion. What a delusion. She ignored the call. Her tendency to leave half full bottles of water in her car would finally pay off. Even though they made her car look trashy, she just never seemed to fully empty one and carry it to the recycle bin.

Now, that was a good thing. She had water with her. One sat in the cup holder, one balanced on the passenger seat and another rolled around on the floor in front of the seat. At least two more on the floor in the back seat. She wouldn't go thirsty and food wouldn't be a problem. She had no appetite. She'd drive until it was dark and then find a truck stop. The facilities should be open. She could sleep in her car. *If* she could sleep. With the doors locked, she'd be safe. And if she wasn't, then let some husky truck driver kidnap her. At least she'd be away from Jake and the FBI.

A new life. A fresh start. It was the only ray of hope she had now. A new name. What should she call herself? She'd always liked the idea that her first and last name began with the same initial. The alliteration was fun. Maybe she'd keep that pattern. Betsy Belle. It reminded her of cow. Sandra Sheller. Down by the seashore immediately popped into her mind. Well, she had plenty of time to think up a new identity. Nothing to do but drive and think.

After two hours on the road, she spied a rest stop. Thankfully, the bathroom was clean. She used the facilities, splashed water on her face and returned to her car, turning when an engine in the distance fired up as she stepped inside her Taurus. The car eased out behind her and then sped ahead of her. A black, newer model car.

A light rain started to fall, which Mackenna decided was par for her life. What else could go wrong?

Another three hours and she could barely keep her eyes open. To be safe, she should rest for an hour or so. A brief nap would sustain her until dark when she stopped for the night. She hadn't gotten much sleep last night, thanks to Jake's incomparable lovemaking. The memory made her smile.

She'd miss that action in bed, that's for sure. Somehow, Jake transformed her into a woman who went through the motions of sex to a willful wild cat begging for more. Like planting a tiny seed, nurturing it, feeding and watering it until it blossomed into a full-grown shrub resplendent with beautiful red rose blooms. She was that rose. She'd always have Jake to thank for that.

A rest area came into view. She signaled her intent to leave the main highway, noticing the car behind her followed. Once parked, she pinched the bridge of her nose and silenced her phone. Jake again. He'd called and left four messages. Whatever he had to say, she didn't want to hear it. There was no believing any fabrication he spun now.

She checked her reflection in the rearview mirror before exiting the car and caught sight of the dark sedan that departed before her at the last rest stop. Tinted windows prevented her from seeing inside. Was it the FBI following her? How could they know already that she was on the run? And why hadn't they stopped her long ago?

Deciding her imagination worked overtime she strode to the restroom, clutching her purse tightly under her arm. She was a lone female traveler and an easy target for a purse snatcher. As with every rest stop on a major highway, travelers rushed about their business ordering food, using the bathrooms, and averting the gazes of fellow road warriors.

Mackenna went unnoticed, which pleased her. Anonymity right now was a blessing. As she emerged from the building, she spotted a large man standing in front of her car, his back to it, smoking a cigarette. No big deal. She didn't plan to bother him. Footsteps sounded on the pavement behind her. A man caught up with her on her left side, grabbing her elbow.

"Let's not make a scene, miss, okay?" Another man came up along her other side and squeezed her upper arm.

Mackenna started to scream, but a white cloth covered her face before she found her voice. The material reeked of fumes that singed her throat. Her eyes watered immediately. Tightness in her chest closed her lungs. The last thing she remembered was a feeling of nausea. And then nothing.

31

J ake was beside himself. Mackenna wasn't answering his calls. He should have gone after her when she ran from his apartment. But his first inclination was to find out what the hell happened at the bank. The few facts he knew couldn't be the whole picture. He prayed—literally—that the scenario he imagined was all wrong. She couldn't be complicit in the robberies.

Demond didn't answer. He left an urgent message to call back. Vicky didn't pick up either. Where the fuck was everyone?

By the time he raced up to Mackenna's apartment, she was gone. Or if she was in there, she ignored him pounding on the door. Emerging from the elevator in the parking garage he checked her assigned spot. The space was vacant. He didn't see her car anywhere on the floor.

Panic grabbed his gut. Why did she run away? Only guilty people ran. But he refused to believe that.

His heart sank when Vinny's name appeared on his ringing phone. Mentally he wasn't in a position to deal with Cabacolli's crap right now. He let the call go into his messages and called Demond again, the tension in his shoulders easing when his colleague answered. Jake dispensed with a greeting. "What the hell happened, Demond? You can't possibly like her for this."

His usual jovial voice was serious. "Doesn't look good, my friend. She lawyered-up on me. I've got a warrant to search her workplace station at her primary bank and we're going to hit her home too. Based on my interview yesterday, and dependent on what we find, an arrest warrant is prepared for the judge's signature. We'll be executing those searches within the hour so, if you're with her, I'd beat feet out of there."

Demond wouldn't go off half-cocked. "I'm not. What'd she say to give you probable cause?"

"She indicated she might know where the deposits came from."

Jake rubbed his forehead to ease the growing tension behind his eyes. *Christ, Kenna, how could you?*

"Jake?"

"Yeah."

"D'you get close to her? Too close to be objective? She there with you now?"

"No, I'm not with her." At least that was the truth.

The breath Demond exhaled sounded like he was relieved to hear it. "My advice would be to keep it that way. She's a cool one. Maybe one of the best I've come across."

Cool wasn't a word Jake associated with Mackenna. Sizzling hot seemed more accurate.

"What time do you think the searches will go down?"

"You know all the hurdles we have to jump. A couple hours would be my guess but who knows."

Jake hoped to hell he found Mackenna before then. Would they target The Hole, or did they know she'd moved in two floors above him? If Jake didn't ask, he wouldn't be obligated to clarify the information if the search team headed to Mackenna's apartment. It bought him more time.

"Run it down for me, buddy. Mackenna said it was a woman this time, but she didn't give me details."

His tone turned authoritative. "Agent Manettia, I thought you said you weren't with her. If you are, you're harboring a suspect."

Jake's shoulders sagged. This was not good for Mackenna. "I'm not with her. Not now. She told me the Good Neighbor Bank suspended her and when I asked why, she told me she'd been robbed again. This time by an old lady. I blew up and she stormed away."

He didn't want to specify that Mackenna had been at his place when this conversation occurred. Demond was no dummy. Once they discovered the empty Hole, he'd reason that Mackenna relocated. With no paper trail to follow, he'd issue a BOLO. Every damn law enforcement agency in the state would be on the lookout for her. And when Demond asked if Jake knew where she relocated, he wouldn't lie.

"That's all I know. Fill in the rest, please."

At first Demond was hesitant, but he finally recounted the details of the Ninth Street robbery. In the middle of his account, Jake's phone signaled an incoming call. Vinny again. Jake ignored it.

"She asked for a lawyer right around the time I showed her the bank balances," Demond said. "She intimated that she might have an idea about the money but insisted on a lawyer, so the conversation ended. I might have been close to breaking her, but then she gave me the feeling she didn't want to come clean about the cash without legal protection. One more nail in her coffin if you ask me. That's why I want to pick her up. Maybe in the face of real charges, she'll crack and give up her accomplices."

"Have you found out anything more about that money in her account?" Jake held out hope that there was another explanation for Mackenna's healthy bank balance, although he couldn't fathom one.

"I don't need to chase those dollars. I want the stolen money and the person who has it. I suggest you focus on the facts, Agent, and for her sake, persuade her to turn herself in. She could be facing time in a federal prison for her role in all of this. I'm willing to back that down if she cooperates. But the clock is ticking."

Arguing that Mackenna was innocent was useless. "If I find her, I'll try to do that."

"Better you find her than me. If I locate her first, I'm adding fugitive to my charges."

Jake disconnected and dialed Mackenna's phone again. It was no use. She wasn't taking his calls. His gut told him something was off. Instead of wasting time trying to find Mackenna, he should focus on proving her innocence. Where had the money come from that poured into her checking account? She hadn't known it was in there. Jake recalled that night at dinner when she described herself as destitute. Who used a word like that unless they truly believed it?

Back at his home office in Alabama, Jake was buddies with a computer analyst who could crack any code, hack any program, and trace any transmission. Asking Cody Wilson to examine the deposits transferred into Mackenna's account without authorization would be an imposition and border on yet another transgression on Jake's part. Not the first time for a reprimand.

His personnel file bulged with disciplinary letters for acting on his own, failing to abide by the rules on two raids when he'd rushed in ahead of the go-ahead signal, and one three-day suspension for covering for an agent drunk on the job. He'd gained a reputation as a maverick, but his track record for solving cases balanced the scale.

The deposits might be a viable lead. Jake only hoped it didn't lead right back to Kenna.

He dialed his long-time ally. "Your ass could be in a sling if they catch on," Jake told Cody after laying out the specifics of the case. "If you want to back off, I understand."

Cody's Southern drawl oozed through the phone. "Let me make sure I understand. These are the bank records of the suspect teller?"

"Yes."

"But this isn't your case."

"No."

"So, it's an unauthorized analysis."

"Off the books, yes."

"Your eyes only."

"Yes."

Cody remained silent a full ten seconds. "Is she sweet?" It was a game they played going through training together as single men who partied hard on weekends. Jake couldn't resist smiling and repeating the expected answer.

"Sweet as sweet 'tater pie."

The sound of Cody tapping keys on his keyboard filtered through the phone. "I'll get back to you."

It was a risk to both their careers. But Cody was the best at what he did. He'd be able to step in and out of the bank's records without leaving a footprint. The only thing that worried Jake was what he might find.

With nothing to do but wait, Jake listened to Vinny's messages. He invited Jake to dinner at the family compound, sounding excited about a business proposition. It had to be tonight, Vinny said. He'd send a car so they could enjoy their meal and countless glasses of Cabacolli's famous homemade wine.

Jake dropped his head into his hands. Why tonight of all nights did Vinny open the door to the Cabacolli family? He had to be available in case Mackenna called. How should he weigh a major break in the covert Cabacolli investigation against working to find the woman he couldn't live without and helping prove her innocence?

One was a given. He'd meet Old Man Cabacolli tonight and finally infiltrate that mob's hierarchy. The case was a career-maker.

The other was an unknown. Where was she? Was she innocent?

While he pondered his dilemma, Vicky called.

"Hey, partner, how does it feel to bring down a major corruption operation? Good, I bet. We couldn't have done it without you."

He thanked her, his mind on Vinny and Mackenna.

"I need one final report from you. I'm offering dinner and drinks to celebrate if you can complete that by tonight."

Crap. Another demand for his time.

"That sounds good, Vick, but I may have to delay our cele-bration by a day. Vinny wants me to attend a family dinner tonight and meet his Old Man. I haven't confirmed yet, but I bet the boss says that takes precedence over a night out celebrating with you. I was just about to call him. We'll have to get our asses in gear fast to set all the precautions in place. I can't imagine he'll want me to pass up this chance. I'll call you back."

Just because Vicky's case was closed didn't mean she wouldn't still have his back. "No need. If you're working tonight, I'll have your six."

32

P ey McCann was nervous. Meeting was dangerous. Up until now, they always communicated by text on burner phones that they tossed often. There was no need for a face-to-face. But his partner was insistent. They'd amassed thousands of dollars from the robberies. Enough to keep them living the high life for months.

He'd split the hauls evenly, aware that his partner had the capability of learning the amount each hold-up yielded to the exact penny. He'd wondered what the man did. He never asked. The man had to be keyed in, on the inside, some kind of corporate bigwig to possess the specifics about the banks that he shared.

From that first day, after the bank rejected his loan application and he stormed from the building at his wit's end, he'd known this dude was smart. McCann sat in a coffee shop, the same one he waited in now, in despair. Without the loan, he'd be homeless.

A deep voice from the seat behind him cut through his misery. "Don't turn around. Just listen to me. I can help you out of your financial jam. It's safe. But not legal. Are you interested?"

He'd hesitated. If he did something illegal and got caught, at least he'd have a roof over his head. Jail offered a cot and three-square meals a day. At that point, any solution was viable. "I'm interested."

And so, their partnership began. He never saw his partner's face, only the back of a tweed overcoat and a fedora worn low over his face. His partner dropped a burner phone in his lap, said "I'll be in touch," and disappeared.

They split each haul fifty-fifty. That was their agreement from day one, although the thought occurred to him more than once that he took all the risks and should be entitled to a bigger cut.

But his partner was the brains of the operation. McCann worked out the mechanics of the heists. So far, his intel had been spot on. Three days after each robbery, he tucked a stuffed envelope into a post-office box at Brighton City's main post office. The activity there was constant. He doubted anyone noticed a well-dressed man routinely checking his box. When his partner collected the package, he didn't know. It was always gone when he next looked inside. In its place was another phone with a pre-programmed number.

After the last robbery, when the grandmother disguise worked flawlessly, they'd agreed to lay low for a while. He was fine with that. Time to sit back and reap the rewards of his work. Exactly why his partner wanted to meet was unclear, but he acquiesced. Now he waited at the same table where it all began.

A text message vibrated his throwaway phone. Out back, behind the building. Next to the dumpster. Red pickup.

Well, maybe he'd finally lay eyes on this guy. He strolled to the driver's side of the vehicle where his partner sat, collar turned up, hat drawn low, wearing dark sunglasses. He stared straight ahead when he spoke.

"Get in. We've got a problem."

Nonchalantly so as not to attract attention, he walked around the front of the cab and stepped into the passenger seat. "The feds are smarter than we thought. Where do you keep your cache?"

The recollection of the piles stacked neat against the baseboard of his bedroom made him smile. The bills now spanned the circumference of the room.

"My place. Why?"

His partner turned and eased a handgun from the folds of his coat. A silencer was screwed to the front of it. "I'm going to need that money."

33

Vinny was impatient and called just as Jake hung up with Vicky. His persistence aggravated Jake. Without clearing it with his supervisors first, he couldn't confirm a dinner with the Cabacolli family. Jake couldn't simply waltz into the restaurant without backup. Striving to conceal his irritation, he accepted the call.

"I got your message, Vinny, but I can't commit yet. I might have plans tonight. You know the kind I mean."

Vinny should get the implication. He always thought with his dick. Vinny snickered into the phone. "You finally gonna tap that chick? What's her name? Kenna?"

Christ, the man was a pig. Instead of responding, Jake faked a laugh.

"C'mon, man, you waited this long. Delay that piece for another night. My old man is hot to meet you. He saw you in your bracelets on TV. Let's just say he's interested in you working for us. The evening will be worth your time if for no other reason than it's a free meal and his wine is superior. And you won't have to worry about getting laid. Misty will be there.

She hasn't forgiven you yet for disappearing on her. Where'd you go, anyway?"

A headache started behind Jake's eyes. There wasn't time to play Vinny's games. He had to find Mackenna. But here was a chance to cozy up to the head of the city's most brutal crime syndicate. He couldn't blow it. This is what he trained for, bringing down the bad guys.

"My head was pounding, man. I think that piece of shit deputy gave me a concussion when he hit me. The beer was sitting heavy. I wasn't about to puke my guts out in your guest bedroom."

"Well, I'm sure Misty will let you make it up to her. I'll send a car at seven, that way we can drink as much as we like."

His laugh sent chills up Jake's spine. Send a car where? He'd never shared his address with Vinny, never so much as mentioned his living arrangements. How did Vinny know where he lived? Jake stared at the words 'Call ended' when the connection went dead.

Jake's boss was elated about the dinner invitation, but uncomfortable about the immediacy of it. Several agents, including Vicky, were on the conference call to discuss the logistics of Jake's dinner. They'd have to hustle to lock the safe-guards in place to protect him. But everyone knew when a mob boss agrees to a meeting, you don't say no.

"We can place a utility van outside and send a couple of agents inside to have drinks at the bar," the boss said. "At this late date, they won't get a table. Cabacolli is right about one thing. His father's restaurant is quite popular. There's always a waiting list for reservations. But a handful of agents inside and out is not enough shadowing, not with these people."

Jake wasn't as concerned. "It's just dinner, boss. I won't leave the restaurant. If it makes you happy, I'll wear the GPS watch too."

"It would make me happier if you wore your ballistic vest."

Jake laughed. "That might prove awkward since Vinny is fond of hugging me when he sees me."

"The hell, you say. I hope he doesn't kiss you on the mouth. Isn't that a bad sign?"

Jake ignored his comment. "C'mon, boss. There's no indication he thinks I'm anything more than a small-time bagman. He could have my address from the news reports. Or if we're right about a mole, some cop on his payroll might have provided it. I hope it was that little shit deputy at City Hall. I owe him one. But you're over-thinking this. Vinny isn't going to shoot me in the middle of his restaurant. Front for the family rackets or not, it's too high profile."

"Make sure you wire up," the boss ordered before issuing the green light for the meet. His cigarette lighter was a high-tech monitoring device that recorded all his meetings. Tonight was sure to be a recording a jury would eventually hear. The excitement of breaking into the Cabacolli underworld was dulled by Mackenna's evaporation. That's essentially what it was. She'd disappeared without a trace. The search of The Hole yielded nothing, as Jake knew it would. But its emptiness lent credence to the theory that she was on the run. And that made her look guilty.

Agents didn't find anything suspicious or out of the ordinary at her home bank. No one had seen or heard from her, not even Sandy. There wasn't a hint or a clue about her whereabouts. It was as if aliens had beamed her off the planet.

Quite smart for the average bank teller, Demond had mused out loud after filling Jake in on the outcome of both searches.

Still, in his heart, Jake knew it couldn't be.

34

Something wasn't right. Vinny's black BMW waited outside Jake's apartment complex sixty minutes before their scheduled arrival. Jake eyed the car from his third-floor window and then, acquiescing to his gut, he walked down the fire exit steps and peeked out the back door of the building. An identical black car was parked outside. The tinted windows prevented Jake from seeing if it was occupied. His instinct told him it was. Vinny's goons were surveilling him. But why?

Jake checked his watch. His backup agents were making their way to Cabacolli's Casaria right about now. They wouldn't arrive for at least another thirty minutes. He eyed the tiny recorder disguised as a thin cigarette lighter that he'd slip into his pants pocket so the entire evening was on the record. Vinny always had a cigarette in his hand. He puffed away all day and night. Knowing the mob's fondness for cigars, Jake started carrying the lighter so he could offer a light as a sign of respect, even though he didn't smoke. Having it on him, with the recording device hidden inside, was easier than concealing a microphone in his clothes or his phone.

Protocol dictated any undercover meeting be recorded. For

him, it was like a safety net. Electronic backup. He'd carried the lighter faithfully. But tonight, doubt gripped Jake's insides. The vibes for this family dinner were off. The Cabacolli family dinners were usually an all-day event on Sundays. Today was Thursday. Why dinner tonight? So suddenly?

He had no intention of parting with his pants for Misty or anyone else who wanted the opportunity to search his pockets. But he'd learned to rely on his gut feelings and tonight, they screamed. Something was wrong. Was it his concern for Mackenna screwing with his thoughts or a matter more immediate? He couldn't sort it out.

Ignoring the recording device, he buttoned his shirt. He'd leave it behind tonight and file a written account of the evening tomorrow. That was acceptable in an emergency and every nerve ending in his body told him tonight qualified. What was one more reprimand?

Once he was dressed, Jake dialed Demond, deliberately delaying his exit to the waiting car. Demond confirmed what Jake already feared. Mackenna's disappearance was flawless, which cemented Demond's suspicions. He apologized while telling Jake that he now considered her a fugitive and had taken appropriate action. The local TV stations received press releases identifying her for the bank robberies as a primary suspect. She'd be the lead story on every newscast complete with a photo and physical description. Every police agency had the same information.

Jake cursed when, once again, his call to her cell phone went unanswered.

Finally, dressed in the suit he wore to testify in court, Jake emerged from his building thirty minutes late, mumbling a half-hearted apology when one of Vinny's goons jumped out of the passenger's seat and opened the rear door. The back seat was empty. The hairs on Jake's neck edged up.

"Yo, buddy," he said after the passenger door slammed shut. "I expected Vinny to be here. Or at least Misty."

Looking straight ahead as the car rolled away from the curb, the goon said, "Something came up last minute for the boss. He's meetin' ya there."

Jake shrugged and tightened the clasp on his GPS watch. "No problem."

35

Mackenna emerged from a foggy stupor in slow degrees. Her eyes felt as gritty as sandpaper. Her tongue was swollen and her mouth parched. She tried to wet her lips, but she had no saliva. Muted piano music filled the room. She blinked at the unfamiliar surroundings. Two windows on a pale blue wall looked out over a lake. She lay on a bed with her right arm stretched over her head.

When she attempted to sit up, cold metal cut into her wrist and she wrenched her head backward searching for the cause. What the hell? Metal handcuffs kept her arm locked to the post of a brass headboard. Using her free hand, she propped herself up into a sitting position.

The room was empty except for a wooden chair and folding table in one corner. A lighted bedside lamp glowed from atop it.

She scanned the floor for her purse and felt her pockets for her phone, finding neither.

Mackenna shook her head to clear her vision. How had she ended up here? The last thing she remembered was the highway rest area. She strained to identify any sounds outside the room. Dead silence.

"Hello?"

Shuffling sounds from beyond the door drew her attention. "Hello? Is someone there?"

The door swung open. A giant of a man poked his head inside. "Hang on, lady. I'll get my boss."

Sweet Jesus! It was the behemoth who spied on her weeks ago at the discount store. Her pulse spiked and her mind raced. That giant had been with Jake's friend, Vincent. Was Jake here? Why would he hold her captive like this?

Footsteps sounded from the hallway. Vincent entered the room. Gone was the polite air he'd assumed in the grocery store and the superior attitude she'd witnessed when he spoke to her and Jake from his back seat in the mall parking lot. He stormed toward her and she cowered in fear, but not before he punched her on the side of the face, blurring her vision and drawing blood when her lip smashed against her teeth.

Tears pooled in her eyes. She raised her hand to her cheek.

"That's so you know who the boss is, Miss McElroy. It isn't my plan to hurt you, but I will if I have to. What can you tell me about your boyfriend?"

Still stunned from the slap, she shook her head. "I-I don't know who you mean."

This time he struck her with more force. Her ears rang from the pain.

The side of his mouth curled up into a sneer. "No? You choose to play dumb with me?" His eyes raked over her body. She drew her knees up to her chest, causing Vincent to laugh.

"You think that will stop me? I can have you naked and spread eagle in a matter of minutes if I have a mind to fuck you."

Fear seized her insides. "Is that what this is about? You brought me here to rape me?"

Vincent sneered. "I hadn't thought about it, but it would sure piss off Jake and right now, that's my goal. To get him here and angry enough that he doesn't think straight."

With one hand he slicked back his coal black hair. Her eyes followed his movements. The notion that he colored his hair flashed through her mind. "Be smart, Miss McElroy. Save yourself from my attentions and tell me what you know about him. What does he do for a living?"

She'd asked the same question more than once and she still wasn't certain. But she doubted Vincent would appreciate that response.

"He's a security guard. I don't know where, but he works the night shift. That's all I know. I thought you two were businesses acquaintances. Don't you know? What's Jake's occupation have to do with abducting me?"

Vincent's forehead creased when he laughed. "A security guard? Is that what he told you? Maybe he's not what I think he is if that's what he's telling you. I hate to break it to you, lady, but your boyfriend is no security guard. He spends just about every night with me, so what kind of night shift do you think he works?"

"You?"

Now his right eyebrow arched at the same time the corner of his mouth rose, as if the eyebrow tugged it upward. "Me and my women. Jake's a real party boy. Didn't you know that?"

She shook her head, dumbfounded. Lies. All the words he'd whispered to her when she lay in his arms, when they stood in the kitchen and he murmured against her lips, every time he spoke, he'd lied. She'd been such a fool.

Unchecked tears made their way down her cheeks.

Vincent sneered. "The look on your face could make me believe he played us both. But you could simply be a good actress. Tell me, what were you doing on the turnpike? My men said you were headed for the state line. Where were you going?

To some pre-arranged hookup with Jake? I'd think right about now he'd be getting out of town if he wanted that phony arrest to look real."

Phony arrest? She'd seen him handcuffed on TV, escorted by the FBI, his name listed among the suspects in the City Hall swindle. Perhaps she was still groggy from whatever his men had drugged her with. She didn't understand Vincent's meaning and she told him so, adding that the news had shown Jake being arrested. He ignored that and repeated his question.

"New York. I decided to take a couple days' vacation to visit my cousin." She dropped her gaze to her lap remembering Jake's observation that she was a terrible liar. But that truly had been her plan.

"Your boyfriend gets arrested, and you leave town to visit your cousin? You expect me to believe that?"

"He's not my boyfriend. He never really was but we're not" ...what was the correct word? Dating? Sleeping together? "... with each other anymore. All he did was lie to me. I know that now. I had enough. I wanted to get away from him."

Vincent eyed her again. "Sorry, Cara Mia, but I don't believe you." He retrieved her cell phone from his back jeans pocket and held the face of it toward her. "He's been calling you. You have at least ten missed calls. That doesn't sound like someone you're not seeing anymore."

Mackenna's heart leapt to her throat. Jake hadn't given up trying to reach her. For what purpose, she was unsure, but at the moment, it didn't matter. He wasn't letting her go. And she didn't want him to.

Just then a man hollered from beyond the door, "Boss, you gotta see this. You ain't gonna believe it. Come here, boss. Quick."

Vinny grinned and pointed his index finger at her. "Don't go anywhere."

He chuckled and jogged out of the room leaving the door

ajar and her mind spinning. Weren't he and Jake business part-
ners? That's what Jake had said. Why doesn't he know what
Jake does for a living if they work together? It made no sense.
Neither did kidnapping her. He might be the biggest jerk in the
universe, but Jake would never abduct her. He'd never hurt her.
On that she'd bet her life. What had Vincent said? He wanted
Jake here and not thinking clearly. What did that mean?

Despite her confusion, her spirits lifted. He'd been calling
her. After everything that'd happened, that shouldn't make a
difference, but it did. Jake would save her. She knew it.

Vincent strolled back into the room wearing an ear-to-ear
grin. His head bobbed as if he'd learned a wonderful secret. "I
gotta hand it to Jake, he's no dummy. A bank teller robbing her
own banks. It's ingenious, I'll say that."

Mackenna narrowed her eyes. "What?"

"So, you were high-tailing it out of town. I bet Jake planned
to meet you somewhere. Am I right? Do you have the money
with you? I'll have my boys search your bags just in case. That'd
be a sweet surprise."

She didn't comprehend his words. "You make no sense.
Please let me go."

"C'mon, honey, your face is all over the news. I bet if I
walked into the post office right now, I'd see your mug on a
wanted poster." He threw his head back and laughed. "It's brilliant. If we hadn't stopped you, you'd be out of state right now.
No wonder Jake was hesitant about meeting me tonight. He
never planned to show."

"You're wrong. I'm not a bank robber and there was no plan
between me and Jake. It's true the FBI questioned me about the
robberies. I think they think I'm in on it but I'm not. I was
running away from everyone, especially Jake. I-I thought he
believed me. But he treated me just like the police."

His head tilted. "The FBI questioned you? Oh, that's good.
Was it Jake asking the questions?"

Her eyebrows knitted. "What?"

"So now, Miss McElroy, you have to ask yourself if all those sweet words he whispered when he was fucking you were true or a ruse? And then you have to ask if Jake was running away with you to live happily ever after on the thousands of dollars you stole, or if he planned to arrest you and make a name for himself? You'd be quite a feather in his cap."

He grinned. "Plus, you're a notch on his bedpost too. I admire the man."

Mackenna stared at him, the meaning of his words beyond her comprehension. She wiggled the wrist cuffed to the headboard. "Please release me. I don't know what you're talking about."

"I doubt that. But it's of no matter now." He extended her cell phone toward her. "Call Jake and tell him I'm in the picture now and I'm changing the plans. Tell him you need his help. When he answers, I'll give you the location where he can meet you."

Vincent's punches manifested a major headache, one that threatened her stomach's stability. This was worse than a bad dream. What did he mean? What plans?

She jolted when Vincent's raised voice filled the room. "Punch in your damn code and unlock this phone so you can call him. Or it won't be only me on top of you in this bed, it'll be every man in this house."

Her hand trembled so violently, she had to tap the numbers twice to type her mother's birthdate in as her pass code. Vincent scrolled through her contacts until he came to Jake's number. He touched the call button. He switched the call to speaker mode, and she listened to it ringing. He placed the phone near her mouth. "Tell him you need help."

After five rings, the call dropped into his voice mailbox. His message was quick. "You know the drill." But hearing Jake speak those four words filled her with a sense of calm. It might be the last time she ever heard his voice. Vincent pressed the phone toward her mouth. "Leave the message."

Mackenna could barely speak. This call would lure Jake into a trap. Even though she hated Jake and never wanted to see him again, she didn't wish anything bad to happen to him. Well, she didn't exactly hate him. God, she thought she loved the man. At the same time, she was handcuffed to a bed and Jake might to be her only way out.

She stuttered. "Ja-Jake, it's Mackenna. I need your help."

Vincent yanked the phone away. "We had a dinner date tonight, buddy, and you're late. I gotta tell you she looks mighty tempting on this bed. I suggest you cease your little undercover game and make it your business to get here."

Vincent reached for her shirt and ripped it with a rending tear. She screamed. Vincent grinned and disconnected the call. He eyed her heaving breasts. "That was the perfect sound effect, Miss McElroy. If that doesn't get him here, we'll take it to the next level."

He turned to leave and she called out, "Wait. Please. I need to use the bathroom. And I'd like some water, please."

She couldn't sit here helpless. If she could get out of this bed into another room, maybe she could lock herself in. Or climb out a window. Anything to get away.

"This isn't a spa, honey." The door slammed behind him and the lock clicked.

Panic gripped her. She yanked at the handcuff, straining to squeeze her wrist through it and, when that failed, twisting to distort its shape and slip her hand out that way. It didn't work. Her efforts resulted in a bruised and bleeding wrist.

The lock turned and Mackenna drew her shirt closed. The behemoth entered with a bottle of water. He strode to a door on the right wall and kicked it open, revealing a bathroom. Then he advanced on Mackenna, grabbed her wrist, and unlocked the handcuff.

"Five minutes, lady." He posted himself in front of the door.

The bottled water was cold. She relished its taste, drinking half of it before taking a breath. It hadn't dawned on Mackenna that her shoes were missing until her bare feet touched the floor. No sign of them either. She stood on unsteady legs and limped to the bathroom. Her knee ached. The oblong window near the ceiling was meant solely for ventilation and not escape. Her head would barely fit through it. She used the toilet then frantically searched the vanity, finding each drawer empty except for a box of condoms. She caught her reflection in the mirror and gasped. Her lip had swollen. Her cheek displayed the purple and blue outline of a fist. The raccoon eyes from her smeared mascara and disheveled hair didn't help.

For one brief second, she thought about overpowering the behemoth when he tried to handcuff her again. But that might earn her another punch. Or worse. And if she ran out the door, what would she run into? A house full of Vincent's men? Men he'd implied would hurt her if permitted. No. That wasn't the solution. She'd have to bide her time and wait for a better opportunity.

When she opened the bathroom door, he studied her, making her skin crawl. She walked at a snail's pace toward the bed, searching the room with her eyes. Nothing that would help her escape. Dejected, she perched on the edge.

She jumped when he barked, "Feet off the floor."

She raised her legs and edged up to the headboard. He descended upon her with a quickness that belied his size, snatched her wrist from her side and snapped it into the hand-cuff. He left without a word, locking the door behind him.

Mackenna's head dropped back against the brass frame. What the hell was this about? What did Jake have to do with it? She recalled the times she'd seen Jake and Vincent together. At the grocery store, when Vincent's attentions obviously perturbed Jake. In the mall parking lot, when Jake ordered

Vincent to leave her alone. He'd said they weren't friends, more like business acquaintances. But Vincent didn't act as if he knew what Jake's occupation was. And Jake had described Vincent as a shady businessman.

What type of business were they in together? Had Jake lied to her about where he went every night? Had he ever honestly said? Vincent said they partied nightly with women. Was that why she'd never seen Jake in a security guard's uniform? Had he ever confirmed he was a guard, or did she assume that? She replayed their conversation in the coffee shop after the first robbery. She'd been an emotional wreck, and he appeared out of nowhere, like a guardian angel. The newscast showing Jake under arrest at City Hall resurfaced.

He was no guard. But what was he? A business associate of Vincent's who planned to double cross him? Why else would Vincent be looking for him?

But if Vincent and Jake were business partners, why did Vincent need Mackenna to summon Jake here? If his men were able to track her and accost her off the highway, surely they could locate Jake. The message she left on Jake's phone only relayed that she needed help. She hadn't given a location because she had no idea where she was. A house of some kind. It must be Vincent's business headquarters for Jake to be familiar with it otherwise how would he find her? If he knew this location, then she could assume he was in business with Vincent, making Jake a shady businessman also.

None of it jived.

Her eyes closed. Thinking about Vincent and Jake magnified her headache. *Focus, Mackenna.* What did she know about Jake? What had he said that day? "You're a smart woman. Think it through."

36

Demond reviewed the police report as he stood in the center of the young man's bedroom. Brighton City police discovered Pey McCann's body behind the dumpster shortly before ten o'clock after the coffee shop prepared to close and an employee hauled out the trash. The young man had no identification on his person. Process of elimination singled out his vehicle. Police checked his license and registration to learn his name. He'd had minor run-ins with the law, both as a juvenile and into adulthood. Driving under the influence and petty theft. He'd recently lost his job as a data management technician when his company downsized. The man had fallen on hard times. The police assumed he was dealing drugs to make a buck.

Nothing out of the ordinary about his murder. Sad to say in that part of town, shootings were commonplace. Especially if it was a drug deal gone bad. No drugs or paraphernalia were found in his car.

It was only when police broke into his apartment that they called the FBI. A wadded stack of one-hundred-dollar bills perched on the bureau in the bedroom, the wrapper clearly stamped by the Good Neighbor Bank. A bank statement bearing the name Mackenna McElroy sat beside the bundle of money, which the police recognized from the FBI alert.

Demond considered the logical explanation that Mackenna was his partner. And since he was dead and she was missing, it was safe to hypothesize that she double-crossed him, maybe even killed him and was on the run. That scenario caused him to shake his head in disbelief. She didn't strike him as the killer type.

Another premise was that she too was dead somewhere, which assumed a third party was involved in the scheme. Jake? No, Demond refused to let his mind go there.

Unless and until Mackenna's body was found, Demond favored his theory that she was a fugitive. And possibly a murderer. So far, there was still no sign of her. She was one smooth operator, he'd give her that.

Jake would be devastated when he learned these new details. Jake had developed feelings for the woman. Demond recognized the gleam in his eyes when he talked about her. He felt partly responsible for that, since he'd been the one to encourage Jake to get to know Mackenna. But Jake should have known better. As an FBI agent you sealed your emotions away and did the job on every case.

Developing feelings for Mackenna McElroy created a conflict of interest for Agent Jake Manettia. Knowing that, Demond should withhold this new intelligence. But Jake was also his friend. He wanted Jake to grasp the whole complicated picture. As if bank robbery wasn't serious enough, Mackenna could be facing murder charges. If Jake hadn't been truthful, and he knew where she was, he should bring her in right away. For his own sake.

He texted Jake's cell phone first, typing a message for Jake to call ASAP. Minutes ticked by with no response. He dialed the undercover phone, a risk he debated but decided to take. The call went to voicemail. He recited a terse message. "Call me, nine-one-one."

Demond searched McCann's apartment. Tucked in a plastic bin in the back of the man's closet he found women's clothing, a blond curly wig and fake eyeglasses. They matched the description of the outfit worn by the female bank robber. Antsy to hear from Jake, Demond glanced at his phone every few seconds. Where the hell was he?

When the phone finally rang, he was disappointed to hear one of the FBI's computer analysts on the other end. His information bewildered Demond. "What do you mean an agent from the Alabama office has been nosing around the electronic files in the Good Neighbor bank robberies? Who is it?"

The tech guy couldn't tell, saying whoever tiptoed through the files was a pro and left no digital footprints. He'd only caught it because he'd been in the file at the same time and noticed a movement on the screen.

"Well, keep an eye on it and if there's any additional activity, let me know right away."

Damn. Jake was based in the Alabama office. What was he up to? Maybe he planned to go over the wall. It wouldn't be the first time an agent strayed to the wrong side of the law for a woman. He didn't doubt that Mackenna McElroy infatuated Jake. Was it more than that? Had Jake conspired with her?

Again, Demond dismissed that notion too. He knew Jake better than that. The kid lived and breathed the FBI.

An hour later and still no word from Jake. For as anxious as Jake was for information about the bank robberies and by default Mackenna's involvement, he should've called by now.

Demond dialed Vicky. She relayed the details about the Cabacolli dinner, which could explain Jake's silence. Vicky said surveillance was positioned thirty minutes before the dinner was to take place and now, hours later, Jake remained a no-show. That wasn't how it was supposed to work. If Jake decided to call off the meeting or delay it for any reason, there were avenues to let the team know. Vicky said the supervisors were conferring about what to do. Her gut feeling was the same as his. This was bad.

An incoming beep ended the call with Vicky's assurance that as soon as Jake checked in, she'd contact Demond.

This was better news. The all-points alert issued for Mackenna had paid off. A state trooper cruising a rest stop on the turnpike found her car more than one-hundred miles away from Brighton City. There was no sign of her and none of the employees working inside the building provided any additional information. Nothing appeared out of the ordinary.

But few travelers parked their cars at highway rest stops for any length of time. The trooper suggested the stop was a meet-up destination. Perhaps a friend picked up Mackenna.

Demond considered the same conclusion. No signs of Mackenna or Jake. Was that a big fat clue staring him in the face? While he arranged to tow the Taurus back, he dialed Jake again and left another message.

"I hope you're not throwing away your career, Jake. Don't do anything stupid. If you're with her, bring her in. I can't keep this under wraps much longer. Call me."

JAKE SILENTLY SWORE at his phone vibrating in his palm. He'd missed one text message and two phone calls from Demond while riding in the backseat of Vinny's car. He'd give anything to know what that was about. Had Demond located Mackenna?

And now, finally, Mackenna was calling. But he couldn't answer her call either, not without his escorts hearing the conversation. He'd allow time for her to record a message and then discreetly listen to it.

So far, this trip had been a long, silent ride, longer than Jake thought it should take to get to the restaurant. But maybe they had to pick up Vinny somewhere first. Not even the radio played to break the monotony. Neither driver nor passenger conversed. Jake had no interest in chatting with them. Lounging in the back seat, he studied the scenery out the back window until the car crossed an unfamiliar bridge. This was a part of town he didn't recognize and it sure as hell wasn't where the restaurant was located.

He leaned forward. "Where are you going, buddy? This isn't the way to Cabacolli's."

The goon in the passenger seat responded, "I told you. Something came up. The boss will meet us." Then he laughed a hoarse, cigarette-smoker's laugh. "Dinner will be late." The driver joined in on the joke.

Jake's back stiffened. His fingers and toes turned cold. This was a set-up. It had to be. Vinny was on to him. But how? There hadn't been any slips, he was certain. Prior to his arrest, he and Vinny never discussed business. They'd been more like fraternity brothers sharing good times. Even when he accompanied Vinny on his shake downs, there'd been little conversation about what happened inside the businesses. Vinny played it safe that way.

Likewise after Jake's arrest, other than that one question about his role in the City Hall sting, he and Vinny didn't discuss the subject. Of course, Jake hadn't figured out yet how Vinny knew where he lived. Was he overreacting? Vinny mentioned that his dad wanted to put Jake on the payroll. It seemed feasible that business like that would be conducted elsewhere, not in a five-star restaurant that attracted every bigwig in town. But the hairs on the back of Jake's neck pinched. Something was wrong.

The advantage was Jake's, however. They thought he was a paltry criminal, not a highly trained FBI agent capable of survival under the worst conditions. *Clear your mind, Manettia.*

Total detachment. That's what you'll need to beat them at this game.

The car traveled fast, too fast for Jake to dive out the door. It wouldn't do any good since he wasn't armed and had no idea where he was. No sense adding to the unknowns of the night. He'd be better equipped to deal with this once he knew the situation. And the odds. He leaned out of the driver's line of sight and retrieved his phone messages. Demond wanted him to call ASAP. What did he mean bring Mackenna in? What happened?

Mackenna's message chilled him. In a soft, vulnerable voice, sounding like a child, she asked for his help. And then she screamed, and Vinny snarled into the phone, directing Jake to cease his undercover game. Jesus Christ, he was made. If that wasn't bad enough, Mackenna was with Vinny. How the hell had that happened when the whole goddamn FBI couldn't find her?

He hadn't wanted this. He should have left her alone as ordered. He never should have taken her to bed, let alone fallen in love with her. She was his Achilles heel and Vinny knew it. Nothing to do now but destroy Vinny, officially or otherwise. If it was the last thing Jake did, he'd kill him for involving Mackenna in this.

Street code dictated honor among thieves. Dragging Mackenna into it crossed the line. If Vinny harmed one hair on her head, all bets were off as far as FBI Agent Jake Manettia was concerned. Meet Jake Manfred, street fighter.

His temper boiled and he leaned forward again. "Hey, asswipes. Call your boss and tell him to keep his hands off her or I'll kill him." Both men laughed and Jake punched the back of the passenger seat. "Do it or so help me I'll kill you too."

"You're outnumbered, don't you think?" The goon on the right chuckled. "I'd like to see you try, though. Don't worry, we're just about there. You can talk to the boss yourself."

Jake peered out the window when the car slowed. They were in the warehouse district on the water but where? By now, his colleagues realized he wasn't showing up for dinner at Cabacolli's Casaria. Someone back at the office had to be tracking him.

Would they find him before a cement stone tied to his feet dragged him to the river bottom? Several disappearances classified as unsolved murders were attributed to the Cabacolli family, although without a body there was never proof. Was this how Cabacolli disposed of his enemies?

The car halted suddenly and a spotlight the size of a car tire switched on, immediately blinding him. Someone yanked open the passenger door. "Out. Stand next to the car. There are three high-powered assault rifles aimed at your head and your belly so don't try anything."

The light blinded Jake. He squinted, trying to focus. Situational awareness was key to his survival. The thug from the passenger seat stepped in front of him, blocking the light and momentarily enabling him to see his surroundings. Three shapes stood outlined in the white glow, each aiming a weapon at him.

"Take off your clothes, pretty boy. Down to your shorts. Spare us a look at your weenie."

A handful of snickers drifted toward him on the breeze and the man stepped aside, once again blinding him.

Had he heard right? Through the bright shaft, a fist full of thick fingers bunched his jacket lapel and forced him to his knees. "Can't you hear? Strip."

Jake eased his jacket off his shoulders and yanked at the knot on his tie. Shirtless, he rose to his feet and dropped his pants. He slipped out of his shoes and socks. Despite the cool night air, sweat pooled under his arms and down his back.

"Hands behind your head. Lock your fingers."

From the shadows, someone marveled at his physique.

Then the scuzzbag who'd ridden in the passenger seat stepped in front of him again. "Stand still and try not to enjoy this." He shoved his hand between Jake's legs, feeling his groin and backside over his boxers. He eyed Jake after he frisked him. "That's a nice watch. Give it to me."

"Fuck off."

The punch to his midsection forced the air from Jake's lungs. He doubled over in pain. The goon wrenched his arm up, unsnapped the watch from Jake's wrist and dropped it in his jacket pocket. Could this night get any worse? Jake prayed his colleagues already were searching for him. They had to be.

The goon shoved his shoulder. "Straighten up. Hands behind your head, fingers laced." After Jake resumed the stance, he shoved him between the shoulder blades "C'mon, pretty boy. Your woman's waiting."

Was Mackenna here? Son of a bitch. This was about more than Cabacolli making Jake disappear. Were they going to murder her too?

Vicky would track Jake's trail to hell and back. Demond was hot to find Mackenna and he wouldn't rest until he closed his case. Jake knew those facts as well as he knew his own name. Vicky and Demond would make Vinny pay. It was little consolation.

Flanked by Vinny's lackeys, Jake walked with them thankfully out of the spotlight's glare and through a door into an abandoned storehouse. He blinked, forcing his eyes to adjust to the shadows. They fell on Mackenna against the back wall, in her bra and panties, her hands tied to a rope thrown over a rafter and drawn tight, forcing her to dangle on her tiptoes.

With no regard for his safety he strode to her, ignoring the minion behind him who ordered him to stop. Even when a gun cocked and a bullet slid into the chamber, Jake advanced on Mackenna.

She clenched her jaw as he approached. Fear filled her tear-rimmed eyes. He embraced her face with his hands, studying it, searching for some sign of understanding. Maybe even forgiveness. At that moment he knew true love and absolute heartbreak.

He couldn't live without this woman in his life. Wouldn't want to. And he was responsible for all the pain and terror she'd endured. How would she ever forgive him? How could she love him back?

He eased his thumb over her swollen mouth and cheek. He kissed her gently.

He stared intently into her eyes. "Did he touch you?" It was scarcely a whisper, murmured so the brutes standing behind them couldn't hear. She was smart enough to barely shake her head no. Relief flooded through him. If Vinny had raped her, the oath he'd taken as a federal agent would mean nothing. He'd honest-to-God slaughter the bastard.

Without moving his head, Jake raised his eyes and assessed the rope that tied her hands, noting the cuts, bruises, and dried blood streaking her right arm. His stomach soured seeing the dark red lines on her fair skin. The rope was thin, like a cord used for a clothesline. That was good.

He took one step back and let his eyes survey the length of her body. No other visible marks or bruises. He moved in closer and cupped her face again. "I'll get you out of here. Believe that, okay?"

A sob escaped her chest, slicing his heart in two. He was responsible for this abuse. All of this was his fault. Her lips quivered. Tears flowed down her cheeks, and he kissed her again before whispering, "I love you, Kenna. Always remember that."

Her eyes softened. She seemed about to speak when loud, leisurely applause cut through the silence. Jake pivoted to find Vinny standing between two oversized men, clapping his hands slowly. The two cronies who escorted Jake into the building were gone.

Three to one. Jake liked the odds. He stepped in front of Mackenna, shielding her from Vinny's lecherous eyes.

"That's touching, Jake. A side of you I haven't seen. I'm sure Misty will be jealous."

"Let her go, Vinny. This is between me and you."

Vinny shrugged. "Maybe. But she's your soft spot, your weakness. That gives me the advantage."

Jake shook his head. "You're wrong. She's a great piece of ass, I'll give you that. But nothing more." It killed him to say that. She had to know what he was doing. She was a smart woman. By now, she'd figured it out.

Vinny laughed. "Oh yeah? She means nothing to you? Then you won't mind if I spend some intimate time with her. You can watch."

Jake stepped forward, waving his hand in the air like a gracious host. "Help yourself." He continued his slow advance toward the trio. "Would you like me to tell you what makes her crazy? Where her erogenous spots are? She screams like a wild woman if you do it right."

All three men leered at Mackenna. Perhaps they thought Jake in his underwear wasn't a threat. Their mistake.

Vinny nudged the man on his left. "Cut her down." The lackey eased a hunting knife from its case tethered to his leg and licked his lips as he started toward Mackenna. "Mind if I cop a feel, boss?"

When he was a half-foot away, Jake launched himself toward the man, startling him and knocking him off balance. They fell to the floor in tandem. Jake grabbed him by the lapels and immediately propped him up into a human shield as his buddy aimed and opened fire, spraying bullets everywhere. Three of them found their target in the man's back. Blood spewed from his mouth onto Jake's neck and chest. Behind him, Mackenna screamed. He prayed she hadn't been hit.

The body became dead weight, heavy enough to throw Jake off balance. He toppled over onto his back but clung to the man's lapels, dragging the body on top of him like a blanket. The bulge of a shoulder holster under the man's jacket dug into his stomach. He reached inside and freed the gun. Using the poor bastard as body armor Jake fired, his sharpshooting skills finely honed. The bullet pierced the shooter's brain, and he dropped to the floor. Jake searched the room for anyone else aiming a weapon at him. He saw no one, including Vinny. During the melee, Vinny must have bolted out the door.

They had seconds before Vinny returned with more of his men. Jake scrambled on his hands and knees to the knife that had flown from the hand of Vinny's goon. He rushed to Mackenna. Terror etched her face. She gasped to catch her breath. He sliced the rope, and she crumbled to the floor. No time to console her. Every second was a matter of life and death. Jake grabbed her by the shoulders and yanked her to her feet. She cried hysterically and he shook her.

"Run! Now! Out that rear door. Be careful." He shoved her hard and she fell to her hands and knees and crawled at first. Then she jumped to her feet and ran when the front door opened and more men than Jake could count rushed into the warehouse, peppering the walls with bullets. He dove to the floor and lay prone, Mackenna's screams echoing in his ears. Had one of the bullets found her? Or had she escaped?

Red-hot pain seared through his left thigh, and his right arm went numb. He managed one last thought before the warehouse went black. *Kenna.*

37

B rambles slashed Mackenna's bare feet when she stumbled out of the building with a barrage of bullets echoing behind her. She hadn't looked back, didn't know if Jake had gotten out behind her.

She ran mindlessly. Faster than she thought herself capable. Sulfur from the gunshots burned her nose. Her eyes watered, clouding her vision. The intense ringing in her ears encased her head in a vacuum. If someone chased after her, she couldn't hear them.

Her steps faltered through muddy grass. Shrubs cut her arms and slashed her legs. She raced blindly onward.

Her escape put distance between her and the building, plunging her into the black night. The odors of the waterfront, dirty and pungent, clogged her airways. She covered her mouth and nose with her forearm. It didn't help. Surrounded by darkness she tripped, fell, catapulted back up, and ignored the burning pain that shot through her knee. She ran to the right down a back alley, barely suppressing her scream when rats scattered at her intrusion. She veered left onto a cobblestone street cast in shadows by one lone lamp post.

Falling against the side of it, she doubled over. She used the pole for support and strained to catch her breath. Her lungs wanted to explode. She swiped snot from her upper lip and looked around for someone, anyone who might help. The street was eerily deserted. What time was it?

She glanced behind her. No Jake. She was on her own. Had to save herself. And Jake. She must find a way to save Jake. Dropping her head back she stared at the starless sky and prayed out loud "Dear Lord, let Jake be alive. There's so much I want to tell him."

The rumble of a car engine jolted her into moving. She took off again running, hugging the buildings to stay in the shadows. She couldn't save Jake singlehandedly. She'd need help.

Agent Crews. It was a costly risk. He was a mean man who wouldn't believe her story. Hell, she was a fugitive. Every police officer in the city probably hunted for her. But she had to try.

She couldn't account for the hours spent handcuffed to that bed once she'd used the bathroom. With nothing to do but think, she'd replayed in her mind everything she knew about Jake. He'd been evasive whenever she questioned him, imploring her to trust him, implying that he kept a secret that someday he'd share with her. Who kept their employment secret?

He'd never admitted to being a warehouse guard. "I'm in security," he'd said, and she'd provided the job description. "Like a guard some place?" she'd asked. "Something like that," he'd said. The conclusion about his occupation had been hers.

She recalled the grocery store meeting when Vincent first introduced himself. Jake hadn't wanted them to meet, had shielded her from Vinny and urged her to walk away, trying to protect her. He'd come to her rescue when Mr. Gleaner plied her with alcohol with the intent of having sex, somehow knowing how to find her. He slipped a handgun in his nightstand. His apartment lacked personal mementos, as if it was temporary.

When everyone was summoned for the photo array at the FBI office, Jake had been the only one in the room who hadn't seemed nervous to be there. She'd thought then that his stance hinted of a military background. Or was it police? He'd encouraged her not to cower in the face of Agent Crews's implications that they suspected her. "They do that to intimidate you," he'd said. Did the average person know that?

Finally, there was the discussion about Mr. Gleaner's sexual exploitation and Jake's insistence that a report be filed even if he had to do it himself. His language. He'd used the same words the policewoman used. When she asked if her friend was a cop, Mackenna answered affirmatively. She knew then that he was.

But he was more than that, wasn't he?

Snippets of what he said surfaced. "You're a smart woman... think it through."

Think what through?

"It's where we find ourselves at the moment, sugar."

What did that mean? Her timing was bad?

"That implies that I lied to you, honey, and I never have." Every answer to her questions had been truthful. *Connect the dots, dammit.*

"I'm one of the good guys." Those words played and replayed in her mind.

Who were the good guys? They were the men who wore the white hats. They were the cavalry. The cops. The FBI.

Despite the cost to her personal safety, her only hope was Agent Crews. Jake had something to do with the FBI. And he was in trouble.

～

JAKE FADED in and out of consciousness. He lay in a puddle of sweat and blood. It pained him to turn his head to see his arm immobile along his side.

A hunk of flesh hung from his shoulder, bringing bile to his throat. He turned away to focus on his leg. The clothesline that had constrained Mackenna was wrapped around his upper thigh so tight it throbbed. Beneath his hip spread a pool of blood. He clenched his teeth, hoping to redirect the pain and clear his head. Where was he? Flat on his back on a concrete floor. The warehouse. Mackenna.

Despite the sword that pierced his brain he raised his head to search the room. No sign of her. Only the mound of a dead man a few feet from him, the guy's eyes wide open and staring at him. Where was Mackenna? Did she get away? Bits and pieces of the night resurfaced. She, half-naked, and Vinny leering at her. Was she tied to a bed somewhere? Had Vinny...?

From behind him, a man's voice. "Hey, boss. Looks like he's awake."

With his ear on the cement, Jake heard the footsteps reverberate as they neared. He strained to raise his head when four chair legs came into view along with the brown alligator penny loafers Vinny often wore. He straddled the seat backward and leaned toward Jake with an uncapped bottle of water in his hand. The bottle tilted and water dribbled onto Jake's cheek, some of it rolling toward his ear and a stream flowing to his mouth. He swallowed as much as he could.

"You disappoint me, my brother. I had great plans for us. Together we could've taken over my old man's operation and lived the high life."

Jake eyed him. His survival counted on maintaining his undercover persona. "I don't understand what this is all about, man. We can still work as a team. I'm still your friend."

"You're a fucking Fed."

Jake's heart surged to his throat. The number one rule of

undercover work was never, ever admit the truth. He'd abide by that tenet to his death.

He closed his eyes and dropped his head to the floor.

"You're fucking crazy."

Vinny snickered. "You think so? You underestimate my old man and his connections. Jake Manfred. Arrested and charged in the public corruption case that went before Judge Truman. True identity Jake Manettia. Real job, infiltrate that City Hall operation and take it down. For the Feds. Your boys should've done better research. Judge Truman and my old man go way back. He owes his seat on the bench to the Cabacolli family."

Jake strived to control his facial expression. "I don't know what you're talking about."

Vinny laughed again. "No? How do you think I knew where you were when you called? How do you think we had your address? I've had an eye on you ever since you turned down my dinner invitation for you and Miss McElroy. Most everyone in this city would kill for an invite like that. You, you son of a bitch, you turned your nose up at me.

"If a door to the Cabacolli family opened, any small-time thief would rush through it looking for the opportunity to get in my good graces or my old man's. But not you. I got to wondering why. I couldn't figure it out, though. You were a puzzle. And then Judge Truman called."

Going on the defensive to argue wouldn't help. Jake shook his head. "You got it all wrong." Jake closed his eyes and prayed that Mackenna had gone for help. Or his colleagues were on their way to his rescue. There was no getting out of this one any other way. But had she figured it out? Did she know about him? Did she care enough to help him or was she long gone? "Where's Mackenna?"

Vinny shrugged. "I have to hand it to that little bitch. I have all my team searching for her, and nothing. Make it easy on yourself. Tell me where she went with all that money."

Inwardly, his heart applauded. She'd gotten away. She was safe. It didn't matter about him and whether or not she summoned help to save him. Mackenna was safe. He could die in peace knowing that.

"I don't have a clue. I told you she's nothing to me."

Vinny turned the bottle upside down and dumped the water over Jake's face. "You lying sack of shit. I saw the way you looked at her. And she had eyes for you. Be glad she got away. She's the only reason I'm keeping you alive. I'm gonna bring her back here and fuck the hell out of her while you watch. And then you're both going for a swim."

He rose and kicked the chair to the side. Stomping away he barked his orders. "Don't let him move so much as a pinkie finger. If he does, fire a bullet into his other leg. And somebody find that girl."

Relief flooded over Jake. Mackenna had evaded Vinny's men. They numbered close to fifty, based on what Vinny had told him about Old Man Cabacolli's ranks. Damn, Mackenna was smart. But was she smart enough?

38

Mackenna limped toward an all-night convenience mart, its lights shining like a beacon at the end of the street. Her knee had swollen to the size of a baseball. Her feet burned from the cuts on the bottom, bruised by countless stones she'd run over. Her ankles and legs were bloody. The muscles in her thighs threatened to seize up with every painful step. But she couldn't stop, not until she found a phone and called the FBI.

She paused a block away from the store to study it. A smile creased her face. Jake would be so proud of her right now. Only one customer, a man leaning casually against the counter in conversation with the female clerk. Was he one of Vincent's men? She'd no way of knowing.

She waited, wondering how she'd explain her lack of clothing or shoes and her general appearance once she entered the store. Well, pride be damned. She had no choice but to go in there, not knowing where the next opportunity might be and unwilling to prolong Jake's rescue. She might already be too late.

Dried blood smeared her torso and limbs. Should she run

in screaming and ask the clerk to contact the FBI? Or stroll in nonchalantly as if being in public barefoot wearing only under-wear was an everyday occurrence and ask in a calm voice to use the phone?

For whatever reason, she smoothed her hair back and straightened her bra. And then she waited.

No telling how long. The customer wasn't a big man, unlike the men who surrounded Vincent. He didn't have that tough guy look either. He flirted with the clerk in an easy manner, both of them laughing. The woman dropped her gaze to the counter more often than not. She must be blushing at his words. Mackenna hoped he was simply an ordinary man flirting with a woman. She surveyed the intersecting streets. Not one vehicle passed. No one searched for her in this part of town. Filling her lungs with the cool night air, Mackenna exhaled slowly and advanced to the front door. She had nothing to lose except Jake. And he was everything.

The bell over the door chimed when she walked in. Customer and clerk turned in her direction, their mouths gaping open as she approached. The man straightened imme-diately and moved toward her. "Miss, are you all right?"

Mackenna raised her hand to stop him and looked toward the clerk. "Is there a phone I can use?" With her face distorted by her swollen mouth and cheek, her words slurred as if she was drunk.

The clerk shook her head. The man reached in his pocket. "I have my cell phone. Do you want me to call you an ambu-lance? Were you in an accident?"

"I need to speak to the FBI."

A nervous laugh escaped him. "The FBI? Who calls them?"

Meanwhile, the clerk reached under the counter. Her bicep muscles tightened and released.

Mackenna smiled, trying to come across as non-threatening despite her appearance. "Did you just press a silent alarm?

That's okay. The police will be better than nothing." She returned her gaze to the man, who seemed more approachable. "Even when the police show up, please call the FBI. Ask for Agent Crews. Tell him Jake's in trouble."

The wail of sirens sounded outside. In the distance, flashing red and blue lights sped toward the convenience mart. Mackenna watched their approach through the plate-glass windows. The trio stood in silence, waiting. No one moved.

Uniformed officers jumped from their cruisers leaving the doors ajar, guns aimed at the occupants inside the store. "Everyone down on the floor, now!"

Mackenna dropped to the floor. The clerk disappeared behind the counter and the man spread out on his belly, never taking his eyes off her.

"Please," she whispered as the cops stormed the store, "I'm not crazy. Call the FBI. Agent Crews Jake needs help."

Bedlam erupted. The clerk jumped to her feet, pointed at Mackenna, and screamed that Mackenna was the armed and dangerous bank robber broadcast on TV.

Really? Armed? Wearing only underwear, she could hardly conceal a weapon.

The male customer eased into a sitting position once one of the police officers searched him and sat studying her, his cell phone still gripped in his hand.

Strong hands grasped Mackenna by the back of her arms. Two men lifted her slowly so that she sat on her haunches, each cautioning the other that she might be hurt. They talked as if she wasn't right there between them.

"Geez, where's all the blood coming from?"

"Where are her clothes?"

"Damn, it *is* her."

"Ma'am, can you speak? What's your name? How'd you get here?"

More police filled the store, guns drawn, searching every

aisle and running through every door. The clerk continued to stare at her. The customer on the floor held his phone up. Was he recording this?

One officer began to question the clerk while another one directed the customer to stand and produce identification, all while two other patrolmen kept their weapons at shoulder level and panned the store.

"My name is Mackenna McElroy. I want to speak to Agent Demond Crews of the FBI."

"Can you stand?" one of the officers asked as they helped her to her feet. She repeated her request like a military prisoner reciting only name, rank and serial number. "Agent Crews. I need to speak to Agent Crews at the FBI."

"Geez, is she drugged?" one officer wondered.

"Can't tell. Let's get her to the unit."

"Ma'am, can you walk? We'll take you to the patrol car. There's a blanket we can cover you with."

Even if she wasn't willing to move, the men forced her forward. They stepped outside the store. Someone yanked open the cruiser's rear door. She slid into the back seat. When the trunk of the vehicle slammed shut, she jumped. A female officer leaned inside and tucked a blanket around her.

"Please call the FBI," Mackenna said. "Ask for Agent Crews and tell him Jake needs help."

The woman stared at Mackenna, her face so close Mackenna could smell coffee on her breath. "Who's Jake? Your partner?"

Sheer exhaustion overwhelmed her. Mackenna's head lolled onto the headrest. Oh, sweet Jesus, why didn't they listen to her? There wasn't time to waste. He could already be dead. "No, no." Her head rolled back and forth. "He's not my partner. He's one of them."

"One of who, ma'am?"

"The FBI. I think he's FBI. And they're going to kill him."

39

Demond spit the stale coffee back into his cup and massaged his stiff neck. His stomach was already in knots. The coffee threatened to sour it to nausea. He was too old for all-nighters.

The office buzzed with activity despite it being two in the morning. That's the way it was in the Bureau. A man was unaccounted for and every agent on the white-collar squad as well as the organized crime squad rolled out of bed to come in and assist. They'd all worked with Jake. He was a brother in trouble.

A team stayed in place at Cabacolli's Casaria, but the restaurant emptied out hours ago and there'd been no activity there. And no sign of Jake.

It took much too long, in Demond's opinion, to rouse the support staff and transport them to the office to track Jake's location via the GPS watch. They finally narrowed it down to a residential address in a ritzy part of town. The local police had the house surrounded, waiting on agents to arrive before they stormed the front door. They reported that the house was dark and speculated it was unoccupied, or all the occupants were asleep. Vicky was with that squad. She assured Demond she'd call as soon as they knew something.

Mackenna's car had arrived at the federal garage and despite a thorough search, it yielded nothing. Not so much as a map to hint at her destination, and no clue about her disappearance. Like the state trooper said, it appeared she parked the car and never came back. But Demond clung to the knowledge that he'd interviewed the woman, seen terror in her eyes and her hands shake in fear. His gut told him she hadn't run off. It was something else.

The switchboard rang his desk and informed him an agent from the Alabama FBI office was on the line, asking the switchboard to contact Demond at his home. Of course, he'd ask that. No one would expect to find him at his desk in the middle of the night.

Demond instructed the operator to connect the call.

When he introduced himself, his Southern drawl sounded just like Jake's, causing Demond to smile.

"Sorry for the late hour, sir, but this is important enough to bother you at home."

"I'm not at home. We have an event here so I'm at the office." Until they were sure what they were dealing with, the Bureau would keep Jake's disappearance on a need-to-know basis.

Agent Cody Wilson paused. "I've been trying to reach Jake Manettia for hours without success. I stumbled across your name in a file I'm looking at for Jake, and I recognized it from my conversations with him. Can you put me in touch with Jake ASAP? None of the numbers I have work and this is an emergency."

"I've been trying to reach him too. What do you mean you stumbled across my name? Where?"

"Um, just some records that came across my desk."

"What'd you say your specialty is? Computer analyst? Are

you the one who's been nosing around in the bank records from my robbery cases?"

On the other end of the line, Cody remained silent. This wasn't the time to play cat and mouse. "Let's lay our cards on the table, boy. I'm friends with Jake's and right now, he's off the grid. If you have information that might help find him, I suggest you share it. I'm not going to bust you for hacking into my files."

Demond waited through the silence.

"This information pertains to a Mackenna McElroy. Jake asked me to review several deposits to determine their origin. But I don't see how this information can help you find Jake."

Finding Mackenna might be just as good. "What'd you see, boy?"

"The deposits into the McElroy account were interoffice. Whoever is behind them spun an intricate web to disguise the trail, one so complex I almost gave up."

"Were you able to follow the path?"

"Yes, sir. The deposits originated from the manager's office, inside the bank located on Mound Avenue."

Demond's shoulders sagged. So what? McElroy must be in cahoots with the manager. "Is that all?"

"No, sir. I took it a step further to determine the source of the funding. That money funneled into the bank through a shell corporation that traces back to an Italian restaurant called Cabacolli's Casaria. Ordinarily, I wouldn't think anything of it except when Jake and I spoke, I had the impression that this McElroy woman meant something to him.

"By the same token, Jake offered that he'd stumbled into a relationship with someone from the Cabacolli family. I find it suspicious that money in Mackenna McElroy's account comes from Cabacolli's restaurant. I think Jake should be warned about her. She might be setting him up."

Demond would've never guessed that Mackenna McElroy

was that devious. Or that Jake could be that gullible. She'd seemed genuinely surprised to see the huge totals in her checking account. "Anything else you can tell me?"

Cody hesitated. "I verified the login each time a sum of money moved from the shell corporation to another account. It's a regular stream into the bank through an employee who signs on as t-gleaner. From what I can tell, t-gleaner diffuses that money into a smattering of accounts in a handful of different branches and moves them around like checkers. I tracked t-gleaner to three different branches. He's careful about spreading it out. But he got careless with the deposits into the McElroy account. They were high dollar amounts and made as direct deposits, creating a clear link. I accessed the bank's personnel records. It appears t-gleaner is one Ted Gleaner, listed as regional manager."

Demond recognized the name from bank personnel interviews after one of the robberies. He shook his head. "Damn. I'm glad you're on our side."

Cody cleared his throat. "Agent Crews, if there's anything I can do from here to help locate Jake, say the word. The full Alabama field office can be there in a matter of hours."

"I'll keep that in mind."

On a separate sheet of paper, Demond jotted three names: Jake's, Mackenna McElroy's and Ted Gleaner. Where was the connection? A love triangle gone bad?

He reviewed Gleaner's statement taken by another agent after the Mound Avenue robbery. Nothing in it raised a red flag. The agent noted Gleaner appeared calm and confident. Unfortunately, he'd never spoken to the man personally. There was little Demond could do until the bank opened later today. If neither Jake nor Mackenna surfaced by then, he'd interview Gleaner.

Demond dropped his head back and closed his eyes. His respite proved brief. Vicky called his cell phone.

Agents had raided the house and found three men sleeping in separate bedrooms, one who claimed to own the house. All seemed in order except for one bedroom where a bed was disheveled and a pair of handcuffs hung from the headboard with obvious traces of blood and skin clinging to it. The owner claimed he liked kinky sex, which might be true, Vicky conceded, but he was wearing Jake's watch. They were bringing all three in for interrogation.

Demond no sooner disconnected Vicky's call than the switchboard operator rang him again, joking that she was rarely this busy on the overnight shift. A local police officer on the line claimed he had Mackenna McElroy in the back seat of his cruiser. She refused to talk to anyone but him.

Demond barely had patience for the preliminary introductions and explanation of how the police came to have Mackenna McElroy in custody. When they handed the phone to her, she breathed into it heavily, as if she was out of breath.

"Miss McElroy, I've been looking for you."

"Agent Crews, you have to help Jake." Her voice was tight, like a piano wire ready to snap. Her words spilled forth in a jumble. "They're going to kill him. I think he's already been shot. Please, Agent Crews. He's in a warehouse. I don't know where it is, but I think I can get back to it. I'll take you there. You have to save his life."

Demond sat up straight. "Slow down, Miss McElroy. Who are you talking about?"

She sobbed into the phone. "Jake. Your Jake. Dear God, there's no time for this. You have to help him."

"My Jake?" Sweat beaded up on Demond's forehead. She couldn't know Jake's true identity and he didn't want to give it away. Was Cody right? Was she connected to the Cabacolli family and part of the double-cross? But if that was the case, why call him?

"Jake Manfred. Or Manettia. I don't know what his name is.

I don't know anything about him, not really. Except he's in trouble. And I think," she babbled now, "I think he's one of you. I don't know why I think that. He told me to think it through. He said I could figure it out. Please, believe me. You have to help Jake." She broke down crying and after momentary fumbling, the first police officer spoke again.

"She's hysterical. But we're fairly certain she's your bank robber. She's half naked, battered and bloody. There's a hospital close by. We thought we'd let the docs check her out. We'll hold her in our jail until tomorrow when you can send someone. She won't be going anywhere tonight."

"What do you mean bloody? What happened?" Jake wouldn't hurt Mackenna. Of that he was certain.

"Looks like she's been assaulted, but she's not talking. She's wearing only underwear. We gave her water. She emptied the bottle like she hadn't had anything to drink in days."

He ejected out of his chair. "Get her to the ER and keep her there. Don't let anyone talk to her except the doctors and don't for any reason leave her alone. Not even while they examine her. Don't leave her side. Handcuff yourself to her if you have to. And for Christ's sake, keep your eyes open. I'm on my way."

HE WASN'T TAKING any chances. Demond immediately alerted SWAT to be ready to move as soon as he knew Jake's location. Then he called headquarters to activate the Hostage Rescue Team based at Quantico. Mackenna said Jake was being held in a warehouse, but since the location and building layout were unknown, a dynamic entry might be necessary. The HRT would blow out the windows, crash through the roof and break down any doors in one coordinated attack, ensuring the occupants inside wouldn't know what hit them. Using their helicopter, they could be airborne within the hour. He zoomed the streets to the hospital at lightning speed. It was easy to do with his flashing light on the car roof and so few vehicles out at this time of night. Or rather morning.

Mackenna looked diminutive resting in the hospital bed, her eyes closed and her head on the starched white pillow that matched the pallor of her skin. Except for the purples, blacks, and blues on the left side of her face. Someone had really walloped her.

A female police officer sat by her bedside and a male officer stood sentry at the door. Demond was happy that the cop demanded and inspected his credentials before allowing him inside the hospital room.

He cleared his throat. "Miss McElroy?"

Her head jerked up. "What the hell took you so long? Don't you understand Jake's life is in danger?" She sat up straighter and tossed her legs over the edge of the bed. She wore a set of green hospital scrubs. He arched his eyebrows at the sight of her swollen feet covered in cuts and contusions. One pant leg crept halfway up her calf. Ugly red scratches lined her legs. Similar cuts and bruises decorated her arms. Gingerly, she eased her feet into paper slippers and attempted to stand.

"Whoa, hold on," the female officer ordered, jumping to her feet to steady Mackenna.

Demond also rushed to her side. "Where do you think you're going, Miss McElroy? Please crawl back into this bed."

She shoved their hands away. "I have to take you to Jake. He could be dead already."

Her words sank like rocks in his stomach, but Demond couldn't let his personal feelings interfere with protocol. Mackenna McElroy was a fugitive and a prime suspect and while she feigned concern for Jake, she could be the reason he was missing.

"One thing at a time, Miss McElroy. You're not going

anywhere until we talk. The longer you delay that, the longer it will take to get help for your friend."

She gasped at his words. "My friend? Is that how you're going to describe Jake? I know he..." She clamped her mouth shut, plopped back onto the bed, and swung her feet up on top of the blanket, grimacing from the effort.

He eyed the crutch by the bedside table.

"Fine. Let's not waste any more time. You want to talk? We'll talk. You want a confession, okay, I confess. Now, will you please help Jake?"

Demond narrowed his eyes at her. "You confess? Confess to what?"

Her hand flew in the air. "I'll confess to anything if it will get you moving in the right direction. I'll confess to the crime of the century. I planned the Boston Marathon bombing. I conspired with O.J. Simpson. I'll say whatever you want me to say. Just please, save Jake."

Beside her, the female cop turned away, trying not to smile. Demond wasn't amused.

"Miss McElroy, you can joke all you want and waste more time if you like. Or we can discuss the situation like adults. If your friend is truly in trouble, then I'll do my best to help him. You have to cooperate first."

Tears pooled in her eyes. She spoke each word as if it was a stand-alone sentence. "My. Friend. Your. Colleague's Life. Is. In. Danger." She smoothed her forehead with her hands, and he noticed the bandages on her wrist. "Fine. I'll do whatever it takes, Agent Crews."

Demond filled his lungs with air and exhaled, concern for Jake making the preliminaries a tedious delay. "I need to advise you of your rights."

Mackenna interrupted and snapped at him. "I remember my rights from the last time you recited them to me. Please get on with it."

"The last time we spoke, you requested a lawyer be present. Are you now waiving your right to have legal representation here?"

"Yes, yes, please. I don't need a lawyer. I haven't done anything wrong except fall in love with a mystery man. And if we don't hurry, I'll never be able to tell him that. Hurry up and ask your questions."

So, he was right about her and Jake. They were involved. But to what extent? There wasn't time to start at the beginning. He slipped a photo from his briefcase of the dead man who'd had a copy of her bank records in his apartment and held it up. "Do you know this man?"

Mackenna squinted, studied the photo, and then shook her head. "No, sir. I don't. Who is he?"

"You've never seen him before?"

"No, sir. I swear to you."

Her body language didn't contradict her words.

Next, he showed her Ted Gleaner's picture. Her eyes widened and she swallowed noticeably hard. She nodded as she spoke. "I know him. That's Ted Gleaner. He's my boss at the Good Neighbor Bank."

She was nervous now. Was he close to making the connection between her, Gleaner, and Cabacolli?

"How well do you know him, Miss McElroy?"

She pressed her lips together in a frown to control her quivering chin. "Not as well as he planned. He tried to rape me in his office. He got me drunk and dragged me home to have sex with him. But Jake was there to stop him. Somehow Jake knew I was in trouble, and he was there, waiting."

Demond knitted his eyebrows as Mackenna started to cry. "What exactly are you saying, Miss McElroy?"

She swiped at her cheeks with the back of her hand. "Mr. Gleaner threatened to fire me if I didn't have sex with him. I told Jake about it. He made me file a police report and an HR complaint with the bank. You can check those. You'll see I'm not making this up.

"Mr. Gleaner promised he'd deposit money in my account if I," she sobbed, "if I slept with him. I didn't remember it right away because of everything that was going on with the bank robberies and quite frankly, I was scared. But I tried to tell you that day in your office when you showed me the balance in my account. Two of those amounts were numbers Mr. Gleaner said he'd pay me for having sex with him. One specifically to cover my rent. But you wouldn't listen."

She'd regained control with those last words and her chin tilted upward. Demond suppressed the urge to grin. Mackenna McElroy had balls.

"You reported him to the police?"

"Yes, sir. Jake insisted. That's when I first started wondering about him because he talked like a cop. He's a master at being evasive, much like you are. That's why I think I know what he is. That's why I called you."

"I'm not sure I follow."

"I don't know what's going on, not really. I met Jake by accident at the coffee shop after the first robbery. He was in the bank when it happened, and he recognized me. I was a mess and he struck up a conversation with me. At the time, I thought he was simply a nuisance. It's a long story but when we ran into Vincent at the grocery store, I could tell Jake wasn't happy and he told me to walk away. When it seemed like Vincent was following me, Jake became angry. That might have been the first time I started to wonder about who he was but with everything going on in my life, I didn't think it through."

She smiled. "Those were Jake's words. He told me I was smart and I should think it through. If I had done that sooner, none of this would have happened and Jake wouldn't be in danger. But it wasn't until Vincent held me hostage that I took the time to think."

Demond jerked upright in his chair. "Who took you hostage? Vincent who?"

She regarded him as if he had two heads. "Didn't the police tell you what I told them? Why I was running through the streets in my underwear? Vincent's men grabbed me at a rest stop. I expected Jake to be more sympathetic. When he wasn't," she paused and a slight grin lifted the corners of her mouth, "when he was acting like a cop, it made me so mad I threw my clothes in a bag and took off. I just wanted to get away from him, to run away from everything. Somehow Vincent's men followed me and, I don't know, drugged me or something. The next thing I knew, I was handcuffed to a bed and Vincent was waiting for Jake."

"Who's Vincent?"

She shrugged. "I'm not certain. I think he's connected to that crime family that's always in the news. To tell you the truth, there was a lot on my mind the day he introduced himself, but I remember recognizing the name. I'd never seen him until that day in the market. Jake said they were business partners, but Vincent didn't seem to know much about Jake. He asked me what he did for a living."

His hands were clammy as he reached into his briefcase to retrieve another photo. "Is this Vincent?"

Mackenna nodded, confirming Vincent Cabacolli's picture.

"Dammit." He eyed the bandages on Mackenna's right wrist. It hadn't been Jake's blood on the handcuffs hanging from the headboard, it was hers. Mackenna studied him, wide-eyed as he rose.

"Miss McElroy, this is extremely important. What did you tell Vincent Jake did for a living?"

She paused. "I-I said he was a nighttime security guard. I don't think he is, but that's what I said."

"And what did Vincent say?"

"He said that wasn't true. He said he and Jake partied every night with women. Vincent made me call Jake. When he didn't answer, he made me leave a message. And then Vincent said something about quitting his undercover ruse and told Jake he had me with him. He said Jake should hurry. There was something about dinner, too, but I didn't understand."

Demond reached for his phone, ready to dial the rescue teams as soon as he determined Jake's location. "And Jake showed up at the house where Vincent took you?"

"No, not at the house. I'm not certain what happened next. It's kind of foggy. I think he drugged me again. But the next thing I knew, we were in some sort of warehouse or storehouse. They hung me from the ceiling by my wrists. I could barely stand. They were waiting for something or someone, I didn't know what or who. And then all of a sudden the door swung open and Jake strolled in like it was nothing. Barefoot and in his underwear."

That explained the watch on the homeowner's wrist. But the wire. What about the wire Jake was supposed to have on him? Had that been the giveaway?

"This is vital Miss McElroy. What did Jake say?" If he'd confessed his true identity to save Mackenna, the likelihood of him still being alive was nil. Demond's heart pounded waiting for her answer.

"He said he'd get me out of there. And he did. I'm not even sure how he did it. He walked toward them and talked about me and the next thing I knew, Jake jumped a man. Guns started firing and I panicked. I screamed. I've never been so scared."

Her composure slipped. She began to shake. "Jake was covered in blood, but he managed to get the knife and cut me down. He shoved me so hard I fell. He yelled at me to run, and I did."

She covered her face with her hands, the reality of the nightmare she'd survived becoming more real as she recounted it. "There was so much shooting. But I ran. I didn't look back. I didn't see if Jake made it out. I don't know if they shot him. I should've tried to help but I was so scared. I didn't know where I was. Someplace near the water because I could smell it and hear the clinking of the ropes on the masts. I don't know if they chased me. I just ran like a wild dog until I couldn't run anymore. And then I spotted the convenience store and asked to call you."

"Why me?"

Her chest rose in inches. "Because I knew you were looking for me. Vincent said my face was all over the news. And I hoped if you came to arrest me, you'd also help Jake. I love that man and he has no idea. I don't much care what happens to me. I'm not your bank robber. I don't think you believe me and I can't prove it. Arrest me if you want. But please, Agent Crews, first let me take you back to the warehouse and maybe you can save him."

Uncontrolled tears rolled down her cheeks. He'd questioned hundreds of criminals in his eighteen-year career and developed a feel for the pros, the amateurs and the innocents caught in a bad situation. Mackenna McElroy was an innocent. He patted her shoulder.

"I'm not convinced you're a bank robber, Miss McElroy. But you're still my number one suspect. I will say I have a new regard for you. You're one hell of a brave woman to have endured what you did and still show concern for someone else. No wonder Jake is taken with you. Excuse me while I make a phone call."

She grabbed his wrist and hung on tight. "But what about Jake?"

He smiled for the first time that evening. "Time to call in reinforcements."

40

Agent Crews strolled out of the hospital room and Mackenna buried her face in her hands in a tsunami of tears. She was still their suspect and that scared the life out of her. But he said he would summon help. That meant recruiting the good guys. Like Jake. If only they weren't too late.

What she wouldn't give to turn back the clock to when Jake cradled her in his arms after they made love. He'd been so tender, whispering that he didn't want to live without her, that he wouldn't let another day pass that she wasn't in, that he needed her more than he needed air to breathe.

They were endearments she'd always hoped to hear from someone and words she never expected to hear from Jake. His declarations left her speechless. All she'd been able to do was stare into his eyes like a doe caught in the headlights, astounded by his admission, and then kiss him again. Of course, that had been enough to ignite his passion for another round of lovemaking.

Why had she reacted so strongly when he hadn't coddled her and cooed his pity after learning that she'd been robbed again? He'd never treated her like a victim, someone he felt sorry for. In the face of everything that happened to her, from the first time he spoke to her in the coffee shop after Robbery Number One to learning about Mr. Gleaner to seeing the dire straits Arthur left her in, Jake approached each crisis logically, not enabling her with sympathy but empowering her with the strength to overcome.

Yesterday had been no different. He'd asked for the facts, as he always did. Yes, he'd snapped at her, unnecessarily reminding her of the seriousness of the situation. And when she wasn't forthcoming with the details of the latest robbery, because she preferred to wallow in self-pity over her bad luck and her suspension and wanted to drag Jake down to those depths with her, he'd refused to follow, instead asking if she'd told the FBI the complete story. She misconstrued that as an accusation that she'd lied when, upon reflection, it was Jake being Jake, standing on the right side of the law. That's where he always stood. That's where he belonged. She was certain.

Given the chance she'd apologize for not believing in him. Because as Mackenna thought back, there wasn't one minute when Jake hadn't believed in her. If only they could get to him in time.

Agent Crews returned with a street map of the general warehouse district. "There are at least thirty-seven buildings in a three-mile radius," he said as he spread out the diagram in front of her. "Where did you last see Jake?"

The maze of dots, lines and words blurred. She'd awakened inside the warehouse, hanging from the ceiling, so she hadn't seen the outside of the building. And she couldn't reconcile the street names with her actual escape route.

"I'm sorry, I've always been directionally challenged. I can get lost in the mall. This map might as well be written in hiero-glyphics. I can't identify anything from this. Why can't I retrace my steps with you and take you back?"

"It's too risky, Miss McElroy. I can't take a civilian into a tenuous situation."

"The way I see it, you don't have a choice. And the longer we debate the matter, the more danger Jake could be in. I beg you. Let me help."

His massive chest expanded with air. When he exhaled, she detected a hint of peppermint on his breath. "Can you describe the interior of the building? Are there windows? Doors? Any idea how many?"

That she could do. She'd hung there for hours, struggling to bear her weight on her toes and cringing in pain in those brief moments when she lowered her feet to rest, thereby straining her shoulder sockets. One mammoth, dark-haired man with a rifle dangling over one arm sat in a chair near the door, half snoozing, one eye trained on her. In no time at all she overcame the embarrassment of being on display in her underwear and had even taken a minute to regret that she hadn't matched the blue lace panties with the white demi-bra that day. Not that her captor recognized the fashion faux pas.

And then, as if Jake whispered in her ear, she'd studied the room, recalling his advice when they rode the bike to the country bar. He'd said it was always a good idea to know your surroundings in case of emergency. Her situation certainly qualified. She'd had enough time to memorize the interior of the warehouse.

"I saw one door in the front of the building and one at the back. Two double garage doors side by side are also at the front. Four windows along the front and two half windows in the rear but they were boarded up, I think. No light shone through them. There was some type of door on the ceiling with a rope and handle hanging from it, like you see for access to an attic. And two interior doors, like office doors, both of them on the left side of the building in the rear corner. Fluorescent lights run the length of the building in three rows. Cement floor. I'm not good at judging distance but I'd guess the size of the entire place is about half a football field."

Agent Crews's eyebrows shot up. "How do you recall all that?"

Heat crept across her cheeks, and she dropped her gaze. "Jake said it was important to pay attention to your surroundings. I didn't do such a good job the first time I was robbed but I tried to pay closer attention after that and provide better details for you. You weren't convinced. Anyway, while they were waiting for Jake, I just hung there, looking around. Like Jake said."

Agent Crews threw his head back and laughed. "Oh, Miss McElroy, you're a precious gem and a bright light in an otherwise dark situation. Excuse me. I have to make another phone call."

She wanted to scream at the exchange of phone calls, none of which she was privy to. They ate up precious time. The door remained partially ajar. In the hallway, Agent Crews threw up his hands, shook his head and punched the air while he spoke into his cell. Finally, he rolled a wheelchair into her room. A nurse helped her into it.

No one spoke until they were in the front seat of his unmarked car. He started the engine. "We'll return to the convenience mart where the police found you and start from there. Hopefully, you can back track your escape route to the warehouse. You'll stay in the car once we get there until I can have a local remove you safely off the premises."

Fat chance she'd let that happen, not with Jake so close. Mackenna strained to look behind them, noting only blackness. "We who? There isn't another car to be seen."

"Don't concern yourself about that. Is there anything else you can remember, any minute detail that might help Jake?"

She shut her eyes tight. Nothing surfaced.

"You say he was in his underwear?"

"Yes. That doesn't ever faze him, though." The admission that she'd seen Jake in his underwear prior to her abduction caused her face to flush. She was thankful the car interior was dark, and Agent Crews couldn't see her. Even as dark as that moment was, when she didn't know if she would live or die, she'd appreciated the man's body when he strode toward her, knowing her hands had touched every inch of it. And her lips. *Please, God, give me one more chance to love the man.*

She directed Agent Crews to slow down. They crawled through the streets once the convenience store was at their backs. "Turn here."

"Wait, back up, down this alley." Each directive was whispered, even though only she and Agent Crews were in the car.

"Around this corner."

"Down here."

And then suddenly, there it was. Her heart filled in a flood of fear.

The warehouse was dark. It loomed like a menacing monster. Agent Crews dialed his phone and recited coordinates he read from a dashboard navigator.

Mackenna squirmed in the passenger seat. "What do we do now?"

"Just wait." With one eye on the building Agent Crews leaned toward her, unlocked the glove box, and removed two long metal objects. Bullets in a clip or a magazine, whatever it was called. He shoved them into his pants pocket. Then he stepped out of the car, went to the trunk, and retrieved a vest that he strapped on and a rifle. Once he slipped into the vest, he returned to the driver's door but remained outside. The windows were down, the night eerily quiet.

From out of nowhere men materialized and trotted by the car on either side, hunched down. Silent. Where did they come from? They wore gray long-sleeved shirts and matching camo pants tucked into ankle-high boots. How could they move so stealthily in those heavy shoes? Thick helmets were strapped to their heads. Heavy vests protected their chests. Each lugged a backpack, wore dark gloves, and had guns strapped against both legs. And they carried intimidating looking sniper rifles.

Agent Crews leaned inside the driver's window and pointed his finger at her. "You stay in the car until a uniformed officer comes to escort you away from here. And Miss McElroy, if you don't go with him, I'll charge you with obstruction of justice."

Before she could reply, he straightened and took off after the SWAT team. Suddenly, the whop-whop-whop of a helicopter sounded overhead. She strained to see out the passenger window. The helicopter hovered over top of the building while she counted four men climbing down ropes and dropping onto the roof.

Like a synchronized ballet, their feet no sooner touched the roof than an explosion lit up the night at the rear door and in the front of the building. An orange glow illuminated the dark, enveloped in gray smoke that clouded the entrance and spread like rolling fog. With the flames as a background, Mackenna watched the SWAT team rush the building, a hail of gunfire splitting the nighttime silence. The noise deafened her. The acrid smell of explosives gagged her. Her eyes watered. She sneezed from the odor.

She jumped out of the car in an effort to inhale more air, her eyes riveted to the scene. Her injured leg gave way, and she braced against the door. Men yelled orders that were incoherent to her. High-pitched screams pierced the night. Somewhere behind her, sirens approached.

A movement to the left of the building caught her eye. She squinted to focus on it. One lone shadow crept along the side of the building, crouched low to the ground. A SWAT team member checking the perimeter? An earlier transmission over the car radio reported the perimeter secure. Inside the warehouse, mini explosions blew out the boarded windows and fingers of flame cut holes in the roof, stretching toward the sky. And still, the shadow crawled away.

Mackenna limped around the rear of the car for a clearer view. She couldn't make out a helmet, or a weapon, or anything that indicated this person was a SWAT member.

No!

In the glow of the flames, it looked like Vincent.

She caught her breath and whirled around, searching for someone to tell. They were all so well disguised, she couldn't distinguish one body in the night. Did they see him?

She spun back to the spot she'd last seen movement. Nothing. The flames roared in her ears. The radio. She could warn them. She jumped into the driver's seat and stared at the mini-computer mounted to the dashboard. No visible microphone hung from it. She touched the screen, but it awakened to display the blue and gold FBI insignia. Headlights flicked on where she'd last seen Vincent and white back-up lights confirmed a moving car.

She couldn't let him escape. This was a man who'd threatened her and may have killed Jake. Spying Agent Crews's key fob in the cup holder, Mackenna started the engine and threw the car into drive. All the anger she'd suppressed these past weeks over that bastard Arthur, the spineless bank robbers who'd pointed guns at her, Mr. Gleaner for trying to exploit her, and possibly Jake's death—it all surfaced, bubbling up in a rage.

She floored the gas pedal and drove straight toward the moving car, screaming like a specter. "No-o-o-o-o!"

With the headlights shining inside the car, she saw Vincent turn, a look of terror on his face. She rammed the driver's side of his BMW.

Airbags exploded around her, stopping her propulsion through the windshield with such force she passed out.

41

Her head pounded. A bright light overhead blinded her. Mackenna immediately shut her eyes tight.

"I think she's coming around."

She rolled her face in the direction of the sound. "Miss McElroy? Can you hear me?"

She raised her arm to shield her eyes from the beam and felt the drag of a wire.

"Careful, ma'am. You have an intravenous line running in your hand. We wanted to push fluids into you. How do you feel? Can you speak?"

Her mouth moved like a cow chewing its cud. Whoever was beside her must have noticed. "Here. I'll prop up your head. Take a sip of water. See if that helps."

Strong hands moved behind her shoulders and lifted her. A straw touched her lips. Mackenna opened her eyes cautiously, glad that the man's body blocked the direct light. "Where am I?"

"You're in an ambulance, ma'am. Do you remember what happened?"

Did she? She drove a car as if possessed and T-boned

Vincent's black BMW, determined not to let him get away with hurting Jake. Her eyes widened and she bolted upright. "Jake! Did they find Jake? Is he still alive?"

And now that deep, intimidating voice she recognized, coming from outside the double doors. "We found him and just in time, thanks to you."

Agent Crews. Somehow, knowing he was close reassured her. She searched the darkness until she found him. She offered a tentative smile and then grimaced. Her face hurt. "Is he okay?"

"He was barely conscious but all he could do was repeat your name. The fact that his name is the first thing out of your mouth tells me you two might just have a thing going on." Agent Crews shook his head, laughing.

"That was the damndest thing you did, Miss McElroy, crashing into that car like that. You could have been hurt a lot worse than you are. We had the area secured. He wasn't going anywhere."

She hung her head. "I-I didn't know. I couldn't see anybody. I didn't want him to get away. I'm sorry."

Now she'd probably have reckless driving added to the myriad of charges against her. What if she had to pay for the damage?

The smile on Agent Crews's face confused her. "Before you arrest me, may I see Jake, please? It's the only favor I'll ask. I have to tell him something, something important."

Thankfully he nodded. "I think that can be arranged. Jake has already been transported to the hospital. He lost a lot of blood and requires surgery."

He issued his orders to the paramedics. "Transport her there, too, and see that she receives whatever treatment required. I'll have an agent meet you at the hospital." Then he looked at her again. "I'll see you there."

The doors slammed and in minutes, the ambulance moved.

Mackenna strained to see out the back windows and marveled at the kaleidoscope of colors shrinking to become less threatening. Red and blue flashing lights reflected off the orange and yellow flames being attacked by firehoses.

Hours later, a doctor pronounced her battered and bruised but not broken. She rested in the hospital bed, waiting for word about Jake. Because she wasn't a relative, neither the doctors nor nurses were permitted to share any information about his condition. She'd asked the agent posted outside her door, but he declined knowing any news and said Agent Crews was en route.

When the big man finally burst into her room driving a wheelchair, she was glad to see him.

"They operated on Jake for a bullet wound to his thigh and shoulder. He's out of recovery and being moved to a private room. He's still groggy but insists he see you. I'd like to see the two of you in a room together myself." He extended his hand to help her sit up and then dropped to his knees, sliding slippers onto her feet.

"Don't blame Jake for any of this. If you need to arrest someone, arrest me. Jake is nothing but an innocent victim in all of this."

Rising to help her off the bed, he harrumphed. "The day Jake Manettia is innocent of anything will be the day I resign."

He referred to Jake as Manettia. Was that his real name? Not Manfred, the name she'd seen on the TV screen the day the FBI arrested him? Was he one of those criminals who used aliases? Or was he really...?

Before she had time to sort through her thoughts or to ask, the elevator doors opened. Agent Crews rolled her down a hall peppered with police and into a room guarded by a man looking much like the agent who guarded her room. Jake was under arrest, same as her. He couldn't be a cop.

Agent Crews showed his identification and signed a clipboard, which he showed to Mackenna and asked that she sign next to her printed name. Then the guard opened the door and Agent Crews wheeled her inside.

Three men circled the foot of Jake's bed. And his friend Vicky, who flashed a broad smile at her. She was the only one Mackenna recognized. Their conversation ceased the minute she entered the room. All eyes, including Jake's, turned on her. He was pale, but his face exploded into a giant grin. He reached for her when Agent Crews moved her close to the bed.

"Hey, sugar. I've been worried sick about you."

Jake looked horrible, his left eye swollen shut and a gash along his hairline held together by five stitches. His right arm was in a sling and at least five colored wires disappeared into the neck of his hospital gown, all attached to various monitors that beeped and pinged in a mechanical serenade.

"Oh my God, Jake." Despite her resolve to be strong, she burst into tears.

Jake tugged on her hand and coaxed her out of the chair. He patted the bed. "Sit but be gentle. This is the leg that has to heal." He removed the oxygen hose from his nose.

She was too distraught to speak. She perched on the edge of the bed and when he tucked his hand behind her neck and urged her closer, she cried on his chest. Through the breakdown, Jake smoothed her hair and reassured her he was fine and everything would be okay.

Finally, she sat up, only then realizing that everyone had remained in the room. At least they'd had the decency to step toward the rear. Now that they were felons, privacy was no longer an option. Jake's thumb swiped the last bit of tears from her cheeks.

"Feel better?"

She nodded and he handed her a tissue. "Blow."

She felt imminently better once her airways were cleared.

"They tell me you're ready to try out for NASCAR, although

Demond is quite upset that you wrecked his car. He's facing a lot of paperwork because of you."

"Who?"

Jake grinned a cheshire smile. "I believe you know him as that mean ole Agent Crews."

She shook her head, speechless. How could he joke when they were both facing criminal charges?

He winked. "Don't fret, sugar. Wrecking a Bureau vehicle is automatic time on the beach but I might be able to pull a few strings with the boss."

"I didn't have a choice. Vincent was getting away. I had to stop him. I thought you were dead."

Jake moved the hair behind her ears. "Why didn't you run away when you had the chance?"

"I was running away when somehow Vincent's men found me. You made me so mad when you didn't believe me about the bank robberies."

"But you had a second chance to get away after you got out of the warehouse. Instead, you turned yourself in."

She glanced over her shoulder at Vicky and the other men listening to every word of her private confession. There was nothing to be done about it. "I realized I'm in love with you. I couldn't leave without at least trying to save you. I thought if I disappeared, in time I'd forget you. I know now that was foolish. I don't think I'll ever forget you."

Jake placed his hand on his chest. "I'm crushed. You love me and you run away from me? That's not how it's supposed to work."

From behind, one of the men spoke. "It wouldn't have helped anyway, miss. Jake's like a bad dream. He keeps coming back. We've tried to get rid of him and it doesn't happen." They all chuckled.

So, he'd been arrested before. No wonder everyone seemed so familiar.

Jake sighed. "Mackenna, let me introduce you to this crew." One by one he named them, prefacing each with the title special agent. "You already know Agent Crews. And Vicky. She's Special Agent Vicky Winston." He squeezed her hand. "Time you knew me too. Special Agent Jake Manettia of the Alabama Field Office, here on assignment in Brighton City."

Her eyes widened and her breathing stopped. "I knew it! I knew you were some kind of a cop." She swatted the arm that wasn't injured. "Damn you, you lied to me. The whole time, it was all a pretense to prove I was a bank robber. And you slept with me. Isn't that some kind of ethics violation? I'll sue you or something. You used me, you bastard."

Jake appeared surprised at her reaction, his eyes expanding. "Hold on a minute, honey. You have it all wrong. My assignment had nothing to do with you."

"I don't believe you." She eased off the bed, using the wheelchair to steady herself. "And to think I thought I loved you. How could I be so stupid?"

Agent Crews's harsh words silenced her. "Where are you going, Miss McElroy? You're still in my custody. I suggest you hear the man out."

She regarded the stern faces riveted on her and looked at Jake, whose mouth edged up in a smile. "Come sit here again and let me explain. And then if you want to walk away from me, no one in this room will stop you."

Really? They would let a suspected bank robber saunter out the door just because Jake suggested it. She didn't believe it. Nevertheless, she perched on the edge of the bed again.

"I came here six months ago to work Vicky's public corruption case at City Hall. I worked undercover as a bagman, which is why you saw me being arrested that day when we finally made our sweep. When I arrived here, I had no idea Mackenna McElroy existed. If it wasn't for a twist of fate that planted me in your bank the day it was robbed, we might have never met."

Tentatively he extended his hand. Hers automatically slid into it.

"I wasn't there as an agent, only as a customer. I was an extra set of eyes once my colleagues arrived. But when an agent is undercover, it's imperative that his cover be maintained no matter what. They had to treat me like everyone else.

"It was a coincidence that I ran into you at the coffee shop later that day. You looked so helpless and, I admit, I struck up a conversation with you to feel you out about the robbery."

He shrugged. "Once an agent, always an agent, I guess. But I did feel sorry for you, which is why I showed up at your bank the next day to check on you. Well, sorry might not be the right word. You're damn attractive and I couldn't stop thinking about you. That was the man, not the agent."

Her heart fluttered. She'd fallen in love with the man, not the FBI agent.

"I was riding my bike one day when a car drove off the road in front of me and I helped rescue the driver, who turned out to be Vincent Cabacolli, from the mob family."

Mackenna gasped. Now she recalled the rumors associated with the name. The Cabacolli family was one of the biggest, most dangerous crime syndicates in the state.

"I see you know the name. I literally fell into the opportunity to make inroads into the Cabacolli organization. It was a chance the Bureau couldn't pass up. Running into you at the supermarket when Vinny saw us was an unfortunate accident, and one that ended up endangering you. For that I'm sorry.

"It was Vinny's interest in you that kept you on my radar." His cheeks reddened. "Well, that's not exactly true. I was interested too. But I was worried about you, especially after I learned about Arthur and your boss. And you kept ending up the target teller in a string of bank robberies."

"Jake, I swear to you. I had nothing to do with those robberies. I know it looks bad, but you have to believe me."

Again, a voice from behind spoke. "We know that now, Miss McElroy," Agent Crews said.

She twisted to see his face. The wide smile etched on it surprised her.

"But I admit," Agent Crews said, "I didn't at first. Jake was the one who kept pleading your case."

She clutched his hand with her other hand. "You believed me all the time?"

Jake nodded. "I did, sugar. But I'm a federal agent. I had to prove it. That's why I kept questioning you, forcing you to relive the robberies. I hoped you'd remember something that would give me a lead."

She contemplated his words. "So, all along, you were just trying to solve another case?"

Jake laughed. "No, ma'am. Somewhere in there I fell in love with you, which only made matters more difficult. I'm not sure what I would've done if it turned out you were a robber. I want you in my bed for the rest of your life, not some prison cell."

Burning fire crept up her cheeks. Such an admission in front of his colleagues embarrassed her.

Jake laughed again. "Don't blush, sugar. We Southern men aren't afraid to love our women and don't care who knows it."

"So, I'm no longer a suspect?"

Agent Crews stepped forward. "No, ma'am. We traced the deposits in your account back to the bank manager, Ted Gleaner, and established an association between him and the Cabacolli family. He laundered the money they made illegally through various bank accounts, usually belonging to seniors who aren't too diligent about checking their activity. It was you who led us to him. If you hadn't mentioned his attempts to sexually exploit you, I might never have made the connection. He was careless with you. You must have pissed him off."

She shook her head. "No, Agent Crews. That was all Jake's doing."

Laughter filled the room. The weight of the world lifted off of her shoulders. They believed her. She was free. Tears filled her eyes when she looked at Jake.

"Is Mr. Gleaner under arrest?"

Jake nodded. "For complicity in the bank robberies and sexual harassment. What he did to you won't be ignored."

Another burden lifted. No more Mr. Gleaner.

"Is that why Vincent abducted me? Because of his alliance with Mr. Gleaner?"

Jake sighed again. "No, that was my fault too and again, I'm sorry for that."

"I don't understand."

"We always suspected that the Cabacolli family had a mole somewhere. It turned out to be a judge who tipped him off about my true identity after the City Hall arrests. Vincent used you to get to me. He knew I'd come if you were in danger. Only he underestimated me and what I'd do to save you. For that matter, he underestimated you and what you'd do to help me. You knew you were wanted by the FBI and yet you turned yourself in. That took guts."

Agent Crews mumbled, "So did ramming my car into the side of his."

For the first time in as long as she could remember, Mackenna looked forward to tomorrow. "What happens now?"

Jake grinned. "Well, my assignments here are done until I have to testify in court months from now. I'll need that time to recover and rehab my leg and arm. My mama has already ordered me to come back home so she can pamper me. I admit I'm ready."

Mackenna's stomach twisted. Jake planned to leave town.

"I'd like you to come home with me. She's going to love you. You can get a bank job in Alabama if you want but I have other plans for you."

Her heart soared. "What kind of plans?"

Now, Jake reached for her head and drew her close so he could whisper in her ear. "First, I'd like you to go off those birth control pills. And then, I'd like you to take my name. I'd love to turn you into a Southern belle." His lips grazed hers in a tender kiss that promised so much more.

Feet shuffled behind them. Agent Crews cleared his throat. "I have some paperwork to catch up on, and a certain bank teller's name to clear." He winked at Mackenna as the other agents began to file out of the room. Vicky squeezed her shoulder and smiled on the way out.

"We'll keep a guard on both of you until all of the Cabacolli soldiers are in custody. Just to be safe. Miss McElroy, you'll have to let us know where you're staying."

She grinned. "I'm staying right here with Jake. Just to make things easier for you."

Agent Crews laughed. "Jake, after all you've put this poor woman through, at least tell this girl you love her for all the world to hear."

Jake sat up straight, winced at the pain and wrapped his arm around Mackenna's shoulder. "I love you, sugar, with all my heart. I'll spend the rest of my life making all this up to you if you let me."

Agent Crews nodded at Mackenna, urging her to respond.

"I love you too. And I think I'll let you do that."

The End

Thank you for reading **Off The Grid For Love**
If you enjoyed it, please leave a review on Amazon, B&N,
Goodreads or wherever you buy books
It's the nicest gift you can give an author.

OTHER NOVELS

BY RENA KOONTZ

Shady Justice
When Push Comes to Shoot
Loving Gia to Death
Locked and Loaded For Justice: Saving Gia
Broken Justice, Blind Love
The Devil She Knew
Love's Secret Fire
Thief Of The Heart
Crystal Clear Love — A contemporary romance
Midnight Deadline —A suspenseful novella
We Have Tomorrow — A contemporary romance novella

Find all of Rena Koontz's books on Amazon, Barnes & Noble
or wherever you buy books

Here's a sample of the multi award-winning **Shady Justice**

CHAPTER 1

The woman was so badly beaten, Steel Chaney vomited his breakfast bagel in the grass at the side of the concrete driveway. So much for bragging that after twenty years on the job, he'd seen it all.

Christ, there was nothing left of her face to identify. Her mouth was a bloody hollow where teeth should be. The tips of all ten fingers were scorched black. Were they burned before or after she died? For her sake, he hoped it was postmortem. Someone sure as hell didn't want her identified.

Chaney spit the last of the sour taste away, wiped his mouth on his coat sleeve, and turned back to the car. The poor woman was stuffed inside the trunk on her back, her legs pinned beneath her. They had to be broken. Blood soaked her clothes, seeping to the area rug underneath her body, turning it pitch black. Her killer had wrapped her in this piece of carpet to transport her from the murder site. Blood matted in her dirty blond hair where her skull was crushed. Caked strands knotted around gold circle earrings. Her eyes were swollen shut, a palette of eggplant purple and midnight blue. A bloodied gold chain fell toward the back of her neck. Robbery was not a motive for this act of violence.

He narrowed his focus to the interior of the trunk. Empty except for three forty-pound bags of cat litter shoved to the rear. What the fuck?

"Steel?"

He turned toward Parker Bentley, the rookie detective he mentored. As rookies go, she was smarter than most and still hungry to learn. He'd balked at taking on a trainee, assuming his seniority exempted him from babysitting. It hadn't. His argument, that a three-month mentoring period was ridiculous given the years and experience most cops already had by the time they expressed interest in the detective bureau, fell on deaf ears, all because two years ago the mayor got his tit in the wringer over some detective new to the job who went rogue and then claimed lack of training. So now, they had training.

He'd checked out Parker Bentley, looking for any excuse to dump a woman hoping to do a man's job. She'd been a terror practically from her first day as a boot, coming up through the ranks in uniform with honors and accolades and an impressive arrest record. Those threatened by her, women and men alike, referred to her as Bitch Bentley. After knowing her awhile, he was certain it was said behind her back. He was even more confident she didn't give a damn.

Bentley shook his hand the first day they met. "I'm not interested in fetching your coffee or fucking you. You're supposed to be the best. I already know the criminal code. What I want from you is every bit of knowledge you have regarding detective work that I can't learn from a manual. I don't give a shit about your love life, your prostate or your wet dreams. In return, I'll make you proud to have mentored me." So far, she had.

She held out a bottle of water. "You going soft on me?"

He smiled. "Maybe. Knew we had a body. Shouldn't have

eaten on the way." His mouth welcomed the cool water. "Any idea who she is?"

"Not yet. No license plate. If this is her car, she's a better woman than I."

"What do you mean?"

"The car is clean inside. I mean immaculate. Not a tissue or an umbrella or a crumbled store receipt under the seat. The trunk where she ended up dead is spotless. Not even a snow scraper left in there from winter. No woman I know keeps a car this clean."

He snickered. "You going sexist on me?"

"No, I'm being honest. A woman's car is like her purse. Anything we might need is in there. If this is her vehicle, she wasn't human."

He loved her sense of humor, even in the face of murder.

He took another swig. "So, car owner unknown for now. What else?"

"Not much. Thank goodness it's cool this morning. I don't think decomposition is an issue."

A polite way of saying the body was fresh. The temperature had dropped last night to the fifties. Fall was trying to overtake summer, but slowly here in the City of Pittsburgh. Today it would be eighty degrees again. They stepped closer to the trunk. No handbag visible unless it was under the body. He should be so lucky to find her wallet and ID. A blood-stained ten-dollar bill peeked out of her ripped blouse as if jammed between her breasts. "Maybe she was a hooker."

Bentley rolled her eyes "An entire crime scene and you focus on her breasts. I have a caveman for a partner."

He was, to some extent. Bentley was dragging him kicking and screaming into the twenty-first century where women were equals. He stood with one foot in the good old days, when he didn't have to admit women like Bentley were superior to him. Didn't mean he didn't respect the hell out of her and women in general. He'd take a bullet for Bentley. Few people he'd say that about, including his two ex-wives.

"I saw the money. Always a motive for murder." One side of Bentley's mouth lifted in a smirk. She wasn't buying it. "Who called it in?"

She pointed toward a young man leaning against his garage door wiping snot from his nose with his sleeve, barefoot, the front of his pants wet. Yeah, finding a dead woman in your driveway would make anyone piss their pants.

"That gentleman, and I use the term loosely." Bentley consulted her mini-iPad. He still preferred pencil and notebook, but she was all about electronics. "Says his name is Dickey Sharpei. Like the dog. Lives here with his parents and sister. Claims he doesn't know the woman, doesn't recognize the car, doesn't know anything about anything. I didn't have a chance to run his name yet to see if he has a record. This is a top-notch neighborhood and, if you ask me, he looks out of place."

Chaney's eyes darted up and down the asphalt street. This community was an upscale suburb just outside the city. Two-story houses with shiny, power-washed aluminum siding, colorful window boxes in full bloom at the end of summer, and manicured lawns. Perennials decorated the paths up to the front doors and varied door wreaths and welcome signs greeted a visitor. The weedy Sharpei landscaping around the single-family lot was less pristine than the neighbors, the siding on the house marred in spots and dirty all over, and not a blooming flower in sight. The entire property appeared slightly sullied compared to the other homes on the street. Likewise, Mr. Sharpei looked marginally below the decency bar in his tattered shorts, his uncut hair, and his dirty fingernails. Plus, he had the shakes. Nerves or did he need a hit of his drug of choice?

"You'll find a criminal history for sure. His face is familiar."

The names didn't always stick, but Chaney recognized him as one of the hundreds of druggies he'd arrested during his stint on the force. Drug possession and grand theft auto, he was certain. How much did the little snot have to do with this woman's murder?

"Who was first on the scene?"

"Unit six-seven over there. Sergeant Wayne Cubb is writing up a report for us now."

"Okay, tell me what you know as fact and what you think in theory." This was how he mentored her, never showing or lecturing, always expecting her to apply her knowledge to sort through the minutia of a crime. She was intelligent, book smart and street wise, and often saw what he didn't.

Bentley filled her lungs and used a stylus to scroll her screen. She printed in tiny block letters, unreadable for his aging eyeballs. He blamed it on the light reflecting off the iPad.

"Call came in at five forty-seven this morning. Dickey Sharpei over there reported an unknown car parked in his driveway. Claims he didn't touch anything, just saw the car and called the police. Says he doesn't recognize the vehicle. He didn't pop the trunk, Sergeant Cubb did. The car was locked but Cubb found the key fob balanced on top of the left front tire."

Sure, that's where every bad guy leaves the key. Chaney nodded.

"Those are facts that I find odd. Normal curiosity would make me look inside the car first for a clue as to who it belonged to if I didn't already know. Would I look in the trunk? Yeah, but maybe I'm unusually nebby."

A dozen years in this city and he still didn't understand Pittsburghese. "Unusually what? Your Pittsburgh accent is surfacing again."

Bentley blushed. She looked good with color on her face. "Sorry. It means nosy."

Chaney agreed. He'd be nebby too.

Bentley swiped at her screen. "Back to the facts. Sharpei says he was out partying last night. Says he was drunk as a skunk when he rolled home. That's a self-portrait. He thinks it was before three." She made air quotes around the word think. "Says there was no car here when a buddy dropped him off. He's having trouble remembering who brought him home. Imagine that. Claims he was intensely wasted. Again, his words. He stressed his intoxicated state more than once. Judging by the wrinkles, he slept in his clothes so maybe." Her shoulders moved up and down. "Never heard a thing until his phone rang this morning about five-thirty."

"Who woke him up?"

Bentley shrugged again. "He says it was a hang up. He took a piss, looked out his bedroom window and saw the car."

"And he immediately called the police? Why?"

"Exactly. The little shit is lying. That's theory. Sergeant Cubb found nothing in the glove box except the owner's manual. A small tin of opened breath mints was on the ground, under the driver's side." She held up a quart-sized plastic evidence bag. "Cubb bagged it so it didn't get kicked around. I was close to Mr. Sharpei. The breath mints aren't his. Sergeant Cubb asked Sharpei for permission to open the trunk, just to follow procedure.

"Sharpei denied recognizing the car or the woman. Cubb said the kid almost passed out when the trunk lid lifted. And he pissed himself."

She smiled at that. Bentley had a knack for discovering a person's weakness. She often used it against them.

"Cubb says Sharpei was adamant the car wasn't his and he didn't know the owner. While he was waiting for us, he called in the VIN number but the identification system is experiencing technical difficulties this morning."

She answered before he asked. "The automatic backup

went into meltdown last night and now VINNY is clogged trying to catch up. I put a rush on an ID."

Chaney studied their witness, then let his gaze roam across the house. "Anyone else at home?"

"No. Parents are away on a trip. Dickey doesn't remember where or when they return. He said maybe today, maybe next week. Said he thought it was a cruise. He said he has a sister but has no idea where she is."

"I wonder if everyone is away by coincidence."

Bentley frowned. "You don't believe in coincidence. Me either. That's all the facts. Here's what I think. Ole Dickey knows more than he says. Who finds a car in their driveway and doesn't look inside? We should bring him in for a heart to heart. I haven't touched the body yet but she's newly divorced, judging by the indentation on her ring finger. Or she was cheating. The autopsy will confirm it, but I don't think she's a natural blond. She needs a root job."

"How can you tell with all that blood?"

"Leaned all the way in with my flashlight. There's gray at her nape. I'm guessing she's middle aged. Anyone can wear tight jeans and a silky blouse but her hands look old. The skin on her neck isn't tight. That shoe peeking out from under her hip isn't what a young woman would wear."

"Maybe she has bad feet." His own shoes were pinching today.

"Always a possibility. My bet is this isn't her car. If it comes back hers, I'd be surprised. It's too damn clean. Possibly stolen. Might as well dump a body and a car all at once, right? But why in Sharpei's driveway? He's a two-bit nothing. What's he supposed to do with it?"

She absently scraped the cuticle on her thumb with her index finger, a nervous habit he'd learned meant she was uncomfortable with a situation. She rarely knew she did it. He'd seen her scratch it until it bled.

"This was a violent act, Steel, not a random carjacking gone bad. Her murder was calculated. I want a good look at her hands. Look at her fingernails, or what's left of them. She fought for her life. Some bastard is walking around with scratches on his arms and maybe his face." She scanned the techs surrounding the car. "I wish these folks would hurry up."

Bentley hated waiting.

They couldn't touch anything until the forensic team finished processing the scene. And they'd been notified an assistant district attorney was en route. Had to be Laquisha Moore, not his favorite. She was the only one who showed up at the location of a crime, acting like she was the detective. It was overstepping, in his mind. She risked contaminating his crime scene.

A forensic photographer already was clicking hundreds of pictures from every angle imaginable, even the underside of the car. Other forensic techs began a grid search of the area looking for evidence. No one commits a crime without leaving some type of forensic evidence behind, a fingerprint, a strand of hair or maybe clothing fibers. The trick would be finding that evidence and then matching it to their murderer.

Bentley watched the techs, wrinkling her nose at the cigarette butts that peppered the front lawn. The techs would collect each one, even though identifying them to the killer would be the proverbial needle in a haystack. The evidence pertaining to this woman's murder wasn't here.

"Why do you assume it's a man?"

Her lips pursed. "It doesn't feel female. That's theory. Too hard to cram this body in here. Our victim isn't a small woman. I guess one-hundred and sixty pounds or close to. That's dead weight and a lot to wrangle with. I could do it, but I train for that.

"Also, a woman plans better." Her hand swept the scene. "She wouldn't simply dump a car and a body in a driveway where anyone could see and hope it disappears. Everyone has camera doorbells these days. This was not the plan. Something changed."

"Maybe it wasn't planned. Could have been spontaneous, an act of passion. Maybe the killer wanted her found." He could see Bentley's mind at work.

"Found but not identifiable? Doesn't make sense. Spontaneous doesn't take the time to remove fingerprints. This is a bold statement, like fuck you. Also, not a woman's style."

Bentley pointed inside. "And this money. Some kind of insult tossed at her after she was stuffed in here. Maybe she was still conscious and could hear whatever words accompanied rough hands cramming it into her bra. Someone not only wanted to kill her, they wanted the last humiliating word."

A homicide was a puzzle and Bentley was good at putting the pieces together. She did make him proud. "Nice, Parker, real nice. I think it was a man, too. Let's talk to our witness."

They walked toward Sharpei. The kid was smoking like a charcoal grill, still crying.

"Long time no see, Sharpei." Steel flashed his badge. "Remember me?"

"I didn't have nothin' to do with this, Detective."

"With what?"

"With that woman."

"Who is she?"

"I don't know, I swear. I never seen her before."

"How'd she end up in your driveway, Dickey?"

"I don't know." He whined like a seven-year-old. "Honest, I don't."

"What about the car?"

"I never seen it before."

"Do you know who owns it?"

"No, no sir."

"You don't find it odd that a random car with a dead woman in the trunk winds up parked in your driveway?"

"I swear I don't know nothin' about it."

"C'mon, Dickey, I don't buy it. You told my partner you were partying last night. Did you come home with this woman and things got a little out of hand? Maybe she didn't want to continue the party and you lost your temper. Or—"

"No, no, I swear to you. I never saw her before or her ride."

"So, the car belongs to her?"

"I-I don't know, man. I'm just sayin' I don't know nothin' about this."

"How about if we go inside? Can we take a look around your house, Dickey? Maybe the lady's purse or jacket is inside."

"It ain't."

"Can we see for ourselves?"

"No, my parents ain't home. They don't like strangers in the house." He started to sob.

Steel laid his hand on his shoulder. "Okay, buddy, okay. How about if one of these officers accompanies you inside and you change your clothes? Let's discuss this further downtown. You'll think more clearly when you're not looking at a dead woman in your front yard. Maybe you'll have a change of heart and tell us the truth."

"Are you arresting me? Do I need a lawyer?"

The right corner of Bentley's mouth edged upward. Chaney chuckled.

"Do you need a lawyer?" she asked. "Only guilty people ask for their attorney. What'd you do to require legal consultation?"

"Nothin,' ma'am, I din't do nothin', honest. But I ain't talkin' no more without a lawyer."

Chaney motioned for a patrolman. Dammit. They wouldn't be able to interrogate him without his attorney present.

"All right, all right, we'll cross that bridge when we come to it." He nodded to the officer. "Escort Mr. Sharpei into his house to find a pair of shoes and clean pants. Make sure he has his cell phone so he can call his attorney once you're at the station. Before you make that call, Dickey, think about whether or not you want to stick to this story."

"It ain't a story, man, it's the truth. I don't know nothin' about her. This was supposed to be a joke."

"So, you do know something about it?"

"I don't detective, honest."

Chaney spotted the deputy coroner approaching the vehicle. "Take this piece of shit downtown. We'll deal with him later."

He nudged Bentley back toward the car. "A dead woman in the trunk of a car is a joke? Please explain the humor in that."

Shady Justice
Available wherever you buy books.
renakoontz.com

www.ingramcontent.com/pod-product-compliance
Lightning Source LLC
Chambersburg PA
CBHW060358260626
47160CB00006B/2354